T0318853

Scions

Books by James Wolanyk

The Scribe Cycle
Scribes
Schisms
Scions

Scions

The Scribe Cycle

James Wolanyk

REBEL BASE BOOKS
Kensington Publishing Corp.
www.kensingtonbooks.com

First Electronic Edition: April 2019
eISBN-13: 978-1-63573-022-7
eISBN-10: 1-63573-022-8

First Print Edition: April 2019
ISBN-13: 978-1-63573-025-8
ISBN-10: 1-63573-025-2

Printed in the United States of America

For Mara.

Acknowledgments

Had this section not been properly tamed and trimmed, a thousand names could've ended up here. So many wonderful people have put their time, energy, and faith (which is perhaps the most essential element of all) into creating this series. I'll now attempt, and likely fail, to name the most crucial parties in the aforementioned process: my family and friends, my incredible mentor Andre Dubus III, my writing buddy David Moloney, my amazing agent Lindsay Mealing, my rock-solid editor James Abbate, and the universe itself for imbuing every moment with a sense of hope and progress. This series is my message to humanity, but it is also the culmination of childhood dreams, battles with *Star Wars* action figures, long nights serving as a D&D game master, and weekend trips to comic book stores and conventions, all of which would not have been possible without an incredible mother and father. It is living proof that anything (and any wish upon a star) is possible through determination and the kindness of others.

Chapter 1

Anna heard the old steward long before his lantern's chalky orange bloom appeared. She'd first sensed his presence from the whine of an oak door farther down the slope, its staccato creaks cutting through the hush of the predawn drizzle, the twisting wail of mountain winds. She waited in stillness by the open shutters, watching the fog shift and creep over blue-black rock, studying the ethereal glow as it grew sharper and nearer. Her legs were still awash in the prickling numbness that accompanied rising from her cushion.

Four hours since the midnight bell, seven since she'd snuffed out her chamber's lone candle and sat to follow her breath.

The razor-mind did not stir, did not blink, did not wander as the steward came to her door and rapped on the bronze face. Instead, it curiously trailed the seed of a thought blossoming in absolute stillness: *Why?*

"Knowing One," the steward croaked in river-tongue, "have you risen from slumber?"

Anna lifted the latch and opened the door. Her steward's wide-brimmed hat dripped incessantly, flopping about with the breeze, but could not mask his concern. Every wrinkle and weathered fold on his face bled a horrid truth. "What's happened?"

"Nothing so severe, I imagine," he replied, wringing his hands within twill sleeves. "Brother Konrad has sent for you."

"At this hour?"

"Yes," the steward said. "Precisely now. Yet the reason for this summoning will not pass his lips, Knowing One. Forgive me for my vague words."

Nothing so severe. She met the steward's blue-gray eyes, full of haunting curiosity, then gazed down at the monastery's craggy silhouette. Few truly understood the austerity of Anna's practice, the importance of cloistering herself for weeks on end. Even fewer knew better than to summon her during the rituals of purification. She counted Konrad among those few.

As she followed the narrow, stone-lined path that carved across the slope, she took in the foggy sprawl of the lowlands and the black clouds blotting eastern skies. It was dead now, free of the ravens and hawks that often wheeled over the ridges, utterly silent aside from their boots crunching over gravel and earth. The monastery was a dark mass, not yet roused for its morning rites. Not even the northern bell tower, a black stripe looming against muddy slate above her, showed any sign of the watchman and his lantern.

Yet something had come.

Jutting out over the lowlands was the monastery's setstone perch, which hadn't seen a supply delivery in close to three cycles. Only it was not empty, nor was it occupied by the violet nerashi that Golyna or Kowak often sent. Anna glimpsed a sleek, battered nerash resting behind a sheen of mist, seated directly above the iron struts that bolted the perch to an adjacent outcropping.

"What is that?" Anna asked the steward, clenching her hood against a howling gust.

"I know not." His words were thick with unease.

In the main hall, a group of Halshaf sisters worked to light the candles lining the meditative circle. Each new spark and flicker drove away another patch of blackness, revealing glimmering mosaics upon the walls, banners emblazoned with Kojadi script, the reflective bronze bowls that hummed their celestial song each morning. The sudden flurry of footsteps upon crimson carpeting did not interrupt their soft, tireless chant in a dead tongue: *With this breath, I arise. With this breath, I pass away.*

After hours of meditation, the monastery always felt like another plane, another realm described in the ancient texts. It was a consequence of the formless absorption Anna invariably fell into, stripping her world of boundaries between things, of objects and observers, of concepts that lent meaning to the tapestry of colors and sensations around her. But the strange urgency in the air divided the world into definite components once more.

In some sense she hoped that Konrad had summoned her to bring news of his progress. Even his occasional plunge into panic, spurred by transient insights into a world birthed from emptiness, shed light on how profound his development had been.

"Do not shy away from existence," she'd always whispered to him, holding the sides of his head as she'd done years ago in Golyna, brushing away the man's tears as they rolled down in golden streaks. "Soon this dawn will clear away the darkness."

He was not the only one who'd changed since the war. His Alakeph brothers had grown still and sharp in the isolation of Rzolka's mountains, perhaps closer to their Kojadi roots than they'd been in a thousand years. At the very least, they were at their most populous, stationed in monasteries and settlements that extended far beyond Anna's awareness. The same held true for the Halshaf. And it had all stemmed from her guidance, they said—without her, the orders would have crumbled.

Yet she could not shake the sense that their central pillar was decaying.

Sleep brought dreams of Shem's flesh breaking apart, dissolving into the nothingness she could only experience in slivers. Flashes of ruins and bodies plagued her breathing during extended sits. Months ago, all comforts had come with a sense of imminent loss, and all pains had arisen with the dread of permanent existence. She felt herself resting on the precipice of something tremendous, something overwhelming, yet inexorable. Something that would shatter her mind if she was not ready.

But for the sake of the orders—for the sake of those who looked upon her as their pillar—she buried those thoughts. She turned her mind toward the mandala-adorned doors that led to Konrad's chamber.

"Shall I bring parchment?" the steward asked. "Perhaps we should preserve your words once again."

Anna grew still with her hand on the door's latch. She turned to examine the old steward, whose eyes now gleamed with expectant hopefulness. "Forgive me, but I would prefer to see Brother Konrad alone."

"Of course." He looked down at her broken hand and crinkled his brow. "Brother Konrad could transcribe your wisdom."

"Another time."

"Very well," the steward said softly. "As the Knowing One desires."

His footsteps whispered off over the carpeting, fading into morning chants from the adjoining hall. Soon there was a storm of footsteps shuffling behind thin walls, moving to wardrobes and chests, padding toward the main hall.

Anna opened the door.

Konrad sat on the far side of the chamber, leaning heavily upon the armrest of his oak chair. A pair of candles burned in shallow dishes near his feet, throwing patches of dim, shifting shadows over his nascent beard and haggard eyes. The return to aging—to true living, perhaps—had been a painful transition. But the worry on his face was deeper than the days when he'd toyed with his mortality. He looked up at Anna with sluggish focus.

"What's wrong?" Anna asked.

Konrad beckoned her to approach. "Close the door, Anna."

Something about his manner disarmed her. It was a consequence of days and faces and terrors that had been stained into her memory, infusing anything cordial with the expectation of pain. She wavered for a moment, her gaze wandering around the chamber's sparse furnishings and shelves of Kojadi tomes, then entered and sealed the door behind her. The air was stale and pungent with sweat.

"Are you leaving us?" she asked.

Konrad squinted, then shook his head. "You saw the nerash, didn't you?"

"Whose is it?"

"Somebody arrived during the night," Konrad whispered. His gaze crept along the floor, edging toward the cotton partition that concealed his sleeping mat. Every swallow was a hard lump upon his throat.

Anna grimaced. "Come out."

"Very well, Anna." A voice nestled in dark dreams. Crude, low, familiar in the most inhuman sense. The song of a bird from autumn woods.

No.

He emerged from behind the covering like a specter assuming its mortal form, letting candlelight wash over his tattered burlap folds, his bloodshot eyes, his twitching fingers. Three years of evading the vindictive masses, fleeing from whatever claws Anna could rake through the Spines and the lowlands, yet now he stood with some twisted semblance of pride.

Of comfort, even.

Anna could not speak. She longed for something—anything—to open his throat and make him scream.

"The years have been kind to you," the tracker said. He reached into the folds of his cloak and drew a rusting, serrated blade, then waved it in the candlelight. "An honest partnership, girl. Let's tie off this loose end."

"He came to settle with you," Konrad said, glaring at the tracker.

"Settle," the tracker echoed. "That sounds fitting."

But the years and pain bore down on Anna, bleeding the last of the air from her lungs. She was faintly aware of drawing a breath. Aware of murmuring beyond ringing ears, the subtle flickers of light dancing upon tempered iron. She moved closer, closer, sensing his shape looming as it had done in those damned woods, stretching up and over her until it consumed her sight, until the weight of his blade fell into her open palm and she was young once again, trapped in the memories she'd worked so feverishly to wrap in linen and tuck away in the shelves of her mind....

Anna drove the blade through his eye.

The tracker's head snapped back, twisting sharply toward the light as Anna forced the iron deeper. There was the low, muffled screech of a boar, then the wet churning of sinew and membranes. Yet the tracker did not advance, nor did he lash out. His burlap visage slowly spun toward Anna, plagued by a blossoming red blot, and its living eye fell upon her with placid interest.

What now, young one?

Again she was weak and helpless, dully sensing the scrape of metal over bone, the familiar yet wicked pulse of hayat's fabric, the fruitless trembling in bone-white knuckles and an aching wrist. All of her measured breaths and ascetic days meant nothing now. She craved *death*, she craved *pain*. There was no watcher behind her awareness, only an animal.

"Never had a taste for formalities," the tracker growled. "Passion. That was what we liked about you."

Hard, broken gasps. Tears winding down in tingling rivulets. Throbbing heartbeats that kicked through her sternum and up into her throat.

"Anna," Konrad said.

It was the tone she'd taken with the girl—not just a girl, but *Ramyi*, the girl who mattered. Collected, sharp, a warning as much as a plea to reason. Something about it cut her to the bone. She tore her hand from the leather-woven grip, fighting for every scrap of air she could pull into her lungs, and stared at the tracker. Her eyes were burning, but she focused through their vinegar sting.

"Nothing to say?" The tracker gently drew the blade from his eye. Spindle by spindle, milky tissue sealed the gaping red incision. "Not the Anna I remember."

She waited until her shoulders fell and her voice found cold stillness. "Because I'm not Anna."

"If it walks like a hound, barks like a hound..."

"You've not felt my teeth."

The tracker studied the blade in his hand. "Spare some forgiveness if I beg to differ, girl." A huff, a ripple of breath across his burlap. "Looks like in the end, after all those banners and bodies and the rest, you'll be the one grinning. Bet you've been dreaming about this since we parted, haven't you? Never seen eyes with that sort of fire."

Anna looked at Konrad. "What is he talking about?"

"Treating me like a wisp?" the tracker asked.

"I have nothing to say to you," she whispered.

"Come off it. A thousand days, a thousand runts prowling in the hills. Every cracked brain from Kowak to Dulstaka knows who slipped their leashes and gave 'em a scent." The tracker shook his head. "Say what you like, Anna, but our silence doesn't suit you."

"He's come for the Breaking," Konrad explained, gazing emptily at the carpet. "I trust his words."

"The words of a serpent," Anna said. Many had sought the Breaking in the ashes of the war, but those who'd knelt before her had been wandering anchorites, guilt-wracked butchers on the verge of madness, victims who'd seen their lives torn away and left with a craving for cessation. And she'd been grateful to anoint them, staring down into blank eyes and blank flesh. It was more than the obliteration of their essence—it was a return to the welcoming void they'd known before the womb, long before existence thrust them into separation and ignorance.

But the tracker was not like the others.

He was a man who'd grown to love his cage of flesh. He'd tasted some strain of that same void, surely, but it had only fed his broken mind, sapping meaning from the world that he knew as his plaything.

Some men were beyond redemption. Aberrations of life, vessels the gods had forgotten to imbue with a conscience.

Killers who took refuge in honor.

"Taking a bite into gifted gold, aren't you?" the tracker asked. "Take what you've been after, girl. Open my throat, scrape out my marrow, stretch my skin out over cursed wood. Dance in the fucking blood, for all it's worth. Grove knows how many spirits are waiting to pick me out of their teeth."

Konrad sighed. "He means it, Anna."

"What are you playing at?" she asked.

"Death," the tracker said.

"Tell me the truth," she said softly, "or we'll carve it out of you."

"Hard work has its day of recompense," he replied. "You gave Rzolka its torch. Suppose that was its last chance, all things boiled down. A few years of glory, a few whelps put under the soil, but now—now it's all in your lap, girl. Way back when I first saw those eyes, I knew you'd wind up towering over bodies. So take your spoils and enjoy it. I'll scream as much as you like."

Anna sensed the rattled edge in his voice like a faint breeze. It was subtle, nearly imperceptible, but the razor-mind caught its warbling tail and shaking timbre. Her lips widened into a thin smile. "No."

His right eye twitched. "No?"

"Death belongs to the humble," she whispered. "Surely a god has no need for it."

"You've grown sick, haven't you? Fine. Let me squeal a bit before you open my veins."

"I'll do whatever I please."

"I know what you want."

"You know nothing about me," she said. "Not anymore. But I'm certain of what you want, because you're a hound. A sad, starving hound. You talk about knowing my eyes, but I know yours. All you crave is control."

"No control in letting you gut me."

"You want to die on your terms," she said, taking a step forward, drowning in his stench of marsh-rot and liquor and bile. "You let me believe I was in command, but you knew what scared me, didn't you? Those days are gone." Another step. "What could you possibly take away from me now? My life? Those I love? Everything burned away, but I remain. And now you'll understand fear."

The tracker's chest swelled with a spastic rhythm. "You watched Volna's men march to the gallows. Don't act like you're not after blood, girl."

"Once I knew a girl who would've given anything to see you bleed," she replied. "But she died long ago. You made sure of that."

Bones creaked along the tracker's wrists. "What do you want, then?"

"Far less than you."

"You can stomp us out. Right here, right now."

"I already have. But your death occurred in council rooms and referendums, not at the end of a blade." She tapped the tracker's chest with a crooked finger. "I want to know what has you running scared."

"Seems clear that I've had my time with running."

"You'll never outrun living," she said. "It's nipping at your heels, isn't it? It must be crushing you. Imagine how shattered your mind will be in a hundred years, a thousand…when you've seen every being rise and fall like stalks in a field, and the weight of eternity finally breaks you." Laughter flared up in her, at once absurd and callous. Yet she held nothing back. "Oh, how I'll weep for you."

"Shattered minds," the tracker growled. "Look what the north did to you. You star-chasing, sand-blinded—"

"What broke you?"

The tracker tilted his head lower, glaring down at her with eyes that spoke of murder, of solitude among broken peaks and howling caverns.

Of *hate*.

"You've taken far too much of my time already," Anna continued. "See him off to his den, Konrad."

Anna surveyed the white-clad brother, her gust of pride taking on a sharply sour note. Nothing pleasant was born of ignorance.

"He knows where the others fled," Konrad said. His eyes flicked up at her with haunting prescience, with the weight of passions he'd learned to bury, yet had not forgotten. The Breaking was a return to emptiness, but those with dark cravings often found a way to regain their appetite.

"And what?" Anna's gaze darted between the two men. "They have no refuge in this world or the next."

"A curious sentiment from the hunter herself," the tracker mused. "How many of your precious scribes have put blades to the inquisitors' necks? Seems you're keen on dragging the beasts from their holes."

"For stability, not vengeance." Some shard of her heart raged against that. There was no denying that Anna had done everything in her power to withdraw them from the currents of the world and its wars, urging transcendence over domination in every forum to which she'd been summoned. But nobody could ignore the parallel truth: The orders were pillars of the new regimes in Rzolka and abroad, a mystical flurry of arms and blades resembling the hundred-limbed guardians in Kojadi murals, ready to sever the head of whatever serpents rose against a fragile peace. And they—she—had proven that in ample measure. "When I said that we have nothing to discuss, I meant it."

"Don't remember what a few bitter men can do?"

Anna's jaw ached. "I recall the cost of compliance far too well."

"They have networks, Anna," Konrad said grimly. "These are the architects. The ones that kept us awake at night. If they could do that to Golyna, right under our—"

"They won't," Anna snapped.

"How can you be so sure?"

"The eyes of the world witnessed their crimes," she said. "It acts as one gaze, Konrad, and it sees everything. Soon every hollow will have its shadows burned away."

The tracker snorted. "Must've been a blind spot everywhere I went."

"You know how a fire rages, Anna," Konrad whispered. "If one ember remains…"

"And if only you knew how the flames were spreading," the tracker said.

"Fear had its time," Anna said, narrowing her eyes at Konrad. "We left it all behind and nothing will drag us back. Especially not something so pathetic." She regarded the tracker with bare pity, looking him up and down as one might examine a lame horse. "Go back to your shadows, and never return to this place. There's mercy in my heart, but I speak for none of my followers, nor the things they'll do once they seize you. Nothing will trouble my mind if they seal you in a place of unending pain. Silence would be my protest." She gathered up the pleats of her robe and moved toward the chamber door, bowing her head as she went.

"Then I suppose the girl will find *you*," the tracker growled.

Anna's foot hovered above the carpet. "What?"

"The girl," he said. "The Starsent."

Her bemusement was raw and swift, burning away any trace of disbelief as it hardened to rage. "Don't call her that."

"Struck a nerve, have I?"

She turned to face the tracker. "You're lying."

"Up in arms over shadows then, aren't you?" His laugh was sickly, hoarse. "But as you want it, panna. No more barks from this old hound. Even if you'll spend your nights counting slats on the ceiling, thinking all the while, 'what *if?*'"

Anna looked to Konrad, but the man's unease rivaled her own. Plenty of nights had already come and passed with the girl weighing heavily upon her mind, threatening to strangle her in dreams of blighted cities and fallow fields. "Where is she?"

"You know my price," the tracker said.

"Yet I trust none of your words."

The tracker gave a wheezing sigh. "All good things in time, eh?" He twisted his neck to the side, filling the chamber with dull cracking. "You get your pup and I get the cuts I'm owed. Swear on that."

Anna studied the man's jaundiced eyes under a creeping shroud of nausea. It was a safer deal than any she'd ever forged, but it still carried an omen of lessons ignored and promises obliterated. She suspected that its suffering might somehow eclipse whatever the girl would bring to bear when she rose from the shadows. The cruelty of a wicked man, after all, had no end, no final flourish. And—

The Starsent.

Even that title was enough to tighten Anna's throat.

"Send a missive to the captain in the Kowak chapter," Anna said to Konrad, still gazing into the dark clouds of the tracker's eyes. "Tell him I'll need their best."

Chapter 2

In the womb of the Halshaf monastery, reborn under every mica-strewn nebula and passage of the shattered moon, Anna had grown to perceive herself as the world rather than its wanderer. In fact, she'd found kinship in the world. She'd fixed it in her mind as some macrocosm of what she was, some seed that had germinated before time itself. No matter how often its shoots and saplings were cut down by the swings of a woodman's ax, it had held fast to its roots within the soil, waiting for the mercy of spring to venture forth once more. But even that had been a concept that she'd wishfully forced upon the world.

It was a child's fantasy, a projection of forlorn hopes.

Soaring high above the patchwork fields and forests of central Rzolka, Anna saw—seemingly for the first time—the truth of her enduring seed. It had been torn from the earth, scorched and cracked, scattered to the winds like the ashes of cities she'd once known. Between masses of wispy ashen clouds, the lowlands stretched out in blackened meadows, in freckled expanses of cut and cleared logging sites, in great tracts of empty huts and halls that jutted from the mires as rotting bones. Most of the sacred groves had been abandoned to overgrowth, or worse, trampled and desecrated by the heretics that had flooded the region in Volna's absence.

Roads that had once been knotted with caravans now appeared as desolate, withering veins, slashed here and there by rusting kator tracks. Furnaces bled their black fumes on the horizon.

Perhaps it had always been this way, Anna considered. Perhaps the higher she ascended, the further back she drew from her insect ignorance, the more the truth of the world revealed itself. But mutation was a constant truth, for better or worse. There were no marking stones for the grave of the Rzolka she'd known—only the soot-stained, oily shrine of what it had become. "What's that glint in your eyes, girl?" the tracker asked. Seated directly across from Anna on a quilted bench, his hands iron-bound and tucked snugly into his lap, it was nearly impossible to avoid his chilling stare. "Not what it was, is it?"

"Your comrades did their work tirelessly," she replied, sparing a momentary glance at his reflection in the window before gazing outward once more.

"My kind? Wasn't a grain of cartel salt in Rzolka before the war."

"Of course," she said. "Mass killings were the lesser evil, I'm sure."

"You laugh, but time'll tell. Mark my word on that. Not even the Moskos managed to sell our flesh at a whore's rate, Anna. Doesn't take a diviner to see the way of it, figure out why the gods want nothing to do with us. Ever learn the word *forsaken,* girl?"

Anna met the tracker's rigid gaze. "I'm no girl."

"The Southern Death's more fitting, eh?"

She looked away.

"Titles, titles," the tracker cackled. "Such a sickness in the world for *titles.* The runts in Malchym would slit their mothers' throats for a fitting one."

"You share the disease of pride," Anna said.

The tracker clicked through his teeth and jingled his iron links, needling Anna's mind with barbs of panic, of latent violence. Narrowed eyes seemed to drink in her fear. "Keep looking for river flowers, *girl.* This entire world is sickness."

At midday, the nerash wheeled over the outskirts of Kowak with a sickening lurch. It sliced through stormy billows, offering vignettes of a black, turbulent sea and a sprawling city that gathered like froth at its shores. Twenty of the order's scribes had deployed there over the past year, but their runes—those that sprouted trees, cleansed wells, reamed in brush fires—hadn't changed the face of the land much at all.

Anna held onto rattling straps near her head as they dove into the downpour. Her stomach knotted like it had in the capsules of the kales, but the sensation soon receded in a backdrop of bewilderment, of screeching wing flaps and crackling eardrums and oscillating iron panels. She wrinkled her nose at the sudden burst of sparksalt fumes; they seemed to bleed from dying turbines, wafting into the cabin and stinging her throat in seconds.

Beneath her the forests swelled, rising up in a stark, threatening mass through screens of mist and smoke. A vast mesa—formed from compacted soil and timber, it seemed—drifted into view in the adjacent clearing. It grew nearer and nearer, fringed by towering pine masts that sharpened to gust-raked canopies, then to quilts of silvery needles, then to ravens perched on gnarled branches and—

The nerash's skids struck the mesa with a teeth-jolting *thump*. Anna's head jerked forward, bobbing with every hop and crunch over the ragged landing platform. She shut her eyes as the nerashif cranked back on his lever, digging the skid's talons into the damp earth and its evergreen skeleton.

They twisted and skittered over the soil, filling the cabin with horrible crunching each time the talons caught a buried log and tore across its bark. Finally there was a clap, a groan from deep within the beast, a hiss as the nerash's cylinders stretched and dampened their halt. The craft rocked back on its haunches, calming the blackness behind Anna's lids, and grew still.

Its turbines slowed with a pup's whine.

"Not dead yet," the tracker said, equally surprised and amused. "Could hardly tell it was an easterner at the helm."

Anna opened her eyes and worked to undo her harness.

"Never been to Kowak, have you?"

She shook her head. "Let's go."

"Swore I'd only visit this pit again when we'd drowned it in ashes," he said. "Then again, you'd know more about that than I would."

"Be silent and hear me well," Anna snapped, snuffing out the tracker's rising giggle. "If you truly desire an escape from your marking, then you'll come to heel. From this moment onward, you'll resist your animal instincts. Not a foul word, not an errant gesture. I have no qualms with casting you back into this world. You are *nothing*."

She undid the final buckle in their newfound quiet.

* * * *

Between chest-stirring cracks of thunder, silence found its deepest notch. That murderous silence, so thick that it leeched the breaths from one's lungs, hung palpably over the inner districts of Kowak. As palpably as the odors of kerosene and rotting bodies, which now lay in heaps at the bottoms of flooded mass graves. It had been impossible to ignore them; they flanked the last stretch of the kator's tracks like pale, bloated flowerbeds.

"There was a riot last night," a ruddy-cheeked militia boy had explained while leading Anna through the moot hall's smoky corridors. "We told them to go home. But that sow's been milked now, hasn't it?"

Anna could not bring herself to look at the tracker's cloaked face. To behold his glee, to know whatever vindicated thoughts he might exclaim with wild eyes.

Waiting in the Chamber of Antlers, she found herself surveying the clusters of empty brown bottles strewn across the table. Their stench, biting and tinged with the same rot that had clung to the drifters who staggered through Bylka, assailed her with every swell of the hearth's dry heat. Amber liquid had pooled into thick, glossy splotches upon the sacred wood of the eastern groves. Decrees and writs and missives were plastered together in stained piles. And high up on timber walls, illumined by grimy lamps that had gathered mounds of shriveled gray gnats, were the dust-covered and club-cracked skulls of the city's earliest pinemen and seers.

This was the seat of Rzolka's eastern power. This was where infallible men had decided the lives and deaths of those with soil beneath their nails.

Anna studied the bitterness creeping through her chest.

The doors creaked open to reveal a mass of grim-faced, heavyset men shambling toward them. They offered little more than nods or grumbles of clan-speak to the flesh-branded young women stationed in the threshold. Jenis was among them, muttering to his captains in a sour, guarded tone, but it was difficult to distinguish the remaining southerners. They all wore the strange pastiche of traditional vestments and northern luxuries that had flooded the region in the past year or so: quilted doublets, the bristly skins of bears and wolves, dozens of layered amulets and trinkets that gleamed with emeralds, amber, Hazani rose gold. Some even had their faces stitched and studded with the turquoise droplets from Nahora's coast, which had been one of Kowak's most demanded *tributes* for bringing aid to their shores.

Upon noticing the tracker, however, their jangling and murmuring fell away. Konrad's old habit of omission was hard to break, it seemed.

"Well," the tracker said, lifting his muddied feet onto the table, "I'm glad you lot haven't been too busy to tuck into your suppers." His laugh was barely stifled. Then his eyes fell upon Jenis and there was an absence of mirth, of base composure. He gazed at the commander with the hatred of a wronged man.

"What is this?" a gray-bearded man spat. "Brought the korpa here to string him up, have we?"

A bald, scowling captain stepped forward. "Honor would be all mine."

"Not yet," Anna said. "Sit. There are matters to discuss."

"Konrad said we had a new trail," Jenis said, shouldering his way to the head of the gathering. His scars were dark and mottled in the lamplight, flashing bright pink as a serving girl moved past them with a dribbling candle and a bushel of bread.

The tracker smoothed out his shirt. "In the flesh."

"Best tell me you're toying with us," Jenis growled at Anna. "This city's already stomped on enough slugs. One more's nothing to us."

"I'll explain," Anna said.

"Explain what?" Jenis asked. "Break his marking. We'll cut him slow and proper."

Anna rose from her chair and swept her gaze across the Rzolkan ranks, making no attempt to uncoil the knot in her brow. "Sit *down*."

The men shared glances and curled lips, shifting anxiously until they found the courage to wander to their armchairs. Several of them, including Jenis, instinctively lifted corked bottles from beneath the table and passed them around the crescent. There was a long stretch of squeaking, fizzling, chugging, all underscored by the hum of sleeping violence with which Anna had grown intimately familiar.

She could almost feel their liquor burning through ulcerous guts, dulling their minds further with every sip and gulp…. "I don't care what's gone on between you," she said, her stare cutting a wide arc around the table. "This day will be immune from your squabbling." Nobody heeded her words as promptly as the tracker, who was quick to straighten his spine and disarm his glare.

"Be quick of it," Jenis said as he wiped his chin with a velvet sleeve. "What's he got to do with the hunt? He ought to be in fetters, far as this city's concerned. Maybe on a stake."

"Konrad was supposed to address you fully on the issue," Anna said. "Yet I now understand his reservations. If finding their remnants is truly your focus, then you'll need to trust me when I ask for your cooperation. You'll need to bury whatever judgments you hold in your hearts."

"Judgments," Jenis laughed. "Look upon him as a babe, shall we?"

The others offered a round of curt, vacuous laughter. It was difficult to laugh—earnestly or otherwise—in the face of men who had taken so much.

"It's our only path forward," she explained.

"That's what splits us, Kuzalem. You tossed your Breaking around to scrape out what's between haunted ears. But sometimes, a man needs his wrath. Any widow here would burn an offering to that."

"What end would come of it?" she asked, examining the rusty age spots and creases on the old fighter's face. His weariness was a constant pall rather than a mask, bubbling up like a spring that merely hinted at some abomination beneath it all. But she understood his breed, his predicament:

An old hound, starved of masters or vigor, knew only of gnawing flesh and barking at shadows. "His death is, and will be, a simple matter. He's accepted that. But he's also the antidote to their pestilence. How many times can you apply the same balm to pox-eaten flesh, Jenis?"

"*Slishaya*," Jenis snapped. "We've made good on giving you silence, girl. Not a doubt that they tore up your soul in the east. But now you drag your mountain mud in our hall, speak to us like our stones are high up in our bellies—not a fucking *chance*."

"Bold words from the Bala," the tracker said.

A rash of curses exploded from Kowak's council, flowing between river-tongue and the grymjek alike until Anna slapped the table with a rigid palm. "Enough. What would you have me do, Jenis?"

The old captain stroked his beard. "Balm. You call our blades and ropes a balm? Your soft-skin girls in the monasteries would let us burn every notch of the flatlands. That's where they're prowling, you know. Everyone knows it."

"Blood begets blood," Anna whispered. "I've seen how you track them down." The term *Kowak confession* had made its rounds in most cities, according to the Alakeph captains still operating across the Hazani chapters. It was no secret that the southerners craved names and names only.

No matter who owned them.

"You'd trust this beast?" asked another man with scar-threaded lips. One of his eyes stared off into the darkness of the neighboring chamber. "Harden your skin, Kuzalem. This is Volna's death."

"I've seen how these movements *die*," Anna said, glaring at Jenis. "They can be hanged and bled and beaten, but they're never truly extinguished. Our victories are what puts divine fire in their hearts."

"Seems she knows a fair bit about us beasts," the tracker said.

She stared into those bloodshot eyes, her lips pursed so tightly that they began to quake. "I do."

Studded soles came clapping down the corridor at Anna's back, muffled by the ancient wood of the chamber's doors. Stillness descended over the gathering.

Anna turned just as the branded women slid the oak bar from its brackets and drew back on iron handles. The doors parted with a deep, aching groan, allowing Konrad to rush into the assembly and its pooling silence with white robes billowing behind him.

"Apologies for my delay," he said, settling into an empty chair at Anna's side.

"Ought to be the least of your regrets," one of Jenis's captains said darkly.

"It was only sensible, wasn't it?" Konrad asked. "How many of the cartel's blades keep an ear to the privy chambers on the Broken Knoll?"

"We're not children," another man snarled. "Hazan's not some beast in the fen."

"You're right," Konrad replied. "They're in every tavern and foundry from here to the plains."

"Lying's a way of life for you," Jenis said, unsealing his second bottle with a faint *pop.*

"He told you what was necessary to bring you here," Anna said. "Now, the choice of whether to listen or bury our words is yours alone. But I caution you against turning us away, Jenis."

"That so?"

"I've come here to safeguard your claim, not usurp it." She watched the old man's eyes flitting around the assembly, weighing his prestige in the eyes of fresh captains, his trust in comrades from dead wars, and his hatred of everything Volna had been, now distilled like some vast reservoir of tar and ash in the tracker's stare. Volna's fall had done more than left the world in need of wardens and governors; it had awoken the ambitions of cruel, long-spurned men with coffers too barren for their liking. "Will you hear me, Jenis?"

Jenis braced his hands on creaking knees and cast his gaze away sharply, almost as though bristling at a bitter swill of his drink. "What've you come for?"

"Eyes and ears," she explained. "He'll give us the shards that have been missing from your operations. All the missed movements, the names, the intermediaries. It's systemic, Jenis, and it needs to be severed at the root."

"Seven hundred marsh-born men went to the plains," Jenis said. "Not one returned. Boys too young to know the feel of a tit are carrying their fathers' blades." In one tremendous swig, he drained the last of his bottle and set it down gently at the edge of the table. "We've nothing to spare your errand."

Anna sighed. "We're not asking for men. The Alakeph can bear that burden well enough. What we need are your breakers, your reports, your—"

"*Your,*" Jenis said, scowling at Anna and Konrad. "Got a knack for that word, girl. Wasn't so long ago that we gave you everything we had."

"And now we'll finish it."

"Quit spying at stars."

"If it's not your problem now, it will be."

"Our problem's with the scalp-trimmers in the bogs," he said, spittle bursting from his mouth as he raced on. "No, no, it's with the mad korpy in the market, raving about spirals and lines and angles, world-eaters and all the rest. Maybe with those province-breakers, burning their own fields." Anna's jaw was aching once more. "You're not—" "Head in the reeds, like all the others," Jenis rasped. "Know how my breakers spent their dawn, Kuzalem? Tracking up and down the Nekresa's banks, dragging farmers out of those shit-stained hovels, asking *who saw what?* and *when was that?* to know about those scribes of yours. Two young ones—must've been eleven or so, says my men—skinned, cut up, left in sacks by the road." He met Anna's eyes directly and at once his gaze was piercing, stripped of its languid veil and haziness, so startling that it forced her to glance away. *"That's* a wild dawn. Something's burning, all right, but not in Hazan. It's in your fucking nursery."

Anna strained to repress the sudden rush of bile in her throat.

A dozen in a cycle, and that tally was still mounting. She should've expected it from those who'd known the war's cost firsthand, especially in the rural provinces, where fear prevailed over wisdom in matters of resolve. That which they could not explain had to be destroyed, lest it destroy them, too.

How often had saviors been mistaken for serpents?

"Done here?" the tracker asked, stretching forth with a dull crack down his spine. "Heard wiser words minced between field oxen."

Anna nodded at Konrad, then gathered up her robes and stood. She studied Jenis's face with dispassion, with doleful rebuke. "Not so long ago, Nahora also paid no mind to the stirrings beneath its shadow." She then regarded the assembly with a placid stare. "I suppose we all find the Grove eventually."

* * * *

At sundown Andriv and his Alakeph company reached the nerashi mesas. They arrived in a pure white beam, a narrow lance that shone like sunlight through the dense fog, distended by swollen combat packs and iron harnesses beneath their cloaks. Their silence, which still must've registered as spectral to those beyond the order, managed to sever whatever disputes had been erupting between the third platform's merchants and Huuri attendants.

"Just how I remember 'em," the tracker whispered to Anna. "In sore need of a fuck."

Crude as it was, those words reflected a grain of what Anna now saw in the brothers. They had grown ruthlessly efficient under the order's new leadership, growing ever closer to a stark, rigorous incarnation only known through the cardinal Kojadi scriptures. But that theoretical return to form mirrored their strength: Not a single monastery or foundling hall had been raided in the past year, which was not to say that zealots hadn't devoted serious time and manpower to such attempts.

Upon each brother's back was a sleek, leather-wrapped ruj, likely bearing the stamped emblem of a cartel based in Nur Kuref or Leejadal. They were vicious instruments, as precise and honed for killing as any other works that had stemmed from the north's postwar patents. No longer were their models burdened by cranked cogs or chaotic sprays of iron. Now they were slotted with tin boxes, their cartridges filled with fléchettes and copper bolts and whatever else the tinkerers could devise, primed to open a man's skull at a hundred paces—or more.

Even their polished ceramic vests had become a vestige of the old ways, no more effective than the straw cuirasses Anna had seen on Gosuri huntsmen. The only protection was a keen eye, a lack of hesitation.

Anna studied Konrad as he made his way over the battered, windswept surface of the mesa, bowing deeply to Andriv near a row of slumbering nerashi. It was impossible to determine how earnest his words and gestures were. She considered that Jenis might've cut to the core of the brother's character, perceiving something within Konrad that she'd overlooked since his Breaking:

His truths were malleable.

His truths were weapons.

"You didn't mention the girl," the tracker said. "Slipped your mind, did it?"

Anna glanced sidelong, watching the tracker's breaths leak through the satin shroud and bleed off as ashen wisps. "I didn't have time to get around to it."

"Strange." He grunted and folded his arms. "Running those pretty lips never used to be a problem."

"He didn't want to hear anything that extends beyond Kowak."

"Huh," the tracker said. "That's the way of it, then?"

"That's the way."

"I'd reckon the old crow would want to know about your sukra." He shrugged. "Then again, you really don't know anything about *him*, do you? You don't know what his hands have done."

"Nobody needs to know everything." Anna turned her head slowly. "And you'll hold that wicked tongue, or I'll cut it out."

The tracker's satin shifted, hinting at a broad, blackened smile beneath the veil. "Wouldn't be the first time."

Chapter 3

Nightfall descended as their nerash broke away from the mainland and thrust out over the Eastern Sea. The remainder of their flock—four weathered Hazani models, bloated to haul immense quantities of freight or fighters—soared alongside them, marked by crimson everburn flares that gave the illusion of abominations worming through black depths.

Anna wasn't certain that the crafts could ever grant her something akin to comfort, nor could she understand the appeal of being sealed in the stomach of a howling bird, but their role was vital. And as far as nerashi went, this design was better than most. Ration trunks, padded inner walls, a heating strip along the floor panel—it was far from welcoming, but it was bearable. She could learn to appreciate *bearable*.

No longer enthralled by the drifting red baubles, Anna slid away from the window and shifted to the edge of her cot. She was dimly aware of the river-tongue flowing between the bunk aisles, so chaste and formal that it had to be among the Alakeph, but the tongue no longer felt like her own. It was the price of constant exile, constant burning bridges, constant rebirths in the womb of meditation.

She suspected that when it was all over, she would not know her own place.

"Kuzalem?"

Anna spun to find Andriv holding a bundle of scrolls beneath his arm. She'd only seen him in passing, but now she noted that he had the sharp, clear gaze of a man with known intentions. That was more than she could say for most.

He was older than Yatrin, but still rather young for a captain, much less a commander. His hair was a dusty brown, cropped and swept to one side. Every feature was pronounced, yet narrow, somehow shrunken; in fact, if not for the deep green of his eyes, pure Hazani blood might've been a fair bet.

"Low suns," Anna said, rising to offer a slight bow. She held onto the aisle's tether as the nerash bucked to the left. "We appreciate your assistance."

"The honor is ours entirely," he explained. "You couldn't imagine my joy when Brother Konrad told me of your predicament. Our tomesmen often recite tales of your involvement in the War of Ravagers and now, to behold you in your corporeal form...."

Anna looked away. "Your chapter has done considerable work for the order, as I understand it. I suppose it was a natural choice."

He offered a meek smile, then gestured down the aisle, indicating a low table cluttered with charts and unfurled missives. A soot-stained lamp swung overhead. "Brother Konrad and I spoke with this tracker of yours," he said, trailing Anna as she made her way along the cramped passage. "His insights were rather fresh, I must say. We had no idea how many of their architects were still inhabiting the flatlands."

"Weigh his speech with caution," Anna said. "He knows what men are fond of hearing."

As they reached the table, Andriv knelt on the cushion opposite Anna's position. He cleared his throat, shifting incessantly, caught in the clutches of sudden and bashful unease. "Lay mercy upon my words, Kuzalem, but such curiosity arises quite fiercely in me: Why have you placed faith in his words at all?"

The girl. Anna channeled that thought into a shallow nod, a delicate smoothing of her robe's pleats. "Not even the inquisitors have managed to make his comrades speak. I would be remiss to surrender this chance."

"As my thinking mind assumed," Andriv replied hastily. "Forgive me."

"Doubt is the sign of a shrewd leader, Brother Andriv. Guard your suspicion well."

He smiled deeply, but did not meet her eyes. "My only task in your service, Knowing One, is to act as the eye that guides your blades."

"Unfortunately, our vision stems from the tracker."

"Of course," Andriv said. "But his words trouble me."

Anna tensed at the newfound edge in the brother's voice. "Speak your mind."

"I would not presume to doubt you, Kuzalem."

"Speak, brother."

Andriv's lips trembled. He joined his hands in his lap, but could not stop himself from wringing them. "He mentioned the Starsent. The one who was Ramyi."

Her breaths slowed and seized in her throat. *Starsent.* That old Kojadi title was like poison. It did not refer to a girl, but to one who could pierce the mind of a man and splay out his thoughts in a constellation. One who would bring about a new world from the ashes of the old.

"Is it true, Kuzalem?"

"What did he tell you?"

"I hold none of these words in my heart," Andriv explained. "But he claims to know where she nests."

Anna gestured to a faded map of the flatlands. "Show me."

"Her notch upon the sands is not what troubles me," Andriv replied. "Her place is said to lie in the den of Volna's engineers. By what divination he knows this, I dare not presume. Nor do I lend him the faith that I reserve for the order, you see. But such a notion pains my mind."

Memories of the girl's essence pierced her awareness. Frigid, searing visions of a world lost to hatred, of words that festered in the recesses of buried dreams. Flashes of the blade she'd put to a sister's throat, of a youthful stare that had traced the lapis lazuli and jade of ceiling mosaics, of blindfolds she'd slipped over a girl's eyes to shroud the skeletons of her kin.

Your violence has come home to you.

"Kuzalem?" Andriv whispered. He was leaning over the table with crinkled brows. "Have I troubled you?"

"It's not you," she said. "Is that all he said? Did he say anything of her purpose in their company?"

"You believe it to be true?"

She shook her head. "Knowing takes precedence over belief, brother. Tell me what he claims to know."

Closing his eyes for a moment, the brother's face grew decidedly somber. His lids flickered with repressed pain, a sense of something hideous and inescapable, as though he'd begun to dissolve from the inside.

Anna knew the sensation all too well.

"She imbues their forces with hellish scars," Andriv said finally. "Those who know of the defiled flesh have given her refuge in their knowledge. Yet there are others, too. Legions of the damned and the savage lend their blades to her cause."

Her fingertips prickled with numbness and the pit of her stomach fell away in a slow, burning ache. Was he truly describing *Ramyi*? It felt like yet another apparition in meditation, unreal; yet as vivid as waking life, jarring her out of time, out of space.

"It wasn't my fault," she whispered, so softly that it was stifled by the nerash's oscillating plates.

Andriv frowned. "Forgive me, Kuzalem, but I heard not what—"

"Nothing," she cut in. "It was nothing." Then came a span of true nothingness, of shared terror in the understanding of what had passed and what was yet to come. "Brother Andriv, I should lead the others in their practice before we put out the lights. I ask you to confer with Brother Konrad and the tracker once more, if only to know her location more precisely. We'll need a staging area."

"Yes, of course," he replied, raking in his charts in a nervous rush. "We have several chapters in mind, though we'll need to pass over Nahora before we enter the flatlands. There are still batteries to the north."

"The chapters won't do," Anna explained. "We'll need to make our presence scarce."

Andriv blinked at her, seemingly in awe of whatever counsel she might offer—nonsense or otherwise.

"A hunter's terror is the surest path to driving a fox into its hollow," she continued, gazing out at the black, misty skies once again. "I won't risk any lives on an assault until we're certain of her position."

Andriv nodded, bowed, and rose from his cushion, sparing a final glance at the table and its scattered documents before he entered the aisle. But his steps were slow, sporadic, nearly dragging between the bunks. Abruptly he turned to face Anna once more, shadows etched across his face in dark splotches. "Kuzalem, do you believe it's actually the Starsent? Will we look upon her?"

"Do not believe," Anna said coldly. "Know."

* * * *

It was a safe house nestled among apple orchards and wide, reed-clogged wadis. Patrols made their rounds six times per day. Two mountains, the transfigured lovers Tuchalla and Qirpek, presided over the compound with the boons of creeping shadows, slope-borne whirls of sand, and treacherous passes. None of the traders or caravans from Nur Sabah had cause to venture there, and even the lowest nerashi runs—whether dispatched by the Nahorans or their neighboring qora—would detect anything worth probing.

That which did not exist could not be killed.

Anna studied the tracker's map of the region, concentrating intently on his dried inkblot. It was plausible enough, and several of the northern-born Alakeph brothers had lent credence to his words.

"Those are foul lands," one had said, examining the countless latches and cylinders of his disassembled ruj with a falcon's absorption. "Death itself could dwell there and he would only find his own." She'd awoken to the hard, biting gaze of Har-gunesh, unsure if she'd managed to sleep at all. Her mind had been ablaze with the tracker's eyes, with his constant stench, which had seemed to effortlessly penetrate the walls of his holding cell. Gazing out at the land beneath them during the night hadn't been bearable, either: No matter how much time had passed, the trampled, shell-scarred remains of Nahora still snuffed out whatever spark she'd nursed in her heart.

Yet now she rested by the window once more, her cheek pressed to warming glass, wondering how many leagues lay between Leejadal and their target. Setting the map aside, Anna turned her attention to a barren sky, to the silvery strands that broke over the nerash's wings and held them aloft. Her instructors in the academy at Malijad had called the substance *danha*, the dissolving matter of the world. They'd said it could not be touched, nor felt, nor truly glimpsed by the living. But it was not the same world her instructor had known, and Anna no longer accepted the truth of others on faith alone.

The danha over Hazan was smooth and still, as stagnant as the parched heat that pooled over its flats and gorges. Hours ago, the endless sand seas had been dotted with the half-devoured corpses of Volna's machines, often encircled by the tent towns of tinkerers and bargaining caravans. Now the land was cracked and naked. Far on the horizon, Leejadal glimmered with its amethyst-tiled skyline, its vast domes that resembled the growing chambers in the kales, its kator lines that spooled out like diamond thread in every direction. Fumes billowed from chasms and pits drilled into cracked plains. At the heart of the sprawling tumor, thrusting up into the danha and beyond its impossible boundaries, seemingly able to pierce the nebulae themselves, was a rod of iron and black stone. The vision was wholly alien, an aberration that her mind could not have fathomed nor accepted in younger years, even after the heights of Malijad.

She watched the flanking nerashi broaden their wings and fan out their leather tails, drifting lower for the approach on the mesas. Sparksalt vapors bloomed in rippling sills beneath the machines.

Andriv came to her side with a patchwork brown cloak draped over his arm. "Merciful stars, Kuzalem," he said. "The quartermaster issued us a spare."

Years ago, leagues away, she'd donned a covering of the same sort. She could still feel the dirt stinging her cheeks.

"Does it suit you?" Andriv asked.

"My thanks," Anna said, taking the cloak and laying it out across her lap. "Though I have my reservations about this place."

"They'll be none the wiser about our arrival." Andriv peered through Anna's window, fixed on the mirror glints of a captain within the neighboring nerash. "It seems that this tracker has comrades in the most unexpected of burrows."

Anna followed the man's gaze, though she found her attention lured by the swelling expanse of setstone and pilfered abundance. Its wealth was little more than an artifice for the ignorant. Such cities had inherited a lineage of mindless indulgence, a haze of decadence, a gluttonous frenzy where goodness could be bought and sold. "It's not so unexpected, Brother Andriv."

* * * *

Nuhra of the Fifth Martyr did not look like the sort of woman who could saw through a throat with ease. In fact, she looked like the sort of woman who was disturbed, even repulsed, by the mere sight of blood. The sort who was decent and virtuous. The trailcarver had highborn flatland features, a lithe form that spoke of restraint in all things, a well-tailored silk and cashmere garment unsullied by mud or drink. She smelled of fragrant oils. Atop her head was a narrow ribbon that bound smooth, glossy hair into a black mass, free of knots or splintered ends.

But Anna could not bow to her, nor could she clasp her hand on the mesa's walkway.

Not after the tracker's words.

"Always said there was no sense in stuffing their mouths," he'd explained as the turbines wound down. "Liked to hear 'em sing."

There was no question of moving in a single unit. The crowds were bustling, swarming at every intersection and junction of shops, flowing overhead on rusting gangways and below in shaded tunnels. Cardamom swirled alongside the odors of scorched stone and flesh. Anna's eyes could hardly track specific faces as they streamed past her: sun-beaten Hazani children, blindfolded Huuri, whip-marked flagellants, henna-streaked women, flesh crowded with beads, piercings, pustules, amulets—it was a vast mélange of rippling fabric and teeth, just as jarring as it had been to her youthful mind.

But it was worse now.

Years of monastic stillness had left her defenseless against every new jolt and sharp cry, every flash of vibrant thread, every sweltering breeze that bled the moisture she'd ceased to cherish. She was skinless, raw, apt to be drowned by every eruption of her senses. And she was trembling. Numbness trickled down to her legs. Spasms burst through her chest. *You are not here.* she whispered to the thinking mind. *You are the sacred watcher.*

Her next breath brought stillness.

And with stillness came clarity, a sour realization of what the war had done to Hazan. River-tongue was plastered over most of the signs and banners. Southerners moved in velvet-cloaked packs, encircled by throngs of hired blades and dancing girls. A presence that had once been fortified by terror was now sustained by salt, by metal, by prestige. In a land with nothing, those with *something* could have anything they wanted. The noble qora, with or without their old masters, had made sure of that. Shop after shop was overflowing with Rzolkan fabrics and gems and weapons, far too lavish to be uprooted or overlooked.

"Can't say they never did anything good for us," the tracker whispered in Anna's ear.

She pretended not to hear him.

At the edge of a spice-peddling row, standing beneath a web of ochre awnings and flapping wings, the city opened into a cluster of earthen paths and shell-pocked setstone. Bodies lay scattered upon the roadways, some crushed and others wilted in on themselves like blistering leather, all picked bare of whatever trinkets or salt pouches had once rested upon their hips. Dry blood was thickening to a burgundy paste in the grooves left by wagon wheels.

Nuhra glanced back at Anna and Konrad, sparing a particularly indulgent grin for the tracker. "Fear not." Her voice was silk and honey. "The holy are spared in this place."

"Comforting," Anna said. She avoided Konrad's warning stare. When dealing with the vicious and the cruel, she'd come to learn, there was no refuge in caution. Intuition had spared more lives than sense ever could.

"Indeed it is," Nuhra replied. "There's little to be gained from the blood of the saltless."

The tracker laughed. "Makes you swoon, doesn't she?"

Scanning both directions of the nearest path, the trailcarver reached into her tunic and produced a thin wooden talisman. She lifted it high above her head, waiting for the bare-legged running boy across the road to acknowledge her and bolt into a nearby alley.

Anna glanced over her shoulder to ensure that the first cohort of Alakeph hadn't been lost in the press. By the time she'd spotted their drab coverings, which did little to obscure the procession of pale flesh and broad frames, a barrage of violent thumps forced her attention back to the path. A hulking machine trundled through the churned-up earth, towering above Nuhra as it came to rest in a wreath of steam. Along its base were oil-smeared, flaking cogs bound by black treads, worked by a set of struts that bore the marks of constant snapping and welding. Squares of overlapping ceramic and dark leather covered its flat sides, forming a pattern Anna could only liken to the shell of a tortoise. Everything about the beast—from its twisting copper vents to its ruj-inflicted gouges—exuded a sense of sheer brutality.

"Oh, Nuhra," the tracker said. "How you spoil us."

The trailcarver blinked at Anna, evidently catching her vague aversion. "A temrus is the most dependable refuge in the Martyr's Ward." A coy, knowing smile cut across her painted black lips. "Unless they learn of the hayajara within."

* * * *

Threading the slender roads and underpasses of Leejadal carried a sense of incurable panic. The world beyond the temrus could only be glimpsed through hair-thin slits in the walls' armor, giving Anna the sense of gazing through a hellish keyhole. Konrad had initially leaned inward to share her vantage point, but his curiosity waned in a matter of moments. It was a blur of cinders and split skin and fur, at once exotic and repugnant. And as the machine rumbled onward, filled with the distant chatter of two old friends and their murderous, half-heard tales, Anna realized she was plunging into an abyss.

An abyss below the densest soil, below the Grove-Beyond-Worlds.

But out of that chaos, which had unraveled over the span of two hours in the temrus's sweltering confines, gratitude had emerged. Their journey concluded at a walled compound on the western edge of the city, steeped in the shade of the impossible spire. Bloated flies swarmed the air and danced over the central lot's kerosene pools. Men clad in rawhide masks, tattered hoods, and veils paced around stacks of crates and twisted scrap, barking to one another in flatspeak variants that Anna had never heard. One by one, the ensuing temrusi chugged through a blackened, iron-patched gate, lining up in ragged succession like behemoths seeking arid land to graze, still bleeding their fumes as Alakeph brothers filed out and paced around the lot.

A crooked, battered structure stood at the center of the compound, rising nearly as high as the bricolage watchtowers in the adjacent ward. Sand-worn paint freckled its walls, standing out amid cracked bricks in patches of indigo and ruby. Every window had been blown out or carved out, replaced by sandbags, firing holes, nail-strewn barricades. Most apparent were the gaping clefts in the upper levels and eastern wings, which left the building's perimeter girded by piles of crushed setstone.

Anna shifted her pack higher onto her shoulders and wandered toward the ruins. Devastation, somehow, brought more security than the city beyond the gates. After all, devastation was stagnant. Devastation had nothing to defend, nothing to lose.

Nuhra appeared at Anna's side and placed a hand on the small of her back, urging her toward the doorway's partition of shredded linen and beads. "Our tea will grow cold, sister."

Despite her best efforts, her spine tensed against the woman's touch. It was not the sensation, exactly, but the suggestion of what her hands had done. "I'll be in soon enough."

"I suspect so," Nuhra giggled.

Anna narrowed her eyes at the trailcarver.

Nuhra gently lifted a hand, turning her ink-laced palm to the sky, and smiled. A granule of sand fluttered on the wind, skittered over her wrist, and came to rest between the smooth skin's creases. Then came another and another, tossed about by a nascent breeze. "The Howling Wall approaches."

Chapter 4

Beyond the shutters was a black, screaming lament. It had materialized as a silent wave, draping itself over the city's wards in beige folds. But the northerners had known better than to watch its approach; they had huddled with tawdry fetishes and carved constellations into their forearms, whispering fervent prayers into the still-gushing wounds. Its thin haze smoldered from cream to mud, then to ruddy soil, then to an absolute void. It battered the compound's doors and shrieked through every crevice, crafting a gloom so thorough that Har-gunesh, cruelest of the northern gods, was driven back into the cosmos. It was the devourer of all things. It was malice incarnate.

Breathe in.

The rug beneath Anna's legs was slithering, hissing, hushing her as the Howling Wall spilled into the chamber and grazed her skin. Her mind was aware of its eternal terror, its primordial sludge that had been nursed and sustained over eons of annihilation.

Breathe out.

Nuhra struck a match, purging the darkness around her chin and bony fingers, then guided the flame to an orb-like lantern atop a serving table. The chamber bloomed with waxy light. Faint flurries of sand and mica seemed to seize in midair, glittering in a sea of momentary frost, then sift down into the shadows.

"Their words align with truth, it seems," Nuhra said. Her stare was wide and eager, her head canted impishly to one side. "You bear the traces of the old ways."

"Whose words?" Anna asked.

"Many speak of you," Nuhra replied, "yet few recognize the marrow that lurks within your bones, Kuzalem. My vision knows it by its true name." Anna met the woman's eyes, sensing a fanatical storm that lurked behind decorum. She was right about the rarity of true perception—Bora, and perhaps Yatrin, had been the only ones to decipher her spirit. Not even she herself could claim that feat. Not yet.

"You were initiated into their folds, weren't you?"

"I've learned not to be vague with my speech," Anna replied.

Nuhra smiled at that. "Abandon your pretense of separation, sister. Does the light of sacred wisdom not shine through our hearts and minds?"

"We are not the same," Anna said. "Hear me when I tell you that we are not sisters. We are not kin. We are not friends or comrades. We are bound by a task and when that task is complete, we'll return to our worlds and never speak of this."

Nuhra drank her tea, taking in Anna's words with subtle delight, then reached across the table to refill Anna's cup. "Which mind compels you to say such things, I wonder? Which mind holds to the illusion of distinct worlds? Do we not breathe the same air and die with the same agony?"

The trailcarver's attainments were obvious: She'd endured the same experiences as Anna, whether through tomes or meditation, and her actions carried a similar aura of efficiency and diligence. Even her eyes reflected the vast stillness of the nebulae. But not all who saw emptiness came away with the same insights, and not all who sought reality were willing to embrace it.

Anna felt her breath trickling across her upper lip, grounding her in Nuhra's words. Every being had a lesson to offer, if one sufficiently expanded their perception. "What do you see in me?"

"Something ancient." Nuhra's voice had grown softer, though no less zealous. "Do you sense it within?"

Yes. It crept toward her lips, but Anna resisted the urge. "Senses can rarely be trusted."

"As wise as it is true."

"The work of a scribe is to know what lurks within every being," Anna explained. "So I caution you against speaking of *certainty* regarding my nature. I am what I am."

The chamber's door opened with a weak squeal, cutting through the storm's moans and bellows. Konrad stood in the threshold, radiant as lamplight shone upon his white garments, weighing the exchange with pursed lips.

"Is everything all right?" he asked.

Anna glanced at Nuhra, taking particular interest in the woman's budding smile. "Yes," she said at last. "We're discussing the approach."

Despite his hunched shoulders, Konrad nodded and bowed his head. "Right. Well, the other breakers have given their support to the strike. Andriv will speak with you when you're ready."

"Thank you."

He lingered in the doorway, probing Anna for some sign of distress that she'd sealed in her gaze or joined hands, then dragged the door shut. The iron latch clicked into place.

"How dutiful he's become," Nuhra said.

"You know little of him," Anna replied.

"Surely you jest. I knew of him when he was a mere boy in the Dogwood and I, a lowly aspirant of my sect."

"Your name never reached his lips."

"We were not permitted to speak with them," she explained, fixing her stare on Anna's scarred throat. "Men of the blade were looked upon as beasts."

"Do you still believe that?"

Nuhra shrugged. "Some may be."

"I've known beasts," Anna said softly, "but not all of them carried blades. And some with blades were crueler than any beast I've known."

"Is that so?"

"Beasts lack a mind capable of understanding wrath, but men—men choose to ignore their thinking mind. There isn't a beast in this world that roams the land, eternally seeking out things to burn or bleed or rape. Men look upon those pursuits as games. Worse yet, they look upon them with *honor.*"

"Ah," Nuhra said, widening her grin. "That's why you hold your heart from me, is it? Do you think that of me?"

"You know yourself well enough."

"We've all done beastly things," she whispered, "but only lambs and sows can survive through goodness alone. Your Alakeph ensure that, with their claws and teeth."

Anna tensed her jaw. It had been a mercifully long time since she'd considered the mind she possessed during war, during slaughter. But it would return soon. It had to.

Nuhra broke the silence with a sweet, delicate laugh. "Your shepherd, Bora, was certainly no lamb."

"Watch your tongue."

"My tongue? I speak of her with the utmost reverence." A surprising mask of hurt, of stinging reproach, suddenly came over the woman. "For a time, she shared my quarters in the sanctuary."

"She was an adherent of Saloram."

"By birth, yes," Nuhra said. "But she was sent out into this world to seek truth in all forms. I knew her when she was barely a woman."

Anna suspended the words in her mind and spun them like wind chimes, struggling to reconcile what Bora had been with the barbarism of what Nuhra was. There was a harsher, more savage element within the adherent. "Now I understand the thread that binds you all together."

"You speak of your tracker, don't you?"

"You know him by a different name."

Nuhra's smile was dim, fleeting. "Does it trouble your heart to know that he was born as a babe like you or I, Kuzalem? That his mother anointed him with the name *Lukas*?"

Anna's breaths ground to a halt. *Lukas.* She rolled the name through her awareness over and over again. After all this time, it seemed impossible that he could have a name at all. That a woman could force him into the world, smeared in the blood of a living womb. That somebody could love him and hold him, and know him as anything other than a killer.

"He used to be so handsome," Nuhra said sadly, her eyes wandering through memories and longing alike. "You never asked him to bare his face, did you?"

Her throat worked to produce words, but they were slow, disjointed. "I have no need for it."

"Lukas, Sixth of Dariyesz." She smiled. "How long has it been since I've spoken those words?"

"I'm certain he's lingered on your mind, by whatever name you choose."

"Certain?"

Anna drew in a hard breath. "The wicked rejoice in one another. He brought you every trinket and puppet you ever wanted, didn't he?"

"It was never him," Nuhra said. "It was you, Kuzalem."

"Be clear."

"Oh, it's glaringly clear for those who have become attuned to the machinations of this plane. Within your thinking mind, my intentions are as clear as dawn."

"I know *nothing* of your intentions."

"Quell your suspicions, sister. You are the tether that binds me to the savior of my lineage. I would not destroy you, nor your search, in this vital hour."

One by one, Nuhra's suggestions and half-concealed truths condensed into a chilling, logical chain. It was never about Anna and never had been. It was Ramyi.

"She won't serve you," Anna whispered.

"Serve me?" Nuhra threw her head back with laughter; the gesture was explosive, bordering on nonsensical, from a source of such composure. "There is no lust for power in my heart, Kuzalem. I seek to shelter the Starsent and nurture her, nothing more. I am her supplicant."

"Forgive me if I doubt your kindness."

"The Kojadi slumbered for millennia, lost to the ravages of those who could not endure or sustain their ways. But once again, their divinity has returned to this world. She will bring about a new age."

Anna glared at the trailcarver, keenly aware of the tremors leaking out across her lips and nostrils. "Volna already has her."

"A splintering of it, yes," Nuhra said. "But I cast off the shackles of their ways long ago. Whatever shelter they could once offer to the Moraharem has fallen away. Now, my sacred task is clear: I must cleanse the mind of the Starsent."

In spite of Nuhra's fervency, Anna detected an undercurrent of something ardent and honest. For a moment she gazed beyond the tales she knew of the woman, beyond the blood that had surely been washed from smooth hands, beyond the stagnant rot of the city and its incursion into her essence. "What makes you think she would accept your instruction?"

"You are a being of light, Kuzalem, but your breed drives out every shadow that it touches. She was woven from darkness. What could you know of her world?"

Anna stared into her cup.

"I would still her bleeding mind," Nuhra explained. "You may not understand our ways, but you know the fate of animals beyond taming. Give my lineage a chance."

"And if I refuse?"

"Then the butchers will do their work." Nuhra gently sipped her tea, studying Anna's eyes over the rim of the porcelain.

Anna lifted her own cup for the first time. It rattled against her lips and the anise tea was cold, bitter. As with all things, whether through volition or the command of existence, there came a point of relinquishment. Ramyi was no longer her pupil, her cherished kin. By now, she wasn't even a girl: The Starsent was as immune to Anna's sway as the cosmos itself. Several moments passed before Anna realized she'd drained her cup.

"What stirs your mind, Kuzalem?"

"I have no guarantee that you won't use her for your own ends," Anna whispered. "Just like everyone else."

"Am I a beast to you?" Nuhra asked, refilling Anna's cup with uncanny precision.

"Everybody wants power. And if they don't want that, then they want to destroy. But everyone wants something, and it damns us all in the end."

"What do you want, then?"

Anna nestled her trembling hands in her lap. "I want this world to be purified."

"By whatever means," Nuhra added.

She let the screeches of the Howling Wall fill the ensuing silence. "Yes," she said at last.

"The Starsent is the survival of our lineage," Nuhra said, glossing over Anna's reply as though she'd taken it for granted. "I would see my bones crushed and my mind obliterated to ensure her path in this world. Do you sense my heart, Kuzalem?"

"You can't prove such devotion."

"Ah, but you have the means," she said, loosening the wrap around her neck. The flesh was stretched taut, yet supple, crawling with a flurry of briar-like sigils. "Dissolve my ambitions, sister, and the core of my being will remain. Let the Breaking affirm my truths to the highest masters of this plane."

Two swift knocks rattled the door.

"We'll be along shortly," Nuhra called, keeping her attention fixed on Anna.

The trailcarver's gaze was mesmerizing, rife with the steadfast faith and fear she'd cultivated over a lifetime in ritual chambers. To such an adherent, death could only be seen as an impediment. Her true path was assured, predestined, a ceaseless progression from seed to sapling to towering oak.

With a gentle nod, Anna reached into the folds of her robe.

* * * *

Nothing definite could be ascribed to the Breaking aside from its mechanism. A lone circle, formed with one flawless sweep of the blade, unwound a lifetime of separation. That was how Anna had described it to her disciples, at least, as the Kojadi tomes held no mention of such things. It sparked revelations about the defilements of a being's old ways, about the harm they'd thrust upon those that they once considered foreign by flesh alone. And in that fateful moment, when the mind bore the weight of horrible knowing, there was no telling what might happen.

Anna had seen hired blades hang themselves from attic rafters. She'd watched concubines chant sacred words for days at a time, and farmers run to their forsaken children, and killers strip themselves bare, offering their garments and ill-gotten salt to the lowliest beggars of their city.

But Nuhra had already been on the cusp of awakening.

Emptiness gazed into her and she gazed back in wonder.

"Will she be able to guide us?" Andriv asked. He was peering through the sliver of the open doorway, examining Nuhra like an animal stalking the confines of its cage. The woman knelt by a bare, pitted wall, staring blankly into some realm that few could hardly envision. "She'll return to us. Won't she?"

Anna said nothing, because she did not know. Yet she was certain of one thing: Despite the appearance of a woman, Nuhra was no longer there. They were looking upon a being without a given name, without memories it could claim as its own, without the host of delusions that had dictated its former path.

"Can we trust her, Kuzalem?" Andriv asked.

"If we couldn't before," she replied, "we can now."

"Does she not seek the Starsent?"

"Soon enough, we'll learn precisely what she seeks. We should turn our attention to more pressing matters." She moved to the threshold of the neighboring chamber and took stock of its dim, candlelit space. Bodies shifted under thick sleeping covers, arranged in rows that bore an unsettling resemblance to linen-shrouded corpses. Konrad and the tracker—*Lukas*— sat near a beaded rug, slumped over a table and its horde of charts. She heard them murmuring about something, exchanging snappy bouts of river-tongue, but hidden words no longer troubled her. Now the world's terrors were raw and plain. "Andriv, are you certain she's there?"

The brother moved to her side. "Beyond question. Even the Gosuri herdsmen confirmed as much."

"Men will say anything for salt and broth in their bellies."

"One of Nuhra's cadre flew over the area just before the storm descended," Andriv replied. "He marked a safe house near the western wadis. It was exactly where the tracker claimed it would be."

"Lukas."

"Kuzalem?"

She shook her head. "Sleep in the refuge of the Pale Crescents, brother. There will be little time for rest tomorrow."

Chapter 5

By the time their convoy of shrub-blanketed temrusi had reached the western expanse, Har-gunesh stared down from his highest perch. Every slat and vent along Anna's transport had been cranked open, bleeding near-boiling air into the sprawl of crumbling stone walls, bushy pines, and scorched soil. It was flat here—threateningly flat. One could gaze over the fields and into the flux of scrambled, faraway mirages, picking out the dark smudges of settlements and peddler caravans alike.

Not that it made any difference now. It had been six hours of crunching over sand and earth and bleached bones, occasionally stopping at dust-shrouded wells to refill the coolant tanks and allow the brothers to retch into dry riverbeds.

Anna's shirt was soaked with sweat, as thick and tacky as a trapper's furs upon her skin. She'd taken a cue from the Alakeph and northern fighters in removing her ceramic vest, bandolier, and rucksack, tossing them into an enormous mound in the rear of their temrus, but even that was a token gesture. Her throat was clogged with fumes, stinging from the arid heat that seemed to leak into her lungs and shrivel her from the inside. Every jolt and bump that rattled through the undercarriage bit into her bones and chafed her flesh, conjuring images of leather stretched over its rack.

Yet as she surveyed the others, noting the creeping dullness in their eyes and the habitual picking at their lips, she understood that she was suffering least of all. A sharpened mind would always outlast a hardened body.

Nuhra sat across from Anna, her face a reflection of dreaming tranquility. Her posture was flawless, as rigid and composed as the guardian statues that had lined the outskirts of Leejadal, seemingly immune to the decay of heat and drowsiness. Sweat trickled down her cheeks in smooth, glimmering bands. Even the northern scribes seated near the front of the temrus, who'd worked under her guidance to apply markings to the better part of the qora fighters, now regarded her as a pariah.

But not everyone was so unsettled. That morning, Lukas had hardly detected a change in the woman. Even if he had, he'd remained mum on his insights. His only sign of knowing had been a drawn-out stare in the compound's lot, carefully weighing Nuhra's silence, her dispassionate lips, her mechanical gait.

"Weird way about her," he'd muttered to Anna as he wandered toward the third temrus, fishing through his pouch for a fresh wad of khat. "Northerners."

But the trailcarver's mission had not been burned away with the rest of her old self. Her every action—indeed, her every step and breath—had become perfunctory rituals, living cogs stripped of all pleasure and craving in service of a grand machine. There was no longer an observer within her mind; there was only a task.

A singular, hallowed task.

Anna was still examining the woman when the temrus bucked, slamming them both into the harnesses. Gaslights sparked to life along the central aisle, casting a pallid glow over rusting wall panels, twisting brass tubes, opposing rows of fighters. Anna clawed at her buckles in disarrayed panic as the others silently snapped to attention, locking the bolts of their ruji and filing toward the stockpiled equipment with unnerving expediency.

No sooner had she wrenched the buckles open than blinding white light flooded the temrus. The transport's rear panel unspooled to the furthest extent of its fraying winch lines, screeching and pounding down upon the soil in an instant.

Sweet, coppery dust wafted up and consumed the first wave of fighters to storm down the ramp. Their brethren trailed them, soon reduced to white cloaks whipping and stirring in the haze.

This is it. This is what we've come to.

She stood and wandered toward her gear, dimly aware of Nuhra striding out onto the field with her men.

Anna blinked at the mound.

A ruj. A ruj for killing. Yes, that had to be hers. She picked it up, looking upon her hands as a puppet's limbs, and slung the leather strap over her shoulder.

A vest to keep her innards off the sand. She'd need that, too. Her hands tingled as she lifted it over her head, pausing in its deafening blackness, then let its weight slap down across her shoulders. She tightened the straps until she could hardly breathe.

Then a rucksack, full of things that would keep her alive. But most men she'd known to wear them did not survive long enough to open the flap. She hefted it onto her back, cinched the buckles, and stumbled toward sunlight. She was halfway down the ramp when she realized she'd forgotten how to kill. Turning the ruj over in her hands, she noticed—for what seemed like the first time—how alien and brutal and unwieldy it was. Point, pull, kill. That was it.

Or had she missed something?

Was it even loaded?

"Kuzalem, conceal your form." Andriv's voice, hard, yet restrained, burst into her awareness. "Their horrors may soon assail our ranks."

Anna turned toward the stream of fighters, who were scrambling off the raised path and into a shadowed underbrush thick with gnarled shrubs and wadis. Tracking their course further into the distance, she noticed a series of beige lumps hemmed in by pines and crooked walls and drooping nets. Sunlight gave the mottled mud structures the distinct appearance of flaking limestone. Some of the Alakeph brothers appeared to her as white glimmers, threading in and out of sight as they traversed the network of canals. She squinted at the meandering company; each emergent head and ruj barrel provided Anna with a more precise calculation of distance, no matter how the heat managed to distort their forms. The compound was a half-league away at most, which put their fighters squarely within firing range.

But such measurements held true for both sides.

Sinking down to a kneeling stance, Anna nodded at Andriv and crept to the edge of a broken wall. Konrad and the tracker were scurrying into a wadi farther down the road, trailed by a detachment of northerners in reed-sprouting camouflage smocks. Their attempt at silence was wasted; even if the safe house was deaf to their approach, slumbering during Hargunesh's daylight pass, the groaning and chugging temrusi had surely revealed their presence.

"Do they know their orders?" Anna whispered to Andriv.

The brother was nervously scanning the path, passing cryptic hand signals to mirrormen and captains scattered along the column of temrusi. "The Starsent will not be ended."

"We may not have that luxury," she hissed.

"The brothers are well-trained, Kuzalem."

"So is she." Anna peered around the wall's chipped edge, straining to detect any movement within the compound. "Your men will know their course when the time arrives."

Andriv settled back against the wall, his eyes roaming the dirt with the telltale glaze of a commander's imagination. A moment later he reached out, patting Anna's shoulder to urge her to remain in position. "We will not fail you."

"I'm accompanying you," Anna said. "It's not under discussion."

"We should wait until—"

"Nothing lurks in the shadows." Nuhra's voice was a faint razor, possessed by the certainty of knowledge beyond her mortal senses. She sat in the center of the road, her legs crossed and fingers twisted into a strange knot upon her lap, gazing raptly at a void beyond the sands. "They dwell in restless dreams."

"Untangle your tongue," Andriv snapped. "Are their watchmen asleep?" Nuhra closed her eyes. "No."

Flickers of encroaching violence filled Anna's chest with hot, painful throbbing, and her heart knocked against the ceramic vest like war drums. Such dread was familiar to the helpless, to the feeble, and it screamed through Anna's mind as silence spread and cemented around her.

Slinging her ruj around and over her rucksack, Anna scrambled down the embankment and into the underbrush in a shroud of dust. Ahead, the fighters advanced in low, sun-dappled ranks, emerging and vanishing with every swell of the ochre haze. Blood rushed through her ears in resonant pulses, as imminent and invasive as the drone of fat red wasps and studded boots trudging through soil. Several brothers called her name, but she hurried under the canopy of budding apples and stunted leaves without glancing back, without wiping the hot sweat that gnawed at her eyes.

This was *her* burden. It had to be.

She probed her awareness for the red lashes of Ramyi's presence, which had once been as tangible as sunlight or scars or the bodies left in the girl's wake. Those days had passed, their memories as disjointed and unreal as a fleeting dream, but she grasped at their power nevertheless. Behind closed lids she honed in on labored breathing, glossy orange biting through blackness, a—

Emptiness washed over her.

There was no sense of stillness, for there was nothing to move, nothing to agitate. No sense of time, nor its imagined passing. Not even blackness persisted in that hollow space.

Torchlight and sullied limestone burst into being. Then came the warm, dazzling flickers of flame and cinders, glowing brands steaming against open flesh, spittle glistening on sharpened teeth. Black pigments, made from the bones that her tribe had burned and crushed during the last harvest, coated the floor and ceiling in the form of glimmering murals, glyphs, inscriptions. Beads of blood and sweat sparkled around her.

Lifting her hands into the light, she found dark flesh banded with pink scarring. The cuts were fresh, still dribbling waxy crimson onto pitted stone. But her fingers were thicker than she recalled, more weighty and callused, capable of clamping around a Gosuri's matted throat and choking it to stillness. Capable of slicing through the thin, pale belly of a southerner. Capable of endless savagery that played through her mind as a tapestry of faces, wounds, howls, an immense wilderness of memories that stitched the divide between the self and the other.

The other.

It was a needle driven into her awareness, a surge of animal fear that destroyed the will to move, to speak, to breathe. *This is not me.* The fear swelled to horror. Spasms tightened her hands to fists, but they were not *her* hands, and that sense of volition immediately felt wasted, illusory, a pathetic attempt of the mind to grasp at flesh beyond its control.

There was nobody to rescue.

There was simply nothing.

Yet every step forward was a desperate scream within, an affirmation of the truth that she was not there, that an abysmal emptiness pervaded all things, that the world flowed around an intangible captive.

The elders threw their heads back, mouths wide and gushing black torrents. Fluted fox bones, protruding from their windpipes in ashen stubs, rattled as the men began their hideous calls. It was a monstrous, baleful harmony, growing ever-lower until it coalesced into a chest-thrumming wave.

Primordial words, stripped of all language and logic, intelligible only to the innermost kernel of awareness, consumed her.

We are.

Anna opened her eyes to dust, to blinding sunlight fighting through the canopy overhead. She was standing at the edge of the narrow wadi, gazing out at the compound's cracked walls and ramshackle wooden gate. Her breaths pooled in her lungs, burning air beyond conscious will, almost as though that vital rhythm had been forgotten, somehow overlooked.

Overlooked as easily as awareness itself, as entire moments of existence:

Crossing over crumbling soil, hunting prey she could not hate, bearing a tool designed to maim and murder.

Anna dropped her ruj and studied its fall, its clouded impact upon the soil. Her hands wandered to her sides, quaking, throbbing, bleeding precious sweat into the earth. She opened her mouth, but did not know the words to scream. Thoughts and senses flickered in and out of complete dissociation. Was it her sight, her terror, her—

"Fuck are you doing?" the tracker snarled, seizing Anna's shoulder— the pain assured her that it was *her* shoulder—and forcing her down to a wobbling crouch. His gaze darted between rows of apple trees and waves of Alakeph brothers, who were beginning to edge along the compound's inner wall with ruji tucked to their shoulders.

"What is it now?" Konrad hurried to them, clutching his ruj by its barrel using a gloved hand. His face was flush, shining with broad ribbons of sweat, as frustrated as it was bemused. "Anna, what's wrong?"

She struggled for gulps of dense, throat-prickling air, staring blankly at both men as she struggled to ground herself. "I don't—" she began. A pause, a shallow gasp. "I don't know."

"Cracked your mind?" the tracker asked.

"No," she said, glaring at him. "There's something wrong with this place."

"You hurt?" Konrad frowned at her vest, her legs, her neck and its ancient scars. "Take it gently. What do you mean by *wrong*?"

A sharp clap issued from behind the mud walls. Their entry was a storm of drumming boots, a smattering of shouts in river-tongue and Hazani, a surge of white shapes flowing into the compound's inner ring. Then it fell away. There was no gargled screaming, no shattering glass, no ruj payloads thudding into mud or flesh with muffled shushes.

Wasps hummed around Anna.

"Think it's over?" Konrad asked.

"I don't feel her," Anna whispered. "Konrad, we shouldn't be here."

Shrill whistling filled the air, accompanied by several Alakeph brothers appearing in the compound's doorway and waving their comrades closer. Most of the men had their ruji slung across their backs or gripped like walking sticks.

But Anna found no relief in their demeanor.

Lukas stood, his knees popping like snapped kindling, and gave a bitter laugh. "Nothing left to raise those hackles, Anna. Just a matter of digging your panna a pit or leaving her for the tribes."

* * * *

A brittle stillness hung over the compound's inner courtyard. Many of the Alakeph were gathered into clumps along a fissure-riddled wall, basking in slivers of shade, overcome by a silence that extended beyond the terse ways of their lineage. Others squatted deep in Halshaf prayer, mumbling ancient words to themselves as Anna strode past. Even the northern fighters, adorned with crudely stitched flesh masks, seemed reticent to stand beside the mud-and-timber house.

The stench reached Anna halfway to the door. It was pus and sun-swollen guts, vinegar and stale piss, bile and fermenting sweat. *Death*. During past campaigns it had become a constant miasma, as tangible and ominous as smoke stirring on the horizon.

It was not the mark of recent death, of course. Fresh blood alone was not so putrid; it was metallic, consistent, woven into Anna's memories of thrashing lambs and errant shells that had left bodies strewn down entire streets.

Anna's stomach clenched.

If Ramyi was inside, the fighters' work had already been carried out.

"Kuzalem!" Andriv burst through the gates with his ruj in both hands, panting like the wild, sunken-ribbed hounds that trotted alongside kator tracks. His eyes were just as fierce. "I feared the worst."

"Trust in my ways," she replied, immediately returning her focus to the mud structure. Somewhere in her periphery, her companions were padding across the dust and clumps of silvery weeds, speaking to the first waves of fighters in low tones. It registered as clearly as the pitter-patter dripping that leaked through the doorway, through narrow windows housing blackness. The normalcy of it all was the most chilling aspect: straight, unmarked walls, a copper spigot protruding through the soil, and a set of nearby furrows lined with still-sprouting herbs, basking in the shade of a red tarp. Had it not been for that fetid pall, it would've been any other home amid the flatlands.

"I'm not certain you should enter," Andriv whispered, almost as though tucking his words into Anna's ears alone. "The brothers assure me that this is a sinister domain."

"I'm no stranger to it."

"Kuzalem—"

"Did they find her?"

The brother's silence bled into the hum of corpse-gnawing flies.

Anna looked sidelong at Andriv, sensing the subtle heat building between her ribs. "Did they?"

"They don't know," Andriv said, lowering his head.

"Their sole task is to know," Anna snapped. "We came here with certainty, brother, and I will not leave without it. Empty words lost their comfort long ago."

Again the brother spoke, his tone rising with the vigor of the chastised, but she did not listen. She moved into the cool, rancid shade of the porch, unable to cease the restlessness in her heart. *They don't know.* Those words sickened her as much as a swell of acidic fumes as they wafted through the threshold. Then she was inside, forcing herself not to inhale, not to think. Her first steps—squelching, wet—echoed with startling effect, and soon the darkness resolved to a bluish, murky landscape, crowded with blunt shapes and—

It had been too long since she'd witnessed such violations of flesh.

Blood covered every patch of the room, oozing and crusting in various stages. Bright red spattering across the ceiling, maroon streaks that stretched from wall to wall, pools of glossy garnet that had been smeared by careless steps. Yet blood was the least of their defilements. Mounds of deconstructed bodies littered the floor: severed arms, bludgeoned heads, maggot-riddled torsos, jawbones and tongues and cracked rib cages, all left in disarray like the remains of an inhuman feast.

Pale, naked bodies had been hung from the walls using iron stakes. Their eyes were raw pits, gouged out by blades or beaks. Their limbs extended from their body with grotesque, impossible length, each bone and socket and fleshy mass stretched out along a line of sinew, resembling the anatomical displays in the academies of Nahoran herbmen.

Anna's throat clenched. The bodies were full-grown, largely men, and the few women among them were marked by southern flesh.

Something scratched, breaking the stillness.

A cluster of knucklebones, still draped in layers of withering tissue, stirred against the soil. They clacked against one another, hovered a hair from the ground, revolved in spastic rhythms end over end. Hayat's scorched odor rose from the bones.

"By the fucking Grove." Lukas's voice barely pierced Anna's awareness. More footsteps tapped over the porch.

The gentle drumming of blood resumed. Anna tracked its source, honing in on the soft splashes and slurping. And as she matched the pattering to the mutilated bodies lining the walls, her skin prickled into gooseflesh.

None of the droplets reached the soil. Nothing flitted downward at all, in fact. She watched the bright, shallow pools beneath the bodies contracting, wadding up into crimson orbs that began an impossible ascent to the ruptured bellies and sliced legs above. Their sounds were erratic, hollow, as though refracted through some warbling membrane and stitched together to make them whole again. Now she could see the floor slithering, churning about in weird maelstroms, spawning pockets of jumbled whispers that swelled and devolved into broken rattling. "Anna." Konrad's voice cut through the gore, the nausea. "You don't need to see it."

But her gaze crept over every bit of marrow and glistening flesh, shutting out everything beyond traces of the Starsent. Near the room's center a set of shriveled lungs twitched and shifted over the soil, exposing the corner of a wooden frame. Shadows lined the inner lip of the boards, hinting at the sort of storage spaces she'd raided in flatland dwellings, the cold recesses of clay pots and honey jars and cowardly men.

"Now, I've known wicked sights," Lukas growled, "but this is something else, girl."

She turned to face the fighters.

They were huddled in the doorway, eyes wide with this proof of true malice, true barbarism, true hatred in the world. The tips of their boots were aligned across the threshold, but none passed it. Several northerners paced along the windows, sparing momentary glances before returning to their ritual chants.

"Did you search the lower level?" she asked them.

"Best have a worldswalker burn out whatever the fuck's seeped into this nest," Lukas said, backing away with his ruj against his shoulder. "Or just put it to the torch. But take this from the bloodied source, would you? That's no place for life."

Konrad clutched at his stomach. "Never thought I'd find a day when our truths collide."

Flowing silk garments dazzled in the sunlight beyond the porch. Nuhra approached like a scalpel's sweep; she shouldered through the crowd with swift, certain steps, maintaining her porcelain visage as she looked upon the bodies and their hexed stirring. As she waded through the remains, her spine rigid and gaze leaping about, her curiosity only seemed to deepen.

"You know what happened here," Anna whispered, "don't you?"

Nuhra blinked at her.

"If you know what's below us, you should speak now," Anna said.

"I see what you see, Kuzalem," Nuhra replied. "My form is blind and deaf to the presence of the Starsent. Yours is not."

Sparing a glance at the fighters, who had now leaned inward, yet still resisted the urge to wander closer, Anna moved to Nuhra's side. Cartilage slid and cracked beneath her heels. "Outside," Anna said softly, "you knew that something was here."

"I knew only of suffering," Nuhra said. "This vessel has an animal's senses."

"So it seems." Moving to the room's center, Anna used her boot to clear away the dissolving remnants of a head and splintered spine. Beneath it was the cover for the wooden frame. It was thin and dripping and resting lopsided over its hole, covered in writhing maggots. As Anna brushed it aside with her foot, it began to vibrate against dampened soil, humming with arcane fervor.

Faded daylight spilled down into the storeroom, illuminating a dusty square of setstone and dried blood. Lining the surrounding shelves were dark, leathery slats and circular bronze caps. *Tomes and scrolls.*

"Just what we need," the tracker mused. "More sacks to haul out."

"Get a rope," Anna said, mustering a forceful voice that drowned out the assembly's muttering. She waited for their footsteps to trot off over the soil, soon joined by whispers and retching and foul southern curses.

Nuhra moved to the frame's edge and peered down. "A most curious crypt, sister."

"What was this place?" Anna asked. "Some sort of ledger archive?"

Her giggle was cold, cutting. "The Nahorans hunted my lineage with undying tenacity. A shelter from the storm was all we had."

Anna narrowed her eyes. "Your lineage held her?"

"No, no, this was a serpent's den," Nuhra said soothingly. "But a shard of our knowledge slumbers here."

Gazing back into the musty shadows, Anna spotted the empty slots and racks that had surely held compendiums, treatises, rites. "Did they bring her here?"

"The serpents were delighted to host the Starsent, sister."

"Then she came for what they had," Anna whispered. All around her the bones scraped and blood slurped and cartilage creaked in decaying sockets, thick with the whispers of the dead. Thick with Ramyi's indiscretion. "She came with help, too."

"You sound certain."

"Even the Starsent is bound by our nature," Anna replied. "Whatever did *this* was imbued with her markings, but it wasn't her. Not alone."

Nuhra lifted her nose and breathed deeply, creasing her black lips in what could've passed for a smile. "Her nature, her bindings. Semantics, dear sister."

"Those bindings are the only thing staying her hand."

"Our lineage believes in liberation from all bonds," Nuhra said. "Even the bonds of nature."

Anna stepped closer to the trailcarver. "What are you saying?"

"The light of knowing will shine upon your restless mind, Kuzalem. This world is a constant act of taking, is it not?" Nuhra bent down, tapping a blade-grooved nail against the wooden frame. Then she leveled her gaze on a scroll shelf riddled with gaps. "One may learn the world from what is present, of course, but one stands to gain insight from what has departed."

* * * *

The smoke was rife with charring skin and lavender. It billowed from shallow, corpse-laden pits strewn across the nearby wadi, twisting skyward in thin black columns that resembled poplar trees in the gloom.

Anna tore off another crust of bread as she examined the northern Falaqor adherents trudging over the road, noting bright splotches upon their gloves and fragrant herb pouches wound into their neck scarves. She was glad for their ways, superstitious or not: None of the Alakeph had been willing to touch the bodies and most of the local fighters—raised in the mires of village rites or Volna's indifference—had unfurled their bedrolls a full pence-league from the compound. Even Andriv was occupied with arranging patrols through the wadis, sentries upon the flanking hills, searches within the winding canals.

"Sixteen." Lukas's dark form loomed at the edge of her vision, waxing and waning as the wind stirred his cloak. "Nine tomes, seven scrolls."

Konrad lifted their iron pot from the coals, his hands wrapped in coarse yellow cloth. "Such impressive arithmetic. You must've been one of Malchym's dobraludz in the academy, no?"

Lukas did nothing, said nothing.

It gouged old fears into Anna's gut.

"How do you know there weren't more?" Anna asked.

"I dunno a lick about it," Lukas said. "Had a spot of help."

Nuhra came crunching over the soil, her hood raised and hands plastered to her sides. Shadows stripped her highborn features of their grace.

Beyond her slim silhouette, the Cruel Sage's Maw continued to devour a ruby sky, growing vast and thick and still as it birthed swaths of nebulae in the east. Its ragged tendrils stretched to mountains and gauzy city lights far beyond the flats.

"Do you fear the darkness, sister?" Her smile was pale, knotted thread in the glow of pulsing coals. Dying wicks glinted in her pupils.

"Take the rest of the works if you desire them," she said to Nuhra, turning her attention to the steaming pot. "We should burn whatever remains of this place."

Nuhra squatted by the coals, bewitched with a hound's ignorance by its heat. "Has it not been desecrated enough?"

"Something lurks here." Anna glanced up at Lukas. "The wicked never abandon the fields they've trampled. We all know the force of rituals."

"This presence will not be banished by flames, Kuzalem."

"Enough of this haunted speak, eh?" Lukas cut in. "Only spirits I'm after come in flasks."

Anna met the trailcarver's bold, luminous eyes. "What was she after?"

"Such answers are beyond the realm of fireside talk, are they not?"

"This is no place for decorum."

"Nor for tongues that wraggle on about truths beyond their reach," Nuhra said, her voice deepening, sharpening in an instant. "This is a matter for those who have given their flesh to the knowledge you seek. But since you lust for the nectar of certainty, sister, know that your answers reside in the cloisters of my lineage."

Wind whistled through the encampment. The woman's words carried a sense of luring, a dreadful prescience that could only lead into the belly of beasts. Years of being used, jostled, beaten, starved—all of it had left bruises that Anna couldn't ignore, even if she wanted to. Salvation was always one stranger's promise away, one kindness she was compelled to take and repay in blood.

Every outstretched hand had been glinting with razors.

"Settled, then." Lukas huffed and yanked Nuhra to her feet, honing in on a nearby coalpit and its crowd of drunken northern fighters. His hands roamed her body. "Put some spring in those heels, *sister*. Had enough of this fucking day." He led the trailcarver off into a haze of shadows and smoke, his footsteps slithering over baked earth.

"Do you think she's holding back?" Konrad asked as he lifted the pot's lid and shied away from the swell of steam.

Anna was still watching their dark shapes slink away. "I don't know." She breathed in curry and saffron. "You shouldn't prod at him, Konrad. He's not the drunken fool you take him to be."

"We have enough history to withstand some ribbing."

"Something's different about him," she said softly. "You felt it when he came to us, didn't you? He's empty."

"There wasn't much in there to begin with, was there?"

"That's what frightens me."

Shaking his head, Konrad set out their clay bowls and began ladling the stew over squares of hardtack. "He's not the wolf that you knew, Anna. Not anymore. I'm not sure what happened to him, but his claws are chipped."

"You also thought he could bring us to Ramyi."

Konrad dropped the ladle into the pot. "He's gotten us closer than anyone else."

"Nuhra did his work," she replied. "There's nothing safe about this. If Volna's keeping ties with him, then I can't turn a blind eye to his role in this. He can't just be an intermediary, Konrad."

"Maybe you have your sight on the wrong threat."

"The Breaking did its work."

"And what?"

Anna clung to that long, stagnant silence, glowering over the coals as coyotes whined in distant hills. The Breaking was all she had left. Her hand began to throb, almost as though remembering that old pain, that death of everything she could have been.

Finally, Konrad sighed. "I'm just asking you to take a wide perspective. Nothing more."

"If she can't be vindicated by the Breaking," Anna whispered, "then nobody can."

"Anna." Konrad set one of the bowls before her, keeping his eyes tucked to the soil as he did so. "I know how much this means to you. I do. I've seen what you're willing to give for the truth in your heart, time and time again. That's precisely why you need to sharpen your ears like never before. Because these people know you and they know how far you'll go, and they'll take everything from you if you *ever* stop baring your teeth."

Anna nodded. "I won't."

"Not even if it comes down to you and her," Konrad pressed.

"Konrad—"

"That's how these things go—trust me. You'll need to look that girl in the eyes, shut out whatever's inside of you, and run a blade through her."

"I've known this longer than you can fathom." As she unrolled her burlap mess kit, digging out a warped spoon and knife and laying them beside the bowl, she wondered who had encountered that truth first. Some fierce notch of the thinking mind was adamant that Ramyi had branded that sentiment upon her very being.

When the time came, one of them would not hesitate.

And with that first spoonful, which trembled so fiercely that Anna could hardly bring it to her lips, she understood the divide between the slayer and the slain.

Chapter 6

Tormented vessel. Moraharem. Most of its adherents wore their disdain for *vessels* plainly, marked by scourges and whips and hammers, breaking their flesh however they could. Breaking it in any way that would shatter the perennial illusion of existing within a body. But the studded turquoise walls and engraved front gates of their jinkaral—the domain of maiming or disfiguring, as Anna's tutors had variably translated it—were as elegant, even as inviting, as Nuhra herself.

"Can you sense its radiance?" the trailcarver asked, taking an Alakeph brother's hand as she stepped out of their temrus.

"I can't sense much," Anna replied. She glanced around, examining the chill, smoky shroud that heralded dawn in Doreshna Ward. Cogs churned and locks gushed open within underfoot canals, filling the street with an incessant, whispered roar. Packs of hired blades and qora fighters, swollen with bulky scarves and ceramic helmets and quilted wraps, wandered past and trickled into crooked alleys, marked by the cherry-blossom glow of their dusk-petal pipes. Ribbon-tagged hawks trotted over banners and awnings, gazing down from the perches that lined the surrounding setstone ascents.

"It's quiet, isn't it?" Nuhra asked.

"Slow morning."

"Oh, anything but," she replied. "Did you not hear the bombs, sister? At least three in this ward." She smiled at Anna. "Although I suppose death is slowness in all things."

Towering black shapes shifted in Anna's periphery. She angled toward them, taking in the colossal form of an arch, bronze gears spinning in sequence upon the walls of setstone canyons, dust raining and metal screeching and skylines shifting in the gap beneath the monstrosity.

Hundreds of bridges, laden with shadowed humanoid blots, crossed the span in needle-thin webs.

"Come now," Nuhra said, clicking her tongue and wrapping cold fingers around Anna's wrist. "We can look upon the market's gowns another day." Anna stole a glance at the second temrus in their formation, noting the beast's sputtering kicks as it sank onto alloy-woven coils and lowered its rear hatch. She found it oddly difficult to center herself without Lukas or Konrad accompanying them, although their task—interrogating another cell of caravan drivers in a market ward—seemed more prudent for the hunt.

Andriv and his men filed out of the temrus in a neat, compact string, gazing up at the enormous walls and calcified aqueducts that now hemmed them in. Their ruji were propped against deflated rucksacks, unloaded, fastened in place by taut slings. But even without that display of force, passersby hurried onto the walkways and stoops flanking the road, pulling scarves across their faces and dragging sluggish children out of the brothers' sight.

A land's tales—especially those spawned among witnesses in charred villages—were truly the most devastating weapon of all.

"Wait here," Anna said to Andriv, using her finger to trace a vague perimeter along the road.

The brother nodded, whistled to his men, and went to work arranging them.

"Will such a presence not cast ripples, sister?" Nuhra squinted warily at the Alakeph brothers. "Leejadal has not forgotten the white cloth."

Anna looked upon the jinkaral's walls and their wind-worn paint, transfixed by rows of lightless firing slits. "I certainly hope it hasn't."

* * * *

Beyond a courtyard of swirling ashes and withered, hornet-laden juniper trees, the jinkaral bloomed as a forest of soaring basalt facades. Concave domes, flooded with red, clotting sand and putrefying bodies, lined the walkway that led to the main hall.

Naked worshippers knelt at the edge of the pits, some with severed lips and others armless, ardently staring down at the bloated remains. A young boy shivered and whimpered as Anna passed, his flogged back heaving with pink crusts of mining salt.

Anna wondered if such rituals were the boy's decision, undertaken after years of study and reflection, or whether they had been thrust upon him by those who equated choice with dissent. She wondered how much *choice* she had given to Shem, to Ramyi, to the hundreds of young scribes who had surrendered freedom to be chained to her prestige. How many doors had been kicked in and how many girls had been dragged away, solely to punish allegiance to banners that the guilty could not comprehend? She'd never had any interest in—indeed, had never even asked—how her forces acquired a constant stream of trembling, golden-eyed initiates.

The thinking mind burst forth to disarm the imminent pain, dissolving her thoughts in a flash of pure focus: She took in the hall's flock of dangling braziers, its obsidian tiling, and its tiered shelves of open jars and wide bowls, stuffed with wrinkled purple berries that Anna recalled from her days with the borzaq. "Feed these to a man," the fighter had told her, "and he'll tell you anything to cease the aching."

Each set of pillars Anna and Nuhra passed offered glimpses of candlelit chambers and steam-clouded wings and barred doors, with one pervading element binding the cavernous space: Silence. There were no screams, no groans—the mutilated figures that roamed the apse and surrounding corridors bore their trials without indulging in the body's laments.

High among the rafters, almost entirely immersed in shadows and silvery smoke, were creatures bound by coiled chains. All that remained of their bodies were sewn lids, marred torsos, stumps of limbs long since removed, rubbery flaps once occupied by ribs and spinal discs.

"Don't the flies get to those?" Anna whispered.

Nuhra bowed her head in reverence as they passed under the display. "The Resolute are deep in reflection, sister. This is their sacred hour."

Her stomach turned. "They're still conscious?"

"Certainly," Nuhra replied. "One might argue that they're more lucid than ever."

After they'd ascended a winding staircase at the end of the corridor, Nuhra led Anna into a cold, sparse study. High windows, formed from thin, swirling glass and latticed black iron, spread pale light over a stone floor littered with wicker mats. A gathering of chests, lockboxes, and tool trays lined the far wall.

"*Ghal'gil*," Nuhra said to a darkened alcove. The word lay on the cusp of the familiar, some vestige of the Kojadi tongue, but its meaning was lost on Anna.

"I've felt her for so long," an old woman croaked. Her voice was leaves crackling in a fire, low and fluid-wracked. "Bring her here, *Kof* Nuhra."

But Anna moved ahead before Nuhra could urge her onward, peering into the recess and its mass of dangling trinkets. Even after the horrors she'd witnessed in the safe house, she was not prepared for the woman's form.

A crude iron cage encircled her head, with lengths of thread binding a needle-pierced face to the encircling bars. Within, clumps of short, matted hair fell over dozens of rings of facial scarring. The raised flesh sills extended down her forehead, through pink, distended lids, parallel above and below burned lips, and down the entirety of her mottled neck, disappearing into the folds of a shirt draped with barbed hooks. One arm was fully removed, while the other had been crudely sawed away near the elbow. The withered, rope-constricted remnants of her legs were folded into an impossible spider's tangle.

But her most telling detail was also the most obvious, the most curious, the most overlooked in light of her state. Her flesh was disfigured, yet bare. *A scribe.*

"It perturbs you," the woman said to Anna, stretching her flesh against its bindings with every word.

"You said you can feel me," Anna said, moving toward the broken woman. "Do you know who I am?"

"I know *what* you are," she replied. "A name is but a shadow."

Anna looked over her shoulder at Nuhra, but the trailcarver remained by the door, smiling weakly at them.

"You are Anna," the woman continued. "Kuzalem to the kneeling, Tungretal to the people of the sun-cracked land, Qes'alur to the Gosuri, the Knowing One to your disciples—"

"Tell me who you are."

The woman's smile was so broad that it pulled a pair of embedded hooks taut, drawing blood from the edges of her lips. "Can you not feel what I am?"

"I long for names."

"Then you may term this form Bamadra of the Eight Rite."

Anna nodded, immediately considering the gesture somewhat wasted, and knelt on the wicker mat before Bamadra. "Nuhra brought me here with a singular purpose."

"Your wanting bleeds from you," the woman said darkly. "Can you sense that gushing void in your being? Will it not devour you in time?"

"Has she told you why I've come?"

"You make no attempt to mingle with what I am," she continued. "Do you retreat from knowing?"

Jagged shards of memory erupted with those words, filling Anna with visions of the blood and rites and blackness, the ceaseless wrath of Ramyi's mind, the terrors of unspeakable things promised, yet left undone. The thinking mind, consciously or otherwise, had sheathed the dagger's point of her awareness. Communing with emptiness was an invitation to entities beyond understanding, beyond mercy.

"No, I don't," Anna said.

"You've surely not come for tutelage," Bamadra said. "Fear itself has delivered you to me."

"We seek knowledge of a different sort, and I'm willing to reward you for your assistance. But if you believe I've sought you out to have my mind picked, then—"

"*Ayrif* Bamadra," Nuhra said, hurrying to Anna with her folded ledger of pilfered writings, "perhaps I might convey our sister's sacred task on her behalf. She knows little of our lineage's tongue."

"Yes," Anna said bitterly, "perhaps that would be best."

Nuhra went to the woman's side, whispering rapidly into ears that seemed swollen by blades and caustic oils alike. There was a rash of murmuring between them, a brief lull, then a labored nod from Bamadra.

"Does she know what Ramyi was after?" Anna asked.

"Beyond doubt," Bamadra cut in, running a thin, scaly tongue over broken lips. "This is the most primal feat of the shepherds."

"The Kojadi."

Bamadra nodded. "She seeks life."

"You speak of her like a spirit," Anna said.

"Rely not on a child's mind," the woman said, scowling. "Unending life, beyond the waxing and waning of time. This is what the Starsent craves."

Anna looked to Nuhra, but the trailcarver appeared equally disconcerted by her master's words. A scribe carried no essence, no vital conduit to the powers with which they imbued others—and Bamadra knew it as well as anyone else. "So she's searching in vain."

Bamadra laughed. "You infer what you please."

"It's not possible." Anna frowned at the coy, lingering secrets buried in the woman's lips. "Is it?"

"The texts she removed were esoteric manuals, more or less," Nuhra explained. "These are among the most *reckless* truths our lineage has preserved."

"Unending life is for the marked," Anna shot back. She found herself rising, pacing over the wicker mats, shaking her head at every fresh implication. "Whatever she took is beyond her understanding."

"You assume that none of our followers have pledged their minds to her undertaking," Bamadra said sternly.

Anna paused mid-step. "Have they?"

"As far as our chapter is aware, no," Nuhra replied. "But we must confront the possibility that the Starsent is pursuing a catastrophic end."

"You're assuming that she can carry this out," Anna said.

"The fear of death is what drives all things, is it not? You've witnessed her methods, sister. I ask this of you: If annihilation is the path to her survival, what is she willing to spare?"

"You're serious, aren't you?"

"The Starsent longs for eternal existence," Bamadra growled. "But to conjure an essence from the abyss of nothingness...the agony is unfathomable."

Drawing in a sharp breath, Anna paused and set her hands on her hips. "Supposing she could grant herself an essence, where would she begin?"

"Such knowledge cannot be placed within a reliquary," Nuhra said. "She possesses but a fragment of the whole, you see. Even so, each step begs the next. Her progress may hasten as she reaches the core of all things."

"Then you know where she'll go next."

"You do not see, sister. This is not a matter of tracing a path. The revelations she seeks have never been transcribed."

Empty terror, empty words: Far too long had been spent in the grips of those with imagined notions about the world and its lurking beasts. "Then where's the threat?"

"These unholy words are passed through direct transmission," Nuhra explained. "A disciple receives the rites from one who has undergone the journey themselves."

"It's an initiate that we're after, then."

Nuhra bit at her lip. "Of sorts."

"Of what *sorts*? If the line is unbroken, we can trace it."

"Therein lies the conundrum," Nuhra said, resting her weary gaze upon Bamadra. "There may be no living holders of these truths, or there may be innumerable splinters. And if they exist at all, then the Starsent will forge a way to them. This is known."

It was all so incredible, so unreal. Yet Anna could now sense the grounded unease in their voices, the dour way of those who dealt with certainties rather than mysticism, birthed by the threat of an entire lineage coming undone. It was not only possible—it was coming. "Supposing she learned the way from a living master," Anna said quietly, "then what?"

Nuhra extended her arms and turned her hands over, making the sigils squirm and dance for Anna. "She would no longer exist in the exalted realm of the hayajara."

"She would have an essence."

Nuhra did not speak, did not shift, but allowed silence to whisper in her stead.

"Could she read this essence?" Anna asked.

"If the ancient texts are to be believed, then yes." Nuhra joined her hands at her lower stomach, then turned away. "Anything is possible beyond that threshold, Kuzalem."

Such a sentiment had slumbered in Anna's mind since the final days of the war. It was not often that she thought of Yatrin—the thinking mind guarded against him and his love, his loss, his pain—yet every dream that summoned his face was interrupted by that blinding burst of light. It was seared into her, a scar that neither faded nor ceased to ache, sweeping · through the endless boulevards and markets of a place she'd once known. It was the merest *suggestion* of what Ramyi could do, especially when restraint vanished from her cuts. Three years was more than enough to delve into reservoirs of pain and wrath.

Blackened skulls burning.

Cities crumbling.

Anger welled up in savage flashes, cutting through the thinking mind and its flow of logic. Anna's breaths grew shorter, shallower, until at last she huffed and thrust a finger at the trailcarver. "This is nonsense."

"If only it were," Nuhra said, still facing the soot-stained wall.

"Why hasn't it been done before, then?"

Bamadra's broken lids shifted, offering hints of the vacuous cavities within. "It has."

"Yet any traces have been purged," Anna said, glowering at the women. "Isn't that right?"

The old woman's laugh was a curt, popping rattle. "Purged? Proof of my words slithers through every facet of this world. Where are the Kojadi?"

"Nobody knows."

Bamadra grinned.

"What's your point?" Anna pressed.

"They shared the aim of the Starsent," Bamadra said. "We will find the same end."

* * * *

Another storm descended in the late afternoon, slithering upon the windows in earthen coils and black eddies and patches of gritty, fizzling blackness. It was not the Howling Wall, but one of its progeny: Ertak, the Flayed One.

Low voices mumbled on in the adjacent chamber, punctuated by bouts of long, fragile silence. It was not in the nature of the Alakeph to speak excessively, nor to refuse the kindness of a host—Nuhra's offer of refuge had left them in a strange state, indeed. The most daring submission to generosity, however, had arrived when the brothers accepted the jinkaral's tea.

Anna wondered if the ushal root would break their stoicism.

"You shy away from focusing inward," Bamadra said. "Sense how your awareness skirts over the sand, Kuzalem."

Anna's eyes snapped open, revealing the black, featureless mass of Bamadra's alcove and rusted cage. "You know nothing about how I've honed my mind."

"Whatever pains you've taken thus far have been inadequate." Bamadra lifted a scalpel from a nearby cloth and drew its blade over her palm, barely stirring as blood ran in dark threads to the floor.

"Do you think my years have been spent without revelations?"

"I'm certain they've occurred to you," she replied, wiping her hand across the hem of her barbed shirt. "You would not be here without attainments, no. But look upon this shell that you scurry under, sister, and know its trappings well. Which mote of your being is under assault by my words?"

Anna looked down at her joined hands, watching the shadows play over her skin in writhing, alien forms. For so long—perhaps too long—she had looked only to herself for knowledge. Without teachers, without guiding hands, it was inevitable.

But renunciation was the seed of growth.

"Your concentration is admirable," Bamadra continued, "but to study a tree's growth is to marvel at the passing wonder of illusions. There is a deeper truth that underlies all formation and all collapse, is there not? Such breaches of the mind's laws cannot be divined through stillness alone."

"It's the only thing that could let me sense her," Anna explained, unable to repress a surge of futility when she grasped the woman's words. Worse yet, when she sensed the sheer *truth* of it all, as though recalling the name of some place she'd known and lost in dreams. Every hour spent in her chambers, delving into the formlessness she'd studied in ancient texts, now felt like part of a foolish pastime.

"A formidable technique, of course, and a foundation one cannot abandon. The lens of the starmen will not focus unless it first comes to rest. Such is the nature of your mind."

Anna brightened at that, though only slightly. It brought her no closer to sensing, apprehending, seizing Ramyi. Perhaps even killing her.

"How curious," Bamadra cooed. Her voice was softer, softer than ever before. "I can sense part of her within you, Kuzalem. Not the Starsent, no: I can sense the one who molded your mind in this new vessel."

Bora. And in that placid void, filled with her name and the blackness and the cool draft leaking from the corridor, Anna's mind settled into some hollow that she'd overlooked for so long. She could feel the northerner. She felt her as clearly as she had in the kales, when her mica cloak swirled and cinnamon wafted freely and—

"Do not chase her," Bamadra said. "She has left this world, yet you remain."

"Did you know her?"

"Deeply," the woman replied. "But the present begs for our will, Kuzalem. All of these shadows, these frivolous comings and goings, act upon your mind so fiercely. Remain with me and only the truth will persist."

The feeling mind clawed at the emptiness, craving, wishing....

Anna nodded.

"Perceiving reality is a matter of stripping away that which deludes you," Bamadra said, showing Anna her still-bleeding hand with an eerily perfunctory display. "Vision, hearing, touch—these are apparitions of your true form. They are a retreat from the center of your being. Projections, if you like. We must abandon our faith in these fabrications if we wish to perceive."

Anna grimaced at her words, her dripping blood. "How can you be so certain?"

"*I* cannot be," she replied. "I can be nothing at all. In fact, my true being will know nothing until its vessel has been picked apart."

"Yet you follow these ways with conviction."

"I've felt you in the space beyond existence," Bamadra whispered. "Three years ago, when the world itself burned and the roots withered and a hundred thousand voices fell silent, I sensed you. Your true form was alive, Kuzalem, and it sang out into that nothingness. Will you speak against this?"

A deep chill set in, worming up Anna's spine and through her chest and fanning out to her fingertips in icy threads. "I remember."

"Just yesterday you felt it again," the old woman said, piercing Anna with raw, familiar terror, with the wild unknowing still seared into her. "You departed for an instant, did you not?"

"I...*I* didn't go anywhere."

"You saw something. But it was not your vessel, was it?"

Anna shook her head. "It was a fever dream."

"Is that what you term your fragments of illumination? Mere dreams, woven by the trickery of your mind?"

"What does it matter?"

"You saw something that extended beyond this plane," Bamadra continued. "Another eon, another vessel, no?"

"It was—" Anna caught herself, sensing the cutting prescience of the woman's voice. There was no hiding from her, no surrender. "It was a ritual of some sort."

"You merged with yourself."

"What?" She had been powerless to stop it. *Yourself.* Nobody, not even Nuhra's master, could understand the imprisonment of that moment. The sense of helplessness, of damnation, of timeless oblivion.

"They will engulf you with mounting fervency as you near the center," Bamadra said. Her voice was even, almost clinical, but it exploded through Anna's awareness. "Your forms will converge, Kuzalem, and there is nothing to cease this process—only a path to hasten it. Hold fast to these cruxes."

"Nothing to cease it?" Anna asked. "You can't envision what I experienced."

"In time, these glimpses will not frighten you so much. A thing cannot be destroyed by itself."

Her own words blossomed from distant memory, welling up in vibrant strands, half-buried flickers of truth: *You cannot be broken by what you are.* A low ringing filled her ears. "What am I seeing, then?"

"Yourself."

"It's not me," she snapped. "Don't you—"

"Not in this vessel." Bamadra's breathing slowed, rattling as a swell of sand glossed over the windows and thrust them into transient blackness. "Remember the lives before this. This may be the last, but it was not the first. Now is a time of binding."

Her throat was swollen, somehow sealed. "They can't be."

"But why?"

"They're just *visions*," Anna cried. "This is my life. Here, now."

"In this vessel. But you've seen the witnessed the flow of your being, Kuzalem, and nothing will halt your ascent. Surrender to the ecstasy."

Tears, childish and long cast aside, bit at her eyes. "They're not mine. I'm a slave to them."

"To master one life," Bamadra said, her voice growing more soothing and measured as light trickled back to the chamber, "is to master all of eternity."

Anna shut her eyes and let the words flow past her. *Eternity.*

"The fear will fade in time," Bamadra continued. "But only if you persist."

"Persist with what?"

"A profound question, yet its answers are trapped within you. What freed you from your delusions, sister? What stole you from this vessel, if only for an instant?"

"I don't know," she whispered.

"Speak it."

"I don't—"

"Pain." Bamadra's voice overtook the rustling and hissing, a thunderclap amid a lesser storm. "It was pain and it always has been. Pain cannot be willed away, nor can it be concealed from the percepts of this frail vessel. When you discern the primordial flow of this world, the chasm from which all pain emanates and castrates you, then you will know truth."

"I've existed in spite of pain," Anna said with a faltering voice.

"Listen without ears, and see without eyes," Bamadra said. "Then you will know the ploys of this vessel. It will scratch and claw however it may to escape what it is. Only the deepest center of your being would seek out pain, sister."

Anna's gaze ran over the assortment of blades and pins and dried herbs set out upon the cloth, certain that she could endure whatever torment the order's implements might induce. It was a meager price to intercept Ramyi, of course. And after all the suffering she'd inflicted upon others—whether by her own hand or with a stamped missive—it was a simple thing to maim her own flesh.

"Very well," Anna said, straightening her back as Bora would've reminded her to do so long ago. "Show me."

Bamadra's hand drifted out of the shadows and into a patch of ebbing, coppery light, hovering over a row of vials filled with black liquid. Her fingers were cracked, stitched, capped by pink scabs rather than nails. She lifted the smallest container at the edge of the cloth and held it up for Anna's inspection. "I can show you nothing, Kuzalem. This will show you all things."

* * * *

The last trace of Anna's neck vanished at the cusp of the third hour. It was a sensation beyond drowsiness, beyond numbness, beyond anything that could even be termed *sensing*. It was simply—in the words of Kojadi tomes she could recite on command—the cessation of the body's self-assertions. Nerves and hairs and blood had gradually relinquished their importance, fading into a pervasive flow that was no longer roused by the stirring of the flesh. Her mind was still cutting, vicious and attuned to every muffled cough in the surrounding chambers, but it had moved beyond the bestial need to probe its own form.

Every breath consumed her awareness, fanning her out into the blackness and nestling her with equal, omnipresent force. Beads of fractal light played across the field. It was a warm haven, a state most of her adherents sought their entire lives.

On this day, however, it was merely the beginning.

"I'm ready." She sensed her own words as the wind howling through canyons, snaking into forgotten gullies and sun-beaten vales. They had been spawned somewhere beyond that sliver of perfect stillness. Beyond herself, perhaps. They thrummed upon her lips long after she'd spoken, rippling out in an effervescent stream, blossoming, becoming *real* in the womb of the formless.

The ayrif did not reply. If she did, Anna's awareness had dissolved the sound and buried it as readily as the Flayed One's screeching beyond the glass. There was only a sudden, burning jolt upon the back of her hand, as fierce and precise as a hornet's barb. Metal slid down through layers of tendons and cartilage, burrowing ever deeper with its lukewarm toxin, materializing in the void as radiant crimson flashes.

And the pain was lucid, breathing down her neck, as inescapable and striking as she'd been promised.

Anna sensed her teeth grinding shut, pressed firmly against pursed lips and the bleeding lining of her cheeks. Tears were budding and swelling and dribbling of their own accord. Each time she detected her fingers curling inward, she forced herself back to stillness, to a state of complete acceptance with the metal's throbbing bite.

There is pain. The words, again, erupted in the experience like a stranger's whisper. *There is the knower of the pain.*

Blood ran down the curve of her hand, its trail warm and thin, and dripped from her palm. She was each droplet and each crack in the stone below, each resonant *plop* that issued from the impact.

Anna forced herself back to the center, back to the wellspring from which all sensations arose and disintegrated. There the pain was a shapeless, burgeoning presence, commanding her attention, her wrath, her—

Far into the swath of nothingness, a dim, tawny light shone. It was less intense than the presences she'd known in Nahora, certainly, but it carried the same assurance of unity. It was an anomaly, something living and fluid in a world of emptiness. Not an essence, precisely, but a microcosm of its weaving. Primordial, unformed, faceless.

The gross, vague ache of the toxin registered at the fringes of her awareness. Beneath that was the frantic ebb of her flesh, coursing in waves that threatened to unmake her into the basest particles and streams of danha. If only she could touch the distant light, the warmth amid chaos...

We are.

She staggered forward, gazing up at flames that singed the cosmos and blotted out the brightest heralds of the northern sky. Flames that licked her skin from a third-league, basking her in heat that sapped her tongue and eyes of their precious fluid, tanning her like a hide stretched out upon crooked racks.

White in the core, blood-red upon its tips and flailing pillars.

It wreathed a mound of blackened shapes, a glimmering, melting, smoldering stack of unholy idols and infernal trappings. Charring, curling flesh. Flesh-borne steam.

Silhouettes wandered past her, bulbous with the skins of bears and cracked-horned goats thrown upon their backs. Shadows nested in the overhang of the creatures' jaws, stretching down and over the sweat-streaked black paint that covered eyes and noses and scarred mouths.

Far above the inferno, unmoved by the whipping torrents of flame and smoke, was the mountainous crest of their temple. Countless obsidian tiers, ornamented with braziers and kerosene bodies upon stakes, winked through the shroud as they neared the domain of the Once-Gods.

Again she opened her mouth to scream, but it was not her mouth. Blackness consumed it all.

Stars flickered into being across the void, their light stretching to the edges of her vision and beyond. Dark green nebulae hung like algae in the nothingness, silent, dead, raking distant suns and moons with emerald talons. Something immense drifted down over the ocean of hazy orbs, blotting them out and forming a mass of pure darkness.

It was not a *thing*, not a slave to whatever titles could be thrust upon it. There was no word for it. No concepts.

Rows of teeth—twisting, vicious teeth, numbering in the hundreds, the thousands—glinted in the light of a dying star.

It loomed nearer, nearer, soundless in its approach, stirring the vacuum with a dreadful hum.

We are.

She had the sense of sinking into some vast ocean, plunging down into depths beyond light and life itself. Here her form was lithe, wavy, billowing out as it explored and teased the loss of boundaries. Only it was not a void, not some barren emptiness, and her fears dissipated in an instant. The fabric that encircled her was living, somehow breathing, molding with every ripple she cast into it. Each of the mass's flutters and waves shaped her in turn.

She knew the presence she sought, even as it wriggled namelessly around her, a junction and binding force that flowed amid innumerable essences. Never before had the patterns been so clear, so immediate, so tangible within her awareness: tiles, thorns, spirals, leaves, diamonds, struts, all congealing and splitting moment by moment. Even in Nahora the essences had materialized upon dark, foggy glass, able to be glimpsed, yet never truly felt. Now they intertwined in the center of her being, joining and departing from her in erratic strands, forming her out of the nether. Perhaps her awareness did not hold them at all. They held *her*.

They made her.

But Ramyi's presence, in spite of its scattered, shapeless nature, held her attention as easily as the pain lancing through faraway tendons. It was a radiant swell, crimson and amethyst and bone-white, creeping out and spiraling as it probed the living fabric.

Anna's awareness drifted nearer.

The vision contracted into an ocean of objects, forms, lights, motion. It was dazzling, nearly overwhelming in its scale. Everything danced around her in a mass of blinking, shimmering eyes, spokes and spindles, starlight and opal globules. Horses whinnied and engines screamed.

"…or I'll slit his little throat." Ramyi's voice was a tinny, resonant wave. "Do you understand me, Zadesh?"

Whimpering. Wet, wheezing breaths. "I do."

"And if you toy with me," she whispered, "I'll make sure that these are the last days of *Uppura Qalefra*, and every spider in its den. Beginning with you."

The Watchful Silence.

Her awareness shut out the spectacle of lustrous, surreal formations, instead orbiting the obscure merchant's dialect she hadn't encountered in years. Thoughts were difficult to bind together, even more difficult to preserve as memories amid the storm of howls and raw sensation and blinding flashes.

The Watchful Silence.

She held onto those words with all the focus she could muster. It was her sole link to the girl, to whatever horrors she'd conjured out of sight, where—

All light vanished.

Sounds trailed off into rattling, fractured echoes.

"I see you." Ramyi's voice was a whisper in her ear, no longer warped and stretched by the emptiness surrounding them. It clawed its way into the lowest, most reptilian sediment of Anna's mind, cleaving through her with an ax's heft. "This is your only warning, Anna. After so long, I believed that you'd seen the wisest course. Now I understand that this silence was just your unskillful ways. So heed my words, Kuzalem: This experience is the basest level of my existence. You are venturing into places you cannot fathom."

Golden eyes stared at her in the blackness, blazing with wicked fire, with a thousand years of torment.

Anna's body was pain.

She did not *feel* the pain—there was simply nothing else to sense. It was razors slipping under her skin, mallets crushing fingers, needles tumbling through her stomach, growing fiercer, firmer, breaking every illusion that love had ever existed, in either memories or her vapid world. *The world.* What was the world? Surely it was an invention, a momentary aberration of this reality, a desperate wish for something other than whipping, breaking, scratching, shrieking. Time itself was a relic from forsaken, fleeting dreams; there was only death, birth, death, birth, revolving with horrific precision until it stripped existence to its brittle bones. Lightless eons came and went. Every nerve screamed, begging to be undone.

"Awaken, sister."

Anna shot up and forward, panting, heaving, her eyes darting madly between beads of candlelight. She slapped her hand against stone, but the toxin robbed the flesh of every feeling aside from the barest ache, the ripples of numbness creeping up to the crux of her elbow. The incision was foul; it had to be excised by any means. She scrambled toward a nearby glint of iron, brushing away the hands that grasped at her, the words that could not soothe her.

Her hand seized the leather cording, squeezing until her knuckles throbbed, but callused fingers pinned her wrist to stone. The blade flailed and grated over the tiles. Pressure exploded in a cuff at the base of her hand, pounding, tingling until her fingers unwound and iron clattered.

"Kuzalem." Andriv was breathless, panting through gritted teeth. "Be still, please. Please."

"She knows," Anna gasped.

"As do you," Bamadra said, still basking in shadows.

The Watchful Silence. It settled in her awareness, coalescing from the froth of pain and disjointed memories. Yes, she knew it, had even dealt with it in wartime: breakers, runners, mirrormen, traders.

Nuhra crouched into view and began pressing a damp rag to Anna's forehead. "Where is she, sister?"

"Here." Anna's teeth were chattering. "Leejadal." She brushed Nuhra's hand aside and cradled her own temples, trembling. "A market, something of its sort. And the man. Zadesh. You need to find Zadesh."

Andriv rose to his full height and moved to the door. He was a pale smudge in the darkness, a moon glowing beyond ragged clouds. "Take heart, Kuzlem. This task is sworn."

Chapter 7

After two days and fifteen bombings, the temrusi trundled back into the safe house's walled lot. It was nearly dusk and as Anna stood by shuttered windows, tracking cloaked shapes to ensure the company's ranks hadn't been thinned, she sensed something guarded among them. Something precious, delicate, invaluable.

They knew something.

It seemed impossible after a half-dozen fruitless strikes, raking through trade depots and markets and auction dens for a man who'd clearly studied the nuances of erasing his own existence. Or, in the minds of those who carried out the hunt, a man who'd never even existed. Each runner and mirror-glint had seemed intent on proving that the lead was in vain, which would've sat all too well with Lukas and the others. Even the most devout northerners had struggled to accept the revelations of the jinkaral's toxin, after all.

But Anna did not—could not—dismiss the ordeal. It was an undercurrent that had staved off sleep, eating, speaking. *The Watchful Silence.* It was the only memory the thinking mind allowed her to know, to sense at will. Beneath it there was a dormant pain, existing beyond all forms and conscious presence, threatening to devour her the moment she forgot its misery. It had been there since Nuhra wrapped her in the jinkaral's blankets, but now it was a fleeting melody, a dissolving shard of some dreamscape, a faceless dread beyond all recognition.

Beyond erasure.

Boots came stomping up the stairwell, shattering her lapse in focus. There was a clipped exchange, a bout of hushing. She turned to find Lukas moving through the doorway and into ruddy candlelight.

Nuhra trailed him, hurrying into the threshold with a flustered expression. "Kuzalem?" Her eyes snapped between Anna and the visitor.

"It's all right," Anna said. "I feel well enough."

The trailcarver maintained her silence, offering little more than a wrinkled brow and a parting nod before she moved down the corridor.

"She's been touchy lately, eh?" Lukas asked, jabbing a thumb toward the doorway. Flecks of bright blood covered his cloak and burlap mask. His garments were torn, singed, dappled with dark smears, sparkling as sand sifted down from their folds. But his rune still granted him that eternal vigor, that freshness in his gait and swaying arms.

Anna had always thought that she'd grow used to it.

"Well?" Anna pulled her shawl tighter across her shoulders. "Don't drag it out—did you find him?"

Lukas stopped halfway across the room, blinking at her through fraying burlap holes. "It cracked you."

It drew attention to her knotted shoulders, her restless lips, her gaping eyes. "Don't speak about what you do not understand." She turned away and sat on the edge of her cot. "Just answer me."

"He didn't make it back."

There was no elation in it. No vindication, no release. "Did you torture him?"

"*Silence.*" He snorted. "Those sukry earn their title."

"Nothing, then."

"Cramming words in my throat, eh?" Lukas asked. "Here's the way of it: He damn well knew our flatlander. Just had to scrape him 'fore he told us every spot on her cheeks." He inspected his gloves in the light, using a long, leather-coated thumb to scrape at a crimson blot. "Seems your girl is in deep, 'cause this Zadesh kretin was a contact. Nothing more than that."

Anna drew in a deep breath. "A contact for what?"

"Well." Lukas wandered back to the door and closed it. "Took a few cuts, but he slipped that she was after a trailcarver. Didn't know what in the Grove she was after, though. Said she was *specific*. He liked that word, *specific*."

"You could've at least brought him back."

"No need," Lukas said. "Left his glyph sets and flash-channels wide open at the desk, you see. An ink trail to this carver, too." He reached under his cloak and produced a thin, ragged strip of parchment. "We've got a meeting."

"Bring it." She shook her head as Lukas crossed the room, intent on the scroll and every wicked thing it had seen to arrive here. "You shouldn't have written to him."

Lukas handed off the parchment. "Think sharper of me, eh? This is the girl's invitation, panna, not ours."

Anna unrolled the parchment and scanned its contents, beginning with the courier's tag in the left-hand corner, then moving to the flash-channel's seal, the mechanical stamping along the edges, the sheen of the cartel's ink. It was all in order, assuming her work with Nahora's breakers had lent any weight to her analysis.

The glyphs were uniformly rigid, a product of whatever stamping press Hazan's tinkerers had churned out in the past year. Such a machine wouldn't have been possible without Volna's patronage—not within such a short span of time, anyway. But war had always meant progress for its survivors. For its sponsors, no less.

She found difficulty in parsing the tongue, which had to be a hybrid dialect of some breed. It had the sharp, terse flow of ruinspeak, but it was coupled with bouts of commanding elegance, which Anna could only liken to—

Bora.

Her heart drummed faster as she took in the glyphs' coordinates, already knowing the impossibility of what she sought. The thinking mind drew her attention to *the Shifting Market*, the day and cycle, the obscure call-and-reply to initiate the meeting.

"Passes your muster?" Lukas asked, removing his gloves and setting them on a low table near the cot.

Anna did not return his gaze. "You're certain he sent it?"

"Sent and stamped by your girl."

"She's not my girl," Anna snapped. "She has a name of her own. We all do."

Lukas grunted, picking at the dark wads of sand and blood beneath brittle nails.

"A day isn't enough to confirm any of this," she continued softly.

"Not enough to know their man's gutted, either."

"Word travels quickly," Anna said. "Nobody in these wards will turn a blind eye to this."

"Won't matter if we get her."

Anna opened her mouth, but found nothing to say. There was some sense in his words: In a hunt, the kill was all that mattered. And there was no guarantee—in fact, nearly no hope—of sensing Ramyi's presence in the same manner, let alone tracking her, probing her intentions.

A wary hound knew the mark of old traps.

"Even Konrad, your sacred runt, has his blades sharp for it," Lukas added. "Got one day, Anna, and we'll use it. Trust that, eh? Won't be a door or droba we don't know about."

"You think preparation is enough."

"That's the way of it."

Anna stared at the shutters, studying flurries of sand as they whirled in dark knots and glittered in through the slats. "You really know nothing about her, do you?"

"Suppose you're right," Lukas growled. "All credit to you."

Wind whistled through cracked stone and fraying cloth.

"No prying ears about, Anna," he continued, sinking heavily into a chair beside her. "Something's burning behind those little lips. Know what she's after, I'd wager."

"You know her aims as well as I do."

"That so?" Lukas asked. "Seems you're peddling death and fire from her, but that's not the root of it. Can't be. If the pup wanted us under soil, she'd paint our shadows on the walls like—"

Golyna. "Hold your tongue." It was red iron in her mind, an immediate reaction beyond control.

"See, I know the way of what happened," Lukas continued. "Whispers spread, eh? Just like you said. Now, if Ashoral and her eastern runts knew what that girl could do, they'd have her strung up yesterday. Last I heard, they were mucking about in Nur Sabah, pinnin' all that ash on Volna. Believe me, panna: If it'd been Volna's tinkerers, we would've cranked those blasts out until the stars were ash."

"Are you finished?"

"Sore business, it seems. Swore I wouldn't mention your boy, and I won't."

Anna swallowed her retort, her lunge toward the hunter's bait.

"My point still has legs," Lukas said. "Bodies aren't all she's after. And whatever it is—whatever those little claws are scratching at—it's got you spooked."

"I see."

"Come off it," he scoffed. "I never bit my tongue with you."

Anna narrowed her eyes. "You brought your world into mine. There were no favors between us—not then and not now."

"Ungrateful," Lukas said, his burlap covering taking on the crease of a buried smile. "You and I were here before all these fucking sukry. Remember those days? Good days, simple days. Bled for each other, didn't we?"

She held up her shattered hand. It didn't ache unless she thought about it. "I bled for myself."

"Living's pain." He settled lower in the chair, gazing distantly at the wall ahead of him. When he spoke, his lips shifted mechanically, glacially. "See it how you like it, Anna, but you've had me since you crawled from the womb. No kin, no warm hearts, no babes—only me. Maybe that's why you won't gut me, eh? Maybe all the other ones are dead."

Anna stared at him. "You long so deeply for that."

"Grove knows," Lukas said. He stood, lingering over the cot for a moment, then stepped away. "Day'll come when you see the way of things. Every runt's got its teeth and if you'd wrench those tender eyes open, you'd see how easily that white fur carries its stains."

"Don't teach me what I know."

His laugh was curt, guttural. "Know? You've got a tough hide, panna, but you don't *know* the world. You've just stumbled through it."

Anna meshed her hands in her lap, waiting until his footsteps tramped to the door and the old hinges squealed. "I know enough, Lukas."

He did not look at her, did not make a sound. When his hand finally slipped from the doorknob and he drifted out of sight, fading into the oily shadows of the corridor, he hardly seemed to have left at all.

* * * *

During the war, a timid man had stumbled into Anna's encampment with tales of an atrocity at the furthest edge of the Flats. He'd told her every detail for a crust of bread and a half-pinch of salt. She never forgot his words.

Sixteen pilgrims, all bearing the ritual beads and dried apricots of Suyuk, the Dead Herdsman, had traveled under the stars in the company of a southern caravan. All along the way, they chanted and sang to the starving townspeople, assuring them of the war's end and burying sacred seeds in the soil along the roads. By the time they'd reached Amaluk, a burgeoning city near the coast, a thousand travelers had come to receive their blessings, crowding the central squares and temples and markets with their hands outstretched. Nobody could resist that divine momentum. It was the panacea to Volna's wrath, to the famine and wildfires that had ravaged their lands.

It was a good omen for their act of revolt.

"You come for blessings," one of the pilgrims had called out, standing high atop the remains of a shattered statue. "And thus you receive."

Nobody knew precisely what transpired after those words, not even the storyteller himself, but he attested that the pilgrims had torn away their trappings, revealing blades, ruji, pale scars from years spent in the service of the Dogwood Collective. Some claimed that they were all marked with Kuzalem's runes, while others swore that only a handful bore her markings.

Later that month, one of Anna's spymasters had confirmed the ending of the man's tale: An entire city burned to the ground, littered with thin, mutilated bodies.

Slaughter disguised as salvation.

Anna could not ignore the tale as she glanced around the café, noting the Alakeph brothers and how unsettling it was to look upon them without their white coverings.

Under dim pastel lights, huddled around tables with smoke-bleeding pipes and splotchy teacups, they weren't so different from anybody else. Once their southern roots would've betrayed them, but the war had muddied that divide. The illusion was refined by their dense black beards, their sun-darkened flesh, their demure way. Assuming one wasn't probing the shape of their tunics too intently, their shortened ruji and yuzeli would go unnoticed.

She herself had submitted to Nuhra's guidance, donning a coiled head scarf, satin mouth veil, and dark red eye powder. It was a trend owed to southern expatriates living among the plains cities, the trailcarver had assured her, though Anna had never seen such women in the flesh. Then again, she had seen mercifully little in her mountain cloisters.

If it had been up to Lukas, Anna would not have even been there. "No place for our precious songbird," he'd insisted, a flask of arak in his grip. But his way did not—indeed, could not—hold any authority. The time of sending men to do their violent bidding was over.

"On with it, on with it," a pale patron barked in river-tongue, sprawled out on the cushions near the back of the café. He was lying between two flatland girls, covered in the drippings of his second lamb skewer. "Never waited this long with Timek in the kales!"

One of the servers hurried to his table with another pitcher of wine. "I'm sorry." His river-tongue was shaky, likely gleaned from the passersby and tenants in this ward alone.

The man leaned his head back and chewed with bovine sluggishness. "I'm sure."

"It should be any moment now," Konrad whispered. He had his arm draped across the back of Anna's chair, his lips nuzzled against her ear like any bold suitor. "If anyone calls out, Nuhra's men will handle it."

Handle it. She had an all-too-precise understanding of what the phrase entailed.

"There can't be any commotion," Anna slipped into his ear. "As soon as they notice us, it'll be flames or flight."

"We have every avenue covered."

"You can't imagine what she learned in the Nest, what she was able to do. She was the only one who could sustain a tether." A tether, after all, was the only feasible way for Ramyi to cover so much ground without leaving a trail. That, or something more refined, more efficient. Something that no army could oppose. "The years surely haven't dimmed her cuts."

"Well, two of Nuhra's scribes are checking markings."

Anna sighed. "It's not enough, Konrad. I trained wolves."

"So did Volna," he whispered stiffly.

She leaned away and drank her tea. It had been a long, fragile while since he'd even uttered the name. But now his voice carried that old weight of the war, the ruins, the wife and child once gripping his hands and trusting him. She still did not know what to say, nor if anything could be said at all.

Crowds streamed past the café's glass frontage, a sea of radiant, colorful threads and fractal sigils. There was no rhythm to the flow, exactly, but the bulk of visitors—sari-draped Hazani women and thin men and timid, bright-eyed children—were moving from the lower concourse to the spice markets. Lurid overhead lamps gave their flesh an oily sheen.

Then the lights dimmed, the third such occurrence since Anna had arrived, and bells chimed along the rafters.

Passersby thronged the shop fronts, eager to have a parting look at this level's intricate, whirring lions formed from brass, its shelves of arak and spiced liquor housed in crystalline bottles, and its rotating menageries of hardy, freshly brushed pack animals, all shining like silk under their keepers' lights. The crowds were still murmuring and jostling, pushing against the barrier of hired blades, when the cogs began their staccato thumps.

Kuh, kuh, kuh.

Bolts slammed somewhere deep within the machinery of the arch, rattling Anna's table, her teacup, her shins and their warped bones. Gaslight ebbed and bloomed above her.

The entire shopfront rose, slipping into the ceiling like cloth running over a gargantuan loom. It was possible that the café itself was sinking, though Anna's stomach was already too shaken to discern motion in any direction. The market's ever-present hum gave her the sense that motion was ceaseless, enveloping, simultaneously lateral and vertical in paths that would've boggled southern tinkerers. But there was no time to be curious. The next level was already ascending from the tiles, its unseen offerings drawing applause and jeers, magnetizing even the most overburdened visitors to the fresh spectacle.

"Anna." Konrad was leaning back, his knuckles furtively tapping upon the table. Something near the swelling crowd had drawn his attention.

A small, sharp blade, running under the green-honey flesh of ripening mango. A thumb pointing toward the northern concourse. Golden eyes weighing Anna through coils of braided black hair. The man's gesture was swift, bleeding back into the flow of onlookers as casually as it had arisen, but it sufficed.

Two tables' worth of Alakeph brothers stood and pulled on their thin, patchwork overcoats, exchanging slate glances that only killers could decipher. It was nonchalant commotion, an awkward shuffle toward the market corridors, a bag of salt left on each tabletop. Next went the northerners who sat on azure cushions by the doorway, rising amid plumes of nerkoya smoke and taking great pains to conceal the threaded barrels in their boots. It was no exodus; it was gradual, demure, less disruptive than an errant spoon striking porcelain.

That was what sickened her the most.

But Konrad was already at the counter and exchanging cheery flatspeak with one of the narrow-necked serving girls. He tapped out the cost of two cardamom teapots, then returned to the table and draped his scarf over sun-cracked lips. "*Shara*," he said, glancing out at the crowds. "I wonder what the markets have today."

Anna's mouth was suddenly dry. "I'm not so curious."

* * * *

It was an animal pack; a wordless, instinctive scouring, a flock of carrion birds cutting through the currents of flesh and henna and homespun wool. None of the fighters—northern or southern or some mongrel blood-breed—were marked by their garments, but Anna could sense their wicked task nevertheless. There was a certain swiftness to their steps, a hurried purpose as they shouldered and rounded and dodged, their gazes cycling between the eyes of passing strangers.

Jashi, another sentry, murmured a string of hoarse flatspeak to each fighter that skirted his stretch of brick wall. He did not meet Anna's eyes, nor Konrad's, as they edged past him. "Sixth booth."

Following the sliver of Alakeph fighters, Anna rounded the next corner and moved under rows of dying gaslights. The walls were a quilt of cracked tiles and splotchy mortar, somehow suggestive of the clientele within the surrounding dens. She refused to peer into the doorways, to acknowledge the broad, leering men standing watch, to indulge her fears about what sent screams and moans leaking through cloth partitions. There was only the sixth lounge, only the Alakeph congregating near its threshold in chilling silence.

She caught herself absently patting the yuzel tucked beneath her robe.

Soft rustling spread through the Alakeph ranks. Thin ruji and jabbing knives emerged from rippled fabric, their silhouettes long and dark against ruddy tiles.

Gruff voices began cropping up at Anna's back, building from drugged annoyance to alarm in moments. But they were mere grunts, hardly words at all, swiftly decaying into glove-muffled cries and scuffing boots and sputtering. Stillness came with a hard crash; Anna turned to find one of the guards lying near the mouth of the corridor, twitching, his glossy blood trail leading back to a group of northerners with curved skinning knives. A dozen other bodies lined the tiles in black heaps.

Anna glanced back, her lips parted and words scraping free, but it was wasted.

The fighters surged through the partition, boots thumping and barrels knocking and cloth flapping.

Thought was now a relic, a luxury.

A hindrance.

Anna swept the hem of her robe back and drew her yuzel, clutching the lacquered walnut grip with both hands. Her thumb flicked the cylinder's bolt into place.

Konrad tightened his sling, swung the ruj round to his lower back, and yanked the drapes aside, allowing Anna to rush into humid darkness.

At the back of the private booth, fixed in the conical glow of a kerosene lantern, stood an assembly of northerners: an armored man springing toward his ruj, a thin youth twirling a blade, hooded women staring blankly, all shifting impossibly slow within Anna's hunting grounds. She saw sweat shimmering upon rigid brows, wild eyes blossoming, their reflections gliding over a reinforced glass pane, sigils—

Scribes.

Blank, goose-skinned flesh breached her awareness in tandem with the hiss of ruji. Sound itself could not outrace the iron.

"Wait!"

But her command was an afterglow, another discordant note among glass cracking and flesh liquefying and debris skittering over saffron carpeting.

Dust plumes and pink mist swirled in the pool of light. And amid that ear-ringing stillness, everything settled: Mangled, stringy bodies were strewn over leather armchairs and fur-draped divans; the shattered glass overlooking the nerkoya den was mottled with red flecks and gray tissue. Yet in the vast wilderness below, glimpsed through a fractured spiderweb, the festivities carried on. Gaslights burned in every hue, blindingly prismatic, whirling and painting the walls in kaleidoscopic washes. Gosuri drums thumped through the carpeting, and resonant tin bowls oscillated deep in Anna's sternum and bodies pulsed against one another in that visceral trance, an ocean of dark, roiling shapes and sparkling sweat.

It all continued as though bodies were not lining the floor.

"I can't see her," one of the brothers called out, rolling over a man with a gaping eye socket.

Anna fought the tremors in her hands, looking upon the corpses as war had trained her to—bone and sinew and hair, nothing more. She hurried past the brothers and glanced at the remnants of the hooded women—no, hooded *girls*—to look upon Ramyi.

Only it was not Ramyi.

None of them were.

Konrad's ruj lowered to his hip. "They're gone."

Anna barely heard him. She was still crouching over the scribes, weighing their mutilated features: They had gentle cheekbones, yes, and the small, oily pores of flatland youths, but they were not *her*. They lacked the pinkish scars, the haggard, deep-set eyes, the marks that would only wither and wrinkle in time. Yet the girl's awareness was an imminent, circling hum, as clear and rhythmic as the den's melodies. It was so close that it bled into Anna's mind, like—

Her periphery swarmed with rapid, distorted forms. She glanced sidelong into the adjacent booth, tracking figures that warped and bent behind a divide of veiny, fractal glass. Luminous runes, golden eyes, bare flesh: the Starsent and her howling mind.

"Not gone," she whispered to Konrad, watching ruji barrels swiveling in the gloom, contorting through jigsaw glass. "Just out of reach."

Rosebud sparks appeared just as her hand seized Konrad's collar. She was still jerking Konrad backward, intent on the black span of the dividing wall, when both panes exploded in a dazzling plume, a spray of micronized glass rippling with rose and azure and teal. Her back slammed against setstone. Pulverizing *thump*s slammed into the opposite wall, distantly registering as an eastern foundry's weighty iron bolts. Each impact was a hoof clopping over stone, a resonant snap in Anna's ears, an Alakeph fighter sublimating into red puffs.

Several brothers hunkered behind sofas and tables, their shouts lost to cracking stone and supersonic pops, but the bolts tore through them and spilled their innards as easily as those of the stacked goose feather pillows.

Anna's gaze snapped to the door. One brother was edging through the threshold, his ruj jutting against the partition, when the frame burst in a cloud of wood and grit and blood. The remains slumped down in a wet, twitching pile.

"Canister!" Anna's voice faltered with the strain; the words seared their way up her throat. "We need a canister!"

Konrad's eyes were wide, ferocious. "How many are there?"

"I don't know." Another brother snapped forward, his skull framed in the light as a jagged, gushing crown. "She's *there*, Konrad."

"Not for long."

Shrieking tones forced their way into Anna's awareness, emanating from the crystalline layer of glass that had blanketed the entire carpet. She watched the globules churning, oscillating, pulsing with the light of the spectacle below, surging up in momentary crests reminiscent of water brought to a boil. Then the glass condensed into a jagged, diamond-like mound, folding in on itself as it wove into tighter and tighter configurations. She sensed the scorched aura of hayat, the latent force ascending with every contraction.

There was no room for hesitation, for terror.

Anna slid along the setstone wall and sank down, kneeling at the edge of the blown-out pane. In one sweep she shouldered her ruj, tilted round the setstone's pitted edge, and took aim at the neighboring booth. There was little to guide her: a murky, webbed wall of glass, a trail of pulsing runes, a shape wreathed in pallid markings.

She fired.

The ruj bucked against her shoulder, fiercer than anything she'd fired since the war. Its cylinders chugged along, *teck-teck-teck*, punching away at the glass in a glittering chromatic haze.

On the fifth shot a spray of blood flared in the den's light. The figure snapped away, runes sinking out of sight, and his crystal shards crackled at Anna's back. She continued to flood the booth with whistling iron, even as she realized there was nobody to sustain the shifting mound, nothing to bind it....

It burst with a sharp hiss. Crushed glass pelted her robes, bit through to the back plate of her ceramic vest, clawed at her neck and scalp and legs, flooded her with hot pain. Within seconds her skin was slick with blood, tacky against her cloth coverings.

The ruj thundered against her shoulder until its bolt slammed back and locked in place, wreathed in a ribbon of steam like a galvanized tongue, hungry for the next cartridge.

Anna spun back against the setstone, still sensing the phantom claps that heralded bruising in the tender crux between arm and breast. A brother's spare cartridge came spinning over the carpeting, clearing a swath through brain matter and gristle, striking her boot with a hollow knock. She fumbled to load it; her gaze was roaming over the carnage, snapping between everything except the ruj.

The doorway was a tangle of arms and shredded bellies. Konrad watched it with ceaseless determination, unblinking, a ruj nestled against his shoulder and blood running in bright stripes down his face. His flesh was glimmering with embedded shards, with the wet daubs of punctures and gashes in need of a suturer's thread.

"Konrad," Anna huffed, racking the cartridge with a slap to the bolt. "We can't force them back."

He fired at a silhouette moving into the doorway. The body slid down in ragged lumps, twisting over itself and sloshing across the carpet. "We just need time."

"We don't have that either." She studied the four Alakeph brothers huddling behind gutted cover, tracking their bouts of returned fire and crawls to retrieve headless kin. One of the men was passing hand signals behind the edge of his shelter, staring up at a glass overlook beyond the enemy position. "What's he doing?"

Konrad glanced at the man, then back at an oncoming fighter, at the plume of arterial blood that drenched the nearby wall. "Talking."

But there was no time to inquire further. The overlook's panoramic wall fizzled into a hail of ice-white shards, cascading onto the den in a soundless, gleaming curtain. Then there were only the white cloaks of Andriv's fighters, the transient flashes of ruji, the iron swarms ripping through the adjacent booth. Black shapes sailed down from the overlook, toppling end over end until they plunged into the enemy's nest.

"Kuzalem!"

Something swiveled over the carpeting, coming to rest at the edge of Anna's vision. She peered down; it was a shalna canister, black-banded and capped with a brass stopper. Anna tossed down the ruj, picked up the device, and—

The first of Andriv's canisters exploded. The adjacent booth's panes burst out in a scintillating wave, leaving only a skeletal frame, a mass of chalky smoke writhing with silhouettes and veiled runes.

A marked man dashed into view, naked, yet blanketed in burning white talons. He raised both hands, fueling the luminous surge of a rune above his collarbone.

It began as tingling upon the backs of her hands. Anna shrank behind cover, flinched, glanced down at the itches that sprouted into stinging and stretching and gnawing between wretched little teeth. Something was squirming in the gloom. Frantic, she dropped the shalna and thrust her hands into the den's whirling colors and blinked in disbelief: Maggots swarmed over her skin, rice-like, fat and molting, twisting as they bore under her nails and wormed out of glossy sores.

Shuddering, cursing, she batted at herself and tightened her hands to stem the flow. But they were still spawning, still shrieking, still churning beneath her flesh. "Konrad!"

The brother could not hear her.

He was clawing at his own hands, muttering mad strings that slipped between flatspeak and the river-tongue, gritting his teeth until spittle ran between them.

Anna shifted away, ignoring the burning patches and white dappling upon her skin. She glanced into Ramyi's booth, where the marked man was still focusing his energy, arms extended and trembling. Behind him was a tangle of murky forms, all moving closer to the shattered panes, closer to the den....

An escape.

"She's getting away," Anna said, dragging herself back to Konrad's side. She glanced at his hands, but—

There was nothing.

Smooth skin, nails leaving red scrawling.

She lifted her own hands, frantically searching for the glossy lumps and pooling blood and thrashing teeth. The feeling mind receded until there was only the hiss of ruji, the den and its flowing hues, the flesh and grit of her palms.

"Konrad," Anna snapped. "It's not real."

The brother's nails raked harder, quicker.

Anna glanced down at the den. Shadows plunged into the masses, hardly stirring the crowds that swelled and meshed around them. A moment later she noticed the thin, subtle ripple winding toward the back of the den, toward the immense curtains and the promenade beyond it.

"They're getting away!" Anna seized Konrad's wrist, holding it before him in spite of the brother's quaking. "Look. It's not *real*!"

When Konrad snatched his hand away, he resumed his scratching, his whimpering. Even those on the far side of the booth were stricken by that madness, tearing at their clothes and shivering behind scant cover.

There was no time for sanity.

Anna scooped up the shalna canister, pulled its cap free, and leaned around the setstone. It was a short span, a throw she'd made a dozen times in war. Just as she cocked her arm back, the marked man stared at her. His eyes dimmed with the canister's release. Perfect stillness, a sense of quiet acceptance.

Metal danced past his feet, skittered into blackness.

The shalna burst in a crackling, bulging mass, jutting out over the den and snaking about in grotesque knots. It hardened into stony brambles, porous and ash-gray and frozen like a shard of some unhinged energy, creeping out to the furthest edges of the booth and twisting through setstone.

"Anna?"

She turned to find Konrad gazing down at dripping hands, running his tongue over bloodied cheeks and gums. Panting like a hound. "Later," she said. "He's accounted for." A glance at the den's chaos, a glimpse of Ramyi's dark sliver burrowing into vague refuge. "We need to get her, Konrad."

Still transfixed, gasping like the others. "Anna, I—"

"Send them down," she said, grabbing a handful of Konrad's collar and tugging it toward herself. "Do you hear me? When they're up, you send them after me."

"After you?" His head snapped up, his eyes bloodshot, bleary. "Anna?"

"Send them." She snatched the ruj up from the carpet, moved to the edge of the shattered pane, and stared down.

The drop was torturous, perhaps severe enough to snap the mottled bones in both legs. Heads gleamed like dark marbles in the throng, alight with every blazing shade of every color she knew—and several she didn't. It was a convulsing mosaic, assailing to every sense, a barbaric thrum that stitched sight and sound into waves of unease.

Compared to what the girl's mind had done, it barely registered.

Anna sat and pushed herself to the edge, then leaned, dropped in smooth succession. No time to hesitate, to listen to Konrad's shouts as she plunged into a hot, gloomy void. Cerulean and rose flashed through her lids; her robes snapped around her, flapped across her face; her boots scraped flesh and—

Pain lanced through her legs, her thighs, the recesses of her hips. She toppled forward, eyes open to the forest of ankles and crushed faces and swishing powders, cracked her knees against setstone. One arm was out, scraping to brace her, while the other kept the ruj tucked, rigidly secure, braced like a small child. Arms and legs brushed over her, against her, their flesh swollen and warm and drenched in sweat. Anna bit back the agony, the throbbing waves racing from her toes to her chest, and pushed herself up.

Then she was carving through the press, shoving and shouldering and sliding, engulfed in the den's ethereal melody. Heads and hands flailed around her. Opal eyes flashed within the shadows, set ablaze by the colors that swept over them in blinding streaks. Nerkoya hung in a dense, cloying miasma, smothering the pain as it saturated her lungs and danced over her lips with effervescent prickling. Her limbs sagged.

Ramyi was a charcoal blot in the distance, a knot of low, wriggling shapes amid bare skin and wafting vapors. *Shapes.* It was not her, not alone. She had their trailcarver.

Chapter 8

Every step slowed Anna, somehow dulled her, as though all the jostling and swaying occurred behind a screen of satin folds. The world was muted, creamy, playing out in honey swells of shadow and sound. Her vision narrowed until it was a diamond spyglass, every wet pore close and threatening and hyper-real, ballooned and misshapen through the nerkoya's lens. But even the dreadful tightness in her chest, venturing toward the inevitable, toward that forgotten, acute fear of death, was simply a feeling—a transient, weightless feeling. There was only the task, her thinking mind assured her.

There was only Ramyi.

Anna broke through a clot in the bodies, emerging into a sparser area littered with swirls of oil and shisha and sparkling glass. She wove easily through the bodies here; they were lurching about with thin, spastic arms, their eyes wrenched open to the flood of lights, shuffling and drenched and breathless as though animated against their will.

Turquoise beams swiveled over the den. The light raked a shadowed pair moving behind the dancers, raining down over long black hair, the pleats of wool robes, coppery flesh devoid of sigils.

Bringing the ruj to her shoulder, Anna hurried after the girl. Her heart pounded between her temples in drowned, frantic knocks, shutting the den and its warbling out of awareness.

A doorway burned into existence as a milky white void, throwing light upon red, turgid faces, ashen wisps, crooked teeth. Silhouettes stumbled through the opening, then cut left, slipped out of sight.

Tears bit at Anna's eyes. The light was too sudden, too punishing. She blinked until the shapes streaming past her were blurry, yet distinct, till the world glowed in pearl tones, till her boots clapped over the promenade's marble tiling. Ringing in her ears gave way to screams, to shouts of alarm in tongues she could not distinguish.

Not that there was any time to heed them.

Ramyi was a distant fleck within the central aisle, an errant fin high above the promenade's waves of shawls and cuirasses. Enormous walls of hexagonal mesh and stained glass rose around her, bathing her in filtered tawny light. Her and her attendant. Her trailcarver.

Most of the crowd was now facing the fleeing girl, wandering closer in a weary shamble, bitterly clutching at their salt and coins, murmuring about foundlings and wastrels. Anna cut through the crowd with her ruj at the fore, dimly aware of the gasps, the curses, the screeches. Her feet clapped harder, faster. Dry breaths withered in her throat.

Ramyi's shape loomed just ahead. Her head dipped below the crowd, emerged, dipped again.

Anna recalled how it looked to drag someone.

Someone she had loved.

"Ramyi!" In spite of the years—the long, bitter years, thick with childish hopes and dreams of singing around campfires—her throat barely functioned. The name was rusty, more of a squeal than a word.

But it was enough.

Calming her steps into a deliberate, even pace, Ramyi glanced over her shoulder. Her feet slowed and ceased over the tiles. The trailcarver squirmed in her embrace, but their resistance amounted to languid swipes, perhaps hampered by toxins or whatever unspeakable things had been done away from prying eyes. Things that had given Ramyi a sense of pride, a sense of fear that she carried and nurtured like a newborn. She stood as though the world itself could not move against her.

The lane was no longer occupied by the commotion, but wholly paralyzed by it. Peddlers pulled burlap over their trays of gleaming forks and berries and tobacco. Children scurried to the fringes of the crowd, their gazes flitting between the black-haired woman and their pouches of licorice sweets. Wrinkled, sunken-cheeked Gosuri beggars cocked their ears toward the budding silence.

Anna hefted the ruj up and nestled it as tightly as the borzaq fighters had always insisted. A stale, familiar ache pulsed through her shoulder, calling her back to critical violence, back to the grainy shapes resolving beyond the stark bulge of the ruj's barrel. The masses around Ramyi cycled in and out of winkling focus, smearing and sharpening the world with every twitch of Anna's attention. Errant breaths caused the aiming nubs to slip out of alignment, to hover above an unmarked skull, to drift over narrow shoulders and roam a wall of innocent flesh.

She moved closer with the lithe, measured steps of a mountain lion, blinking through the sawdust in her eyes. Her hands were slick and cumbersome upon the ruj's lacquered wood. Hauling the trailcarver up by a bloody collar, Ramyi shifted heavily toward Anna.

The man was gaunt, likely starved; it was nothing for the girl to pull him to his feet, wrench his head back against her chest, and fix him in place. Her stare was colder—more detached—than ever before. It was not stirred by the man's sobs or torn face or trembling legs.

"Ramyi," Anna said calmly. The name was foreign now, a wind screeching out of some ancient hollow in her mind. Nearer, nearer—creases emerged beneath Ramyi's eyes, around the broad bridge of her nose.

Metal glinted above the trailcarver's throat. It was a flatland blade, short and narrow and fanged, tucked along the wiry sprawl of Ramyi's fingers.

"Let him go," Anna said. "He's nothing to you."

Ramyi pressed the blade into sallow skin. "This isn't how I wanted to speak with you." Her voice was not all pride and enmity and distance; there was a note of shame, of earnest disappointment.

"We can speak," Anna replied, "but not until you release him."

"He's needed. If only you could *fathom* his role, Anna."

"If you take him like this, then nothing good will come of it."

Ramyi blinked, her lips wringing in apparent confusion. The bewilderment in her gaze spoke of experiences immune to the shackles of time, of space, of knowing itself. "What are consequences?"

"Can you trust me?" Anna did not lower the ruj, but she softened her brows, her rigid jaw. "If you help me, I can help you."

"All I need you to do is walk away."

"You don't understand—"

"Do not speak to me about *ignorance*," Ramyi hissed. "My mind is not the sum of my years, Anna. You should know that better than most."

"I know that you're hesitating."

"Any moment now...."

"You don't want to see any more violence," Anna cut in.

"You're so hopeful," Ramyi said, nearly cooing her words. "That's why you'll never stop them. You're too good to put terror in their hearts."

"*Their?*"

"Everyone," Ramyi said flatly. "Everyone who brought the wars into being."

Anna's finger teased over the trigger. "You're no killer."

"You always thought you knew me. But even I didn't know what I was, Anna. Nobody really knows themselves until the world bestows their true name upon them."

"I remember your true name."

"So you say, Kuzalem," she said sharply. "So you say."

Anna sensed the threat in their proximity. She thought of the black, springy birds that had once trotted near her father's fields, apt to flee at the gentlest arising of footsteps. She thought of the blade in Ramyi's hands, of the trigger's coils tensing against her finger, of the heedless power granted to a weapon's wielder.

"What are you waiting for?" Ramyi pressed on.

"I've come to listen." She advanced, suddenly weighing the utter stillness of the crowd, the clamor of doors crashing open and river-tongue exploding down the concourse.

Ramyi gazed past her. "How many ears does it take to listen, Anna? Especially when I've told you what to do." She stared at Anna, into Anna.

"Release him."

"We're leaving."

Heads and shoulders jostled about in the gray mass beyond the girl. A pale-skinned, lean northerner slid into view, blatantly bearing a string of runes that roamed her throat and the broad field of her upper chest. Her white cotton shirt was banded around the waist, torn in some spots and patched in others. Black hair spilled unevenly over her shoulders in thick, shining bunches. She was older than Ramyi, but still young—far too young for the pristine, haggard gloss in her eyes, the mirthless imitation of a doll in Malchym's shops.

Anna's focus hung on the third rune. It was a shallow crescent, laced with vertical slashes and an outer ring of spokes. A rune Anna had often seen, yet never been able to mimic. A rune that had stirred the war's ashes and preserved a thousand lives.

The tether.

All it took was one touch, one instant of perfect stillness. The marked woman stood five paces from Ramyi. She treated Anna and her pointed ruj with quiet scrutiny.

"If you move any closer," Anna said, sensing the footsteps thundering down the concourse toward them, "I'll have to shoot."

Ramyi retreated two steps, dragging the trailcarver in turn. "You're too *good*, Anna. That's how I know you won't."

"I'm warning you."

"As I warned you."

Another step back. The marked woman tensed her legs, balled up her fists, cast furtive glances at Ramyi, all the while weighing the distance....

The trailcarver shut his eyes and tilted his head skyward. Toward burnished light, toward curtains of sand skittering over glass. Tears clung to the rim of his cheekbones, glowing and celestial for an instant, drying as swiftly as they settled. *"Sha'laqam, gul kelaf an shawar."*

His words awakened something in Anna long before she became conscious of them. Before she recognized the dialect of the midland qora, before she embraced the sacred acceptance in his voice, before she was thrust into memories of the monastery and its tomesroom, where such words had crowded the annals compiled by long-dead Saloram thinkers. No, no, all those were aftershocks. The first arising, lancing through her mind with a needle's precision, was a murky portrait of a woman with shaved hair, cinnamon fabric gathered around her neck, the impassive stare of a perched hawk.

Bora.

Then the moment was over, labeled with wretched clarity:

Distraction is death.

Anna's awareness snapped back to Ramyi, to the three paces separating her from the marked woman. She could track every subtle movement between the women, every nascent breath and swiveling pupil.

Alakeph fighters fanned out along Anna's periphery, distinguished—even in her narrow, nebulous band of vision—by their earthen tones and raised ruji.

"I knew it, Anna," Ramyi whispered. "You don't want to kill me." Another step, this one smooth and undaunted.

"I don't want to," she said, "but I will."

The heel of Ramyi's foot arched, slid backward. Her hips gently twisted toward the marked woman. "You won't, Anna." She shifted her weight to one foot. "You won't, because you're just too—"

Anna fired twice.

A pink haze, an arcing spurt of garnet blood and sinew. Screams, a crowd dispersing like a stone-struck hive, Ramyi's eyes in gilded bloom. Both bodies slumped to the tiles, fabric torn and flesh stringy and mouths wide in disbelief. The trailcarver contorted and rolled free of Ramyi's embrace, his shoulder ripped open, pulsating, reddening the floor and its intricate maze of grooves.

"Kuzalem!"

She noticed the marked woman's maneuver too late. There was a wink in the air, an anomaly as slight as a gnat sweeping in and out of her vision, then a sudden clearing among red smears.

The trailcarver writhed and groaned and stared perplexedly at what remained of his upper arm. He was bleeding rapidly—so rapidly that the Alakeph did not wait to secure the surrounding booths, but instead rushed to the man's side, arguing in their hushed tones and tearing strips of cloths from their robes, binding the man's arm, binding his chest, calling for assistance, bickering about the temrusi and how far they were.

Anna forced a breath through shaking lips. She lowered the ruj and turned away and did not listen to those who vied for her attention.

The concourse was deserted. War had instilled grim haste in those who survived the shelling, the shooting, the seizing. Stragglers slipped out of sight, fleeing down market lanes and onto the open-air decks. Footfalls retreated in a fading roar.

"His breaths will depart." The flatspeak sprouted between hushed, sullen men, but it was deafening to Anna. "If we bleed him now, we might be able to—"

"He's coming with us." Anna rounded on them, glaring. "Where are our scribes?"

"With Brother Konrad and the second unit," one of the Alakeph captains said. His sleeves were as bloody and shredded as the others. "Their wounds are grievous."

"We need their assistance."

"There's no time for them, Kuzalem," he replied. "The temrusi have already received them near the promenade, and Brother Andriv will rendezvous with us in the neighboring district. Our fate remains."

Anna stared at the trailcarver's gaping wounds, which were now framed by a lattice of bandages and poppy tinctures, prodded by red hands and rags. She'd seen worse, but none that their victims had ever survived. The flesh was slashed open in clean furrows, split as though by a fisherman's blade, shining with blood that welled and gushed and oozed. Severed muscle bands twitched among shards of bone and cartilage.

His eyes lulled open, closed, open, closed....

"How far is our temrus?" Anna asked.

One of the Alakeph herbmen stood, wiping his hands upon an ochre smock. "Our mirrormen sent for it."

"That's not an answer."

A whistle sounded near the doors to the outer decks. One of the northern fighters waved them closer, his ruj tucked beneath his arm and canisters stacked near his boots.

"It's here," the captain said to Anna. "He will not survive the descent, Kuzalem."

"If he dies, then the world has willed it," she whispered. "But neither of us will assure such a thing, brother."

The captain gave no response, but was quick to crouch down by his men, delineating orders and gesturing toward the exits and weaving Halshaf prayers into every command. Within seconds a team of Alakeph brothers had lifted the trailcarver in a cotton bundle, ferrying him toward the doors in a cautious, mechanical rush.

Anna absently toggled the bolt of her ruj, gazing around at the sprawl of fighters and blood and cowering bodies. It was all too static, too settled. Within minutes there should've been a flood of Leejadal's urban units, or perhaps the qora companies that protected bloodlines and investments alike. Rumbling boots, wailing klaxons, black-clad sharpshooters—anything at all.

But their crime trickled on in silence, forgotten, as though the great cog of order had expended all its motions and run itself into changeless oblivion.

It was surely the war that had done it, Anna considered. War had drowned the world in apathy, made it some horrible machine so preoccupied with survival that it could not function. Until the end of days it would shamble on, cracking and crumbling and shedding its rust to the wind, only thinking to mend itself at the cusp of annihilation. And even in that final hour, the engineers would bolt their doors and clutch their blades, because that was all they knew.

Anna's gaze tracked the trailcarver in his swaddling, the Alakeph brothers unfurling ropes behind the musty glass walls.

Perhaps it had all begun long before the war.

A sharp *tick* issued from above.

Anna stared up at the vague, burnished speck perched atop glass. At first it appeared to be some shard of scrap that'd been blown adrift by the winds, fluttering and skating over the rooftops until it came to rest on the Shifting Market's enormous covering. There had to be hundreds of them scattered up there, sun-bleached and forgotten. But there were not hundreds; it was the only one.

Anna squinted until she discerned a pair of tucked brass wings, stubby legs, a hooked beak. Suddenly the marks of its maker—the precise machining, the intricate, sleek shape—were as obvious as what it heralded.

The whirring bird's head tracked from side to side, rose briefly, then hammered down.

Tick.

"Let's go." Anna did not call out; her broken cords produced something akin to a hound's bark. A glance at the Nahoran bird, at the chilling stillness around them. "I said *go.*"

Several brothers passed her questioning looks, but they held their tongues, gathering up their gear and hurrying out to the deck with their captains in tow. There was no time to probe her urgency, after all: Death did not wait for understanding.

Anna slung her ruj across her back and moved to the door, weighing the bird's every gesture as she went. She'd scarcely emerged into hazy tangerine light and kerosene fumes when the first crack sounded in the distance; she could not place it among the hissing sands, the looming setstone, the surreal, verdant expanse of cypress trees and hedges, all passing beneath them as the Shifting Market trundled along.

She rushed to the balcony. A handful of men were descending on their ropes, reduced to dark bulbs in the maelstrom of grit, shrinking toward the amber stain of their temrus. She noted the soft curtains of dust spilling from the tires, the slow, haggard crawl of the beast as it kept pace with the monolith above. The shell whistled somewhere far above her.

"Faster," she urged, seizing one of the ropes and shifting over the edge. Her gloves slipped and whined and caught on the fraying coils.

Whump.

Her hearing was washed away with the impact, scattered to the wind like the billowing black rose that swept over the balcony and choked her. Bits of crushed glass and pulverized setstone pattered down across her hair.

Anna did not look up, did not look for the brothers who had been waiting to descend at their tethers. She was intent on sliding, on the vicious burn through the gloves, on the stinging rain that pelted her cheeks. Moments from street level, she peered down and into the open hatch of the temrus.

Countless shapes scurried around the vehicle, fleeing and cowering and dashing for cover. Ash rained over the crowds.

Another blast rang out as Anna's feet brushed the hatch. This time she glanced skyward, noting some deep growl and shudder within the market itself. Then its cogs did not churn, and the rope did not hum with its breaths, and the beast fell into a disturbing slumber.

Anna felt their hands tugging at her ankles. She slumped down onto the edge of the hatch, breathless, studying the cavernous blackness beneath the arch, the elaborate clusters of lanterns and luminous tubes and pumps that had functioned just moments ago. The air was still hot.

"Kuzalem, come," one of the brothers said, extending an arm toward her. "This is not the end."

"It isn't." But in her own mind, the words were a question, some lingering doubt.

The temrus chugged toward the rusty shard of daylight in the distance.

Chapter 9

The man seemed intent on death. Not on rushing toward it, precisely, but on surrendering himself to it, tasting that peculiar numbness. It was a certain thing now. None of the herbmen could lay their hands upon him without being scratched or spat upon, much less the scribes. It had been that way since he'd awoken on the musty cot, sweat-shimmering, drowned in some feverish swell of pain and terror.

Anna lingered in the doorway, studying the bundled cotton sheets: deepening crimson, soil splotches, the sour, off-yellow rings of old urine. She knew the shades and odors well enough—not only from war, but from living itself, from old men shivering away and babes left by the roadside.

Death.

Nobody knew how long he had left, but there was fair certainty that his breaths would slip away before the coming dawn. The brothers had dutifully opened the slats of his chamber's windows in case they did. In the temrus there had been talk of drugging him with nerkoya, marking him before he even knew what had occurred, but Anna would not allow it. If his words were guarded in the approach to death, they would be incinerated by hayat's kiss.

Even so, such drastic measures had plagued Anna's mind for hours. She was desperate for something—for anything—to lend meaning to what had happened. There was no vindication in the groans that issued from sealed doors, nor in the bright, swollen scratches covering Konrad and his brothers. There were no assurances, no finalities. Hours of muttering and hushed rebukes between Andriv and his captains had shown her the inefficacy of it all. She found herself missing the sterile, monotone business of war, with its casualty numbers and analyses and forthcoming plans. Nothing and nobody at the downstairs table had made any sense of the chaos.

The dying man squirmed under his coverings, igniting every question she'd bit back among the fighters:

How did Nahora know?

Where is she going?

Have I killed her?

The final question hung above all others, tucked among her fears like a pulpy gray wasp's nest, threatening to break and devour her with the slightest prod.

Anna glanced down both avenues of the lightless corridor, waiting for the shadows to warp and loom toward her, for prying eyes to catch a stray lick of candlelight. Certain she was alone, Anna moved into the dying man's chamber and gently closed the door.

Nothing shifted beneath the blankets.

Anna moved to the bedside, settled into a chair with chipping blue paint, and meshed her hands upon her lap. Her breathing quieted until it resembled that of the dying man. Then the stillness was somehow profound, all-encompassing, as though there was only the room and the covered man, unspoiled by an observer in any form. Perhaps this was how Bora had felt in the kales, looming over Shem in sleep and sickness....

"You should take their marks," she said. After she had spoken, muddying the silence in a manner that needled her with discomfort, she wondered if he'd heard. She knew the man was not dead—that was to say, not dead *yet*—because ringed sigils trudged over his exposed neck. Still, a beating heart did not guarantee the preservation of the thinking mind. There were endless badlands between the realms of dying and death, many of which Anna had explored herself. Places where words were songs and time held no sway.

The man opened his eyes. They were small and hooded, almost icy in the candlelight, yet stunningly lucid. "Do not need."

Anna moved to the edge of the chair. "Tell me your name."

His gaze wandered to the far side of the room, not quite curious, not disinterested. Northern faces were difficult to read in that sense. Even his features—small, sun-beaten, set in tight alignment like a jeweler's studs—said nothing definitive about his bloodline. He did not *look* like a wicked man, but Anna knew she'd been wrong before.

"We're not trying to harm you," Anna continued, glancing at the bloody bandages covering his shoulder. "We just need to find the woman who hired you."

"It will do nothing," he said somberly.

"But you know what she was seeking."

He did not speak for a long while. His eyes drifted shut, joined by the shallow drifts and dips of his chest. "There is nothing to remedy what has been done," he explained. "I have failed my people and my sworn oaths in the same life."

"It's not too late to undo it," Anna said. "What did you sell her?"

"I sold nothing. It was taken from me."

"Taken?"

"She forced my mind open," he whispered. "She glimpsed things that could not have been spoken, even if I'd willed it. Such malice was foretold by the forbearers, by—"

"She was seeking the ritual, wasn't she?"

The man's nostrils widened. His breaths grew shorter, sharper. "To what end does Nahora seek this knowledge?"

"Nahora?" Anna drew back, puzzled. "We're not with Nahora."

"Impossible," he said. "Nahora is the only hound still seeking out Kuzalem. Surely you were deceived as I was."

Anna went silent, running his words over her tongue as wind howled into the chamber. *Seeking out Kuzalem.* She looked at the man and his broken body, at the promises he'd surely held in his heart. "You thought you were meeting Kuzalem."

"The Starsent knew her signs," he said weakly. Tears leaked from the creases of his eyes. "This shame cannot be locked away, you see. Not even death will purge it from me."

"*Shara kan jalandri, nal shukra hal'karef.*" Anna softened her stare. "I recognized your way when you spoke. You're a good man."

He blinked, let out a wheezing breath. "You know of Saloram?"

"I know its heart," she said. "You can still preserve this world."

"Who are you?"

Anna straightened her back and leaned closer. "Look upon me and you will know my name."

His lips quaked. "Kuzalem."

"I'm here," she whispered. "I'm here with you and no harm will come to you. This is my promise."

"I waited for you. Cycle after cycle, I waited for your whisper through the silence. I always knew that someday…" Here he paused, slipped into a lull of sorts. "…someday the world would send you to me, to us. And so I waited."

Anna set her hands upon the man's blankets, searching for the subtle flow of his breaths. She could hardly sense them. "Why?"

"To guide you," the man sobbed. "I had nothing to teach you, Kuzalem, but everything to show you. It was foretold."

"You can still show me."

"My time in this world is fleeting," he said, "and I will not clutch at my breaths like an animal."

Just like her, Anna thought, unable to steer her thoughts away from the shepherd. Yet the word *us* was also lodged in her mind. "We have maps of the territories."

"It will not be enough." His lids lowered until his eyes were crescent slivers. Even this effort was monumental. "I wanted to bring you, Kuzalem. Forgive me."

"What more do you need?"

"It is within you," he said hoarsely, "yet without, too. Our tongue fails us."

Anna felt the breaths widening, faltering. "There are more of you, aren't there?"

"More of us." His whisper was a hollow echo.

"Stay with me," she said, pressing a hand to his forehead. It was hot and sweat-streaked. "Did you know Bora?"

The woman's name wrenched his eyes open. He stared at her, seemingly into her, as though Anna's memories of the northerner had been dried and strung out before him. "Wait for her, trailcarver, wait for her...Bora, forgive me." Sweat ran down to his pillows in thick rivulets.

"She told you I was coming?"

"She—" There was a coughing fit, a stippling of bright blood across the sheets. "Death loomed for her, Kuzalem. She could not know."

"She told me nothing."

"No time," he mumbled, "to initiate you. In time you were known."

"In time? What are you talking about?"

"It was you," he said. "Always you. My people have known you in dreams."

"Where are they?" Anna asked. She was nearly frantic now, fighting to relax her eyes as she looked upon—as she held, even—the answers that had eluded her for years. Hot blood coursed through her temples. "Look at me, look here. Where are your people?"

"Tell her, Bora." He closed his eyes and passed air through his lips. "Bora, she will not find her way. It's too dark."

"Where *are* they?"

"She will find her way." His tongue was lolling now, pasty and cracked. "She will go to the Apiary, and she will know herself."

"She?" Anna pressed. "You mean me?"

"She will go...to the Apiary."

"I don't—"

"The Apiary," he moaned. "The Apiary, the Apiary."

"Wait." Anna held the sides of his shoulders and stared at his gibbering lips, the lumps in his throat, the sporadic flickers of his eyes as they swept under falling lids. "Look at me."

But a low, seething rattle was all that slipped from his throat, robbing the last of his breath as it went. His gaze grew still and his fingers tensed into bony talons upon cotton swells. Everything settled with that same haunted silence, and at once Anna was reminded of the apple orchards sprawled out below the hills and crags and paddocks of her memory, those strange and endless swaths of childhood, where wind did not stir the leaves for the better part of summer and nothing—not even the gnats or bluebirds—flitted through the treetops. For a thing could die there in that stagnant heat, unnoticed and forgotten, as though it had never existed at all.

* * * *

Nerkoya. Its moldy pine odor hung heavily in the corridor, awakening fears of tomesrooms and bloody throats long before Anna reached the tracker's door. But she was not afraid, not anymore: Anger left no room for such things. Now she stalked toward the door with aching lips, with bitter words squirming in her throat, carving wretched grooves across her tongue: *You should have known, Lukas.*

She shoved the door in.

Lantern light carved out a greasy yellow blot, streaked with naked bodies and their sheens of sweat, their pockmark flesh freckled with bruise-pink scars, lesions, growths sprinkled by coal-black clusters.

The monastery had been full of such visions. Captivating, distracting visions. Anna flicked the lantern down, pinning her sight to the blackness near her boots, gravely aware of the cat-like eyes scurrying just beyond the lantern's wash. Then came the rustle of fabric over flesh, the hushed murmuring. The air was hot and pungent.

"He's dead," Anna hissed.

"Eh?" His voice was raspy, almost whining from the smoke.

"Her trailcarver," Anna said. "He died. Just now, he died." But he did not know what she meant; how could he? He hadn't even known of her return. It did not seem to matter who had returned from the market and who had not, or whether his information had spilled innocent blood, or if they'd even found the girl.

"Huh." The silence mulled and flattened as Nuhra clothed herself at the edge of the shadows, listening. "She dead?"

"I don't know."

"Have you brought her?" Nuhra's eyes flashed open.

"No," Anna said.

"Don't know if she's dead?" The tracker's burlap fluttered with a hard breath. "How's that?"

"She knew."

"Knew what?"

"She knew that we were coming and she made us pay for it," Anna snapped. "How did she know?"

The tracker looked to Nuhra. "Dunno."

"And Nahora knew, too."

"Fuck."

"I want to know *why*."

"I told you," he said, thrusting a finger toward her. "I don't know."

"That was your task."

"My task?" Lukas leaned back on his sprawl of bunched sheets and square pillows. "If memory serves, your task was to put the korpa under soil. I did my share."

"You do not command me," Anna whispered.

"No command," he said. "That's the heart of it, eh?"

Anna's breaths were sharp, hot.

"Your boys in white know their blessings more than blades," Lukas added.

"And you know nothing." She stepped toward them, her attention snapping to the resin stains on still-smoldering glassware. "This *task* is vastly more important than your life. You should treat it as such."

"She got you rattled, didn't she?"

"Mind your tongue," Anna said.

"Something she said, maybe?"

Anna took another step.

"You must've gotten close," Lukas cooed. "Close enough to touch her."

Another step.

"That's it," he said. He was bathing in her shadow now, small and strange without clothing. "Come and bleed me. That was our deal, girl: I get her to you, and you open me." She could hear his shaking breaths. "That was our deal."

"Was it?"

A hard swallow. "Honest dealings, Anna."

"I never said I was honest," she whispered. "Perhaps I'm something more horrible than you could ever fathom. Perhaps I'll make you walk this world to the end of your days."

Lukas's eyes snapped to Nuhra, but the woman did not look at him. She sat on the edge of the bed, eyes scampering back and forth amid chaotic thoughts.

"Do you think these comforts will save you?" Anna paced around the gloom, running her fingers over the tables' spreads of flowery nerkoya piles and smeared ashes. "What happens when you lose your taste for these base stimulations? Will you turn to carving your own flesh, just to *feel* something?" She loomed over him, her lips aching in the curve of something that was not quite a smile. "I own you and you will not be released until we have her." Anna glanced at Nuhra. "Either in shackles or in the Grove."

"She must be preserved," Nuhra whispered.

"Shut *up*," Lukas said, whirling toward the woman as though he intended to strike her. "You and your scarred sukry can burn in the flats, for all I care. Only deal she's got is with me."

Nuhra's gaze did not falter. "Her life is—"

"Heed my words," Anna said coldly. "She's lost to the sands. This is no time to speak of her fate—not yet. If she lives, she's wounded. But she'll burrow now."

"Burrowing," Lukas growled. "Seems you've mastered that."

Anna folded her arms and drew a long, bitter breath. She could not hold rage within herself; not as she once could. After a moment of creaking floorboards and brittle silence, she leaned against the wall.

"Did the dead man speak?" Nuhra wandered out of the nerkoya haze and into the light, her eyes bold and questioning.

"Barely," Anna said. "His breaths were fleeting."

"He revealed something, then."

Anna looked away. "He knew Bora. He said she waited for me." She met Nuhra's eyes, sensing the woman's bewilderment, then looked to Lukas. "Did you know about this?"

Silence returned.

"He was all we had," Anna continued. "His people are out there. They could help us, I know it. Bora's people."

"Didn't have any people," Lukas snapped.

"So you believe," Anna said. "Spare me your ignorance."

"Perhaps his face is known to our breakers," Nuhra said. "They could come by morning."

"Perhaps." Anna thought of the man and his pain, of how he'd refused the runes that could've preserved him time and time again. Few men held such conviction. His death felt like something ancient, something she'd learned about in the kales and memorized like a poem, thick with his fading words and pervasive stillness. Some of his words cycled into her awareness, lingered there, pricked at her: *the Apiary.* It roiled up from the maelstrom of the day's violence in a black surge. "The Apiary," she said softly.

Nuhra tilted her head. "Sister?"

"He spoke only about that," Anna said. "The Apiary. That was all he could think to say."

"Perhaps you misheard." There was a coy edge in Nuhra's voice.

"What is it?" Anna glanced at both at them, reading the subtle cues that they passed between themselves. Something dark hung in their stares. "He said I would know myself there."

"And what?" Lukas asked. "Doesn't matter what you know. The girl's the aim."

"He said I could find his people," Anna said to Nuhra.

"Initiation," Nuhra whispered.

"Abandon this vagueness," she said sharply. "If you know what it is, you'll tell me."

Nuhra offered a gentle, trembling bow. "I'll have a runner sent to the nerashi platforms. Prepare a pack, dear sister, and spend the darkened hours bringing stillness to your mind. You will need such clarity for what lies ahead."

"A nerash?" Anna blinked at Nuhra. "Where are we going?"

"To the kales of the fallen Emirahni."

The name was old, rusting over in her mind. *Emirahni.* She recalled its jagged edge as Lukas cleared his throat.

"We go alone, no boys in white," he whispered. "Malijad surely remembers their scent."

Chapter 10

It was difficult for Anna to hate Malijad. It was not a testament to the city's allure, a concession to some conflicted note within herself, but rather a blunt, practical truth: It was the nature of men and deeds to be hated. Malijad was an entity beyond fixing, vast and convulsing and woven from the flux between things, blossoming into and out of hateful affairs.

Or so her memory had assured her.

But as the nerash cut down over the mesa's shoulder, unveiling an expanse of shadow-raked flats and cracked basins, all of it arid, desaturated by the wooly drift of the evening's cloud cover, she realized that Malijad had died long ago.

All that remained was a cancerous husk with its pustules spread to the horizon. The skyline was craggy and eroded, swelling up from districts fanned out like black rose petals below. Every canal was dry and dark, an infected vein, snaking out into the gullies that ringed the basin.

She did not hate it; she feared it.

"Seems like yesterday," Lukas said, his burlap face pressed to the window. "Does it call you back, Anna?" The engines thrummed. "Calls me back."

"I didn't believe what had been said of this place," Anna said. A set of terraced cliffs passed beneath them, cluttered with the ragged encampments of Gosuri tribes. Below the flesh-walled tents she saw fire-lit droby pacing within their pens, Huuri and manskin alike, gazing up at the nerash in mute wonder. "We never marched on Malijad."

"You severed its head. Wasn't long after that when it marched on itself."

It had crossed her mind once or twice while in the monastery. Somehow Volna had always seemed insatiably evil, sustained by its own wrath, far beyond the consequences of assassinations. She'd envisioned new leaders rising from the depths of the hive and clawing their way into power, seizing whatever gaps had been left in the wake of death. But that did not occur. It had only taken a year for their territories to devour themselves from within, to splinter and dissolve into something malleable for the new order. Nobody dared to mold Malijad with their hands, however. It was a rotting corpse, still crowded with blood-bloated flies, withering into dust under the Cruel God's stare.

Nuhra's breathless chanting bubbled up through the engines' drone. It was strange to hear her voice after a day of silence. She'd been withdrawn since mentioning the Apiary, not only wordless but numb to the world at large, tucked away in a shell of constant meditation. If she had anything to say about their destination, she seemed resolute to stifle it. Lukas only mirrored her reservations, and at times he'd appeared hesitant to harm her with that truth, deeply concerned by what it might do to her.

That was the most unnerving thing of all.

"You know what it is, don't you?" Anna asked. There was no time for further pretenses, for comfortable silence. There hadn't been any semblance of those things since Anna had left the brothers and entered the jaws of a beast.

Lukas was slow to answer. "Little to be gained in what I know."

"Tell me what it is."

"It's northern madness," he said. "You really think Bora's kin are drifting around? That we'd find 'em like this?"

"*This*," Anna echoed. "What do you mean, this?"

"It's all built on whispers and smoke," Lukas said. For a moment that seemed to be all he'd surrender, but eventually he glanced down the aisle toward the nerash's operator, paused, then checked if Nuhra was still in her trance. His voice lowered until it was a razor upon iron. "You know the flatlands, don't you? All that harping on fate?"

Anna nodded.

"Back before the pup, the Emirahni were headed by the old hound. Real fire in his eyes, I'll tell you. But he lived for the days of ruins, you see, with all his relics and broken jars and tongues that sleep in dead cities. Drove him to the edge."

"The Kojadi," Anna said, recalling the vast galleries and sealed chambers she'd once explored in the kales. "Their relics were from the Kojadi."

"Don't tell me you believe it."

"They left their markings upon this world, did they not?"

Lukas sighed. "Doesn't matter, when you reach the thick of it. The Orzi's cracked head was stuffed with it all. Wanted to know the old rites, the old ways...wanted killers from the old breed."

Even Anna's gaze fell upon Nuhra, wondering if the northerner could hear the tender words passing between them.

"See, in the old way, it wasn't a qora's business to sort out corpses from saviors," Lukas continued. "They had the Apiary for that."

Anna's mouth was dry. "Is it alive?"

"In a sense," he said. "Make it out and you've got the weight of the stars behind your blade. If you don't leave, your trail ends there. The purest test, he called it."

"I don't understand."

"You think I do?" Lukas shook his head. "Not even Teodor would set foot in the fucking thing. Still had bones from the last sukry they tested."

"But he was certain," Anna whispered, remembering the dying man's fervency and haggard breaths. "He told me I would find something here."

"Don't get your truth from me, then. This is Nuhra's realm. *Korpa*'s mind might be gone, but she has a way of things."

"You wouldn't have let her bring me here if you thought it was for nothing."

Lukas leaned his head against the glass, folded his arms stiffly, and shut his eyes. "She has a way."

* * * *

Even while traversing the nerashi strips west of the city, where retaining walls cast ripples of deep, frigid shadows over the flats, Anna sensed Malijad's reluctance. It was reluctance in a stark, opaque form, as tangible as the fumes that streamed up into cooling air. Travelers trudged past with heavy shoulders and heavier brows, scowling at the embers of daylight on the horizon.

At the nearby terminal, they boarded a kator that had trundled out of the northern expanse. It was soldered in spots, blackened in others, stippled with the bite marks of shells and ruji alike. Flesh-peddlers claimed the rearmost pods, smoking pipes in the doorway while their crop of fresh bodies stirred and groaned in the darkness.

The only place to stand was a patch of rusted railing, well within eyesight of several provisionary fighters. There was nothing threatening about them, not yet: Most of the new breed were young, orphans; if not merely living like them, eager for salt or a minor land writ or a morsel to eat. They did not seem to know Anna's face, and if they did, they did not care. The vacuous nature of their stares suggested that they did not care about much at all.

Their kator howled with the crack of bursting cylinders, then lurched and squealed forward, chugging along a mottled track.

Metal rattled beneath Anna's feet, but it was too dark to see anything aside from her hands gripping the rail, thin and ghastly, almost glowing. Her vision was consumed by the city, by its skylines and shattered towers, by the sun smoldering like red filament as it shrank away, by every ruined peak rising and darkening by the instant. But the city lent her the gift—that rugged, fearless defiance of death—that she had cultivated as a girl she no longer knew. She gazed at the lights now flickering in distant recesses because she was curious, not beholden. She considered how small they were, how insubstantial they seemed when weighed against the city's lightless veil. For a moment, she felt that she could lift a finger, touch it to the yellow blots, and snuff them out one by one.

They arrived at the terminal, but even there, Anna could not shake the strange sadness of that thought.

Malijad colored them in turn, sapping Lukas of his barbs, pulling Nuhra deeper into whatever state she'd reached on the nerash. Near the markets, a lanky, sallow-skinned guide exchanged brief words with Lukas before leading them to a group of rib-lined horses near the markets. The shallow glint in his eyes practically sang for Volna's return.

"Quick on their feet," the man babbled in river-tongue, droning off as though he'd forgotten he was even speaking to them. "Not ones to spook, either."

Anna noted the pink scars wreathing their torsos. It was no wonder that they'd lost their fear. What puzzled her, above all else, was how the man had kept them out of a butcher's stall. Most of the monastery's horses had been stolen over the past two years, carved up or otherwise sold in Kowak, but there was no sense in punishing the desperate.

They rode in a column under the pink baubles of hanging lanterns, moving in a nervous canter between the districts that were not lined with high, serrated fences and perched marksmen. The silhouettes of discarded machines, haunting and black and teeming with sparrows, ascended from the ruins around them like an iron forest.

There was danger here, Anna knew, but somehow she felt above it all. She rode with her hood down and the mare's reins loosely in her grip, slumping back so she absorbed the saddle's every thump. To these people, she was nobody, another faceless killer they judged from the shelter of shuttered windows and latched doors.

But when they reached the gates of the kales, she was a girl once again.

Not *a* girl, but *the* girl, the one she encountered in dreams and warm, fleeting memories of spring fields and blackberries. The girl who had slept with teardrops drying on her cheeks, waiting, wishing for the day when wicked men begged her to kill them. The girl who had not seen wickedness in herself.

They descended from their horses and stood beneath the arch. There were gouges in the masonry, entire blocks removed where hinges had once been fixed.

"Best to be quick," the guide murmured. He gathered the horses by their reins and led them across the road, pausing briefly to eye the Huuri beggars huddled nearby.

It was difficult for Anna to remember how the courtyard had looked—it was empty now, picked bare of whatever tools or tiles had been left for the scavengers. All that remained was a stretch of darkness and silvery moonlight upon broken soil, and behind that, the looming shape of the kales. Smoke did not leech into the skies as it had during Anna's stay, nor did lanterns burn in the countless notches and chambers of the southern facade. There were a few guttering fires that shone here or there across the upper levels, but they did not belong to the artisans and poets that had once graced the halls.

"Do you feel it calling, sister?" It was Nuhra's devotion, not her abruptness, which made Anna flinch. Surely she felt that *call*—her voice was even, smooth. She looked at Anna and blinked.

Anna's hand strayed to the yuzel beneath her cloak. "Let's go."

* * * *

The emptiness was truly what gnawed at her. War had familiarized her with darkness and stillness, even the sort of stillness that caused every step to screech and snag on her attention, but it had never lent comfort to desolation. In its death throes the kales had remained seemingly immortal, writhing and crumbling, but never able to be killed. In fact, Anna had occasionally wondered if it took some delight in the spectacle it hosted. But as she wandered past scorched marble frescoes, shattered statues, and fountains buried by mounds of windswept sand, she was struck by the tragedy of it all. Now it was a gallery of dead things, dead times, of man's foolishness in believing that beauty could endure in such a place. Every chipped banister and blackened parlor carried a sense of guilt beyond explanation.

Lukas and Nuhra were the only shapes that moved around her in the gloom, marked by lanterns that swung on whining metal hooks. Anna had not heard anybody else during their ascent. It was an enormous structure, certainly, but even the most delicate sounds—a muffled cough, a foot scraping over stone—could roll through an entire wing with ease. She wondered if the scavengers were asleep in spite of the city's nocturnal tendencies, then wondered if they had stumbled upon other visitors before, and had simply learned to hide from those who would hurt them. She chose to believe that they were sleeping.

Halting at the top of a narrow staircase, Nuhra lowered the lantern to her waist and stared out into the blackness. Her eyes had a milky gray gloss in the scant lighting.

Anna examined the woman sidelong. It was not indecision, as far as she could tell. She'd never seen this wing, had not even known it existed, but Nuhra's steps were too assured to cast doubt on her familiarity with the kales. The woman had led them in constant ascent, taking them far higher than Anna's former chambers, pausing only to listen to the wind that raked through colonnades and shattered oriel windows. They had to be nearing the rooftop gardens that Anna held at the fringes of her memory.

"Keep those boots shuffling," Lukas growled at Anna's back. "No place for you two to lay a bedroll."

"The call," Nuhra said gently.

And in the breathless quiet that followed, Anna heard the call, too. It was a muddied drone, rising in dull crescendos, withering to a weird hum, folding in on itself in sporadic cycles. But it did not call her to come forth—it warned her.

Just ahead, scarcely illuminated in rusty shades by Nuhra's lantern, was a thin wooden door that had been sealed with crossbars and flaking latches.

"This is the farthest I'll go," Anna said. She looked at Nuhra, then at the blackness gathered around Lukas's mask. "I've given you both grace in holding back your words, but this is where it ends. Tell me precisely what's ahead."

"Clarity," Nuhra said, as though it somehow eased Anna's mind. She studied Anna's hard lips, her furled brow. "None have been called to this ritual in a hundred years, sister. But this world has chosen you. You will be our warrior."

I've been everybody's warrior. Yet the zealous gleam in Nuhra's eyes was far from what she'd seen in wicked men. There was no lust for slaughter, for wealth, for territory. There was only the faith—the raw, bleeding faith—that Nuhra had exuded from the moment Anna met her. Long before her Breaking, before she'd ever become enamored with the depths of her own mind, there had been that faith.

"Do not veil your words," Anna whispered. "What are you asking of me?"

Nuhra smiled. "To endure. There is nothing else to do, Kuzalem, but to endure. This is the way of revelation."

"It sounds like a way of war."

"Once, it was," Nuhra said. "The sacred beja earned their names in such trials. But this is a new age. It will extend far beyond the way of blades."

"What did it show them?"

"The beja?" Nuhra asked. "It showed them their path. There is no room for doubt in the mind of an enlightened killer. Who must die and when? When must they bare their own throats? It whispers all these things, sister."

Anna's throat tightened. She'd learned centuries of history in this place, but all of it had been a mélange of blood and fire. No matter how old the world grew, killing seemed to be an inescapable urge, if not a divine pattern.

"Take refuge in yourself," Nuhra continued. "When they peer into you, it will be the only sanctuary. All other things will fall away from you."

"I've already reached such states." She thought of the black liquid in the Moraharem chamber, of the things and faces it had shown in nightmarish vignettes. But even that had been preceded by past attainments: She recalled the total dissolution that hung in her memory like a window's faint reflection, forever calling her back to the war and the chaos that had blossomed into serenity. "None of them brought an end to this."

Nuhra hummed. "You tasted it, sister, I can see that in your eyes. But this will set you on an irrevocable course. It will light the way to your purpose."

"You're steadfast. Perhaps you should endure it yourself."

"I was not chosen," she said, suddenly tight-lipped, terse. "He would not have uttered its name if he did not know your true nature." She looked away. "If he did not feel that you were *becoming.*"

"Becoming what?"

But Nuhra did not seem to hear her. She proceeded over cracked tiles, her lantern's frothy bloom coating the forest of vases and grotesque statues that guarded the path. After a moment, Lukas's burlap brushed Anna's ear.

"Chosen," he said, though not without an edge beyond Anna's recognition. Fear, disbelief, mockery—she could not place it, but it chilled her nonetheless. "Knew that from the start, panna."

She twisted her head away from him, then moved up the final steps and through the tangle of brass arms and serpent heads. When she joined Nuhra at the door, she was curiously breathless.

The humming had swelled to a constant, frenzied pulse against the door, rattling the wood until its grain was distorted, phantasmal, in flux between two indistinct planes. It bled into the tiles in muffled waves, caressing Anna's sternum and ribs.

"It's natural to cede to your fear," Nuhra said. "At some stage, it will be inevitable. Surrender with trust, sister."

"Nuhra." Lukas's voice was faraway; hoarse, yet tender.

"Hold onto the deepest pillar of being," Nuhra whispered. She stared at Anna with bulbous, frantic eyes. "You must be firm, for—"

"Nuhra!" His voice clapped through the blackness. "Bring her back here."

"What?"

"Bring her."

"She was chosen," Nuhra hissed.

"Always another way. But this," he breathed, "this isn't it."

"What has seized you? This is the hour of her awakening."

"*Chodge*, Anna," Lukas said, extending a pale hand into Nuhra's lamplight. "I know you'd kill to get your girl, but there's no trail here. Nothing but the Grove. So walk away." His fingers wavered. "Anna."

Anna surveyed Lukas's hand as though from a great distance. She had never encountered the earnest fury he now buried in his voice; it was beyond matters of greed, of power, of domination. He needed her, of course, but he'd needed her before, and he'd kept her through cruelty. Now his words struck her as wounded, pleading, the sort of helpless cry a beast emitted on the verge of death.

Nothing about the door suggested that it would bring salvation. Its dreadful song guaranteed pain and terror. No matter what she endured in its confines, and regardless of how certain the man had been about her path and his people and Bora's wishes, Anna—or at least her thinking mind, that sliver of perpetual awareness—knew that it wasted.

But perhaps death was preferable to the world Ramyi was forging.

It was deliverance from the ruined dwellings and fading faces that played through her mind.

"Open it," Anna said to Nuhra. She did not look up at Lukas, but her body was angled toward him, frozen. "If I'm the only one who was chosen, then this *is* the way."

Latches clacked open. Crossbars slid over their brackets with coarse grinding.

"Northern madness," he said, raising his voice. "Just like I told you, isn't it?"

"You want me to free you," Anna whispered.

"It's not about that."

"It always was. Just tell me it was."

Lukas stepped forward. "Not now, not here. Set your head straight."

"I'll do it," she said. "If you want the Breaking, I'll do it."

His voice stuttered, stopped. "It's not fucking *about* that."

Hinges squealed and lukewarm air drifted over the back of Anna's neck. The humming was deafening now, rich with a million distinct voices, shrill and buttery and grating in the same instant, melding together until Anna seemed to breathe their song.

"Endure," Nuhra said. The woman took Anna's shoulders and forced her back in a swift, blurred motion.

The door's square of lantern light fizzled with black shapes, black clouds, flitting like a sandstorm over her skin and before her eyes. Anna jerked forward, but her mind was numb, blank to the survival instincts she'd worked so hard to hone. Her last shard of lantern light carved out the burlap stitching of Lukas's mask. She swore that tears were shimmering in his eyes, but the mind could not trust itself.

Then the door slammed shut, its creak and thud lost amid the droning, and Anna dissolved.

There was only the swarm.

Vicious wings and hair-thin legs danced over her flesh in a hot, ecstatic wave. Every sensation was sharp and encroaching. She felt them prodding her lids, crowding the warm curves of her nostrils, fluttering over her lips. Again, she was seized by that paralyzing terror, by resignation that held back her screaming and swatting. Every breath was a short, cutting stab for air, whistled through her nose or lips.

Is it over?

The question sparked a dreadful realization with her—it had only been seconds. Suddenly she was cognizant of her body trembling, shuddering in the cage of their antennae and mandibles and waiting barbs. They could smell her fear. She'd heard that from a girl near her father's post once, but she could not recall the girl's name. She could not recall anything, not anymore. There was only her skin and its effervescent tingling.

Soon she could not hear her thoughts. Her lungs cried out for air. Her eyes watered and ached. Blood thumped through her ears, pounding against the hum that would not subside, would not ease, would not—

Her skin evaporated.

The swarm continued to surge and hover and probe, churning against a body that was not Anna's, but calmness began to bleed into the blackness, into the void that had once confined her. She did not feel trapped, for *she* did not feel anything. Only sensations remained. Every scratch and hum flowed into a cloth that embraced her, somehow *became* her, settling with familiarity and longing that she could not fathom. She had been here before, abiding in that perfect stillness, in the center of all things, studying a stranger's thoughts as they roiled up and shrank away into a froth of nothingness....

Bliss trickled down to thin fingers, made quaking lips widen with abrupt joy. Who had shed the tears that now wound down burning cheeks? What animal had looked upon death as an end, a threat that towered above all others?

Laughter knocked through a flowing chest.

Droning thickened in the blackness, ascending to a unified tone beyond comprehension, swelling, leveling until it was a singular resonance.

Then the world vanished.

Visions emerged as though gliding past a keyhole: a wooden door streaked with Nuhra's lantern light, the creek where she had seen a coyote lapping up water, blankets bundled up to her chin, the verdant heights of Golyna. Sensations registered at the barest edge of consciousness, muted, smothered by velvet dullness. And as the world revolved in her mind's eye, her body warping between childhood and adolescence in undulating contractions, the scenes did not appear so disjointed. Anna softened her gaze until she did not cling to the sphere of passing light and color; she watched without admiring sunrises, without resisting the iron that pierced her flesh. Soon the equanimity was all-consuming, coaxing her away from the spectacle until her life transpired in wordless beauty. It ran together as a shimmering stream, unbroken, effortless, playing out in a single experience that was at once eternal and ephemeral.

But the moment teetered on an impossible crest, and soon the stream quickened to a blur of pure light, a flash that burned away years and faces and names.

Her mind settled in that blank, boundless plane.

For a moment—an hour, a decade—there was nothing.

Then raw shapes formed amid the sprawl, conjuring moonlit earthworks that some splinter of herself recognized as Malchym. Yet she, Anna, had never been so close to the city. Alakeph marched past her in milky shadows.

Dread gripped her in cold pangs. Memories exploded through her in blinding pulses—not her own, but those that she'd witnessed near a safe house, or sprawled out upon stone tiles. Rising flames, bones jutting from flesh. The fear was inescapable, rampant, compounding its own dread by the moment.

Her body hurried alongside the fighters, thundering over blood-streaked tiles, but it was not animated by her will.

She could not move her hands, could not blink.

Help me.

Then she was in some buried, crushing place, wreathed in mica that whirled and dazzled before her eyes.

An enormous silhouette towered over her. It was vaguely humanoid, its shoulders and head bulging in dark growths, shrugging faintly, glacially, with breaths that stirred the dust and grit around Anna's ankles.

Now she did not fight the helplessness. She surrendered to the weird majesty of the figure, to the cavern's stale heat and crackling force.

"I have waited." The words exploded through her mind, not spoken but heard, understood in a way that transcended every tongue she knew. "Come forth, my child."

Stars whirled before her, tracing the passage of days, weeks. Hills, riverbeds, forests—the terrain was fresh, yet evocative of things long known and traversed, possessed by nostalgia she could not understand. An old woman's eyes stared into her own. Ramyi materialized with a misty gaze, a blade in hand, her shoulder wrapped with—

A hand—perhaps her own, perhaps not—touched her stomach. Her fingers came away with blood.

Violet fabric, boots pounding up chipped stairs, Nuhra shouting…

Anna's eyes opened to blackness, to the rhythmic hum of the swarm over her hands and her face and her neck. She curled her fingers, eased into a long, smooth breath, and felt the prescience slip away like a fading echo. The world did not feel real, but it was accessible, malleable. She was still trembling.

Distant memories dissolved to their former skeletons, stripped of the vivid, unknowable things that had filled her—*her*, for she knew no other word—mind just moments prior. Yet the path forward remained. She was certain of every step, of every rise and valley that lay between her and Bora's people.

Screeching hinges jarred the swarm upon her lips. Faint, ruddy light spilled through the doorway and gave form to the circling wasps.

"Sister!" Nuhra's shout was frayed. "The easterners seek our end." The woman's lantern lowered to her waist. "You truly were chosen," she said with unexpected softness. With a bittersweet edge, even. "You have seen your nature."

But the glow of the experience still radiated from Anna's chest, suffusing her with warmth and clarity that transcended fear. The alarm in Nuhra's voice swept over her like the wings that kissed her skin. She did not speak, for language seemed so unwieldy, so unnatural.

Screams rose above the humming, joined by iron clattering against stone and commands issued in Orsas.

"Show me what you've seen," Nuhra said. Entranced, she wandered into the chamber and its thrumming cloud. "Sister, please." The wasps danced over her skin. "I must *know*. My mind is pure—it stands on this sacred precipice!"

Anna raised her hand, but it was too late.

There was hardly any time for Nuhra to flinch, let alone scream. Her eyes and mouth vanished in a convulsing black mass, and soon her entire body was rippling with that monstrous shell, staggering forth in spite of the pain, the inexorable end, the blood that dribbled over the lantern's glass and pattered across stone tiles. The swarm's voice was hateful, screeching.

Nuhra sank to her knees, her face—a mask of chitin, beady eyes, gnashing obsidian teeth—catching the edge of the lantern's glow.

There seemed to be a smile beneath it all.

Cracking iron rang out beyond the doorway, piercing the dampened hum of the swarm.

That was all it took for Anna to tether herself to the world. She practically felt the cogs of the thinking mind churning within her head, locking in place, scheming, flooding her body with the terror and savagery one could not survive without. Sidling around Nuhra's wasp-laden corpse, Anna hurried out of the chamber and toward whirling bands of light.

Everything was brash, disorienting, close in a way that made her feel like a suckling fawn in woods she had never roamed. Lantern light swabbed pockmarked columns and chisel-gouged mosaics, birthing the world from the vast nothingness that encircled her.

She heard grunts and scraping boots and murderous, half-choked taunts as she neared the stairs, all the while clawing at bunched robes to free her blade. For the first time in years she was aware of her hand's broken nature; it was a curious sensation, a rediscovery of a body she had accepted and somehow forgotten. But the blade slid free and she clutched it at her side, creeping forward, struggling against a barrage of alien thoughts:

Is this my blade?

My?

What is mine?

Light washed out her vision, boring into her skull with its dull ache. She did not hear the violence that had passed between flesh and jagged edges just moments prior.

"It's her."

Anna understood the meaning of the hard, pitiless Orsas long before she knew which tongue had been spoken. Ragged breathing soon overtook the silence, and blackness seeped back into her world as the light dimmed, raked down her robes, came to rest upon the blade she could hardly feel herself holding.

"Disarm yourself." This time the Nahoran employed flatspeak.

She did as instructed, but she did not hear iron striking the tiles. Instead, there was only a fierce, sustained whistling, reminiscent of the shells that had claimed her hearing in countless engagements. She blinked at the murky shapes below.

The tracker was easiest to discern; he was fixed in the overlapping beams of lantern light, coiled up on his haunches like a waiting mongoose, his overcoat and mask flapping where blades had bitten through to his flesh. At his feet was a discarded yuzel, still venting steam in boiling strands. Blood stippled the tiles and severed limbs around him.

Anna understood the man's surrender when the shadowed Nahorans crept inward, revealing their true strength of ten, perhaps fifteen, fighters. She recognized the featureless coverings on some of the men, which marked them as hunters beyond equals, as a tool not since seen since wartime—as *Borzaq*. One of them was aiming a ruj at her skull. She met the man's eyes evenly.

"Anna, First of Tomas, hereby judged as Kuzalem," the Nahoran said in flatspeak, "you are sought for insurgency involvement in the territory of Leejadal. The state and its benefactors have requested your presence." A long, peculiar pause ensued, as though the fighter had expected— or even feared—a reaction. But Anna merely stared and listened. "Is this understood?"

She nodded, but his words were nothing more than hollow, imprecise sounds.

She understood *everything*.

Chapter 11

Hours passed in damp, stifling blackness, marked only by the breaths Anna whispered through her cloth covering. They guided her gently, almost reverently, from walking paths to horseback to a nerash's cushioned bench, occasionally exchanging Orsas she could no longer grasp. She heard neither Lukas's words nor dragging steps. And though that void had once induced terror, devouring her with all of its vagueness and starved senses, she was no longer afraid. She observed the hours as shifting lights, noises, thoughts; a ceaseless composition of moments arising and passing away.

Then the cushions fell still beneath her and the nerash swayed upon its haunches, and silence sparkled in Anna's ears. Fabric scratched around her. After a pause, the sack lifted, drowning her in milky light.

Silhouetted figures crowded the cabin of the nerash.

"We are honored to look upon you once again," a man said. It was so quiet, so still, that his tongue's wet clicking echoed between them.

But Anna was already transfixed by the copper wisps rising off the platforms. She watched them dancing, eddying in the shade of a city woven from rust and glimmering fines. Several of them soared until they led her eyes to an impossible spire.

It was Leejadal, undoubtedly, but *she* did not know such a place. It was a lingering artifact, alien and vestigial, no more familiar to her than the jinkaral's dead visions. How could it be? After all, she had not felt its soil, had not tasted its air. It was yet another *thing* she understood through memories that were not her own.

"To look upon *me*?" Anna asked, surprised—even amused—by her own voice. *"Again?"*

* * * *

Death was not the worst fate a thing could suffer. Anna had known that truth long before she'd encountered the Apiary, but now it was a plain axiom, as vivid and striking as the sunlight streaming through the office's windows.

A dead thing had peace, after all. It could rest in the hollows of nothingness, free of its obligations, its burdens, its weary tasks it had performed in life. It was granted the somber, unshakable respect that eluded the living.

When Nahora died, the world had looked upon it with fresh, forgiving eyes, recalling the violet legions that had held mountain passes, the soft-tongued suturers, the cities that had been sacrificed for victory. There had been a vast effort—free of any one creed—to reclaim its grave and clear away the ashes, to return life to the hills and valleys Anna had traversed with a ruj slung across her back. In some ways, there had even been a sense of potential. The womb of war had allowed the state to be reborn, unfettered by the dominance of its forefathers.

But Nahora had not known of its own death.

Within the monastery's shelter, Anna had envisioned the state as a starving, rabid hound, pacing the flats for a kill that never came, gnawing at its own paws when the hunger grew unbearable. It was without a den and without pups. Now there was the hunt and only the hunt.

Yet in the years since Anna had convened with the remnants of the state, relying on sparse missives and the Alakeph's breakers for news of the world beyond the monastery, new masters had risen from the chaos of uncertainty. Perhaps in the end, that was all the hound had desired. A leash was salvation from death; a leash was the omen of a fresh hunt.

"Would you care for some tea?"

The Nahoran attendant's river-tongue was crude, yet passable. She sat beside a barren bookshelf on the far side of the office, her back achingly straight and eyes inquisitive, weighing Anna with equal parts awe and mistrust. She was a pureblood citizen; that much was plain from the highborn curves comprising her cheekbones and jaw, the emerald depths of her eyes, the olive flesh that had grown dark and splotchy in the cradle of Har-gunesh.

Yet she was distinct from the eastern sisters that endured in Anna's memory, almost tainted. Her belted amethyst dress, in spite of its crushed velvet and lace cuffs, was already fraught with loose threads, torn fringes, the stains of mud and drink alike. Golyna had imbued Nahora with a sense of the pristine, even the divine, but such illusions could not last forever.

"No," Anna said softly. She noticed that the woman was kneading her fingers, suppressing the urge to shift, to blink. Those old eruptions of fear—conscious or otherwise—had now become glaringly apparent. "Where did they take my companion?"

"Such a matter is not within my domain," the attendant said.

"Will they kill him?"

Her pause was considerate, weighty, riddled by thin fingers picking at the lint across her lap. "No," she said eventually. "I don't think they will."

"Oh."

The woman regarded Anna as though she had said something insightful. "These inconveniences will soon be resolved."

"Inconveniences." Anna chewed the word, recalling the inexorable path she'd glimpsed in the Apiary's confines. Every occurrence was yet another thread in the fabric of time, of reality itself. *Inconveniences.* She couldn't suppress a dim smile.

But the attendant was no longer surveying Anna; she was staring at the office's oak door with a shrewd, concerned face, one ear cocked toward the patter of muffled steps.

Then the brass handle dipped and the door swung open, revealing a woman with braid-bundled dark hair, sharp, study features, and amber eyes. Ga'mir Ashoral stood as poised as ever, but her face was lined now, agitated. Her violet tunic was sun-faded; it clothed her loosely, airily, hanging over flesh that had grown lean, yet dense in the flatlands. Several pendants—brass, iron, tin, still gleaming with the touch of vinegar and sand—glinted along her collarbone.

"Ga'mir," the attendant said in a hushed voice, rising with eyes fixed forward and hands pressed to her sides.

Ashoral did not acknowledge the woman. She moved to her desk and sat in her chair and looked toward Anna as though she did not see her, as though she were entirely alone. Her desk was bare, aside from a tall, graceful wine decanter resembling a swan's neck. "Have you slept?"

Anna could not tell if she'd been addressed. "At some point, surely."

"Many in my ranks assure me that you've been rather diligent," Ashoral said. "They were perplexed by your descent from the mountains." She paused, examining the gouges and scratches that endured as bright scars across the desk's varnish. "I knew better, of course. The greatest toil of a hare is to rest its weary paws."

The mountains. It was hard to believe Nahora's claws still extended into Rzolka, let alone the craggy recesses that had originally been chosen for their solitude. "Your breakers must have fire in their bones."

"There was ample warmth by your monastery's hearths."

A lump throbbed at the back of Anna's throat. It was not fear—no, *fear* was still a separate, bestial thing to be dissected by the thinking mind—but rather, chagrin. She had been meticulous in combing through the inducted Alakeph brothers, inquiring about the splotches upon their flesh, the distant threads of their bloodline, the satin lilt in their river-tongue. Her mind edged toward darker plots, toward black-haired foundlings and—

"I haven't brought you here to threaten you," Ashoral said.

"You can understand my confusion, then." Anna squared her shoulders and straightened against the chair's cushioned back. "What have you done with the tracker?"

"Nothing," she said. "Yet."

"And you'll sustain that decorum, if you expect my cooperation in any degree."

"I fully expect it," Ashoral said, reaching under her desk to produce a twine-wrapped scroll. She set it on the table between them, but did not nudge it toward Anna. "Our aims may align more closely than you suspect. Grant me your faith in this matter, and you will see it rewarded in turn."

"If only you knew how often I've heard such words."

Ashoral held Anna's stare, one corner of her lip crinkling as she did so. "My hope, Kuzalem, is that this occasion will express its own urgency."

"This *occasion*?" Anna squinted, leaned forward. "None of my fighters were naïve enough to see altruism in the state's course, even while they shared trenches with yours. Recent events have only vindicated what I know."

"You're referring to the market."

"As are you."

A stretch of brittle silence followed. Ashoral glanced down and smoothed the folds of her tunic, then cleared her throat. "You believe we were hunting you."

"No," Anna said. "A shell knows nothing about its target. I know that you intended to kill, however."

"Do you realize—"

"Our actions in the market had nothing to do with your insurgency," Anna cut in. "It's not my business to meddle in the affairs of warring killers. But I would caution you against meddling in mine."

For a moment, her words—indeed, her threat—appeared lost on Ashoral, perhaps even placating. There was a deep stillness in the easterner's eyes. "You know little about this insurgency."

"With due respect, Ga'mir, I have more pressing concerns than Leejadal's affairs."

"As do I."

"Forgive me," she said. "I've forgotten that the state's aims precede all others. Tell me, what has Nahora gained from these ventures? Prestige? Filled coffers?"

"We were summoned here."

"By whom? Those who saw an opportunity among rubble? The cycle deviates, but it never ceases."

Ashoral took a slow breath.

"You can be direct with me," Anna said. "Has this occupation lined your own purse? Is there—"

"Enough of this ignorance." The measured restraint in the ga'mir's voice, surely cultivated in the service of endless councils and tribunals, evaporated with those words. Her eyes were narrower now, more lucid. "This is not a sanctuary, Kuzalem. You do not know these lands as you know your sacred Spines, nor do you understand how much of our blood was spilled to preserve a culture that wishes for our annihilation. If you wish to sit before me and disgrace the work of the state—of my brothers, my sisters, my bearers before them—I will hold my tongue." Her nostrils flitted in and out, widening. "But you turned your back on this world. You cannot vilify that which you created."

It was true, in some sense, but Anna did not know herself as the girl who had once fled from her hunters. That girl had died time and time again. Yet that old form, which she now regarded as something illusory, perhaps even false, now carried the burden of ancient wrongs. Had it truly flayed the world? She considered that the world itself was not as precious as the pupil she would kill.

"What were you seeking in that market?" Anna asked softly.

"That which drew you out of your mountain refuge," Ashoral said. "We are not the blind beasts you've forged in your mind."

The ga'mir's eyes were earnest, knowing. Anna's chest felt as though it had imploded. "I never thought you blind."

Ashoral glanced at her attendant, whose eyes had grown creased with acrid thoughts. "*Rosna an'dregol,*" she whispered.

The attendant's grimace was brief, nearly disguised as thoughtful consideration. She rose, offered a perfunctory bow, and exited the office, all without meeting Anna's eyes.

"Let us cast aside our veils, Kuzalem," Ashoral said. "The dawn of the Starsent is upon us and we will find no reprieve in coyness. This is only the beginning of your task—you would do well to accept the wisdom of seasoned hunters."

"Seasoned?" Anna asked. "Be plain."

"The Defiling of Golyna revealed precisely what will move against us. Since that day, we have not slept. We have been relentless." Ashoral shut her eyes for a moment. "Yet she eludes us."

"You never sought my aid."

"The state was certain she would return to you, given enough time," Ashoral explained. "I did not share its optimism."

"What gave you confidence in Leejadal, then?"

Ashoral eyed the scroll between them. "This tracker remained in contact with old cells. It was simply a matter of extracting the whispers that flowed between the hunted."

"She isn't with Volna," Anna said. "She sought their knowledge, but little else."

"We are aware."

Anna studied the slate certainty in the easterner's gaze, pondering how many missives and embedded operatives it had taken to assure them of such things. "You think she's leading an insurgency."

"Involved with one," Ashoral corrected.

"You don't understand a thing, then." Anna watched the Howling Wall coalescing far beyond the city's limestone maze; it rose from the flats in a gauzy amber wave, creeping closer, closer....

"Enlighten me, Kuzalem. The state only wishes to align its blades with your own."

The moment descended on her with eerie prescience, electric, fizzling across her scalp with memories that were not yet memories, a vast foam of all things that had not coalesced into being. The Apiary's revelations welled up with razor-teeth, beckoning her. *This is how it must be.* "She seeks an end to all things," Anna whispered. "Make no mistake, Ga'mir: She will not waver in her course."

"Naturally. If I doubted these words, you would not be here."

Anna's laugh was curt, hollow. "You simply can't *grasp* it. In your mind, you see another war approaching, don't you? You see a threat to Nahora's bones. But this is devastation beyond the devices of man, Ga'mir." She shook her head. "My course is clear. Leave us to our task and we will do what we must."

"You know I can't allow that," Ashoral said softly.

"None of your schemes will prosper against a goddess."

"And hyperbole will get us nowhere, Kuzalem. This is the domain of conquerors and the conquered—I'll not wander into mysticism with you."

"Mysticism?" Anna hissed. "What exactly do you make of her bid for power?"

"We *make* nothing. We know of her designs, her allegiance to Kowak, her—"

"What did you say?" The words were hollow in her mind, devoid of the echoes that blanketed all other phenomena. Had it been foretold, foreseen?

"Kowak," Ashoral repeated. "The Starsent has turned her gaze upon its banners."

"You're lying."

"Is that what you wish to believe? Each of us is free to choose their deception."

Anna's hands tightened upon the chair's armrests. She could *feel* herself—Anna, that limited, separate thing—burgeoning back into awareness, severing the vastness of the world. She was a bundle of unease and tension and scheming.

"Kowak had infiltrated Golyna long before their aid arrived," Ashoral continued. "You should understand, I imagine, that we rarely preserve our sources for such information. The extraction of buried words supersedes mercy for a broken mind."

"They stood to lose just as much as you."

"And just as much to gain from the Starsent—is it not so?"

Anna regarded the ga'mir warily. Nothing was impossible, she admitted, but accepting that truth was an invitation to deeper pain. "Who spoke these words?"

"One of their captains," Ashoral said. "We'd suspected a network for some time, but his missive was the first we intercepted. And his truths cast light upon a shapeless world, Kuzalem."

"You tortured an ally."

"An operative," the ga'mir corrected. "Kerlis, third of Jakub. You might be interested to learn that he was a member of Jenis's front-breaker cadre during the Weave Wars."

Bitter pangs erupted in Anna's stomach. "What are you implying?"

"Recall the commander that presides over Kowak, and you will know their designs."

But Anna's lips could not form *Jenis*. Her mind would not, could not, turn toward it. "He has nothing to do with this."

"How has the Starsent managed to sweep the snow over her tracks? Has she not moved with the swiftness and guile of mountain beasts?" Again, the ga'mir's voice was hardening, fraught with some undercurrent beyond dissection. "A war is not constructed in a vacuum."

"You're hunting shadows," Anna said. "You crave anything that will vindicate your fight; I can see that well enough."

"They turned her," Ashoral snapped. "Her mind, and her chaos, and all that's contained within her. Do not blind yourself to this. To broken men, she is the true prophet."

"You have no idea what she seeks!"

Ashoral's eyes drifted back to the scroll. "An end to this world," she said solemnly, "and the birth of something new. A world without the trappings of history, of masters, of belief in anything, new or old. They offer power to the powerless."

"She serves herself."

"Jenis, herself—what does it *matter?* The truth remains, with or without your lenses: She will destroy that which is known to us. She will destroy that which is precious."

Anna rested in that frail, sour silence, unable to resist the ga'mir's conclusion. When all frames collapsed, there was only the certainty of devastation, of things scourged from existence. It did not matter what—nor whom—had acted within the girl's orbit. Cessation was the only path.

And yet she recalled Nuhra's words, those small and cautious things that had steered her mind away from bloodshed:

I would see my bones crushed and my mind obliterated to ensure her path in this world.

But now Nuhra and her mercy were gone. There were no champions to guide the Starsent, to bring about whatever salvation had once been assured. A hunt could only end in death.

"Make no mistake," Ashoral said presently. "I have brought you here in good faith. If the Spines offer you divine refuge, our bindings will not fix you to this task."

Anna's mind churned at that:

Perhaps she could seek the girl rather than hunt her.

"Together, however, our forces could bring this to its end," Ashoral continued.

Perhaps she could save her.

"Very well," Anna whispered. "But I know the path. Not *a* path—*the* path. You must be prepared to die for it."

"Thousands of prophets have uttered your words."

"We did not seek her in Malijad," Anna pressed on. "We sought the light of knowing."

"Knowing."

"Yes," Anna said, "knowing. The knowing of all things, at all times, in all worlds. For a moment, I was *that*." Her lips quivered. "This is the domain of the hayajara and the hayajara alone. I will not teach you the ways of war, and you will not teach me the ways of existence. If you can accept this, then your cause is mine."

Ashoral opened her mouth, but did not speak. Then her chest heaved and she breathed out, exhausted, drained of that ardent spark. "So it is." Ashoral paused. "Yet I must ask your aid in one matter."

Anna frowned.

"Your presence would be invaluable at Malchym's upcoming convergence." Then, noting Anna's deepened confusion: "I suspect that the head of every family, cartel, and coalition will be in attendance."

"As I've told you, the path is clear," Anna said. "There's no cause for divergence."

"Even so," she replied, as though the phrase itself could settle the debate. "Perhaps such affairs weigh faintly on your mind, but once the ashes of this task have fallen still, those of us who lack *knowing* will need to preserve this world."

"What qualifies you to do so?"

"Such words are irrelevant. Our intention is simply to maintain balance, and our task reflects this. If the Starsent remains at Kowak's side, their dominance is assured."

"And if you break our path, nothing is certain," Anna said. "Not balance and not the world."

Ashoral did not seem to hear her. "Killing is done in shadows, Kuzalem, but peace is forged in light. You have your path and I have mine. All I seek is your presence."

"Have you mistaken me for an ambassador?"

"I assure you that your prestige speaks for itself." Ashoral's gaze softened. "Urge them to stand together, and a thousand years of peace will blossom."

"They'd sooner see each other torn open."

"And thus, I implore you to sway their hearts. You will not wear our colors, nor speak our tongue, nor preach our axioms—you will preserve our world."

Before that moment, Anna had not questioned the abrupt conclusion of the path before her. Her visions had raked through the abyss of time, but they had not stretched beyond Ramyi's face, the blade, the blood. They'd flowed into absolute nothingness, beyond perception and being itself. She considered that her course was crippling to the mind, and that it had done everything in its power to turn away from such trauma. After all, that imminent task was so disturbing, so unlike anything she had ever known, that it did not seem possible for the world to endure in its wake. But it was the way of all things to change and wither and bloom, and in consideration of that wisdom, Ashoral's truth remained: *Who will pick up the pieces?*

"Very well," Anna whispered. "But I will not stray any further."

Ashoral pursed her lips, nodded. A smile nestled between ease and weariness came over her. "Enough of it, then. Come."

Anna crinkled her brow.

"It would be improper to dine before you've seen your quarters," Ashoral explained.

"My comrades are—"

"Here," Ashoral replied. "*Brother* Konrad is eager to speak with you."

"The tracker?"

"Sedated, for the time being," Ashoral said. "He was not interested in compliance."

Nothing stirred within Anna's chest. She had known Nahora long enough to adapt to its treachery, its endless reach, its ploys. Long enough to understand a core axiom:

Leaders held land, but the state held the world.

Chapter 12

"I trust your visions over their pledges." Konrad sat across the low table with his hands gathered in his lap, his stare roaming, restive. "Do you think it's the true way?"

Anna remained silent, mired in contemplation that had not lessened since her afternoon in the ga'mir's office. Now her quarter's high windows were sills of blackness and rippling grit, impenetrably dark, a reflection of the maelstrom coursing through her mind. Three hours of speaking had strained her throat and tongue, but they had not been sufficient enough to explain what had *really* happened to her old mind, to Nuhra, to the stillness of the Apiary. An eternity could not convey it all. But she lacked the force to continue, to make Konrad comprehend such things beyond surface impressions. This new mind was not accustomed to exhaustion, she supposed.

Konrad displayed none of that fatigue. He had been frantic—predictably so—in the wake of Nahora's arrival, even while relaying the tale to Anna, but that energy had sublimated in moments when he recognized his master's attainments.

Now he was eager to know the truth of things, to know his course, to know what part he played in the cosmic dance. *This* was what he'd forsaken his old ways to uncover.

But Anna had not seen him.

"I know it's the truth," she said, pausing to sip her jasmine tea. "This is the crucial hour, Konrad. This is when I'm forced to demand faith from the brothers."

"They'll lend their faith to you, but Nahora's a hard sell."

"Not to me," Anna corrected. "To the path."

Konrad shifted on his cushion. "Of course."

"How are their spirits?" she asked. Distantly she thought of Ashoral's words—Kowak, Jenis, that slow rot from the bogs—and soon found herself scrutinizing every action of those in her company. Konrad began speaking, but she did not listen. She held Andriv's face in her mind's eye, wondering, ruminating....

"Anna?"

Her attention snapped back to beige walls, steaming teacups. "What tasks has Andriv overseen?"

"Tasks?" Konrad was at a sudden loss, stunned by something—though Anna did not know what—in her voice. His brow twitched. "What's the matter?"

"Try to recall them."

Confusion faded to grim deduction. "What did she tell you?"

"It doesn't matter," Anna whispered. "Where has he been, Konrad? What has he done beyond your sight?"

Konrad shook his head—was it in disbelief, in realization?

It was maddening how swiftly her mind had devolved. She was unable to decipher the subtle swells and dips of his chest, to discern lies from truths through the oscillation in his voice. She hadn't expected her mind, like any blade, to hold its keen edge eternally, but her severance from the Apiary's revelations was palpable. Painful, even.

"He was monitoring missives," Konrad said after a moment. He sounded shy, almost wounded. "That's all he did, Anna."

Then she understood his beaten tone: It was her mistrust of the order. He had never heard her accuse a brother of anything, least of all on the word of an outsider. She herself had placed her faith, her life, in their ways. But in times of war, there were no sacred laws to uphold. Anything good and known and perennial was apt to be shattered.

"Do you trust him?" Anna asked.

"Trust," Konrad said weakly. "That's a sordid word for an operative."

"Still your mind and speak."

"I trust what the world has given me to trust."

Anna set her hands upon her thighs and inhaled. "Did Ashoral mention Kowak in your meetings?"

Konrad shook his head. "What's this all about?"

"She claims that they're in league with Ramyi." The ensuing silence was strange, protracted. "And if her words are true, then Jenis—"

"You can't be serious," Konrad snapped, practically wincing at his own flurry of the feeling mind. He took a moment to compose himself, to lower his voice to conspiratorial depths. "From Ashoral or otherwise, the state has shown the ways of its hands time and time again."

"This isn't about power," Anna said.

"It isn't? Ever since the war, that's all they've wanted. Desperation toys with decent minds; it destroys them. Everything and everyone becomes a tool."

"Ashoral's words are steadfast," she said. "It's not so hard to believe that after all we've known, men would crave a new order, even one born of flames. The Starsent is the avatar of our world's dissolution."

"You know Jenis and you know Andriv."

"I know the nature of desperate men. Kowak has the most to gain from the death of the old ways."

"So says Nahora, with a blade to your throat."

"They didn't coerce me."

"Yet there was no invitation to this place," Konrad said. "For any of us."

"You didn't hear her words, Konrad."

"Misdirection is their *art*. If a herd turns against itself, then the wolf's work is done." Anna opened her mouth to reply, but Konrad lifted a finger. "I would know better than most. You should, too."

"And what if it's true, Konrad? What then?"

"Then we destroy them," he said. "But not on Nahora's word."

"Kowak prospers from our inherent trust."

"Only if you assume that they're moving against us. Look at the whole of it, Anna—they've tended to their own affairs, the same as the others." He sighed. "And even if they turned, it wouldn't say a lick about the Alakeph. They can't be bought."

"They are not gods," Anna whispered. "They are not beyond the sway of causes."

"None of us are."

"Precisely," she said. "So nobody, and nothing, should be exempt from examination. Can you lend your heart to this?"

Konrad did not meet her eyes. "I can."

"Then tell me how Andriv has proven himself."

"I won't get into this, Anna."

"You *must*," she growled. "He could have killed her in the market. What was he doing on the upper levels? Was he biding his time?"

"Anna—"

"I can't see him," Anna said softly, her gaze growing dull, vacuous. "Just like you, Konrad. You simply aren't there. The path moves around you, but where are you?"

Konrad did not speak for some time. He merely stared down at his hands, those calloused, knotted things upon his lap. "I'll be with the others, should you require my counsel. Low suns, Anna." Then he stood, bowed, and left the room as a gliding shadow.

* * * *

The mind was a fickle, defiant thing, though Anna had forgotten that fact in time. It hadn't taken long, really—a year, perhaps two. Before those liberated days, her mind had played host to the echoes of abominations and split faces, to all of the odors and shrieks and regrets of war. On nights when she'd woken herself with screams and slick flesh, swatting at the covers for a man who would never be there again, she found refuge in the monastery's Kojadi tomes. *The mind, a sister of the sea, exists in its waves alone—stillness and turbulence are occurrences rather than natures.* Those ancient passages, reduced to soil-dark scrawling in her chamber's candlelight, had granted her the comfort to return to dreamless sleep.

But on that evening, the mind asserted its chaos.

Even with her eyes shut, Anna's concentration was lost amid the deluge of sensory percepts—the wafting aromas of mint and fearful sweat, the low voices, the clinking glass, the dry heat, the embers crackling and popping in the adjacent chamber.

There was no center, no relief.

Anna set her hands on her lap and gazed around the dining hall.

Everyone was absorbed in their private tasks, picking at roasted lamb or glancing about darkly or exchanging muttered flatspeak, paying mercifully little attention to Anna and her captains. It was expected, she supposed: In Hazan, hunger had always taken precedence over trust. Only the most wretched wanderers turned their backs on a host's offerings. Still, it was eerie to observe how quickly the Alakeph—not to mention the northerners, some of whom had marched under Volna's banners—had taken their seats among the Nahoran fighters. It was a living dreamscape of the war and its muddied lines.

She wondered if they had been misled, deceived in the same vein as any others who'd shared meeting chambers with Nahoran officers. Perhaps they'd been told that this reunion was natural, that it was good, that it was Anna's personal endeavor.

"Are you well?" Konrad stared at her over a plate of turmeric-tinted rice, his spoon hovering below his lips. His words since their meeting had been sparse, functional. Now there was a pall of worry.

"Of course," she said, though her mind did not align with that instinctive response. It was still at odds with Andriv's absence. His attendant's assurances—*he'll be along shortly*; *he's bathing*—did little to soothe her. And where *was* Lukas? There was no prudence in causing undue alarm, she supposed, but the silence regarding his condition chilled her. That, and the mere observation that she was concerned for him at all.

It all felt wrong.

"The storm's fading," Konrad said as he raked his plate. "You should step out, you know. This air is dead."

"Don't worry about me."

"Someone should." He sighed, set his spoon down. "Long days and long nights, Anna."

Again, she looked around the room, gauging smiles, scowls….

"You need to take care of yourself," Konrad continued.

"Myself." The word was vapid to her. "Things are playing out as they must." But Konrad had received the Breaking long ago, and he did not remember that taste of selflessness, so fluid and ethereal. "How can I say *I'm* tired? This body is moved by the cosmos."

Konrad's brow tightened. "Get some rest, Anna. Please."

She held her tongue; there was nothing she could say to placate him, after all. The Apiary and its truths had transcended the very concepts that comprised his mind. Her logic—indeed, her realm of perception—was as foreign to him as language to a beast.

Anna stood, pulled on a subtle smile, and started toward the doors.

She felt herself drifting past them, past everything….

In the corridor she stood by herself, her back pressed to cool stone and feet joined beneath aching hips. Hundreds of footsteps skittered through her awareness, above and below and between the walls. She searched for herself amid that wilderness, but there were only shallow breaths, muted heartbeats, the tacky feedback of sweat upon flesh.

Then something intruded that wreath of oneness.

It began as a whisper, an intuition nestled in the base of her skull:

Your errors are incessant, Anna. Ramyi's presence was a screaming void. *Does your mind turn away from destruction? Only the frailest beasts would leave breath in their prey.*

The Starsent's presence burrowed into Anna, raging through every notch and warren of memory, of feeling, of intention. There was nothing to hide. It was all sliced open and hung before her in blackness—the path to sacred knowledge, the progression of the world into that finite future.

Their divide collapsed.

The Apiary's revelations dangled in that boundless expanse, glinting like the shards of a broken mirror, bathing their shared awareness in hayat.

You've seen it, Ramyi howled. *How could you? Your form was always unworthy of divinity.*

Silence pervaded Anna's world; it drowned her, stifled her.

Perhaps this was always your purpose, Ramyi continued. *Nobody else could illuminate my path.* Images fluttered between them—boots stalking down dark corridors, white fabric rippling in their periphery, beard-shrouded lips curling to form river-tongue....

Don't do this, Anna managed.

We all have our path to walk.

Anna's fingers scraped over stonework. *I spared you.*

And this is your reward, Anna. This world will be reborn in new light.

Pain burst up Anna's throat. *They're using you. They did it to me and they'll do it to you, too.*

When I ascend, there will be nobody to use. Stand aside, Anna—your death will be the end of a bitter nightmare, and nothing more. Can you not feel it? Wake up from this long sleep.

Anna's attention turned inward, clinging to the hard breaths that flowed past the rim of her nostrils. She focused until Ramyi's awareness was a dim shadow, another phenomenon among many. And in that place of stillness, whirling before her in a rosebud of gray light, the girl's hold dissolved.

Her eyes snapped open to the sight of an empty corridor.

She had no thoughts, no fears—only certainty.

They were coming.

Anna burst through the dining hall's wicker doors and froze, overcome by the sea of candlelight and ruddy faces. A terrible quiet fell over the room, amplified by the weight of countless stares. She could not shout the proper words, or in fact, any words at all; her voice grated and stirred within her as though rising from timeless sleep.

But the Apiary's path collapsed upon her and suddenly it did not matter.

Brother Andriv wandered into the doorway on the far side of the hall. His eyes shone like pearls, bulbous, brimming with waves of horror and ecstasy. Sweat glimmered upon his cheeks and forehead. He carried a loaded ruj, though it did not immediately frighten Anna.

She was accustomed to seeing the brothers carry their weapon that way, after all. Tucked against the shoulder, barrel raised, a finger curling over the trigger. There was only one difference now and it did not feel so significant:

This ruj was aiming toward her.

The brother lingered for an instant, a horrible fragment of a second, returning Anna's gaze with the emptiness known to men who had killed and found solace in killing. Then he seemed to remember himself, to remember whatever task he had been issued, and his focus returned.

Andriv leveled his ruj at a tall, dark-haired easterner leaning over a clay bowl, blowing gently on the broth in a waiting spoon. The easterner was facing Anna, but did not notice her. He did not notice much at all.

Then the man's head evaporated; it burst into a dark, glistening mist, stippled with bits of mind, skull, gristle. It was silent aside from a wet *pop*, a gentle drumming. Gazes swiveled toward the body, but the second shot—and a third, a fourth—registered long before anybody shouted. They came as a steady *chk-chk-chk*, biting through pottery and oak and stone alike, slackening bodies and liquefying flesh.

Anna stumbled backward, groped the doorway, studied the mad determination in Andriv's eyes. Her lungs would not cycle air. Pressing herself to the doorframe, she sank down and craned her head around the corner.

Screams erupted from the hall, undercut by the din of chairs clattering against tiles. Bodies were scrambling and shoving toward the corridor, but there was nowhere to flee—brutish figures surged into the hall from the northern wing, severing the flow of the exodus in moments. Bottles exploded, each crack high and discordant amid the flowering panic, the wailing Orsas, the flatspeak that ceased without warning. Dark shapes worked their way through rows of tables and still-squirming bodies.

There had to be *something* to do, some way to—

Anna noticed the runes shining faintly through neck-wraps and painted flesh.

She cursed under her breath, edged backward. Iron raked the doorframe and showered the tiles with splinters. It felt impossible to move, let alone intervene. But then came the rumble of steps in the adjacent corridor, far too disorganized to belong to the southerners, all streaming toward the compound's barracks. There was still a chance to force them back; and if not, a hope of escape.

Konrad.

His name entered Anna's mind like a glowing brand, purging every other instinct, every shred of self-preservation. It beckoned her to the smoky, wailing depths of the dining hall.

She crept nearer, nearer, but the thinking mind resisted.

He is gone, it whispered in that wordless way. *His path has ended.*

Anna pulled a hard, bitter breath through her lips, acknowledged the wrath now budding in her chest, and set off running down the corridor.

Ramyi snapped at the edge of her focus, luring, watching....

A deafening clap rang out at the far end of the corridor. Black smoke twisted into a fat, pooling blossom, snaking around the ankles of those who passed in its wake. Four, five, perhaps more, all bleeding into the haze, all screeching the vicious strains of river-tongue Anna had not heard in years.

She spun right, dashing into the narrow cleft of a passage that led into darkness. Her world was reduced to hoarse breaths, clapping footfalls, a constant and tinny ring deep within her ears. But the beasts' cries nipped at her heels, never too distant to fade....

Why are you running, Anna? Ramyi's voice trampled through her awareness. *You've distasted dissolution—you know its sweetness.*

Anna drowned herself in the sensation of breath, that fleeting gray light that summoned her back to—

Large, slick fingers clamped around Anna's throat.

She wrenched her eyes open to find Andriv staring back at her, his face beaded with sweat, twisted into a bemused scowl. She was struck by the sense—if only for an instant—that this slaughter was unknown to him, that it was demanding upon such a chaste mind. Then her pity was gone and there was only that animal panic, a pulse dribbling through his grip, her hands scratching and swatting to no avail. Her face burned, ached from within. Blackness encroached at the edges of her vision as she watched his brow churning.

"I'm sorry," he said. His fingers dug into her skin, eased, tightened once more. "I didn't—forgive me, Kuzalem."

Her fingers grew cold and dull. They dragged along the brother's skin, even raking over sweat-streaked cheeks and lips, but it was all done in vain. Numbness throbbed at the crown of her skull; breaths creaked up her windpipe and thickened in the notch of her throat.

Everything sank into a deeper gloom, losing its crisp edges, its vibrant sheen. She saw only the black squares of doorways arrayed behind Andriv's silhouette. Her world receded into that gray light, withering....

Then it all fell away—the hands, the pressure, the gulf of nothingness.

Air surged into her chest.

Anna staggered back, her knees buckling, vision blackening, and sank down heavily against stone. She struggled to stand, gasping, but only managed to press numb fingers to her throat. Her limbs throbbed in chilling electric surges.

Candlelight bloomed in her awareness, illuminating pleats of swishing white fabric, the long, thin profile of a blade, limbs thrashing and teeth glinting and sweat shimmering. Was it one body, two? The white fabric seemed to bleed together, binding them until—

She did not trust what her vision revealed.

Konrad was pinning Andriv to the wall, his blade piercing the flesh just below Ramyi's rune. His boots shuffled over stone, gradually ceding to the marked brother's tenacity, but he did not relent: He screeched through gritted teeth, sank back into a lynx's crouch, and shoved upward, driving the blade forth until its hilt dug into Andriv's jaw.

Andriv cried out, choking on blood that was swift to retreat and vanish with hayat's binding. But pain was a passing deterrent, an illusion that could be dispelled if experienced for too long, and soon the brother grew calm. He huffed around the blade, around his split tongue, his stare leveling and brow settling. His fist swung up in a wild, heavy arc, striking Konrad's neck with a *whump.*

Anna watched Konrad stumble back, wheezing. She was distantly aware of the ruj lying near Andriv's feet. Shouts thundered down the corridor, breaching the constant hum in her ears, forcing her to claw at the wall and clamp her jaws and rise on shaking legs.

A blade's edge swept past her face.

She leapt back, hands raised in frail fists, studying Andriv and his stark silhouette, his swaying iron, his wide, fearful eyes.

"You don't need to do this," she managed. "You can resist."

His chest heaved, unaware that it did not need to breathe, to function at all. "This is hard enough for me. Please, be still." He moved closer. "Please."

There was a hiss—that of sand shifting within an hourglass, or a windswept dune—and Andriv's torso burst outward, a dark, thick jet of rib cartilage and innards, punching away the brother's spine. He sank to his knees, twitching, screaming as fresh organs sprouted into existence and settled behind walls of budding flesh. His blade skidded across cracked tiles.

Konrad loomed over the fallen brother, advancing with Andriv's ruj beneath his arm. He squeezed the trigger; it wrenched back with a dull scrape, a hollow *click.* Tossing the weapon aside, Konrad reached for the narrow blade, his—

A short knife, sliding from the inner lip of Andriv's boot, glinted in the candlelight.

"Konrad!"

But her voice was broken and Konrad was a slave to his bloodlust.

Andriv torqued at the waist, forcing his blade up and inward with a practiced thrust.

Anna had no idea how deep the strike had gone; she noted Konrad's strange surprise, the bestial manner with which he jumped back and patted his stomach and blinked at Andriv. She did not hesitate, did not think. Her only instinct was to kill. She rushed forward, raised her knee, collided with Andriv's regenerated spine.

The brother pitched forward and slammed down upon the tiles. He hurried to stand, his boots and knuckles scratching over stone, but Konrad's boot crushed the back of his skull. There was another stomp, another, each impact wet and sickening, until Konrad's foot slipped amid the blood and chipped bone.

Then Andriv was on his back, squirming, rolling, his knife slashing and spearing wildly.

Anna snatched the longer blade from the floor, marveling at its weight, its polished sheen, its serrated edge....

"Break him," Konrad growled at Anna. He sidestepped the brother's strikes, grimacing through the cuts that skimmed his shins and thighs, his hands dancing around the iron as though catching a fish in summer streams. "Now, Anna!" Seizing Andriv's wrist, he sprang nearer and drove his knees into the brother's stomach.

Anna rounded the two men, fixed by the knife's spastic twists. She was a phantom to them, a passing presence that no longer registered in their periphery. But she would not forsake her task—not again.

Just before Anna could kneel near Andriv's head, the knife slid free of Konrad's grasp, flailing about between flesh awash in sweat and blood. The iron vanished into the tangled folds of their robes, and soon there were grunts, howls, curses—Anna could not separate the dueling voices.

"Hurry!" Konrad gasped.

That was all she needed. Her hand guided the blade to Andriv's throat, to Ramyi's marking, to the tendrils of hayat that roiled free of its cuts. A sole sweep, flawless and rapid, snuffed out the rune's luminescence. She studied the sigils beneath his flesh as they dissolved, decayed....

Andriv's hands ceased their struggling. His stare rolled back toward Anna, pure and hopeful in the afterglow of birth, glimpsing her as though it were the first time. "By the Grove," he whispered.

She did not pause to examine his smile, nor to cherish the light that now swelled in his glistening eyes. She lifted the blade, angled its tip between his eyes, and thrust downward.

Everything grew still.

Turning away from the body, Anna realized that she was not breathing, that the stifled croaking in the air was not her own. "Are you all right?" she whispered.

He made no reply.

"Konrad," she said, glancing sidelong at his robes and shadowed face. His back rose and fell in weak cycles. "Konrad, speak to me."

"Are you hurt?" he mumbled.

"Look at me."

"Hurt," he said. "Are you hurt, Anna?" Fluid crackled in his throat.

"No."

"Good." Gasping feebly, he slumped forward and rested his forehead on Andriv's chest. A steady rattle pervaded his breaths. "It's my fault, Anna. I was wrong. About them and him, I mean, and—"

"Enough." Her tears did not feel like her own. It had been so long since she'd cried, since the feeling mind had intruded on her suffering. "Give me your arm, would you?"

A rivulet of blood drained from his lips.

"Give me your arm," she hissed. "Don't be stubborn."

"You're wasting time."

"Let's go, Konrad."

He sputtered, stippling Andriv's robes with red blots. "This will be easy for me," he whispered. "A long rest." His lips, trembling and crimson, edged toward a grin. "Finally."

"We're not finished yet." She swiped at her eyes, at once angry and perplexed. "Don't you *hear* me?"

"Your Apiary was right," he said.

"No, it wasn't."

"My path…it was here, always here." The rattling swelled to a constant, mechanical *click*, echoing beneath shouts and ear-cracking blasts. "Yours is somewhere else, Anna. Somewhere there. So go."

"We just need to leave," she said. "We, us."

But the rattling faded away and his robes did not shift, and his eyes lingered on the cracks between tiles, where his blood pooled in thin, glossy threads.

Anna braced her hands on her thighs and leaned back. "Us," she whispered.

Canisters exploded in the distance, clouding the corridor and dulling her hearing once more, but it did not matter. Death was so near, so welcoming. So simple.

She focused her bleary stare on the silhouettes storming through the haze, waiting for their iron to eviscerate her. There was no fear in that moment, only the promise of liberation, the end of some wicked dream. She studied their forms as they loomed nearer: sleek limbs, wrapped shawls, bulbous packs.

They would not grant her death.

The Nahorans flowed around her like a living wall, fanning out to the furthest reaches of the corridor, the edges of alcoves, the shadows of every passage and doorway in sight. Their efficiency—so swift and orderly in the midst of collapse—verged on incomprehensible.

"Kuzalem," a woman barked, hurrying to Anna's side with a ruj slung across her back. Once kneeling, she tore away her black covering to reveal dark hair and piercing eyes. Ashoral's gaze was neither frantic not tranquil; it reflected the even vigilance she had carried in realms of peace and violence alike. "Are you capable of walking?"

Anna nodded, still transfixed by the easterner's eyes. Had they ever known devastation? Had they wept?

"Come," Ashoral said, offering her hand as she examined both avenues of the corridor.

"Where is Lukas?" The easterner studied her face, frowning, and only then did Anna realize that she'd spoken the name before considering it. Her hands shook upon her lap as she examined the motions of the thinking mind, the adherence to the path that the Apiary had laid before her. *He* had been present in those visions, an irreplaceable cog in things to come. Sacred, somehow. The mere impulse to abandon him clouded her mind with murderous vignettes. "The tracker," she corrected, sickened by her words, her obedience. "We can't leave him."

"Time is bleeding away, Kuzalem."

She looked at Konrad's body. "We can't."

"If we return for him—"

"If he falls into their hands," Anna cut in, meeting Ashoral's eyes with sudden clarity, "he's certain to surrender his knowledge."

The ga'mir turned to one of her fighters and grimaced, surely acknowledging the truth that was woven into Nahora's fighters: Most captives would supply—or betray—anything of value to ease their torment. One of Volna's former leaders would have no qualms with such an exchange. In fact, he might welcome it.

And the depths of Lukas's knowledge far exceeded the business of war.

Ashoral shouted a string of Orsas, sending her fighter darting down one of the corridor's bisecting passageways. She glanced back at Anna, wary. "He will be retrieved," she said gravely, "but any further delay is fatal. Stand, Kuzalem, and protest no further. Compliance will be your survival." The ga'mir extended her hand.

Anna took it.

Chapter 13

Wind howled through the rooftop crenellations. It was a living assault on Anna's flesh, a ruthless barrage of grit and mica, billowing up from the darkness far beyond the compound's expanse. Within its wailing, the lower floors' screams and supersonic thumps and huffing flames fused into the voice of fear.

It was the voice everything Leejadal had repressed and left to rot in the war's aftermath.

Anna pressed her cloak to her mouth and shut her eyes, her attention anchored to the tactile shifts accompanying each step. Indeed, she carved a path forward by the press of her boots alone. Years in the monastery had kept her rooted to such mundane movements, but now her attention was frayed, split between memories of a southerner's face, a faraway *kales*, the vast, gaping void—

"Kuzalem, remain with us," Ashoral shouted. Her voice was a whisper among the gusts.

She peered through scrunched lids, saw the black forms of the borzaq hurrying through sheets of fizzling ocher.

Leejadal's skyline rose in black slats before her, as ominous and alien as the monoliths she'd once glimpsed in dreams. Directly ahead was the spire that appeared to slice the world into mirrored halves, its setstone peak ascending through the shroud, through the gloom of churning cloud cover, up and beyond the celestial realms unknown to the living.

Anna wondered, in thoughts that she despised and was quick to dispatch, whether Konrad and her brother Julek and all the others resided there. She had seen too much to believe in those fantasies; she had seen the brutal truth of emptiness, of nothingness.

What could this world offer her?

The storm suddenly dwindled, wilting as though gathering ancient breath, its gusts whining and tracing serpents into mounds of sand. Darkness faded to billows of cloudy amber. A lantern's ethereal glow materialized at the end of the platform, blanketing a nerash's hull in dim, freckled light.

A pair of Ashoral's borzaq fighters pried open the latches along the side of the craft, releasing the main doors with a wisp of pressurized air. Crimson light filled the nerash's cabin as filaments sparked to life within looping glass tubes.

Anna trudged onward, the wind rising in her ears once more. Vague shapes hurried around her, taking up positions behind chimney stacks, low walls, reinforced domes. Everything seemed to be an extension of the sand, whirling, spiraling, and decomposing in grainy vapors. Mere paces from the nerash, she spotted Ashoral within the cabin.

The ga'mir was waving her closer, shouting something that the storm was swift to bury.

A blast rang out at Anna's back. It reached her as a rolling clap, a wave that kicked through her and suspended the grit in momentary stillness.

She was running before she understood the noise. Before she experienced fear, in fact. Wind roared in tandem with the southern cries. She pushed herself to move faster, lower, to ignore the iron that whistled past her and gouged at the nerash's outer plates. Her boot caught the lip of the doorway; she slammed forward, ribs and knees and hands striking metal, her breaths stolen in an instant. Hands seized her robe and dragged her into stillness, away from that whipping maw.

"Don't go," Anna breathed. Her words barely emerged. "Wait for him." Rolling over, she found herself staring up at the strange bulbs, at borzaq fighters shifting about and sidling toward the doorway.

Even Ashoral was leaning out of the craft, her shoulder thumping back as she cycled through the ruj's bolt cartridges.

"We can't go," Anna said, louder this time.

Ashoral glanced at her over a padded shoulder. "He will be extracted."

The floor panels began to rattle beneath Anna. Then came the engines' mewling inhale, the nose-prickling sparksalt fumes.

Anna sat up against a dividing wall, her head pounding. "Wait."

"We will not convene here," Ashoral replied, her voice gaining an edge of reproach. "Ready yourself, Kuzalem—our aim will be achieved. But now is the time of resolve."

Craning her head toward the nearest window, Anna saw their end approaching:

Dozens of ruji ignited, scarring the haze with dark blemishes.

Iron sparked through the cabin. Glass tubes popped in cloudy pink wisps. Several fighters slumped over, their faces reduced to oozing flaps, as the cabin door began its descent. Grit flooded the nerash, swooping into the forming vacuum like the Apiary's wasps.

Anna touched her face, brought her fingers away with smears of bright blood.

"*Sheluk!*" Ashoral's command reverberated through the sealed cabin, vanishing into silence so sudden that it was unsettling, almost maddening.

Ruji fire crackled along the hull as the engines flared, their collective force punching down into the craft's landing skids, bleeding out through an undercarriage of elastic cables and cylinders.

Anna braced herself, waiting....

There was a snap at the nerash's rear, a sudden *whump* as the cogs locked in place and shifted the chambers. They rocketed upward, gravity receding in an instant, the air itself condensing, stiffening.

Her stomach ached, dense with acid and primal confusion.

She'd barely grasped the overhead cording when the nerash banked hard to the right, slamming her shoulder against the wall. The impact was numb, only made prominent by the sheer absence of pain. As she steadied herself, she watched the world shift beyond the windows, the burnished cityscape drifting in and out of twisting shrouds, ascending, sinking in rhythm with the craft's maneuvers. It took her a moment—and the sight of smoke bleeding from blown-out windows—to recognize the fortress they were circling. She had never witnessed the compound's exterior.

"Where is he?" Anna asked.

Ashoral stood near the cabin door, hair plastered across her blood-speckled face, one hand bracing her ruj and the other wound up in cording. She was studying the compound with remarkable composure. "There," she said decisively, nodding toward an arrangement of terraces. She lowered her weapon, retrieved a small stone from her pocket, and examined it as the craft dipped toward the upper levels. "We won't have a second opportunity, Kuzalem. Understand this well."

But Anna perceived only the stone. Its mint shade was diffusing, darkening toward emerald in the easterner's palm.

A tracking stone for a tracker.

The terrace fanned out below, all of its statues and shell-gouged craters gaining vivid clarity as their nerash pierced the haze. Borzaq fighters clustered near the doors, kneeling, murmuring, shouldering their ruji with unblinking focus.

The landing skids crunched over stone, grating up through the floor panels, through the soles of Anna's boots.

Dust wafted past the window, unveiling a sprawl of silent killing: Fighters dismembering one another, black wads of smoke twisting skyward, hayat manifesting as prismatic flails and ethereal warbling.

The main door hissed open.

Screeches and charred air flooded the cabin, shattering the quiet that had enveloped them like a dreamscape. Synchronous ruji fire erupted from Ashoral and her unit. Within moments, however, slugs tore through a fighter in the doorway; his body jerked and slumped out of the craft.

Holding firm to the cording above, Anna crouched lower and studied the encroaching slaughter. Her heart hammered in the base of her throat, driving her mind toward rage, toward thoughtless panic. *Where was he?* Every shadow and spark leaped out at her within the carnage, melding into formless clouds, dividing—

It all vanished in a black shell.

The air thinned and windows cracked and the nerash bucked, the old minutiae of scraping and breathing lost to a wavering ring in Anna's ears. She touched her own lips, her cheeks, unsure if she had died in that sudden mask of smoke. But the world returned to her in faint measure, drawing her attention to the bare presence of her senses, of life. She staggered toward the doorway with her hands at her side, devoid of fear, of any need to exist. Ashoral was speaking to her, thin trails of blood running down the curves of her neck, but Anna was focused on what had endured through the blast. She noted the cracking emerald stone lying near a borzaq fighter's body, glanced out at the haze.

A lone figure was shuffling toward the nerash—a man, tall, naked, his rune and torpid essence glowing with bittersweet familiarity.

Anna shrank away without knowing why. It was him, after all, and she had sought him out. *Hadn't she?* It was only when the haze sifted apart, sharpening her vision of Lukas and his labored steps, that she understood: Without a face, he had been a monster, not a man.

Now there was no illusion.

No refuge.

Reality did not wait for her to embrace its defilement. Several borzaq fighters rushed out to meet the marked man, hoisting him up and hauling him into the cabin in seconds. The door shut with a squeal of air, a crushing stillness. Blood pattered down from the ceiling.

Anna watched him with her lips pursed, struggling to reconcile his matted amber hair and broad, swollen ears with the fiction she'd constructed in her mind. She wished that the fighters would continue to encircle him, perhaps sealing him away behind some new veil. She wished that he would remain on his stomach. Most of all, she wished she understood the Apiary's plans.

But wishes seldom came true.

The nerash's engines clapped beneath her, severing her thoughts as the craft shuddered and sprang skyward. She gripped the cording with both hands, her eyes shut to the nauseating blur of the storm and webbed glass, leaning into every lurch and pivot of their ascent. She only dared to peek when the cylinders ceased their screaming, leveling out to a steady burn over rooftop bazaars and obsidian mausoleums.

The spire was still etched into the skyline, firm and precise against clouds of shifting beige. A dark bead plummeted down from its heights, burning a swath into the storm, drawing Anna's eye toward a fading compound.

She saw the impact before she heard it: an expansive bulb of cinnamon and tar, a shock wave filtering out through the streets, leveling structures, statues, entire blocks of tents and awnings, consuming everything in its wake. A deep, horrid groan engulfed the nerash.

Suddenly she felt a gulf in her chest, a terrible longing for things and faces she had never encountered.

But the impacts continued to blossom throughout the city—near, far, in districts known and unknown. There was no longer a safe house, no longer the sanctified jinkaral, no longer anything that had once held mercy for Anna.

There was only obliteration.

"Do not look upon it," Ashoral said darkly, her footsteps thudding nearer. Distant explosions thumped and snapped as she sidled into Anna's periphery. "We must endure now, Kuzalem. This is what we are called to do."

There was nowhere comforting for her to look. The world itself tore through every barrier she'd constructed.

Perhaps, then, the only salvation was to destroy her own boundaries.

Anna pulled in a long breath and worked her way down the cabin, wordlessly passing borzaq fighters with soot and blood smeared across their faces. She moved from cord to cord, her eyes intent on Lukas. She studied his back's tremors, splotches, jutting ribs—and fear. That was it, wasn't it? The way he writhed upon the panels, turning away from light and eyes alike. Fear. It should have strengthened Anna, but it only chilled her. A frightened thing was a living thing, a pitiful thing.

And he did not deserve her pity.

That realization sparked something deep in her chest. It was disdain beyond words, stitched from memories she'd long since abandoned. Memories of what he had done and where he had taken her and how he had used her, gutted her. How dare he expect her to feel anything for him? He was a beast, and he could not feel anything—not truly, anyway. It was another work of theater, another fiction. Emotion was the sharpest tool for the dead-hearted.

"Stand up," Anna said flatly. She moved closer, noting Lukas's fingers curl and scratch over metal. "Stand."

"Kuzalem," Ashoral said. "He will be restrained."

Anna bent down, aware, yet unafraid of her restraint bleeding away. She reached out and gripped Lukas's chin. His flesh was warm and sickening. Then she wrenched his head to the side, her eyes piercing, her jaw aching with—

Red, glistening eyes stared back at her.

Sallow flesh, a wide nose, dark, ragged scars running from his forehead to his lips.

Anna's hand jerked away. She stood, wandered back through the cabin, faced Ashoral with bile in her throat. Sensations arose, but she did not allow them to coagulate in consciousness, to color her mind with anything other than hatred. Without hatred, there was chaos. There was everything her boundaries had held at a distance, suppressing and twisting and denying to grant her some measure of peace after so long.

"Take him to the rear brig," Anna said in a low voice.

Ashoral nodded, gesturing to fighters behind Anna. "You wish to speak with him?"

"No," she whispered, "but I will."

* * * *

For several hours she lay on a cot, staring up at the craft's warped alloy ceiling. She'd resided in that curious cleft between awareness and unconsciousness, her thoughts trickling into dreams and vice versa, every waking moment plagued with memories of burlap and hayat's monoliths. When she eventually rose and stood before the windows, twilight had deepened to full blackness, and they were drifting somewhere above southern Hazan. The land below was flat and arid.

She focused on the warmth in her palms, the breath rolling in and out through her nose. There was stillness in her mind, but it was of the dull, numbing variety. It carried none of the serenity she had known in the monastery. Thoughts of Konrad welled up in her, but the thinking mind crushed them and scattered them to the fringes of awareness.

Not now, she assured herself. Perhaps never.

There was still too much to consider. It now seemed bizarre to have spent so long with the tracker—an easier name to stomach than Lukas—without ever confronting the shadows that had lingered in his presence: Words unspoken, days forgotten, crimes absolved. And why now, of all times? She did not need closure; she had told herself this, anyway, and it had been sufficient for the intervening years. She had reached deeper states than most of the Moraharem, and she had glimpsed truths that the Kojadi themselves had overlooked. So why now?

The answer arrived while she was gazing through glass, through her haggard reflection.

Soon he will be undone.

There was no need to analyze the answer. It had come from a reservoir deep within her, resounding with its own logic, its own proof.

The tracker would be erased and there would only be a man.

A reborn man, an unconditioned man, existing within a conditioned body.

Such an answer did not appease her. What of her rage? Where would it go? Much like secrets intended for the dead, forever buried in scrolls and sour hearts, that rage would endure as terrible longing. It had to be manifested while it was still possible. And if not manifested, transmuted.

But into what?

She left the bunkroom, the question still playing through her mind, and went to the brig.

Ashoral had not posted anybody near the door, though Anna suspected that was a pragmatic decision. Only ten fighters had survived the takeoff, and two of them had been relegated to the sole suturer's care, their stomachs packed with gauze and stitches.

Anna studied Lukas through the latticework of bars and welded panels. She'd seen his head bob slightly when she stepped into view, but now he feigned disinterest, perhaps even sleep.

He was slumped against the far wall with his knees tucked to his chest, his head bowed, bathing in a patchwork of dim, bluish light and shadow. He wore the linen tunic and trousers that the easterners had provided. His rune pulsed steadily.

"They say Jenis turned tail," he said.

Anna moved to the bars and rested her hands on them. They were colder than she expected. "He did."

"Your boy in white, too." He clicked through his teeth. "Yet you've got me in a cage."

"Nobody's aims are beyond questioning."

"Maybe," he said, "but have the straight way of it, Anna: This affair's not orbiting me."

"Pain follows you."

"Does it?" he asked. "When I was in their cell, they went on about what happened to Nuhra. Chewed up, far as they could tell. Not even the Grove would take that body." His terse breathing drowned out the silence. "They dunno know how it happened, of course. Nobody but us knows why she went in there. Well, nobody but you."

"Get to the heart of it."

"See, she whispered a lot in my ears. Things that would turn the stars over. She told me your girl could cut into your mind, see what you want, where you're resting your pretty legs. Just a few days back, I called her cracked." He shrugged. "Seems she had the truth."

Anna gripped the bars till her knuckles throbbed. "What would you know about truth?"

"I just know how to follow a trail."

"And what?" she demanded. "Does it make you pure?"

"Everyone else tried to carve you up, when it came down to it," Lukas said. "But not me. Nothing more to be said, nothing less."

"You've done far worse."

"Still came to me. Tongues flap and twist, girl, but you've known my banner this whole way." He snorted, straightened. "Come to think of it, I used to know an herbman who said that the cruelest deed was to bundle wicker 'round your heart. Birth to death, never showing anyone that pulsing little core. Well, you know my heart. More than you can say for the others."

"Perhaps you assume too much," Anna said. "You couldn't possibly understand the goodness of someone's heart."

"Someone like Konrad?" he growled. His name was vinegar and needles. "Brother Konrad. Where's he now? Jenis's side, same as the rest?"

Anna listened to her breaths sharpening, shortening. "He's dead."

"Ah," Lukas said. "Finally showed his heart, then."

"He went back to find me." Pressure swelled behind her eyes. She had not recalled that moment—that slow, painful separation—until now. "He died for me."

Lukas dropped into an unusually long silence, wringing his hands upon his knees, nodding. In anybody else, it would've been discomfort. "Expect me to sing a song for him, then?"

"No. I don't expect anything from you."

"Strange visit, then," he said. "Eastern korpy said you dragged me out of there, too."

"We all have our aims."

"Here to skin me, then? Maybe—"

"The Apiary showed me my path," she said coldly. "It revealed every being, step, and action that lies between me and my task. You are nothing but a stepping-stone. Understand that and do not deceive yourself: Your existence is the means to an end."

"You're more cracked than she was."

Anna loosened her grip. "They'll tell you when we land."

She turned away and started back down the corridor, imagining his stare as it crawled over her back and shoulders.

"All these years," he said, "and you never asked to see what was underneath."

She paused mid-step, glanced back. "It wouldn't have changed anything."

"You were never even curious."

"I was," she said, "but everyone has their reasons."

He drew a sharp breath. "Reasons?"

"To be afraid."

His sigils took on a nervous, dancing edge.

"It made you weak," she continued softly, striding toward the bars once more. "That's all a mask does, you know—it proves that your fear has beaten you. Why else would you seal yourself away?"

"Clever girl."

She had expected him to lash out at that, to curse her. Her breath hung in her throat. "I hope you live in fear."

He nodded, sighed. "Haven't been scared in a long while."

"You would be, if you looked closely," Anna said. "Do you see mirrors in your dreams?"

"Eh?"

She blinked at him with a slate expression. "All this time, you were never hiding your scars from the world." He did not look back at her. "You were hiding them from yourself."

"Finished?"

Anna lingered in the corridor's crimson glow. She was unsure if she had finished, unsure if she had done anything at all. It took her several moments to notice the subtle, yet persistent tic in Lukas's brow. "Yes," she said at last.

The seed was there, after all, and it would sprout and bloom when his mind was at its weakest. It would worm its way into every fissure of his memories—she knew that all too well herself. Her realization did not bring pride, however; it left her hollow, haunted. That was the eternal price of possessing a heart.

Anna moved away from the bars. She was not looking at him anymore, either. "Remember to rest."

* * * *

Each plunge into tranquility was marred by the promise of waiting jaws. Several hours of watching the breath had burned away the fetters of time and space alike, leaving her suspended in a realm of formless light, an abode far beyond whatever fears her mind had concocted. There were no longer feelings, nor a body to perceive them. But it was nothing compared to the Apiary's bliss.

There was no true release; there couldn't be.

Release was lethal.

No matter how deep she delved, Ramyi's presence remained with her as an orb of gray light, revolving, circling, whispering at every moment. The Apiary's revelations had awakened something within both of them. Something dormant, something horrifying. Now it was an ordeal to simply obscure herself from Ramyi, let alone combat her awareness.

Within, without—escape was a childish fantasy.

"We've crossed the strait."

Ashoral's voice tore Anna from her rapture, returning her to a world of tense, burdensome flesh and devouring thoughts.

"Are you certain of what you're doing?" the ga'mir continued, approaching Anna's back with graceful steps. Despite her apparent composure, there was an undercurrent of worry in her tone. A suggestion of weariness, even.

"I am," Anna said, though that admission terrified her. She opened her eyes to her window-framed reflection and the silvery clouds beyond it. "You should speak openly with me, Ga'mir. The age of pretense is dead."

Ashoral's blotted form lingered in the glass for a moment, then shifted out of view. "Do you believe in eternity?"

"I've felt it."

"Yet it now exists beyond your reach," the easterner said. "Is it not so?"

"Division is a concept, not an experience."

"Your Kojadi conditioning has told you as much."

Anna lifted her head, breathed in stale air. "Their words have taught me nothing," she explained. "They point toward wisdom, but they do not assume its form."

There was a protracted lull, a moment of pure anticipation as Anna waited for the ga'mir's prodding. Thoughts were never exchanged without purpose. There was always an element of power, of victory in one form or another. But Ashoral's presence was not triumphant—it was broken.

"Does it wound you," Ashoral began quietly, pausing to swallow, to tease out each word, "to know that you held it in your palms, but could not retain it?"

Anna rose from the floor and turned to face Ashoral. The woman's face was ashen, lined with oozing scabs and lesions. "It is not the nature of things to be retained." Anna paused, expecting to counter the easterner's ruthless logic, but Ashoral did not speak. "What answer did you seek?"

"Questions seldom have answers." The ga'mir headed for the doorway.

"I did not speak of divisions as a mental exercise," Anna said. "Make no mistake, Ga'mir: Extinction will not separate us by our flesh. I can hear your mind in turmoil, and I will listen. The others will not."

"You would not understand the way of my mind."

Anna studied the fear bleeding through Ashoral's stance. The same fear that corrupted all creatures, scattering gazes, rattling fingers. "Your mind? Are you the only one who's lost something?"

"Not something," Ashoral said quietly. "Far more than that."

"We've all lost our soul."

"That would have been a small price, Kuzalem." She opened her mouth, paused, finally glanced away. "Forgive me for breaking your concentration."

But Anna's stare did not falter. "Do you look upon me as a machine? Do you think concentration has returned anything the world has taken from me? I'm not broken, but perhaps I should be. Pain is my only constant." She pulled in a slow breath. "Long ago, I learned how to survive: Surrender everything. This world destroys what it wills, and it destroys that which clings to its ruins."

Ashoral leaned into the corridor, gazing back and forth to ensure they were wholly alone, before settling primly on the edge of a nearby cot. "We sought existence and nothing more," she said finally. "Our cause in the flatlands was just."

"You speak as though your cause has ended."

"Perhaps not our cause," she said, "but our lifeblood. The State has no place in this world."

"Your people are resilient."

Ashoral set her hands on her knees. "My people are dead. They are starving. They are ill with a thousand maladies, both of the mind and body." Her eyes lost their focus, staring through the metal panels, through the swirling danha that encircled the craft. "Did you see how easily death came to them?"

"Yet we endure," Anna said. "Their sacrifices will not be in vain."

"I embraced that sentiment when Golyna fell, but hope is brittle, Kuzalem. At least within the city's confines, my people died with the State in their hearts. Now, here, they died like animals. And for what?"

"Existence."

Ashoral's sullen eyes did not brighten. "Are you aware that Nahora blossomed from the branches of the Kojadi?" She shifted her lips, exhaled. "Our forerunners enshrined their knowledge, but they rejected the doctrine of dissolution. Nothing can be built atop sand, after all. They preached that our State would abide in eternity, immune to the floods and fires of time. Our people lived and died on that promise."

Anna's mind swirled with axioms unspoken, with harsh, dogmatic reminders that the world and its contents were little more than the shifting sand Ashoral had disparaged. But she could not bring herself to lecture the easterner. Some lessons were too painful to be taught. They had to be experienced, to be withstood, to be embraced and accepted as intuitively as the flow of the tides.

"I believed in eternity, Kuzalem."

"Believe in what's real," Anna said. "Believe in our task."

"What will remain, should we succeed?"

There was no immediate answer to a question of that nature. Anna had pondered it before, both in waking life and in nightmares of barren fields, but all of her theories were ultimately speculation. Only the Apiary's vignettes—which had terminated with unimaginable finality—were beyond doubt.

"Speak to me," Ashoral said coldly.

Anna blinked, suddenly cognizant of the gray light prowling behind her lids. "The present will remain," she whispered. "The present slept before us, and it will return to its slumber if we pass out of existence, empty of dreams or dreamers. We must remain awake."

"Do you not feel the long sleep calling to you?"

"I do," Anna said. "I always have."

"Perhaps it's time for us to lay our heads down."

"Speak on your own behalf," she said, only noticing her harshness in the silence that followed. "I've lost everything, but my eyes remain open.

If you can't weather the destruction of the State, I will understand. But I'll offer neither praise nor honor."

Ashoral's strength left her in an instant. She bent forward, bracing her elbows upon her knees, staring forth absently. "Without the State, there—"

"Have you witnessed a sunrise? Tasted honey? What about holding a babe?"

"Kuzalem, please."

"Phenomena remain, with or without the walls you've constructed around them. *That* is the only certainty. But if you desert me in this hour, all things will return to the void of the uncreated." She fixed the gray light in her mind's eye, studying it, tasting it.... "This is your choice, Ga'mir."

Ashoral's nostrils dithered, flaring out, shrinking in. Her eyes listlessly combed the panels. Despite the quarters' fume-laden heat, her shoulders were bunched and shivering.

Until that moment, Anna had considered the resolve—indeed, the cutting, silent equanimity—of the borzaq to transcend mortal fetters. It was a dormant force waiting behind stone veneers, fueled by childhoods bereft of mercy, of pity, of thoughts that did not concern the State and its desires. But the ga'mir's demeanor hinted at the embers they had failed to extinguish. It hinted at humanity.

And although Anna saw herself in the easterner, and she felt her pain as if it were her own, there was nothing to be done. The will to persist could not be impressed upon another mind; by its very nature, it had to be seized.

When Ashoral rose from the cot, Anna understood her choice.

"Your words are illuminating," the ga'mir said, unable to meet Anna's eyes directly. Shame was always a warrior's most severe wound. "I should prepare the others for the task ahead."

A smile warped the corner of Anna's lips.

"Are we drawing close?" Ashoral added.

Anna shut her eyes and surveyed the formless expanse before her. An ethereal hum stirred at the edge of awareness, beckoning her nearer, nearer, into the vast web of the Apiary's whispers.

Her presence strained toward the core, toward truth.

Filaments of her being stretched, aching—

Gray light exploded through her. *Just where I thought you were,* Ramyi cooed. *Don't be alarmed, Anna. I know precisely where you're going. There's no need to run any farther—just rest now.*

Anna did not shy away from the presence, nor did she turn inward. She studied her fear with the impassive lens of the Kojadi, no longer a victim, but a watcher. *You've warned me many times,* she whispered to Ramyi, *but this warning is mine.*

Her mind sank deeper into that limitless space. Energy raked up her spine, coursing through folds of tendons and brain matter, flowing around the gray spark that now revolved in the crux of awareness. Blissful warmth throbbed along her fingers. Then a kernel of pure light materialized before her, its threads expanding and overtaking the gray disc within her mind's eye. White fire purged the somber shades, the cacophony of voices, the dreadful presence that spoke of ripping flesh and writhing maggots.

Ramyi's presence vanished.

Anna opened her eyes, but the nerash's interior was not what it had been. Moments prior, it had been sparse, even claustrophobic, and crowded with rows of flickering crimson tubes. Now it was a sphere of raw light and motion and dazzling colors, a domain of stillness and infinite wonder that occurred to her as a return rather than an ascent. It was as though she had always known this place, had always been a part of its fabric, but had simply forgotten the trail home.

"Kuzalem?" Ashoral was now standing over her, frantic, searching for whatever intangible force had taken hold. "Can you hear me?"

"We should alter our course," Anna said.

"Have you seen something?"

"Alter it."

But the world functioned in a trance that did not impede the mind. Its torpor trickled all around Anna, dragging, resisting, wasting precious moments. She envisioned a fox's paw sinking onto a spring-loaded plate, oblivious to the waiting iron teeth....

An ear-splitting crack rang out beyond the windows.

Banking heavily, the nerash moaned through its cylinders and lanced downward. Metal crates and scrolls and bundled packs cascaded down from the storage racks. Ashoral slammed to the floor, grunting, grasping at anything rooted around her.

Anna clung to the cot's iron bars until her fingers burned from the torque. She watched the clouds whipping past, the bright flashes of shells, the sills of fog and frost that crept up the glass as they swooped lower.

Wind screeched over the wingtips.

Shrapnel tore through the canopy and hull with hissing claps.

Cold, violent wind streaked past Anna's face, cluttering her vision with a tangle of blond hair and tattered fabric. Her mind danced around the litany of protocols the tinkerers had mentioned during her first flight: *If it's in free fall, seek shelter in the back.* Or was it against the sides?

The windowpanes cracked and burst.

Boundaries dissolved in an instant; the skies came howling in, bone-chilling, glittering with crushed glass and nascent snow crystals.

Anna's head struck iron.

The world revolved, but it did not vanish.

There was a vast, impossible tundra, knotted with the shapes of distant herds and their pursuers. Her breaths whirled before her. She was exhausted, worn down in the thickest marrow of her bones, every limb shuddering and aching. The surrounding snow was stained with red blots—blood, her blood. Limping forth, she noticed the glasslike sheen of her flesh, the ease with which she peered into striated muscles and pockets of cartilage.

I am not a man-skin.

Terror seized her, but she studied it curiously, patiently. It faded as quickly as it had arisen.

I am Huuri.

Blood dribbled down past her navel, over her thighs, her toes.

The world cracked again.

She flailed through dim, cloudy water, her lungs screaming, vision tracking the bubbles that tingled through her lips and climbed toward shifting light, toward air—

A blighted landscape emerged through the clouds. She dove downward, fanning out her wings, scanning for prey—

Her trousers were soaked in piss. She could not scream for help, could not raise her voice to beg for mercy. Her pulsing innards were gathered in her hands. She looked up to find the smoldering eye of a ruj barrel, and beyond that, the pale skin and scarred throat and bright, gold-fire hair of the Southern Death, the one called Kuzalem, the one called Anna—

Everything dimmed to blackness.

She opened her eyes—yes, her own eyes, she could feel their nearness—and glanced around wildly, for it was the only movement she could manage. Crumpled, frost-veined metal hemmed her into a maze of hard angles and shadows. Milky light and snow spilled through gashes in the walls—shattered windows, scarred metal panels, great chasms bridged only by skeletal iron beams, all framed by a backdrop of vague brightness. *The nerash.* Memories returned to her in a fearful rush, a spur of panic. *Ashoral.* The quarters were canted, perhaps wholly rolled over, though Anna could not tell which way was up or down, above or below, left or right.

Her entire body throbbed. Blinding pain rocketed up her limbs and nested in her joints, blazing garnet red every time she shut her eyes, blinked, breathed.

Survive.

Anna wriggled her foot; the shushing of fabric was an ocean wave in the stillness. The stillness. She shut her eyes and recognized the stillness as intimately as Yatrin's touch. Tears streaked down her cheeks, though she did not know why. Stillness. It was like fluid in the air, thin, formless, snaking past ancient oaks and overgrown fields. It carried the faint sounds of life itself: branches creaking and sagging and snapping, swift paws treading over powder, fathers calling for their daughters.

Focus, she reminded herself. She had heard such voices before. Some had spoken during midnight meditation, haunting her on the precipice of sleep, while others had awoken in the uncanny silence of Hazan's flats.

But she was tired, so tired, and rest was so near....

Konrad, Nuhra, Yatrin, Shem, Bora—their faces formed and unraveled on the stage of consciousness, dancing before her, welcoming her into endless reprieve.

Do not rest. The voice cut through the froth of pain and dullness, so clear that it seemed to manifest in the very seed of Anna's mind. *Awaken and go forth.*

She sat up, straining toward her toes in spite of the stabbing pulses down her spine. Cramps tore through her stomach. Every nerve and muscle worked against her, prickling, jerking. She pushed herself onto her knees, nearly biting through her tongue with the effort, then stood with her body flat against a crunched wall panel. The metal numbed her cheeks and palms.

The quarters were strewn with snowcapped remains—most of them shredded, dented, singed—but the dark form of a body made itself known. It was gangly and lopsided, its bronze flesh poking up through cool blue mounds, still emanating rare, thin wisps of breath.

"Ga'mir," Anna croaked, edging along the wall with leaden fingers. "Ashoral, can you hear me?"

There was only the mewling call of the winds, the skittering of snow over ice.

Anna picked her steps over crates and canisters, approaching the easterner's body with silence that felt increasingly absurd, if not wasted. Breaths did not guarantee survival. She squatted down beside a tangle of dark hair and cracked shoulder plates, then gently turned the ga'mir's face toward herself, guiding her hands by sight alone.

Ashoral's lids quivered like those in the grips of fever. Her lips were dark and turgid. Anna ran her fingers across the woman's forehead, whispering soft promises to preserve her, but the stillness persisted. Shallow breaths crept in, bled out.

"Wake up," Anna whispered to her. She lifted Ashoral's hands from the snow and swaddled them in her robes. "You can't go yet. We aren't finished."

Yet, even as she worked to rub life into sallow flesh, she found herself dwelling on the inevitable: Death was always near. Her gestures began to feel mechanical, almost ritualized. She had seen life vanish often enough to understand the frailty of a body.

But Ashoral opened her eyes.

She had the alert, disoriented stare of an animal, her pupils swollen to black buttons.

"There," Anna said, stunned herself. "Keep your eyes open. Don't let them close, do you understand?"

Air creaked down into Ashoral's throat. She nodded.

Anna clasped the woman's hands and glanced upward and tried to stop shaking. "I need to find help." Yes, that was a good start. It was what one did when death was circling. "Can you move?"

Ashoral pinched her eyes shut, seemingly against a swell of pain. "No," she managed.

"It's all right." She rested a hand on the easterner's shoulder, then searched the heaps scattered around her. There was a folded wool blanket beneath trays of ration tins. Anna pulled it free, brushed away a film of snow, and draped it over Ashoral's back.

"You should go," Ashoral said quietly. "They will come."

"We can resist them."

"No. The Starsent knows."

"Just wait," Anna said, rising to her full height before the easterner could protest. "Don't sleep and keep your hands close to you. I'm here. I'm staying here."

She staggered into the nerash's crumpled corridor, where ink and blood coated the wall panels like the cave drawings she'd found as a child. *Did I find them?* There was a fine divide between her own memories and visions, but she could barely sense it now.

Footsteps scraped behind the walls. Before Anna could even locate the source of the noise, metal squelched and groaned to her immediate left. A door drifted open on bent hinges.

Two borzaq fighters stumbled out of the blackness, their faces blank and streaked with blood, muddied by cobalt shadows. They held their weapons at their sides. Behind them were the shapes of mangled bodies, some twisted over on themselves and others torn in two, all without breath, without movement to discern them from fallen tins and scrolls.

"Is this it?" Anna asked, her stare sweeping from fighter to fighter.

"We should make haste," the taller fighter said.

"Not without the others," she replied. "Ashoral needs attention. One of you should see to her."

"That may not be wise," the other said.

Anna studied their faces, noting the grim, wordless efficiency she had always associated with the borzaq. She understood their sentiment well enough—a hound's bark always preceded its bite.

The shorter fighter drew a small compass from a leather pouch strapped to her thigh. "There's a garrison less than ten leagues east of here."

"Ten leagues," the tall fighter repeated sourly. "They'll be on us before nightfall."

Their comrade pocketed the compass. "That's why urgency is of the essence."

"We can't leave without them," Anna said, though such words felt feeble when she saw the resolve in their eyes. Survival did not require mercy; victory did not demand compassion. "I need help."

"Come with us," the shorter fighter said. "Our task was issued and it shall be completed."

A bitter moan echoed from the opposite end of the craft.

Anna spun on her heels, though what she found did not frighten her. In fact, it suffused her chest with curious warmth. She spotted the tracker squirming in his cage, his head lolling against the wall, fingers dangling through iron bars. He had never been so pathetic, nor any more deserving of death. It was the end she had fantasized about during those early years, those nights when rage and hatred and blood had dominated her mind. When agony had seemed like the sole panacea for all the wrongs he had committed. This was the end he had earned, after all: Sealed away like a beast, unwanted, left to howl for whatever wicked men came to inflict suffering upon him. It was the culmination of a young girl's prayers and offerings and hopes.

But the thinking mind did not share that girl's delight. He was a tool to the Apiary—she had not lied about that—and tools were not to be discarded. They were to be used, to be worn down. Only then could they be tossed aside.

"Fetch me his key," Anna said to the fighters, clutching at the aching bruises along her own ribcage. "One of you should see to Ashoral's wounds."

Lukas was a prowling beast at Anna's side, pointedly studying her bloodstained robes and bruised flesh as they approached the crew quarters. His stare was reminiscent of those she'd observed among packs of thin-tongued coyotes: focused, pitiless, hungry. But those were thoughtless; his was calculated.

"Just give me your arm," he sighed.

Anna tightened her fist around the key. Its chipped point protruded between her fingers like a fifth knuckle. "There's no need."

"You're limping."

"Don't concern yourself with me," she said, suppressing a grunt as her innards throbbed.

"No way we'll cover any ground like this," Lukas said. "Even if those legs keep pace, they'll follow the blood. Give me an arm."

She despised the thought of his aid nearly as much as realizing his words had merit. It wasn't as though she had a choice in acceptance, however: It was becoming impossible to avoid her broken, shambling gait.

"I'm fine," Anna whispered.

By the time they returned to Ashoral, the light beyond the nerash had dimmed considerably. The fighters were huddled over her body with gauze and tinctures and needles lying nearby, their hands flowing briskly amid shadows, passing hushed Orsas between dusk's whistling breezes.

Lukas wandered closer. "Stitching a corpse, aren't you?"

"Enough," Anna hissed. She knelt beside the fighters and tried to ignore the bloody smears on their hands. "How is she?"

"She will not survive," the taller fighter said.

That truth should not have stung as much as it did. Dealings in Hazan had been circuitous, so blanketed in mistruths and euphemisms that she'd forgotten the way of a frank tongue. Perhaps it had always been that way, she considered. Witnessing death was far easier than acknowledging its approach.

"Kuzalem," the other said presently. "Ga'mir Ashoral would not trade her life for our task."

"She isn't making that choice," Anna said.

"I am." Ashoral could barely speak; her words terminated in a popping wheeze. "Leave me. Death will not squander its opportunity."

Anna glared at the easterner's sluggish lids. "If they come—"

"They will," Ashoral cut in. "But I will bleed them for their choice."

The taller fighter stood, unwrapping the suturing thread around their wrist and casting it aside. "Gather up your supplies."

"Nobody is to be abandoned," Anna said quietly.

"Let it go," Lukas said, his footsteps clanging nearer. "Slim chance we'll make it anywhere with your rattled bones, let alone *hers*."

The shorter fighter, still attending to Ashoral's lower back, glanced up at that. "How severe are your wounds?"

"It's nothing," Anna said.

"Over ten leagues, nothing becomes everything," the fighter replied.

"It's *fine*," Anna said. "Lift her up."

The fighters did not move. Instead, they looked to Ashoral expectantly, their faces unaffected, resolute.

"Seek refuge in the nearby hills," Ashoral whispered, straining to peer at Anna through bloodshot eyes. Her ensuing commands were a flood of Orsas, at once forceful and soft. Her fighters listened with due reverence, nodding. "They will return for you, Kuzalem." Breath whined through her lips. "They will return."

"Yes, they will," Anna said. "And they'll find *us*."

"Cease this," Ashoral groaned. "Blood demands a body. Kowak's men will hunt until they have their kill."

"You know who they intend to kill," Anna whispered.

Ashoral shut her eyes. "And I," she breathed, "will ensure that they fail."

"There we have it," Lukas said, clapping his hands will a tinny echo. "Death for the dying, breath for the breathing." He turned away and started toward the corridor.

Anna scowled. "Where are you going?"

"Not much time to pick the bodies clean," Lukas called back. "Pair of helping hands is always welcome."

Anna could only blink at Ashoral, at the bright blood seeping into snow, at the fighters standing and stuffing their packs. Again, she remembered the coyotes that had stalked the hills south of her home, gazing aimlessly— perhaps pacing, panting, licking themselves—as their kin withered before them. Kojadi words tugged at her thoughts: *Pain is birthed within the perceiver, never the perceived.* She had waited years for that axiom to provide solace. The war should have made death easier, even mundane, but it had only made it more senseless. Countless bodies, countless families, all ruined in the name of lasting peace—and where was it now?

Perhaps it was better to scourge it all, to begin from ashes....

Anna seized the roots of that thought before it could mature, holding it apart from herself, dissecting it. A chill burrowed through her chest.

"Kuzalem." Ashoral's broken voice roused Anna from her dwelling. "Leave me my ruj."

"You don't need to remain," Anna said.

"My ruj."

"Your garrison can return for all of us," she pressed on. "With or without a body, she'll know that I live. If you—"

"Do not tarnish my end," Ashoral snapped.

Anna held her tongue, resigned to the fire in the easterner's stare. Nothing could turn a Nahoran away from their path to death—or so she assured herself. She stepped back and watched the fighters going about their work, stalking in and out of the quarters, leaving swollen leather packs within Ashoral's reach. Anna did not need to imagine their contents: Shalna's supersonic crackling had been seared into her mind.

"Do you have kin?" Anna asked faintly.

"I did," Ashoral said.

"The State will embrace you," Anna replied, though the words did not stir in her heart, in her soul. The easterner lifted her head; her eyes were swollen, gleaming. "It will not end with you."

"Guard your speech against such assumptions, Kuzalem."

"It's not an assumption," Anna said. "It's a promise."

Chapter 14

As a child, Anna had heard stories of the hunters that roamed the winter hills. They were hard men, red-cheeked and leather-palmed, draped in the fleshy strips of birch trees. They did not speak the same tongue, her father had told her, for they knew only the tongue of the trees and herds. They gleaned poetry from heartbeats, from the slithering of shadows, from pained breaths. But a man-skin could not understand the language of prey without becoming its domain. Burned figurines, crowns fitted with antlers, breathing that approached hibernation—it was an elaborate dance, a merging with the fields and groves that surrounded them. Once they reached that sacred state, the land itself—or perhaps Chalsuya, the Silent One—made its offerings known. Every trace of life was a ripple upon a still pond.

But as Anna stared out at the mass of dark pines across the valley, her vision coalescing into pockets of blackness and luminescent snow, she realized that she was deaf to that primordial tongue. She could no longer see Ashoral's fighters, nor the subtle trail that their steps had carved away from the nerash's wreckage. Soon she would see nothing at all: Daylight was receding into a veil of stars on the horizon, bringing darkness with neither allegiance nor pity.

She settled into her notch of granite and tried not to think of Ashoral. It was a wasted effort, of course—her mind was shaken by the recurring sense that she had forgotten something, and she knew precisely what it was.

"You're too exposed," Lukas said. Anna glanced sidelong to find him squatting near two holes he'd dug in the frozen soil, his arms laden with kindling and deadwood. "First sukry to come through that pass will tear you apart."

Anna shifted away from the precipice of the overlook, nestling herself deeper among stone and mossy boughs. It was a firm position, or so Lukas had assured her, but it gave her the sense of being bait rather than a watcher. They occupied valuable ground, after all: The forest flattened out below them, sloping into stretches of icy creeks and ravines, and hills formed a thorny crown far in the distance. Anybody determined enough to scale the overlook's slope would find it treacherous, yet feasible, especially under the cover of darkness.

"What's that for?" Anna asked, nodding at Lukas's pile of sticks. "We can't make a fire."

"Never been in a forest fight, have you?"

She shook her head.

"*Chodge.*" He began packing kindling into the base of the first hole, followed by a mound of thin cotton strips and evergreen needles. Using his knife and a block of flint, he set the pile aflame, then covered it with a crude lattice of branches. Finally, he laid smooth, flat stones across the branches. "Not a trace of smoke."

"No heat, either," Anna said.

Lukas grunted. "Give it some time. Hot stone's your only god on nights like this."

It was hard to imagine that any gods could reside in such a place.

"Come closer," Lukas said, hanging his hands over the branches and stones. "Chill's only going to worsen."

Anna pulled her wool blanket higher across her shoulders. "I'm fine where I am."

"Now you're just being stubborn. Nothing new, I suppose."

"We should keep our voices down."

"Those shells didn't soar 'til we were over the foothills," Lukas said. "Long fucking march to here, even without the snow. Sit back, be easy. We've got time."

Time. What use was time when it was all thrown away?

"So what happened to your lot?" Lukas asked, startling her.

She had a suspicion of what he meant, but she did not want to think about that, let alone speak of it. "My lot."

Lukas nodded, rubbing life into his raw, pinkish fingers. "Heard rumors you'd kept thick company during the war." He gestured to the trees and scraggly underbrush around them. "Seems your ranks are a bit thinner these days."

"It was war," she said quietly. "Nobody's alone in war."

"Where're they now?"

"Gone."

"Gone *how?*" he pressed. "Heard your Huuri burned himself to ash."

Anna gripped the edges of the blanket. She studied the anger rising in herself, tracking its swells and heat across her face, only to find that it was not anger at all. It was pain. It was everything she had buried in shallow soil. "I killed him."

"Eh?"

"You heard me."

"Known you too long to swallow that," Lukas said. "Killing's not in your blood."

"It's all I know," she said. "I destroy those who trust me."

"Best lay your head down, gi—"

"I thought it was only Julek," she whispered. "After him, I thought it was all over."

"Rest the name."

But there was no choice in the matter. Anna let the cold seep into her bones, staring idly at the stones and threads of smoke winding between them, wondering how it had all slept so long within her. "It wasn't you," she said. "It was me, my foolishness. And I've accepted that. I've tried so hard to do that."

Lukas's lips contorted. He let his hands hang over his thighs.

"But it was Bora, too," Anna continued. "She died for me. I still remember that night, believe it or not. I told myself that nobody would ever die for me again." She did not know why she smiled. "It never ended."

"Enough of it," Lukas said.

"Do you know what else I remember? You asked me to think about sharing a life with somebody." She waited for the easterner's face to form in her memory, but his features were muddied now, forgotten. "I nearly had that. *Love.* Can you believe it? If he hadn't died, maybe there really would be children clinging to my skirts."

"*Enough.*"

Her eyes sharpened, cutting into Lukas so swiftly that the man averted his gaze. "You have no right to tell me what's enough."

"I've been down these roads," Lukas said. "Nothing but night there."

"Night? I learned the nature of night through you." Anna fought to control her tears, but it was fruitless: They came unbidden, itching along her lids. "And I've had to *kill* so much more than you know."

"Just come off it, Anna. Meant nothing by it."

"I did," she hissed. "We were going to have a child. We were *supposed* to have one. But when I understood what I was, and when I understood this world, I knew that it could never happen. So I went to the herbmen and I chewed the bleeding roots, and I held that miserable truth behind my lips." Her tears grew brittle and cold upon her cheeks. "All this time, I believed Ramyi was the herald of death. But it was *me*. It has always been me."

Lukas met her eyes, but he did not speak, did not smirk. His eyes softened and his lips parted slightly. It felt as though some vast wall was preparing to collapse. "You should sleep," he said at last. "I'll keep watch."

And when she had finally stopped crying and laid her head on wool and shut her eyes, the forest was dark and full of birdsongs.

One of the stones Lukas had warmed over the fires was nestled against her stomach, bundled in thin fox furs, slowly bleeding its heat. It did not take her pain away, nor did it erase the faces and voices that clouded her mind. But it was a good thing—a good, fleeting thing that belonged to her.

She clutched the stone tighter.

* * * *

She opened her eyes to the void that existed between dreams and waking. It was a realm of infinite space, its black swells all-encompassing, ever-changing, writhing around her like liquid coal. Behemoths lurked at the fringes of her vision, freckled with gossamer starlight and dwindling nebulae.

Anna lifted her hand and studied it. Her flesh was a mass of shifting sand; writhing, swirling, flowing playfully in the presence of her mere attention. Yet the longer she examined it, honing in on the dunes and furrows across her palm, the more she dissolved. Patches of skin broke apart and flayed themselves, exposing the living fabric that lay beneath. The fabric that ought to have been there, anyway. She found no blood, no bones. In its place were granules, misty hayat, droplets of pure sound— but where was *she?*

"You've come so far." The voice was neither that of a man nor a woman. It was not even composed of words. Upon dissecting the sound, Anna perceived it as the roar of ocean waves, the creak of ancient pines, the sizzle of rainfall on a parched plain. "Think not of what I am, Matrasa. Know only that we are."

Her mind revolved around the word, tasting its strangeness, its inexpressible nature. *Matrasa.* It existed in none of the tongues she'd acquired. But it was not meaningless; it was overwhelming, replete with celestial light and eternity and bliss, a blinding spark amid darkness. *Matrasa.* Its rapture ended as swiftly as it had begun.

"I can't see you," Anna said.

"Cease the search without," the voice replied. "Turn your sight within."

Her breathing slowed, easing the motion of the enveloping black spirals in turn. An enormous shape—featureless, shrouded, unending—materialized before her. She knew it before the thinking mind could decipher its form.

"You," Anna whispered. "You granted me the visions."

"We did."

"*We?*"

"All will be revealed," it said. "You have glimpsed the rays of the great star, but it is time to look upon the orb itself."

Now her head swam with visions of what lay ahead, increasingly sensing that this was *it*, this was *truth*, this was the ascension that abided beyond words and concepts. It was what Ramyi had sought for so long. Something numinous and primal. "You were with me in the Apiary, weren't you?"

"I am in all things."

"But you spoke to me there. You guided me."

"You are the one that has been sought," it said. "Soon there will be neither inner nor outer, light nor dark, life nor death. Come forth, Matrasa, and act without fear. This is the hour of becoming."

She recoiled at the word *becoming*. It was a reaction embedded deep within her, more ancient than the mind itself. "Where do I go?"

"Follow the path."

"I can't glimpse it anymore," she said. "I brought us here, but now—"

"You still expect an *I* to answer your calls. That which does not exist has no voice."

Anna listened to the boundless, pervading stillness at the core of her being. "This is a dream, isn't it?"

"Awake, dreaming—the mind holds no divisions. There is nothing beyond that which is perceived." A roaring echo, spawned from the depths of Anna's visions, began to fill the void. "Rise, Matrasa, and become."

Radiance consumed her world.

* * * *

Anna opened her eyes to cotton light and shimmering beads of ice and hard, throbbing pressure across her lips. More than pressure: the cold leather cup of someone's glove, trembling. She spun over, panic sharpening her vision, her hands straining toward—

"Hush." Lukas squatted beside her in a beige Nahoran smock, his wolfish gaze fixed upon something in the lower valley.

She breathed heavily through her nose and listened: Ice melting and drumming over snow, birds chirping overhead, southern voices carrying in the thin air....

Lukas glanced down at her and nodded, his hand easing against her lips. She nodded in turn.

When Lukas's glove fell away, Anna carefully drew her legs inward, bristling at the blood flowing into deadened limbs. She knelt upon her bedroll and scanned the white expanse below.

A cluster of fighters, draped in white smocks and pine needle netting, were picking their way through knee-high snow. The wares of Kowak's tinkerers covered them: slender ruji barrels, lined with the holes of a flute; gloves glinting with razors; distended packs housing gaping mortar tubes. Breaths streamed through their homespun wool masks.

Lukas pointed toward a stand of tall, wind-bent pines spanning the hills several leagues beyond the valley. There was nothing immediately remarkable about it. But as Anna studied the dark slopes, her attention continuously sliding back to the brutish pack below, she saw what the tracker had seen: strange, shimmering patches mingling with dense canopies.

Sparksalt fumes.

Her vision snapped from thicket to thicket, cliff to basin, suddenly cognizant of the ripples playing out across a motionless land. It was not one nerash, but many. Far too many. Some of the fumes stirred just over the adjacent rise.

"Let's go," Lukas mouthed.

It was the wise thing to do, perhaps the optimal thing. Even so, Anna's thoughts lingered with Ashoral. She wondered if the easterner was still lying in wait, nestled in her firing position like the mountain lions that prowled the steppes. It should've been easy to suppress the mind's wandering, to tether herself to Lukas's suggestion. After all, it was likely that the ga'mir was already dead—if not from cold, then from her open wounds.

And yet....

Fanning out into a wide horseshoe, the southern fighters advanced with the slow, threatening steps of a stalking hound. They aimed their ruji at the windows and blackened scars arranged along the chassis' sides.

"Anna," Lukas whispered.

But Anna could not move. Her mind—indeed, her entire body— screamed inwardly, seized by the assurance of something dreadful, something fundamentally *wrong*. At once the forests and snow and faces appeared to her as a living nightmare, inescapable, woven from the black thoughts she had always overlooked. Bile flooded her gut. There was no reality beyond this fear, this cosmic suffering, this droplet of eternity that engulfed her in its maw, whispering *pain*, only *pain*.

The moment diffused into gray light. It refracted through her mind, coursing out to the horizons and cavities of awareness, screaming to find *her*, *her*, *her*. It pounded against Anna's focus in brackish waves. She refused to break; she couldn't.

Then a hooded figure trudged out of the tree line near the nerash, the curve of their left shoulder utterly absent, accompanied by even more of the white-clad fighters.

The trance shattered as Anna's mind came to the point of realization: *Ramyi.*

Lukas seized Anna's arm. "It's time to *go*."

Anna pressed herself to the snow and edged forward, wedging herself into a stone crevice near the overlook's precipice. She surveyed the wreckage as the southerners began filing through its entrances.

With her breath high in her chest she waited, listened.

Blood sprayed through one of the rear windows.

Metallic claps and screams echoed from within the nerash, sending Ramyi's forces scrambling toward the slaughter. Cylinders burst with supersonic thuds. Smoke twisted out through gaps in the hull. But within moments it was still again, having reverted to that uncanny, natural silence that pervaded the forests.

Southerners staggered out of the nerash with their ruji slung across their backs or gripped like walking sticks. Many of them had fragmented vests or bare limbs, exposing sigils that now pulsed with hayat's fervor. One man, nude aside from the scraps of his cloak and singed trousers, proved what Anna had already suspected: They'd been marked.

But just as Anna moved to shift away, she recognized Ashoral.

The easterner was being dragged by a pair of southerners, her legs limp and trailing over the snow. She left a pinkish rut in her wake. Her face was hidden beneath a tangle of matted hair and blood and gashes, and she did not open her swollen eyes. Thousands of similar corpses, some far more disfigured, had been assembled and catalogued on the shores of Golyna.

But Ashoral was not a corpse; her sigils limped over frost-blackened flesh.

Anna could not breathe. Her mind swarmed with the brutal possibilities, the myriad punishments Ramyi could inflict upon her lesser prize. A living Nahoran was a rare indulgence for those who'd studied the art of torment. Even the words of the State acknowledged as much:

In the absence of victory, embrace death.

The fighters hauled Ashoral before Ramyi and kicked the back of her legs, forcing her to kneel on red-freckled snow. The others converged around her like a restless pack of hounds.

Snow crunched as Lukas shifted closer. "She's buying time," he said in Anna's ear. "Let's get moving."

She could not look away.

Ramyi stood before the easterner for a long, painful while, examining her prey with slivered golden eyes. Nothing about the encounter felt real. It was a jarring pastiche of Anna's dreams—the frozen, lifeless hills, the Starsent shrouded in white cloth, the blood—all presented through the eyes of some celestial hawk, circling far above the terror.

Ashoral's head lifted slightly, angling toward Ramyi like a blind pup. She did not speak, did not shiver.

"Where is she?" Ramyi's voice was high and brittle.

The easterner's only reply was a stream of wispy breaths.

"I don't want to hurt you," Ramyi said, "but I will."

Shaking, Ashoral straightened her back and revealed cloudy red eyes. "Then hurt me."

"Anna," Lukas hissed, gripping her upper arm.

Ramyi extended her right arm to the nearest fighter. Her gaze did not stray from Ashoral's broken body.

The fighter drew a glinting blade from a sheath strapped to his thigh, then placed it in Ramyi's waiting palm.

No.

"He's going to mark her," Anna whispered, her tunnel vision widening, blotting out everything beyond the blade and the neck and the pink snow.

Lukas's hold tightened. "Fuck, Anna." He jerked her arm backward, but she would not—no, could not—shift in turn. "No *time* for this."

"If she isn't here," Ramyi called out, her voice now swollen with sickening guile, "then I suppose she'll have no objections to this." She pressed the tip of the blade to Ashoral's throat and held it there with a gentle, dainty touch.

Anna's fingernails scraped over wet rock. The gray presence filtered back into her awareness, beckoning, seeking.... "Bring the ruji."

"What?" Lukas's hand released her arm. "Do you—"

"Bring them," she whispered sharply.

"Trying to be brave?"

The gray light expanded in her mind's eye. "Hurry."

Ramyi tilted the blade, settling its edge along the curve of Ashoral's throat. Dim, oblong sigils drifted toward the iron, almost as though gorging themselves on the Starsent's latent force.

Anna spun around, her body primed to kick and claw, but there was no need: Lukas squirmed toward her with a long burlap sack, his lips pursed and eyes hard. When he drew near, Anna lifted the sack from the snow and set it on the rocks near her feet. She undid its knotting drawstring and pulled out two ruji and locked their segments in place, all in the grip of frantic silence.

Lukas seized the barrel of Anna's ruj. "Fuck're you doing?"

"Take one," Anna whispered, unable to shut herself away from the gray light. She glared at Lukas. "I need you to trust me. Take it, and aim at Ashoral."

Lukas's mouth churned, cycling through curses, taunts, challenges. The muscles in his neck tensed and rattled.

After a moment, he took the ruj, loaded a tin cartridge strip from the sack, and shouldered it. But merely holding the weapon seemed to unsettle him. He studied it at length, perplexed, peering down at its barrel as though it might devour him. It was not what Anna had expected of such a man. Time bred experience and experience bred numbness.

Numbness was what she now needed.

Anna loaded her own ruj and sank deeper into the rock notch. Laying the barrel into a lichen-ringed fissure, she twisted and bent until the ruj's wooden stock was nestled against her shoulder, then squared Ramyi's head between the pincers of the aiming nubs. Her vision excluded everything that she would not kill.

"Aim," Anna said softly.

Fabric rustled, iron scraped over stone, and the branches creaked high above them.

Lukas grunted. "Tell me when."

Anna clenched her lips and sealed the air deep in her belly. A faint ringing awakened in her ears, throbbing to the pulse of the gray light. She saw the blade sweeping across Ashoral's flesh, pirouetting with a tinkerer's precision, leaving hair-thin threads of blood in its wake, venting hayat into—

"Now."

Her finger curled around the trigger, but with the spring's *click*, that nascent flicker of violence, of budding terror, her concentration shattered. The gray light raged through her mind. *I see you.*

Ashoral's head burst, clouding the air with pink mist.

Anna's ruj kicked against her shoulder in tandem, excising the billow of gray light, but the moment had already passed.

A shell of snow erupted around the nerash, wrapping up and over into a crackling dome. The ruj's slug clapped and sizzled against ice. Steam wafted over the breeze.

Anna drew herself up from the lichen and stone, staring with wide, tingling eyes. She had witnessed such a shell before, but in earlier days it had been formed from sand, too low and narrow to envelope more than a cluster of fighters. Now it was enormous, its curves pristine and forged with inhuman perfection, glimmering like a bone-white star sprouting from the valley.

"Go," Anna said. She gazed at the shell as it thrummed, shedding its patina of loose snow and diamond frost.

"What in the Grove is—"

"Just go."

"*Korpa,*" Lukas swore, rising and slinging his ruj across his back. "What'd she do?"

Anna hurried past him, her ruj in one hand and the burlap sack in the other. Frozen moss and slush squelched underfoot. Despite her mind's wild churning, there was nothing to grip or understand—it was a menagerie of panic and impulses and startles. Every branch and root jutted out at her, grotesque and threatening.

Do not be afraid. The voice jarred her as she tossed the equipment over the slope and began working her way down a spur of granite. It was not Ramyi's; it was hardly a voice at all. *Focus yourself on this moment, Matrasa.* It was the whisper of dreamscapes, the hum of roiling seas....

Her hand snagged on a thorny outcropping, but the pain was a dull echo. She pulled it away and stared at the pale flesh, stripped of fear, of thoughts themselves, watching her blood wind its way into her palm's grooves and the sleeves of her robe.

Abide in my stillness, it whispered.

"Anna," Lukas snapped, his boots scraping the lip of the overhang. "It fucking *broke*. They're coming."

Anna nodded, though she did not comprehend his words. That immortal voice still resonated within the deepest locus of awareness.

Lukas dropped onto the snow beside her and loped toward the valley's slope. "Get moving," he snarled.

Move. The instinct moved through her mind, alien, endogenous, manifested by something that was not her. She watched the tracker's form gliding through pines and snow-bent boughs, dissecting every memory and urge that his image evoked. Then came crunching steps and river-tongue, and with them a flood of fear, and the world drowned her once again.

She sprinted after him, her lips and mouth burning, stinging with raw air, her boots dragging through every patch of crusted snow. Branches scraped her cheeks. Mossy bark and odors of sap and birdsongs flitted around her.

Lukas was a dim shape in the distance, but—

Flecks of lightning punched into a nearby oak, grazing her arm with splinters and fibrous chips.

"*Cease it!*" Ramyi shouted, her river-tongue echoing down the slope. "She should be breathing."

Fresh terror surged through Anna, sapping the strength from her legs in an instant. It was mercifully numbing.

She pushed further, gasping, wincing—

"Keep on." Lukas was pressed against the back a nearby pine, his ruj concealed along the fold of his trousers. He grimaced at Anna's slowing steps. "Said keep on, didn't I?"

Anna staggered forward, straining to whisper. "Come."

"Thick ears, girl," Lukas said.

"You can't—"

"We're evened out," he hissed. "Now run. Don't let me see that face again."

She could only blink at him as she stumbled past, wondering if his eyes were pinched against the cold or unbidden thoughts. His sigils moved with more grace than ever before. She thought to thank him, but she did not know why. He was undeserving, and yet….

Now it was too late anyway. She was kicking her way through thick snowdrift, wading at the deepest stretches, her arms wearily flailing. How far could she run? She recalled earlier days, warmer days, when Julek's weight had been so welcome.

She closed her eyes and listened: ruji tearing through timber, wild screams, boots crunching and branches creaking and wind whistling, all—

Her body pitched forward.

There was an instant of pure weightlessness, the wind reaching out to meet her, before her cheeks crashed into snow and ice. Then she was rolling, blinking through screens of cool blue and white and black, bracing against every crack and cut, grappling to fold over on herself.

But the land was flattening now, growing denser and pitted beneath her. Anna twisted onto her stomach and clawed at the ice with throbbing hands, her lips scraping against cold heat. Her legs swung over a sudden edge. She scratched harder, grunting, fighting as her stomach and arms and chin cleared the precipice.

Then it was gone.

It took her several moments to recognize the sensation of free fall. It was a phenomenon from nightmares, a vessel into wakefulness. She opened her eyes to a white sprawl below, to legs and arms swiping through nothingness, to the misshapen blots of trees and fields and ponds. Her ears rang with the screech of wind.

And as she plunged through an evergreen canopy, she did not think of anything, nor did she need to.

Death's whispers soothed her.

Chapter 15

When she awoke—she had always been unsure if the dead could indeed sleep—she saw only the Grove-Beyond-Worlds. It swallowed the boundaries of her vision, vast and ink-black and glittering with the light of untold dimensions. There were clouds of milky ruby and cerulean, too, expanding before her like the irises of dead gods. Or perhaps they *were* gods, all of the gods, the ones she'd cursed when her mother and cousins had sung their deeds by the hearth.

It streamed before her like a prismatic river, unbroken and luminous, marred only by the spiny black shards that rose up on either side. Their silhouettes reminded her of summer evenings, where she'd lay under the quilts of stars and silhouetted trees….

A snowflake whirled down onto her cheek and melted, leaving a cold kiss in its wake.

I'm alive.

She worked to flex her fingers, but it was done in vain: Chills wriggled out from the center of her chest, fixing her limbs like alloy struts. Her flesh, raw and dissociated, busily throbbed with whispers of false warmth.

All she could manage was opening her eyes and gazing up at the nebulae, at the passing trees and clouds that—

They were passing. Moving. Suddenly, she was cognizant of the earth hushing beneath her, and of her body stirring with subtle tremors, cresting and sinking gently, possessed by waves that were not her breaths.

Fear swept over her, its pall as severe and tangible as the pain in her frozen legs. Had *they* found her? She glanced hungrily from side to side, biting into her tongue to calm chattering teeth, but the darkness occluded everything except the pale glow of frost and fog. Her mind was free of the gray light, but it meant little—if Ramyi were near enough to look upon her, there was no sense in projecting her awareness. Or so she convinced herself. Trapping her breaths in beaten lungs, Anna closed her eyes and listened:

Crisp snow, steady steps, the twinge of taut rope.

But the steps were too nimble for the southerners and far too few in number. She counted four legs, perhaps six, all landing with the painstaking coordination of birds in flight.

Anna paused, gathering her strength, before craning her neck upward and peering down the length of her body. She was draped in a narrow fox skin. The varnished wood of a sled—perhaps that of a herdsman, or a peddler—stretched alongside her, its reins leading toward a collection of silhouettes several paces ahead.

None of the figures wore the packs of Kowak's men, nor did they carry ruji. They were thin, their heads shaved to reveal a tapestry of dim sigils: jagged, twisting roots spiraling out into blossoms, nearly—

No, not nearly. They *were* identical. Not only to one another, but to the markings Anna had glimpsed so long ago in Galipa's inn. Identical to the hawkeyed woman who had delivered pain and prescience in equal parts.

"Bora." She hadn't meant to speak aloud. It was a hoarse, rusty gasp, indistinguishable from the breeze's mournful tones.

Or so she had hoped.

The figures halted their steps, allowing the sled to glide several paces before coming to rest over trampled snow. They turned toward her in unison, their sigils growing brighter, swifter beneath shadowed flesh.

"Do not be afraid, Matrasa," the tallest figure said. His river-tongue was firm, yet comforting, warped by the same ambiguity she'd once detected in Bora. An ambiguity that suggested no home, no culture, no kin. "The long journey is over."

Her lips trembled, but she did not speak. She was too broken for that. Tears sprouted in burning strips along her lids, unwanted, inevitable. She lay her head against the sled's planks and watched the stars stream overhead.

* * * *

She awoke to waterfalls of molten gold. Firelight whirled upon the plates and bowls and chalices before her, its glaring sprites luring her eyes to a spread that she could only liken to a flatlands mirage.

Mounds of luscious grapes, roasted seeds, breads and apples and wine flasks—it was a more bountiful feast than Anna had encountered in years, all of it unmarred by the blemishes and rot that had ravaged the growing regions in her youth.

Her stomach gurgled in anticipation.

Ravenous hunger overtook her, brandishing its dizzying talons after days of fear and squelching bile. It emptied her mind of everything that she could not peel or chew or drink. She was weak, far too weak to resist it.

Her lips were caked with jam by the time she noticed the figures standing along the walls. Much like those who'd drawn the sled—though the vision did not, or rather *had* not, seemed real until that moment—her watchers had shaved heads, buckskin coverings, and barbed root sigils. They were all smiling at her, their hands clasped and legs joined, as stoic, yet warm as any of the kales' bathhouse attendants.

She dropped a handful of blackberries, blinked at them. "Who are you?"

One of the women—it was not Bora; it could not be, for her gaze was too childish, too soft—stepped closer to the table. "Eat, Matrasa."

"Who *are* you?" she repeated, although some mote of herself assured her that she knew the answer and that she had always known it. She studied the unwavering warmth in the young woman's stare. "Why have you taken me here?"

"Do you not recall this place?" the woman asked. She looked at the others and were quick to look back at her, all of their faces furtive, apprehensive, lined with crooked smiles.

"I've never been here before." She took stock of the room's mottled walls: bits of leaf litter and clay and wicker, all packed into the wedges between curving birch trunks. The sole entrance was little more than two flaps of hanging leather.

"Did you not see it?" the woman asked. "Comb your mind, Matrasa—have you not experienced this moment already?"

Anna gripped the gnarled arms of her chair. She could not divorce the woman from the one who had carried her sigils. And how could she hope to? Flesh came and went, shaped by blades and plagues and flames alike, but sigils...sigils persisted. Sigils separated the dead from the living, and the wicked from the kind, and—

"You see her, do you not?" the woman asked presently.

"I need to breathe," Anna whispered, but she could not stand. Her legs screamed in pain at the barest thought of movement.

"You're thinking of her," the woman said. She was suddenly crestfallen, almost wincing. "She is still here. If only you could hear her..."

Anna met the woman's gaze directly. "What are you?"

"A wave," she replied. "We are all waves and nothing more, Matrasa."

"You know what I mean."

The woman smiled at the others. "We are those who have waited for you." They looked at her encouragingly, waiting for something, anything, but Anna—

It all fell into place.

Her vision imploded into a black whirl, a stream of images and sounds, all laced with the Apiary's neon threads. Voices streaked past her as though receding and expanding in the same instant. She watched the tables, the faces, the sigils, all converging like the pieces of some vast puzzle, fulfilling….

"Do you see it?" the woman asked. "Has it returned to you?"

Anna's hands shook as she stared at them. "How could you know?"

The woman nodded to a man beside her, then stepped aside to allow him to open the tent's flaps. "Eat your fill."

"I've had it," Anna said softly. "I just want to *know*."

Several of the attendants moved toward her, their hands extended in warm invitation.

"As I told you," the woman said, "we have been waiting."

"What are you doing?" Anna's chair crunched back over the soil. "Don't come closer."

"Trust us as you trusted her," the woman said evenly.

"You aren't Bora."

"Yet she was us. Be at ease, Matrasa. Give us your arms and we will carry you to the plane of completion. All will be revealed."

Nothing had ever seemed so threatening. It was not death, not anymore— she had been prepared to die for a long while. Perhaps too long. Now she stared into the jaws of something strange and numinous, a void beyond the horizons of living or dying or slumbering. It was tantamount to kneeling before the cosmos, baring her throat like the hordes of wartime captives who'd been put to the blade. But even captives could die running, riddled with arrowheads or iron. A broken body robbed her of that choice. There was only surrender, only passage into a world beyond the mind's comprehension. She trembled at that visceral fear of the unknown, cursing fate, cursing herself, cursing the weakness she had nursed for so long. How many others had faced the Breaking with barren eyes? It was not so different, and yet….

"Very well," Anna said, her voice disembodied, an echo of her own. "I'm ready."

* * * *

Their village was a dreamscape molded from dense, towering pines and snowy deerskin and pulsing coals.

Everything rolled past Anna in wispy shapes, the pine limbs long and drooping above her. Even the hands upon her back—lifting her, embracing her, carrying her through the maze of tents—were a vague swell, less defined than the waves that had stirred her hair in Golyna's harbor. Every step and jostle reverberated up from the mass below, reminding her of the village's woman, the tall man.... She could not count them all, but there was no sense in division anyway—they all carried Bora's sigils. Even more of them lurked on the fringes of the path, mute and skittish, their luminous shapes pressing through the fog like clouded moons.

She found herself wishing for death, though the thinking mind recoiled at its very idea. But it was a known thing and a simple one. A logical one. After all of the pain, all of the faces she'd scourged from her memory, what was left to embrace? Who could endure in such a world?

"Are you ready, Matrasa?"

Anna opened her eyes to find that she was no longer in the village. The forest was silver-black in her periphery, but ahead there was only a dark mass, a sheer cliff of sorts, lined with icy veins and knuckles of white rock.

And amid those granite talons she saw herself: murals of a woman with hair like straw waterfalls, with wide, diamond eyes, with briar-tangle scars across her throat. Each image was set against a blizzard of cosmic radiance and innumerable reaching hands, its paint hardly faded by rain and vicious years.

A pale, prickly silhouette rose along its base, opalescent and stark in the moonlight. A facade woven from cracked skulls and femurs and knuckles came into sharp focus. Moss blanketed the ossuary's rib-cage lintel. At its very center was a maw-like door, oblong, framing an ink-black pool. Its stagnant water gazed back at her, invited her.

Perhaps this was where it would happen. Anna stared at the structure, wondering if it was the long, dreadful dream of a girl who had never left home. Perhaps she was still in the throes of her fever, kicking and clawing on Galipa's straw mattress. It had to be so. Otherwise, there was no meaning to the suffering, no conclusion to the days and nights she'd bled in service of something better. To dissolve was to be free.

"I'm ready," Anna whispered.

They moved her closer, tucking a whispered chant under their breaths and the snap of fallen branches.

She watched the stars and moon gliding over the ossuary's pool, warping....

They released her.

Frigid water surged up and through her cloak, and at once her body was heavy, inert, burning in the darkness. She gasped, trying to curl in on herself, but it was no use. The water seemed bottomless. Fabric ballooned up around her, trapping her arms and legs and neck, making every breath near and fleeting. Then came the dying warmth, the warmth her mother had always warned her about, trickling into her fingers and down her throat and into the hollows of her ears. As she sank lower, her hands becoming misshapen, bloated orbs beneath the surface, she looked toward the forest. It was an unbroken wall of sigils—of Bora's sigils.

Mothers, fathers, children, babes; all watching, all silently comforting her in the time of death. Soon Anna did not feel anything, and while the water rose up past her chin, her lips, her nose, enveloping her face with blissful heat, her mind drifted toward their presence alone. Just before she slid under, she noticed the pale blots of smiles upon their faces.

The blackness was calm, quiet.

She did not turn away from it. She faced it until she sensed herself dissipating, drifting away from the heaviness of flesh and feeling, of everything she had ever despised and craved and devoured.

Awaken.

Anna collapsed on her hands and knees, sputtering, shaking, screaming into the void that was no longer a void. No longer water, even. There were only her pale fingers and grains of crystalline sand and locks of golden hair. She forced a breath in, spat it out, screamed again. Life, death—there was no end, no escape from its lunacy, and—

"Be without fear, Matrasa," the voice whispered. Anna's fingers clawed into the sand. "This moment has already occurred, and it is one of boundless perfection. You are not dead, for you are nothing. Look upon me, and you shall look upon the womb of all things."

Chapter 16

Anna lifted her chin and searched for the voice's source. It was impossible to perceive too far in any direction, for the warm, phantasmal light that enveloped her could not sift through the veil of twinkling mica, nor the darkness that lay beyond it. Soon her eyes adjusted to the shimmering rain, however, and she discerned the long, twisting fangs of stalactites overhead. Gentle sand dunes stretched out before her, gradually receding into a murky cinnamon haze. There was nothing natural about this place. Time was powerless. She could feel it in the hum of her body, which was now painless, without—

She paused, staring down at the movement of her once-broken hand. Her once-scarred hand, in fact. But where were those marks now? Her fingers were straight and supple, a living memory of how they had been in the days before tending her father's fields.

Everything was flawless.

She began swatting at herself, probing for every blister and gouge she'd ever received, but there was nothing to find. Her skin was soft, smooth, pale, as though it had never endured the stare of Har-gunesh.

Death did not hold dominion here.

There was only calmness.

Only her.

Anna stood easily and wandered into the shadows, listening to the soles of her feet as they shushed and drifted over the sands. She began to strip away her clothes, though she did not know, and soon she was naked in the darkness, alone, unafraid. The air was warm and silky.

So she walked, and walked, and walked….

After a long while—minutes, years?—she came upon something other than blackness. It hung before her like a thunderhead on a summer night, broad and ashen, known only by the nothingness that surrounded it.

"I'm here," Anna said. Her words fanned out within the void, addressed to nobody and nothing in particular.

But they awakened something nevertheless.

Sunbeams splintered the darkness, streaming down across a craggy dome, then mountainous, sloping shoulders, glacial elbows, every feature grotesque in its immensity. It had to be a statue. Nothing else could be so stagnant, so grand.

Then it breathed.

Its chest expanded with a groan, grating stone upon stone, sifting the powdery scabs of moss and encrusted stones through shafts of light. The bridge of its nose fluttered with streaks of luminescence. Both eyes rolled open, infinite, blinding in their purity.

Anna gazed into the dual stars, sensing more than ever that she was not there at all. She was a shadow at nightfall.

"Matrasa." The being's stone lips did not part; every sound was a ripple in Anna's mind, at once nonsensical and gripping. "Lay down your burdens. Every path will be known to you."

"That isn't my name. You keep calling me Matrasa, but—"

"The Living End."

"What?"

"I call you by your true name," it said. "Matrasa, the Living End. That is your nature, but I would not expect you to remember it so simply. This cycle of birth and death has clouded your purpose."

"I have no purpose," Anna said softly.

"How can you be certain?"

"I've come to stop those who believe in purpose."

"Then you've closed your eyes to the signs of the cosmos."

She stared up at the being. "What is this place?"

"It is not a place," it replied. "It is the absence of places."

"Then it *is* death."

"I've watched you in dreams, Matrasa. You wove a world away from that of flesh—you have walked the very plane that you now encounter."

"I didn't create it," Anna said. "It was—"

"Hayat." Deep, startling laughter filled Anna's mind.

"Yes," she whispered. "What are you?"

"No answer has ever resulted from this query," it said. "Can anything be said of *me*? There is only that which binds my form together, and that which has passed before me. There is only hayat."

"You're a scribe, then."

"Once, perhaps I was." There was a sober note to its voice, a faltering stork's cry buried amid whispering. "But listen intently, Matrasa. I am that which remains when all else is stripped away: names, flesh, perceptions. I am that I am.

"Avert your mind from fear, Matrasa," it pressed on. "You have known this wellspring of the void. When everything was stolen from you, what endured?"

"I don't know."

"Speak not from your mind's vacillating, but from truth."

Anna allowed herself to bundle her words behind quivering lips, no longer feeding her thoughts, but merely studying them, squinting at them. How long had it been since those glimpses of ineffable stillness? She could still feel them thrumming within her, beyond all perception, beyond both discrimination and distinction. Moments that had emptied her of herself entirely, leaving behind only—

"The world," Anna said. "The world endured."

"And what lends form to this world?"

Again she paused, listening intently to the echoes of a slowing mind. *Time. Concepts. Vision.* Nothing served as a satisfactory answer; nothing sated the ravenous question.

"Hayat," she whispered finally.

The being pulsed with cobalt veins. A luminous wreath sprouted over its stone flesh, its mineral tufts, its eerie, wavering edges. Suddenly, it did not appear to be a contiguous formation at all, but rather a fluid expression of *something*, drifting apart and congealing moment by moment, its form distorting until it resembled a living waterfall. Each instant of destruction was a spark of creation.

"Hayat," Anna repeated, this time more firmly. "But that is not *your* nature."

"Where did your mind acquire this certainty?" The being waited, but Anna did not deign to reply. There was nothing to assert, nothing capable of being proved. "The deeper you gaze into yourself, the less you'll find. Soon enough, the emptiness peers back at itself. It knows its own name."

Anna blinked at the being. No, not a being—it was neither a thing nor a process. It was Hayat. "But once, you had a name."

"All things carry a name," Hayat said, "but these are titles that distinguish the strand from the whole. Without the mapmaker's ink, there are no seas to speak of. There is only water."

"What was it?"

"My name?" it asked. "The world is dying, Matrasa, and we are its cure. Where is the prudence in studying the shade of our tincture?"

"But once, you were me," Anna said. "You were once a scribe, and—"

"I am all things," Hayat replied. "A scribe, a carcass, a sapling. Expand your mind, Matrasa, and see the boundaries dissolve. You will know that I am you and that you are me. You will know our nature."

"Was that what I saw?" she asked faintly. "In the Apiary, I saw—"

"You saw reality."

"But even before that, I had visions. Strange visions."

"The lives before this moment," it explained. "Every strand of your being—both past and future—is realizing its true nature. Soon, their existence will converge. You will awaken. You will *become* for an instant, a bead of all-that-is, but you will become."

Anna lifted her hand and turned it over, aghast at the rippling flesh that spoke Hayat's truth. *Where am I?* Beads of newborn skin and nail and hair churned in soft eddies, bound by rivulets of hayat. By threads of that which now spoke to her, through her.

"Do you see it?" Hayat asked. "That is your true essence, Matrasa. Nothing can touch you. Nothing can harm you. You are and shall always be."

Notions of eternity flared through her. Lightless eons, the deaths of everything and everyone she had ever—

"Cease this storm," Hayat said, smothering the faces in her mind's eye. "It is their nature, too, but you will not believe me. Your form has forgotten reality. It craves birth, death, gain, loss…but there is only change, Matrasa. You will grasp this truth when the time demands it."

"It doesn't make anything easier," Anna said. "Truth never has."

"If you realized the weight of my words, it would."

Anna eased the tension that had gathered across her shoulders. Every glimpse of cessation had demanded a leap toward madness, toward the void, and time had only made the sacrifices more severe. At least in past days, the path had been illuminated by one who knew its price. It took Anna a moment to understand the curious longing in her chest: *nostalgia*.

"You remember her," Hayat said. "She cared very much for you, Matrasa."

"How do you know?"

"Because a mother knows its children. She was never separate from me, even now."

A mother, a child. The revelation scraped against the hairs of Anna's neck. "Those are your people," she said. "You marked them."

"No," Hayat said. "I created them."

"What?"

"A seed cannot sprout in arid soil," it said. "Eventually, the purifier of this world would come into existence. But without guiding hands, it may have taken eternity. How many beings would suffer before this instant of ascension? How many eons would be squandered in violence and desolation?"

A chill came over her. "So you created tools."

"This is how the darkened mind may perceive them. Consider this, Matrasa—you would not exist without her. She would not have existed without you."

"She *died* for me," Anna seethed.

"Your burden is an illusion. I am all things and in time, I will claim all lives. Birth demands death."

Anna tried to listen without feeling, without even thinking, but it was unavoidable. Bora's nature shone through Hayat, and Hayat had shone through Bora. They were intertwined in the core of its luminescence, its sacred axioms, its wisdom disguised as callousness.

"Much can be said of Bora," Hayat continued. "Her brothers and sisters obeyed my command. They toiled in these hills, waiting for the day when the Living End realized her true nature. Waiting until you returned to us. But even as a girl, Bora was not content with the assurances of her forerunners. One night, she laid out her things and left us to pursue her own path. I still recall the laments of her mother and father. How could they have raised a child so faithless?" Hayat's voice unspooled, fading into the drone of wasps and crickets. "Now I understand her way, Matrasa. It was the way of the cosmos."

"You could have sent more of them," Anna said. "You could have saved her. You watched the war and you—"

"Do not speak to me of war. You have known a thousand wars, both as conqueror and the conquered."

"You seem to know so much about me," she whispered, recoiling at its bite. "Where did you come from?"

"We have always been."

Anna gestured to its neon threads and humanoid protrusions. "This form hasn't."

"This form was birthed, no different from those that have preceded it," it explained. "Yet I can recall little of that life. All that remains is the knowledge of a homeland and the horrors that ravaged it." There was a long, haunting silence. "You may know the Kojadi as masters of the mind, but this is an incomplete portrait. They—we—were ravenous. Those who knew the way of the luminous flesh became entranced by its power. Hayat was their weapon."

"And you?"

"I withdrew from their wars," it said. "In those times, there was only death and domination. Cities and empires burned in the wake of the marked ones. The hayajara who understood their own marks chased existence, whatever the cost. But they did not understand the futility of their pursuit."

Anna walked closer, basking in its cobalt haze. Something about the tale resonated within her, as jarring as the name of someone she had once been, or a lover she had known....

"I tasted reality, Matrasa: Hayat itself, stripped of its veils and boundaries. But tasting it was all I could do. In our wild game of arrogance, I accepted my own defeat. That which I encountered surpassed all limitations. To bend time, to conjure new worlds—these are rudimentary tricks compared to its true potential. And so I sought the one to harness it. I sought the one who would undo the wickedness of this world."

"You sought me."

"Yes," Hayat said. "Within you, I shall germinate the answer to all things."

It was daunting, if not crippling, to comprehend. Countless years of warfare, of empires devoted solely to the mind and its inner workings—all of it ceased with her. With a girl from Bylka, who was not pure, who was not good, who had spared the wicked. "It can't be me," Anna said weakly. "If you can truly control time—"

"To what end?" Hayat asked. "To spawn more cycles in ignorance? I am not the ultimate expression of the cosmos, Matrasa. This title is yours. All of my force was expended on merely existing, waiting for this sacred moment. Now I am that which sustains my mind. Alone I am nothing, but within you, I will be everything."

Anna's hands shook at her side. "But what *is* it?"

"Be precise."

"Hayat," Anna said, the word stinging her tongue. "Is it living?"

"It simply is." Filaments of light whirled around its eyes. "An eternal fabric, a wheel, a river—words are blunt, useless tools in the face of its splendor. There has always been hayat and always shall be. But we have forgotten how to awaken. We dwell in the perpetual dream of suffering, Matrasa."

"You think suffering isn't real?"

"The hayajara exist on the cusp of waking," it continued, unmoved. "You perceive the cracks in that which is presumed whole. Do not close your eyes and do not rest. Soon you will know the real from the unreal."

Her fingertips tingled with the promises of what awaited her: The end of suffering. The birth of a new world, a just world. It was so near, and—

And it could not be bloodless.

"Through killing," Anna said pointedly. "That's what you want me to do, isn't it? You turned your back on war, but what came of it?"

"You speak of Tanrasa," it said. "The Devouring End."

"Her name is Ramyi."

"In this incarnation, perhaps."

"But you knew what she was," Anna snapped. "You could have looked for her."

"And then?"

"You could've killed in the womb, long before *this*. Before she lost anything, and before her life was pain, and before—"

"This world plays out as it must."

That truth was acrid, perhaps fundamental, but Anna stared back at it blankly. "And now I'll need to kill her."

"As mice perish beneath hawks, and as darkness consumes light. Would you stand against the turning of the stars?"

"She was my *sister!*" Anna caught herself panting, trembling. A broken sigh slid through her lips. "She was mine."

"Your bond is deeper than you can fathom," it said. "When the hour of trial is upon you, you will understand. You will recall this sorrow as a cloud in open skies."

"Perhaps you've forgotten what it's like to love something," Anna said.

"Love?" Hayat asked. "When you speak of love, what does the word conjure in your mind? Prizing one being above all others?" The sand between them skittered in glimmering coils, its granules rising, pivoting, fanning out like a serpent's hood. Steadily the mass compressed, budding into the facsimiles of arms, legs, a head and torso. Hayat swept over the sand in a luminous curtain, then faded to reveal—

Him.

Yatrin wore the smile that had always broken her heart. It was not the smile itself, but the memory of it, the warmth it had provided in better days. His eyes were softened by the sleep he'd craved in wartime. Every pore and scar and hair was precisely where it should've been, a living mirror of Anna's memories, of wishes made on long, somber nights.

Anna moved toward him, trying to remember everything she'd wanted to say....

He collapsed in a plume of sand.

"That which is granted," Hayat said flatly, "must be returned."

"Was it him?" she asked, still staring at the spot where he had been, her vision melting with hot tears. She swiped at her eyes. "Was it?"

"Did you ever truly see him?" Hayat asked. "All you have ever known is flesh arising, forming, and dissolving. You love the illusions of this world."

"Enough."

"Love will endure, Matrasa, but you must set aside the love your form has come to understand."

Anna gritted her jaw until sorrow was yet another ache. "Why are you doing this?"

"That which can be taken away was never part of you."

"They were," Anna whispered. "Once, they all were."

"Do not mourn," it said. "The twilight of this world is at hand. Place your fate in the hands of the cosmos and all will be fulfilled." Again a stream of sand funneled up, twinkling in the glow of Hayat's stare. It twisted and thrashed and shrank until it was a gritty cloud, then a bulb, then a spindle, each incarnation growing narrower and denser. When the last shroud of mica fell away, only an obsidian scalpel remained.

She stared at the blade's slivered edge. "Stop this."

"I see your nature," Hayat said. "As you have manifested the nature of others, I shall manifest yours."

The blade drifted closer to her neck. "I can't do it."

"Trust me, Matrasa. Trust that which created you."

Emptying her mind of rabid, fearful thoughts, Anna watched light streak along the obsidian's edge. "I want to." She lifted her chin, closed her eyes.

There was a flicker of pain, white-hot and demanding, its touch howling with echoes of hayat. Warm blood trickled to her collarbone. Every nerve screamed against the blade, clawing toward escape, toward some semblance of reprieve, but Anna did not heed their cries. She focused on the splitting of her skin. On mosaics of ice-blue hayat behind her eyelids. On bestial terror. All of it flowed through her, past her.

Then the blade's touch vanished. A subtle current wound its way to the tips of her fingers, calling attention to newfound stillness.

Anna opened her eyes, but there was nothing to see. Blackness encircled her, endless and skin-warm, unsullied by anything that might've lent it form: shadows, vapors, echoes. She found herself gazing at the void where Hayat had once dwelt. Or had it? The mind was known for its tricks, those

ceaseless tricks, all aimed at keeping itself in motion, at chasing, chasing....
Nausea rippled through Anna's gut.

It was real, she assured herself. *It* is *real.*

"Are you there?" In that instant, she knew that it had happened. It must
have. Her voice carried that nascent strength, ringing clearly, truly into
the depths of blackness. She lifted her hand and probed the span of her
neck for the being's cuts. But her skin was as even as parchment, and—

Light.

There was no wrist in her periphery, no fingers, no nails. There was only
pale, pristine light that had arranged itself in familiar shapes. Its edges, like
those of Hayat itself, frothed and ebbed in fractal jigsaws, simultaneously
creating and destroying shapes that Anna had gleaned in fleeting dreams.
No, not in dreams—in meditation. And they were not just shapes, but sigils.
She gazed deeper, honing in on their wild tangles and celestial geometry,
but each pattern dissolved in the moment before recognition.

In you, I will be everything.

Fear drained away. What did it mean to be alone, to be afraid? She was
everywhere, everything. She was beyond harm.

Turning her mind toward its seed of bliss, Anna sat on the infinite plane
and rested her hands—her living, radiant hands—upon lustrous thighs.

Awaken.

Chapter 17

Distended shapes crowded over her, backlit by a field of stars and milky nebulae. Thorny air scraped down her throat. She willed herself to sit up, but it was impossible: Her hands and feet squirmed dully over snow, lifeless, throbbing in feverish waves. Beads of ice water snaked along her skin.

"*Chalnish soya?*" a man asked.

The river-tongue thrust her into alarm. Her eyes flitted around, taking in the moonlit heaps of bodies that had been lain out at the water's edge, then mammoth, silvery trees, then the silhouettes of ruj-bearing southerners.

She studied her own panic with a newborn's feebleness. The fear of death was a blunt, substantial thing at the bedrock of awareness, but there were more immediate concerns that did not adhere to logic, nor to analysis. *Am I alive? Am I here? Do they see me?*

Snapping twigs ceased her mind's chaos.

"She's breathing?" Ramyi's flatspeak was as stiff as the night air. She moved nearer, but remained out of sight, still obscured by Jenis's fighters. "Good."

A nerash's engines moaned in faraway blackness. It trampled over the last wheezes of Bora's kin, and the gruff laughter of the southerners, and the creak of a thousand swaying pines.

Anna shut her eyes as gloved hands descended upon her.

Nothing can harm you. She clung to that belief with all her focus, ignoring the terrors her mind conjured and paraded before her. *Nothing can harm you....*

* * * *

The world passed her as a motley stream of sensations, raw and ephemeral, stripped of all the illusions that had once made it bearable. Survivable, even. On many nights she'd retreated into the refuge of memories, and on others, into the hope of that which had not occurred. Time itself had been her opiate. But the old mind was dead, as were its comforts. The only thing that had endured was the eternal *now*—infinite, shapeless, assuming countless forms without ever becoming them.

"Will you not speak?" The southern fighter, who'd been perched on his stool for nearly an hour, draped his hands across his thighs and regarded her sourly. He held a thin knife by its blade, though he seemed reticent to carry it at all. He was too young to torture. "They just want to know," he added timidly.

Anna let herself sag down against the oak post, grimacing as her shoulders bore her weight and rope dug into bloodied wrists. She was not afraid; there was too much bewilderment in her mind and too little assurance that this was, in fact, reality. Even pain had lost its immediacy. Her body was suffering—there was no question of that—but she observed its plight as one watched a caged beast, frowning quizzically at the whimpers that escaped her own lips.

Look outside yourself.

What was there to see?

The hut's interior was a bizarre pastiche: warm, flickering firelight upon velvet deerskin, effigies of Anna formed from crushed pigment and foliage, bloodstained tables, entrails strung out along packed earth.

"Whatever you saw," the young man said presently, "it's not worth dying for."

Anna grinned.

It certainly seemed to be worth harming—if not killing—for. Withstanding their questions had become an exercise in patience, above all else. *What did you see? How did you mend your flesh? What is this place? Where did the passageway go?* Each question had been met with silence and, in turn, a visit from one of the southern liaisons, who'd passed yet another fruitless query into the questioner's ear.

"I don't want them to do their work," he added. "My brother fought in your company."

"Is that why they chose you?" Anna asked.

He nodded. "He wrote letters about you. Gabris, that was his name."

The name plucked a cord deep in her memories: A stout, snub-nosed boy who'd carved toys for the foundlings between strikes. She had never forgotten his charred body. "You should be proud of your brother," she said after a moment. "Do you think he would want you to do this?"

He furrowed his brow and looked away. "I just want it all to be over."

"I do, too," Anna said. "But killing is a false hope."

"We're only killing the right ones."

"You're killing yourselves."

A high, wailing breeze quieted them.

"Why couldn't you just stand with us?" he asked finally, glancing up with red, bitter eyes. "We're your blood, but you'd rather throw your blade in with the easterners, or the flatland babes, or *anyone* else, wouldn't you? Gabris said you were good, but he must've lost his mind. At least Volna cared for us."

"Volna would've slit every throat in Kowak."

"Yeah," he said, snorting, "maybe. It would've been better than what came next."

Anna had heard tales of the famine, but they told her little in comparison to the southerner's gaze. The war had bred corpses, but its aftermath had stolen the world's spirit. How could she blame him for his wishes, his delusions? His mind was like her own—a product of all it had endured.

A tangle of voices rose just beyond the hut's leather flaps. One voice stood out by virtue of its strangeness, its absence from her thoughts....

Ramyi entered the hut—or so it seemed.

There was no flesh to speak of, nor eyes, nor lips, nor strands of hair. Her entire body, peering out beneath dark cloth and a crumpled hood, was a mass of pulsing energy. *Hayat.* It hummed as though attuned to some resonance in the air, cool blue and scintillating, so utterly hypnotic—indeed, so familiar—that Anna could not look away.

I am you and you are me.

She rested her head against the splintered post and began to laugh. It was a deep, side-aching laugh, the sort she hadn't known in too long. She laughed through the thumping of Ramyi's boots, carrying on until she was breathless, until tears muddied her vision and spilled down wind-scratched cheeks.

"Did you crack her?" Ramyi asked the young man.

"No," he said hastily. "She just—"

"It's so simple," Anna cried, her hair strewn across her face. "It was always so *simple.*"

Ramyi faced the young man. Her hayat condensed into a firm, oscillating sheen. "Leave us."

The southerner gave a jerky nod and ducked through the flaps. His frantic steps crunched over snow, tapering away until they bled into the wind's whispers.

"It's over," Ramyi said. "Is this what you wanted, Anna?"

Anna. What did it mean to be Anna, to be Ramyi? They were halves of a whole, something unbreakable and indivisible, their voices flowing between them like vibrations along a string.

"Don't you see it?" Anna whispered.

Ramyi cocked her head to the side, studying Anna as though she were a deranged, pathetic beast. "I didn't want them to die that way. You brought this upon them—you made me into a scourge."

"You don't understand," Anna said. "I see what you—*we*—are."

"Whether or not you're cracked," Ramyi replied, moving nearer and squatting at Anna's eye level. "I need to know what you encountered. That knowledge is *mine*, Anna. It was always meant to be mine. I don't want you to suffer like them, but we're all bound by what we must do."

"We're hayat, Ramyi. Nothing more, nothing less. That's our nature."

"And what? *Hayat* sutured your throat? It set the bones in your hand?"

She nodded.

"Do you think I'm a fool?" Ramyi whispered.

"No."

"It gave you its blessings," she said, almost choking on the words, "and now you disgrace its name?"

"There is no *it*. We are it, Ramyi."

"Where are its cuts? Where's your essence?"

There was no way to make her understand. Even an essence was a barrier, a wall between *it* and others. No better than words, Anna supposed.

The northerner's almond-shaped eyes, now gleaming like pearls, scrunched into wary slits. "You must believe yourself to be divine," she said quietly. "All of these *effigies*—and for what? A coward?"

"Ramyi—"

"Once, I cared for you. I could spare us from this pain, Anna, but you resist me at every junction."

"We can still preserve this world."

"What's worth saving, Anna? The selfishness? The wars? The pain of it all?"

"There are no boundaries," Anna said hoarsely. "We are all of those things."

"We are *not*," she snarled through gritted teeth. "I don't know what you've done with your time, but since my birth, I've sought one—just one—thing: To survive. This world takes and takes until we're nothing but dust. We're forced into birth and dragged into death. Why, Anna? Why?"

"Nothing survives forever."

Ramyi's hand slashed across Anna's face in a powder-blue flash.

Her ears rang and her cheeks stung, raw with the bite of bony fingers. "You asked me what I saw," Anna said, using her tongue to probe the bloody lining of her cheek. "I didn't see anything, really. How can I explain it to you? Before I wasn't seeing—I was living in a realm of illusions."

"Then you'll die with clarity, won't you?"

Anna watched the northerner's form swaying vigorously in the candlelight, splendid and cobalt, alluring by virtue of its utter strangeness. "If you wish to kill me."

"Is this what it comes to, Anna? Making yourself into a martyr? Is that why they've scrawled your image on these wicked stones?"

"Perhaps," she whispered.

"You can't even make use of its power."

She felt the air stirring over her skin, the warmth in her fingertips, the kernel of hayat in the center of all she was….It coursed through her entire being as a silent symphony, formless, limitless, a seed of all that could ever manifest. "Yet."

"Show me its truths," Ramyi said, "or I'll bleed them out of you."

"Start cutting."

Ramyi stood and squared her shoulders. "After all these years, it doesn't surprise me that you'd squander this sacred knowledge. In my hands, it could shape any world we desired. We could purge every wicked being."

"You, not we," Anna said. "My life is not worth annihilation."

"You must think I'm seeking the revelations for my own gain."

"Jenis is. He used me and he'll use you, just like—"

"Keep his name out of your mouth."

"Like Gideon," Anna finished. "It ends here, with me. We've paid for peace in blood."

"My sister's blood."

"She never would've wanted this."

Ramyi's eyes narrowed. "How dare you speak of what *she* wanted? Her purpose lives on through me, and through me alone."

"Her only wish was to spare you from war."

"Ignorance," she hissed. "That's all you cling to. You've never known the way of her circle, nor their aims."

"They were *her* aims, not yours," Anna said sharply. "Perishing is not peace."

"If she were here, I would know everything: every word and wish she ever had. But she's gone, Anna, lost to the void for which we're all destined. You sent her there. But the vision of the Starborn will not be killed so easily. I'll ensure that it comes to pass. A world without whips upon our backs, and without the poison of blasphemous tongues."

Again, Anna listened to the silence—the silence in her mind, in the wind, in the encircling forest. She met Ramyi's stare until the room darkened around them. "When I'm given the chance, I will kill you. Forgive me."

The northerner's flesh took on a static haze, burgeoning with something just beneath the surface. Something furious, something vile. Ramyi pulled a blade from the inner folds of her cloak. "This will be your penance."

* * * *

Near the end of the first hundred cuts, Anna lost count. The marks were short and shallow, evoking the ridged flesh of the crocodiles Anna had seen in the kales' menagerie. At times she imagined she was still in Malijad, still in the Apiary, still young and afraid of everything. But now she was drained of fear. Pain was a liquid sensation, a second skin that sheathed her and radiated from the crown of her head to the cracked nails of her feet, tethering her to *now*, to this eternal instant.

She'd spent an hour watching Ramyi, trying to parse the torpor in the northerner's eyes between every prick of the blade. There was nothing to decipher, however. Ramyi worked mechanically, wordlessly, seeking out bare patches of flesh like a crow prowling worm-laden fields.

Anna's attention now lingered on her upper arms, which were webbed with veins of trickling blood. She was captivated by the sight: bright red upon hayat's opal tones, a weird landscape of rivers and cracked-flesh tundra and energy. *Is this how I dissolve?* She'd experienced the mind's unraveling, of course, but a body was something tangible and fragile. It heightened its own senses, almost as though courting death, tempting it with percussive heartbeats and swells of ecstasy.

Then the slicing ceased. Ramyi stepped back, her form reduced to a shadowy blot in Anna's periphery.

"Enough of this," Ramyi said meekly. "Please, Anna—just teach me."

Anna felt the blood race down to her ankles. "I am."

"No, you're dying. Why are you making me do this? Do you think it brings me joy?" Tears flowed over her cheeks in crystal threads. "I just want the pain to end."

"Come closer," Anna whispered. "Let me teach you everything."

Ramyi approached her post with timid steps, almost as though being dragged forward, compelled by something foreign to her own mind. She came so close that her breaths, warm and faint, tingled over the gashes on Anna's neck.

Anna craned her neck forward, grimacing through the pain. She couldn't decipher the bulge in the easterner's eyes—was it fear, regret? It didn't matter, did it?

She kissed Ramyi's forehead.

"What is this?" Ramyi whispered, jerking away in an instant. "Why?"

But the strain was too much. Anna's head slumped forward, her vision suddenly dark, thick with impending death. Her chin rested upon slick, stinging flesh. She smiled faintly at the pressure across her lips, although now it was a memory, a fading, weightless thing.

Shouts rose in the nearby woods.

Anna opened her eyes to the muddy sight of figures streaming into the hut, unable to discern anything beyond the sloshing of snow and the drumming footfalls and a large, intrusive silhouette.

"Stand him up there." The speaker's river-tongue commanded familiar attention, still carrying the rasp of every order it had barked and every watchtower fire it had tended.

Jenis moved into Anna's field of vision with the jingling of buckles and chains. He smelled like wet straw and ale. "Seems you've had better days, Kuzalem."

She glanced into the man's tangled, shadowy features. "I've known worse."

"Southern, through and through." His belly laugh clawed at Anna's ears. "The sooner you share, the sooner we cut you down. Figure you know the formula well enough by now."

"You're in for a long wait, then."

Jenis seized her chin. "Listen here, sukra." He squeezed till her teeth ached. "Haven't forgotten the days in the Nest, have you? Said you'd do anything to win. Anything to break their backs. This is *it*, this is the time. Hero or traitor—what'll it be?"

"We won," Anna managed through the blood. "There's nothing left to break."

"Soft belly you've got. You think ashes mean we've won? Babes starving, our men in fucking chains? Is this what we buried our sons for? We're not dead, girl, but we're not alive, either. Just got new handlers. Don't you think we've fought under their banners long enough? Malchym, Kowak, Golyna—they fancy us as hounds, nothing more. Now we'll seize the yoke."

"And how will you take it? Killing those who have never harmed you?"

"Never harmed us," Jenis sneered. "Happened the same as it's gone to you—a thousand little cuts: writs, selling land, binding families. When nobody's got blood on their hands, they all do."

"You do, too," Anna said. "You've just given Volna new life."

"We've cut away the fat."

"You mean Hazan."

"And all the rest," Jenis said, leaning ever closer. "No more masters. They won't use us again."

"You don't want any masters," Anna breathed, her tongue slick with a film of blood, "but you're still a slave to the hatred in your heart. Death will liberate me."

"Still believing those bedside tales, Kuzalem? Prayin' for the Grove and its soft moss?"

"I don't believe," she said. "I know."

"Then you're more fucked than the rest of us."

Jenis angled himself toward Ramyi, briefly affording Anna a glimpse of the hut, the assembled southern fighters, and the towering slab that had been propped up near the doorway. The latter sight was the only thing alarming enough to capture Anna's attention, however. The rest of her world was washed-out, transient: Light and shadow smeared together as a blurry canvas; dull, knotted voices crept past her. Focusing through a wildfire of pain, Anna examined the rusted back panel of the slab.

A pair of limp, muddy hands protruded over the upper lip. Prickly blossoms, fifty-pronged and immediately recognizable in spite of the distance, wormed over their fingers like a second skin.

It was one of the few sigils she could never forget:

A tracker's essence.

"No sense in drowning the unruly pups," Jenis said with a nod toward the slab. "Just need to change the hand that feeds."

Anna strained against the ropes. "You won't gain anything from him."

"Oh, it's well past gaining anything," Jenis said. "Time to build a new order, Kuzalem. And orders need throat-cutters just as sorely as visionaries."

Ramyi pushed through the cluster of fighters. "Jenis—"

"Bogat," he snapped, rounding on the northerner with clenched fists. "What's it now?"

"If she dies, we lose it all," Ramyi whispered.

"No way 'round it," Jenis said, glaring at Anna. "Not the first time her ilk's been stretched out. Stubborn ones, that's what they are." He paused, eyeing Ramyi with disdain that soon crumbled into groans. "Perk your ears: If she won't make her marks here, she'll do it on some other scrap of soil. Simple choice."

"We can take her with us."

"What for?" Jenis asked. "Want us at her feet, slack-jawed and needy? Just how she wants you—just how she's had you."

Ramyi's lips tightened. "Let's finish it."

Glancing at the slab's attendants, Jenis stepped aside and gave a shrill whistle. His beard was liquid silver in the candlelight, still damp with its crust of melting snow, so thick that it nearly buried a savage grin. It seemed that he'd never known a greater pleasure. He squirmed as the slab rotated, his eyes hungry, passionate….

Anna understood why.

Dozens of thin, rusting stakes jutted up through Lukas's flesh, pinning him to the slab as though he were nothing more than a doll, or a butcher's latest carving. Living, dead—the distinction felt arbitrary. His sigils pulsed along in a torpid rhythm, but his body was curiously still, as slack as any beast lifted by the scruff of its neck. A forest of blackened tips sprouted from his eye sockets, his lips, his tongue, his throat, his chest, his belly, his manhood, his fingers and legs and the expanses between them.

"What've you done to him?" Anna whispered.

Even Ramyi's stare traversed the ceiling of the hut, desperate to flee somewhere, anywhere. Her throat bobbed spastically.

"Done nothing to him." Jenis clapped a palm against the slab's back plate. "Couldn't do a thing if we wanted it—this kretin's rune has bought a name of its own."

Anna's breaths were hot, short. "Take him down."

"Just what I had in mind." Jenis whistled again, this time adding the flourish of a mocking bow.

The southern fighters gathered around the slab, gingerly angling their hands to grasp Lukas's punctured limbs in a sea of points and oxide-crusted stumps, then began working to free the body. Even as they strained and tugged and tore, Lukas was slack, silent—the hut filled with soft squelching. Blood frothed around vanishing wounds.

Then, in one concerted tug, they lifted Lukas's torso from a row of stakes, leaving his eyes and cheeks and tongue freckled with blubbery crimson tissue. Spinal fluid crackled in fresh cavities.

Jenis pointed to the packed earth before Anna. "Here."

Still gripping his arms, the fighters carried the body as instructed and stood it upright. For a moment, Lukas remained unresponsive, his fingers dangling and blood twisting in whirlpool pinpricks. Then his nostrils twitched.

Lukas jerked his head back and let out a bestial scream, but the pain was surely nothing more than a fading inconvenience: Patches of split flesh converged; his sigils leaped to startled attention; eyeballs sprouted like lustrous eggshells, their sclera clouding as a raw stream of pigment birthed irises and pupils.

Anna shut her eyes. She should've been able to watch—perhaps been able to enjoy it—but she couldn't. It wasn't like her dreams at all. In that world, she had despised him, blamed him, wanted him to suffer as badly as herself. She had torn out his teeth and burned his kin. Yet now, with the mental constructs of the old mind vanquished, what remained? There was no villain, no victim—those were labels she had imposed upon reality. There was only a living being in pain.

There was hatred toward life itself.

"Ears still sharp?" Jenis cooed, propping up Lukas's chin with a single finger. "Dunno how much you caught of our jabbering."

Lukas gazed at his once-comrade. "All of it."

"So, what'll it be?" Jenis asked. "Slit the sukra's throat and you'll be pissing wine in Kowak by the full moon."

"If not?"

"If not," Jenis echoed, laughing at the suggestion. "You fell in with the wrong lot. This is how you redeem it, boy."

"We should've stomped you out."

"Us?" Jenis asked. "Interesting eye for history, you've got." He turned toward Anna, gesturing up and down at Lukas's shaking form. "Hasn't told you a lick about where he's from, has he?"

Anna met Lukas's eyes. She saw the hurt, the shame.

"We put his daughters in the ground," Jenis said coldly. "Screeching wife, too. This is the face of your master, Kuzalem—tucking tail when we marched on him. Same masters who've always had a blade to Rzolka's neck." He smirked. "I knew your scent the moment you set foot in Kowak, Lukas. Masks couldn't shield you forever."

"You fucking worm."

Jenis snorted. "Think I wanted 'em did in? Orders, Lukas, orders. Same orders you gave to your men. Only spot of difference is which line you're holding."

"We fought for Rzolka," Lukas whispered, his eyes huge and wild.

"No, you fought for the old blood. So did we, and your clan peeled off my boy's skin for it."

"It was war."

"That's just it. Never wondered why I threw in with Kuzalem? I was just itching for a new war—had been since the ink dried on the peace writ. I was waiting to wipe you out. You and your entire breed." He leaned toward Lukas like a probing wolf, his teeth gritted and brows furrowed. Then he shrugged. "Bygones be bygones, though—time to break the cycle. No matter how many corpses we stacked in Nahora, we never purged the infection. They built it that way: War keeps us in line, keeps us kneeling to our saviors. Enough of that. Behead the serpents and a new world'll follow."

"Blood and salt's never been new."

"Earned in your own name, it is."

"You think I've been with her for salt?" Lukas hissed.

"Hope so," Jenis said. "She's not so pretty anymore."

"Fuck your wine, and your salt, and all the rest. World's grown tired. I'm living to die, you old sow."

Jenis's knuckles crunched into Lukas's nose. Blood sprayed over packed earth before squirming back into the man's ripped nostrils.

"You listen here," Jenis whispered. "Unless she gives our Starsent what she's on about, we'll saw off that head of hers and the hounds'll have a nibble on her bones. Gives you all the time in the Grove to prattle on with your wit." Lukas glanced at Anna, but there was nothing to be said, nothing to be shown. "We can put you back on your skewer, drop you to the bottom of the fuckin' sea, and we won't miss a wink at night. Or, you can show your teeth. You open her belly and you'll have everything Volna never put in your palm. Let the dead ways crumble. Creation's death, isn't it?"

Lukas's stare wandered the dirt floor.

"Always were a wise one, I can't darken that," Jenis continued. "Pick your eternity well, eh? Blackness or starlight? Cold water or warm thighs?"

Or death, Anna considered, somehow perplexed by her own involvement in the dilemma. Everything, for her, led to death. She wasn't afraid of that end—it was something that now felt overdue, blindly seeking her day and night. Absurdity was the worrisome thing: The absurdity of indecision in her brother's killer, the absurdity of loyalty and everything she had associated with it, the absurdity of dueling over who would take her life.

"Time's burning," Jenis said presently.

Lukas regarded Anna once more, this time with the vapid stare she had come to know so well. But now that emptiness was fullness. It was an answer that had masqueraded as a question for so long. I don't want to kill you, it whispered, and yet…

A *bang* thudded somewhere in the distance, trailed by low, gravelly roaring. Several of Jenis's men edged toward the hut's flaps, their faces dour, cagey.

"Must be the trees," one said, breaking the silence. He looked at Jenis and shrugged. "Always falling."

But it was not a tree. Anna knew that with certainty. Her childhood had been full of trees crashing down, plummeting through the underbrush with their tinny rattling, and none of them had ever made a grown man flinch. This sound was just as familiar, but for entirely different reasons. It was an itch on her tongue, a forgotten lullaby.

She knew it did not come alone.

"Now or never," Jenis told Lukas.

Two blasts ripped through the surrounding forest in rapid succession, their echoes rolling outward and deepening like a monstrous heartbeat.

Anna's ears rang dimly with the percussive force. Closer. She studied the gathering's collective confusion: flitting, skyward glances, loosening grips, pacing bodies. Their ignorance wouldn't last forever. High above her, so slight that she nearly mistook it for wind, a nerash's engines whined.

"Stop," Anna cried. "I'll give up the rune."

Ramyi barged into the group's clearing. "You will?"

"I don't want to serve anybody," Anna whispered. "It was Nahora—they turned me against you. Against all of you." Her gaze swept over the assembly, lingering on Lukas with a pointed edge. "I couldn't see it before."

"Fuck're you doing?" Lukas growled.

"Making my mark on this world," Anna said. "I wouldn't expect you to understand."

"What d—"

"You have Volna in your heart," she pressed on. "That's why you've taken so much from me, and from them, and from Rzolka. You made them do this."

Jenis's scowl began to widen, revealing a set of thin, brittle teeth.

"You're cracked," Lukas said.

"No," she said, "just free." She nodded at Jenis, feigned a weak smile. "All I ask is to unbind his rune. Let me carve him open for all he's done."

"The famous Breaking," Jenis said, scratching at the knots of his beard. "What's tugged at your heart, Kuzalem?"

Another blast rang out, this one nearer and sharper.

"Pain," Anna said.

"No better teacher."

Her palms ached, remembering the feel of iron, the tackiness of blood….

"Korpa," spat Lukas. He raged against his handlers, twisting, grunting, no tamer than the beasts that prowled the deepest woods.

But as his head flopped forward, glossy with its sweat-sheen, Anna gleamed the way of his tongue. There was a playful twist in his brow, a budding fire in his eyes. He passed her a muted nod.

"Cut me down so I can gut him," Anna said evenly.

Jenis cackled and clapped like a giddy boy, even as his fighters convened near the flaps and passed hushed words among themselves. He didn't react to the next blast, nor the one that followed it. "To it, then," he snapped at a nearby fighter. "Get those ropes off."

The man hurried to Anna's side, then sidled around till he was out of sight. His blade sawed through the dry, fibrous cords, its motions humming down through the bones of Anna's arms.

Ramyi watched from a distance. Her face—particularly her luminous eyes—did not waver, offering the illusion of inner silence. Surely she could mislead the others to that end, perhaps even warp their perceptions directly, but Anna glimpsed the turmoil manifesting beneath her physical form. Maelstroms of hayat crept over her flesh and marred her silhouette. Even her eyes spoke in that ineffable way: *What are you planning now?*

Anna's arms fell forward, numbly spilling into her lap. Sensations returned as tangibly as the streaks of blood running from her elbows to her fingertips.

"We should send a few out," one of the fighters said to Jenis. "Getting louder, isn't it?"

Jenis paid him no mind. He stood with his arms folded, engrossed by Anna—her weakness, her blood, her surrender. "Help her up."

"There's no need," Anna said. In spite of her injuries, which now throbbed like beads of hot tar upon her flesh, she was more capable than she'd been in years. All of her old agonies had vanished, replaced by a sense of fluidity, of childlike grace and tenacity. Her bones felt thick and sturdy. Her lungs flowed in effortless rhythm. Mind, matter—the dualism converged in the fabric of her being. Hayat lent its strength and pervaded her awareness: It revealed her screaming nerves to be a hallucination, a mere fever dream of death. She studied that fear as she rose, each motion smooth and assured, never allowing the pain to break her mask of equanimity. *You cannot be broken by what you are.*

Several of the nearest fighters shifted uneasily. They were hard men, coal-eyed and stubbled, but torture gnawed at men in a way that killing did not—especially when the tortured resembled their daughters, their sisters, their wives. Not even war could suppress that instinctive revulsion.

Every stare harbored pity for the wretch and her glistening wounds, quietly pleading to end the suffering, to show mercy.

That would be their downfall.

She felt as though she were gliding toward them, her pain ceding to a blissful haze, an effortless cosmic dance in which there was no need to act, only to be. Shoulders scrunched and brows furrowed as she stepped before Lukas, but the fighters kept their distance, wary. Anna's mind strayed toward visions of their blades ripping through her. How did it feel to be extinguished? There was no time for that fear now, of course. Her path was known, even essential—destruction always preceded creation.

A fighter lightly took Anna's hand, then coaxed her fingers open and curled them around a blade's bone handle. It grew immediately slick with sweat.

Two men held Lukas still, though he'd ceased his struggling long ago. Now he was tranquil, meeting Anna's stare with melancholy that she could not dissect. It was something bittersweet, something undone. Something that would rob his Breaking of the freedom it ought to have granted.

More blasts crackled in the forest.

"On with it," Jenis groaned.

Anna lifted the blade and pressed it to Lukas's neck. Donning a soft smile, she surrendered her hands to fate. To hayat, by any other name. She watched the blade pirouette in a smooth, flawless sweep, instantaneously snuffing out every trace of his essence.

Then he was not there.

His flesh vanished in a surge of frothy blue-white hayat, leaving behind a burning core that was no different from Anna's own flesh, from Ramyi, from the energy that stirred in every being. It warped and shimmered and stretched until it birthed a new form, a living effigy of the man it had once inhabited.

Tears dribbled down Lukas's cheeks.

"Don't," Anna whispered. She lifted her hand and wicked away the droplets, all the while smiling, marveling at the hayat's dance. Her voice was high and tight. "Please don't."

"That's that," Jenis cut in, nervously eyeing the flaps and the rumbles beyond them. "Chodge, Kuzalem. Give her your cuts."

Lukas hung his head and sobbed.

"It will pass," Anna whispered. She did not look at him; there was nothing more to be done. Nothing beyond the confines of his own mind, more accurately. She moved toward Ramyi with the blade at her side, her thumb sticky and stained red upon the iron spine. The girl's luminous form consumed her vision.

"What does it look like?" Ramyi asked, her eyes brimming with terror and awe in equal measure. She stood so close that Anna could feel her own breaths curling back against her. "My sigil—tell me what it is."

But where Ramyi expected trees, Anna saw only a vast forest. She saw pulsing hayat that had been issued a name, a history, a sacred task. How could anything straddle the boundary between divinity and ignorance, radiance and depravity? "You'll see it soon enough."

You'll see yourself.

With a heavy swallow, Ramyi lifted her chin and peered at Anna over the slopes of her cheekbones.

Anna set the blade against the girl's opal jugular. Swift, pattering heartbeats ticked beneath the iron, incessantly calling Anna to that wicked task. She could do it. She had to. What difference did it make—to bleed a lamb, to slash a girl's throat? But she could hardly distinguish her own hand from Ramyi's flesh.

Forgive me.

She squeezed the bone handle and held her breath and ripped the blade across soft skin. There was a subtle snag, a—

Anna's hand hung in midair, trembling, entirely divorced from her control. Divorced from feeling, even. It was a dead zone in her perception, a static, gangly bulb crawling with hayat's waxy patina. She watched a bead of blood well up and streak down the curve of Ramyi's neck.

No.

Several fighters edged closer, their arms outstretched, their runes in utter tumult. Sweat glimmered on their brows. They'd been waiting. Hoping.

"You never learn," Ramyi whispered. Stepping back, she touched a finger to the bleeding nick, then studied it closely, soberly. "Your eyes speak what sleeps in your heart."

Every limb grew useless, cold. Anna could neither flee nor fight nor scream—the fighters' runes fixed her like an alien vise, drowning her in stillness, that fatal stillness. It seeped into her chest until her lungs felt choked with tar and setstone. Until every breath was a shallow wheeze. Her eyes—growing slower, ever slower—flitted downward, drawn to the blade as it tumbled from frozen fingers and thumped onto packed earth. Raw, mindless panic erupted in her, but she watched it arise like clouds in a distant field, moving over her, away....

"Not your sharpest choice," Jenis huffed.

"It's enough," Lukas said, squirming at the edge of Anna's vision. "Enough!"

Ramyi's placid mask did not shift. "Is it?" she asked calmly. "After all she's done to me?"

The next blast reached Anna's ears like a fissure deep beneath the waves, at once muffled and thunderous. Her vision wafted in and out of blackness, suffused with the warmth of childhood, of happiness beyond causes, and in that silky descent toward death, silhouettes raced about and bolted toward the flaps and shouldered past one another.

It was near, but it was too late.

Death seemed to envelop her in a soft, humming quilt, urging her to let go, to fade into the nothingness from which she'd arisen.

Her vision settled on a patch of candlelit earth. She studied a pebble in its center, the way it cast a miniscule shadow and glinted faintly and remained still in spite of the carnage outside. Blackness encroached until the pebble was but a keyhole, and—

The pebble lifted.

It hovered just above the earth, turning silently, gently, as though a child were inspecting its every notch and crag.

As Anna's hearing dissolved into a wash of muted tones and vibrations, she tethered her focus to the pebble; rather than fearing death, she was transfixed by the phenomenon. It was so whimsical, so unreal—it robbed her dissolution of its terror. She willed the pebble to lift higher, just a bit higher….

It rocketed toward the nearest fighter, then vanished.

This was a dream—it had to be a dream.

But a moment later the fighter dropped his ruj, toppled to his knees, and let his head hang like that of a discarded puppet. A thread of blood trickled from the entry point in his forehead. Bits of his brain freckled the tent flaps.

One of Jenis's men shrank away from the body. "*So korpa?*" He let out a shrill scream just before the pebble severed his spine.

Anna tracked the stone's hum through the air, flicking it about and burrowing it in bones, organs, eyes—it was a curious game, more a test of will than survival. Indeed, she recognized herself in the stone. Not as a projection, but merely another limb, a lost sense that had faded amid the chatter of living. It was the final refuge of her mind. She felt her body withering in the black silence of its end, but what was a body, anyway? Some flesh, some fluid? The pebble—*she*—orbited the room, beautiful and swift and blood-soaked.

Suddenly the binding force broke across her body, dissipating as though it were darkness pierced by dawn, a thunderhead crumbling into fog. How can hayat hold me? the thinking mind whispered. *We hold ourselves.* Air flooded her lungs. Clarity expelled the blackness in her vision. Her fingertips flexed and stretched in warm, golden effervescence, the sensations experienced both within and without her, at once immediate and impossibly distant. She—in all her totality, her name and speech and form—now seemed to be an extension, a mere vessel of that which animated the pebble and her body alike.

"What are you doing?" Ramyi seethed at the marked fighters, her voice slipping under the rumble of advancing blasts. She worked her fingers into feeble, strained shapes, but it was fruitless—the fighters' hands jittered and contorted and cracked with sickening pops.

Anna watched their knucklebones churning beneath pale flesh, jutting out within rings of blood....

Their screams were like birdsongs.

Settling into the stillness that pervaded chaos, Anna looked upon the gathering with a soft smile, a graceful mind: fighters staggering back through the flaps, their faces half-charred and smoldering; bodies slumping in red pools; Jenis screeching at his captains; Lukas eyeing the bodies of his former handlers, huffing, wiping at the blood that freckled his face and neck.

And in the center of that soundless cosmos, a luminous galaxy.

Ramyi's eyes bloomed to wild orbs. She stumbled back, grimacing as she severed the link with her marked fighters, then shoved her way toward the tent flaps.

"Girl!" Jenis howled. He lurched to snag her collar, but came up short. "Sukra! Get the nerashi up."

Several of his captains, so intent on the thunder of killing that they did not notice the corpses by their boots, were quick to heed the command. They dashed out through the flaps, ruji raised and voices hoarse, leaving behind their breathless commander. Another round of shelling thrummed the tent's walls.

Doubled over and wheezing, Jenis faced the flaps with his hands clasped to his thighs. He gave a sickly laugh. "Brought friends, did you?"

Anna let her arms rest at her sides and moved closer. Her steps were light and careful. She eyed Lukas—that humanoid spur of hayat, of herself—but he was catatonic, his mouth wrenched open and eyes creased with scarlet blemishes.

"We'll gut them, too," Jenis rasped. "We'll gut every last one if it means we're free."

Still trembling, Lukas knelt down, retrieved a dead man's ruj, and rose to face Jenis. The weapon hung loosely at his hip.

"You can cease this now," Anna said. "No more bloodshed, no more pain."

Jenis turned with a pronounced limp in his right leg. Silky orange light painted his beard, his sour lips, his still-burning rune—Anna's hands itched with the memory of its cuts. "Think you can put me down like all the rest?" he growled. Then his stare shifted, his shoulders scrunched. Fear rippled across his brow. "Korpa."

The marble eyes of his fighters gazed up blankly from the earth, alight with the reflected droplet of flames, of tears half-cried on the horizon of death.

Lukas aimed the ruj, but his eyes were vacant, fixed on visions far behind Jenis and the forest.

"What are you?" Jenis whispered. He drew a short, broad blade from a sheath on his thigh.

"I am," Anna said. She moved closer, picking her way through the mass of bodies and bloodstains, overcome with waves of ecstasy that arose from nowhere in particular. There was no way to repress her smile, nor her bright eyes—she felt only love, only light, only joy, all shining through the colored glass of her flesh.

"Tell 'em to tuck their teeth," Lukas said, passing Anna a warning glance from the corner of his eye. His words leaked out, half-hearted, the Breaking's nascent awareness recognizing the chain of each thought as it rose from the echoes of his conditioning. That which he now was observed all that had corrupted him. "W—who's out there? Easterners?"

Jenis glared at him. "Won't matter if you never get to them."

"It's over," Lukas spat. "We can dance if you want, but let her go."

"We've got more blood than you think, boy."

"You might," he said, "but they'll wring out every d—drop if they can't find her. Breathin'. That's the long and short of it."

A series of rattling blasts settled into the grooves of the southerner's silence. In Anna's mind the moment was an unbroken stream, a twisting mesh of hayat that assumed a thousand forms in the span between blinks. She was transfixed by its majesty, its simplicity—how had she never seen it?

"Go, put our people in their pits." Jenis lifted his blade and swept it lazily toward the forest, his eyes blister-red, bleary.

Anna lingered in the gulf between the bodies and waving flaps, scanning Jenis for the pride of a beaten man. Such virulent things resisted oblivion.

And when she finally moved forward, conscious of the rage in his fist and the venom in his pupils, she did so with understanding of the animal's nature. A serpent was called to strike; a bear was called to devour. Men were called to kill.

She stepped past him, immersed in his warmth for the briefest moment....

"Anna!" Lukas's voice sprouted in the crux of pain and knowing.

Then the blade was cold heat in her belly, wriggling, violating the old mind's boundaries of self and other. Jenis's hands were white-knuckled. She blinked at the iron's splinter silhouette, then at the beads of blood freckling the tops of her feet, at the crimson streams slipping over the crest of her hip bone and snaking down pale thighs. She looked into the man's eyes. Tried to look at them, anyway—his stare was downcast, seemingly oblivious, and—

Jenis's skull burst in a glistening shell. Gristle-pink, scarlet, bits of discolored gray: His mind blanketed the tent's wall, but only for a moment. Even as the pulp dripped over soil and his body collapsed and his legs spasmed, hayat worked to reassemble him, to sprout something new and vivid from that sordid heap.

Anna gazed down at the blade. Pain flitted around her head like a gauzy crown, thick and numbing. "Help me hold him," she calmly told Lukas. "I need to Break him."

But Jenis was already rising to his feet, his face slick and bright in the afterglow of birth.

"Help me," Anna repeated. She stepped back, cradling the blade as she went, wholly focused on Lukas in spite of the agony. Agony. It was just a word now, a concept woven from rejection of that-which-was. Her agony was nothing compared to that of Lukas; she glanced up at bulging eyes and wet, clammy skin, his Breaking screaming out against everything he had done, everything he was doing, everything he held—

Yet Anna was not bound by its weight. *I am all things and in time, I will claim all lives.* Birth demands death. There was no creation, no destruction. No question of what had to be done. She wrapped her hands around the blade and extracted it from her belly, surprising herself with her own wince. Her wound gushed with a tinge of déjà vu. How many times had this occurred? How many times had she rejected the sacredness of the moment, the experience?

Lukas edged toward Jenis with sharp, skittering movements, his face twisted into a mask of revulsion. His mind was too raw with the sting of the Breaking—it was sunlight ripping through a black morass, a dose of truth so potent that it could crush him under the weight of things left undone: To harm another was to harm oneself.

But here, now, foretold in realms that eluded his perception, violence was necessary.

"Let me free you," Anna said, seizing Jenis with a fistful of blossoming gray hair. She struggled with him until he knelt in silence, baring his teeth, huffing, gazing up fanatically at Anna and the thing she had become. She did not hate him; she pitied him. Anna set the blade across his throat.

"Do as you like," Jenis said as he lifted his chin. "Whatever breed you are, you bleed like the rest. Prickle at the same blade-coats, too. Not an herbman in the world who'll stitch that gut."

The Apiary had already told that truth, and now her flesh tingled with its echoes. She felt the toxin seeping into every pore and gash and severed vein. It was a wicked brew, an amber sap distilled from brittle yolar leaves and rattling serpents, mashed in a rusted vat somewhere south of Qersul, spoon-churned twice a day by a wrinkled widow, a woman who had miscarried thrice, who would have named her children—

Anna rooted her mind to the task at hand. The blade seemed to sweep on its own accord, carving easily through the sagging skin and stubble.

Jenis's sigils winked away, replaced by the ensuing flood of hayat. His entire body shimmered, its form both fluid and fixed, a living extension of Anna and Lukas and the countless masses that had arisen and perished in ignorance.

"Do it," Anna said to Lukas. She marveled at the chill of her own voice. "Do it now."

Opalescent eyes stared up at her. Begging, wondering...

"I can't," Lukas whispered.

Neither of the men could. They were blank, shuddering creatures now, their minds purged of all that had given the world its meaning and horror. Their bodies had ties, of course, but how could those bindings relate to them? They had no families, no memories, no preferences or comforts or urges. Not yet, anyway. Not of their own accord. And in shedding the artifacts of the old mind, they also shattered the perpetual, savage instinct at the core of every beast—the need to kill. It was all they had ever known, not only in this life, but since the eons of mud and caves, hunting and being hunted, slaughtering to avoid being slaughtered.

Without it, what were they?

Anna released the man's hair and looked at Lukas. She found him shuddering, his ruj lowered and fingers far from the trigger.

And as Anna bore the weight of what stood before her, the righteous violence that had shone through the Apiary's visions, her breaths slowed to a crawl. Did he need to die? She studied the southerner and his tired body, his drink-laden eyes, his hands and their aging tremors. He'd burned every comfort to stand by Anna's side, and what had he received in turn? Pain. Whatever occurred now would be a hollow attempt to find solace. How could it heal them, after all? Time would do their work with vicious ease. Even if he were butchered by their hands, that which they would kill—the entity peering through the eyes that Anna now met with her own—was not Jenis, nor could it be. He'd died in the Breaking, banished to—

Horror trickled up from her gut.

I will claim all lives.

She stepped back, overcome by the magnitude of it all. There was no need to open throats. No reason for bloodshed or torment or even cruel words. Killing was merely the dissolution of an ephemeral form—the Breaking was apotheosis.

It destroyed that ravenous, lonesome beast that knew itself as *I*, blindly roaming and eating and stealing to sate an endless appetite. It replaced an illusory cycle with eternity. For one who corrected that fundamental misunderstanding, who ceased the dream of existing in the world, rather than being it, birth occurred every moment, swallowed and renewed by a thousand subtle deaths, forever ongoing, forever abiding in the benevolent stillness of *now*, of *here*, that infinite dimension Anna had come to inhabit. She understood it so clearly, so completely, that no other thought could arise in that instant. The Apiary—indeed, Hayat—had conveyed that basic truth, yet it was so simple that her mind had corrupted it: When a single entity evaporated, what remained?

Everything.

Hayat.

Ramyi needed to die, but there would be no murder—only the end of a timeless nightmare.

"It's enough," Anna said, smiling dimly, tearfully, at Lukas. "It's time to go."

Lukas did not stop aiming his ruj. There was still an animal strain in him, an instinct circling in the abyss of awareness, calling him toward the habits of that old, dead mind: *Kill.* His face churned between scowling and sobbing. The Breaking showed the way, but not every man could take that first step.

"He's dead," she pressed on. "Him, who he was—he's gone now. Come, let's go." She extended a hand toward Lukas.

With quivering lips and bulging eyes, the southerner lowered his ruj and set it awkwardly against his leg. "All right."

Nerves failed along the backs of Anna's legs. She felt her body crumpling, sagging down into itself, unburdened by pain, yet wracked with frailty. Not only frailty, she realized, *death*. The death of a body, an ancient shell. She tracked its dissolution with stoic curiosity—swaying, sinking....

Warm hands clasped around her.

"I've got you," Lukas whispered, lifting her and resting her cheek against his chest and settling her, babe-like, into the crux of his arms. Heartbeats pounded behind his skin and birthed birdsongs in Anna's ear.

And as Anna was carried into that brisk night, snowflakes wilting upon her skin and vicious light stabbing through the trees, she surrendered to the procession of fate. Whether she died now, or in an hour, a day— she smiled with acceptance. Birth demands death. The words caressed her, embraced her.

Boots crunched through the snow and with them came the hard, striking tones of Nahoran fighters. They thundered past Anna, intent on Jenis and his lonesome hut.

"Wait," Anna wheezed into Lukas's chest. "Wait."

But the wind faded for a moment, a single breath, making way for the thrum of nerash engines and southern screams and stiff, croaking pine branches. In that sleeping void, three subdued snaps issued from the hut.

What had they killed?

Anna's vision darkened, cycling between buried sounds and memories of fields and blackberries.

"Get her in," a Nahoran called out, rousing her to violent wakefulness. She heard the hiss and whine of a nerash's doors. "Hurry, in."

Hands swam over her, under her, working in tandem to lift her into the fume-laden darkness of a cabin. Dozens of breaths, too-near and suffocating, echoed around her.

"Where is she?" Anna whispered, her eyes shut and lips throbbing.

"Lay still," Lukas said quietly.

"We need her," Anna said.

A Nahoran halted his commands in Orsas, swallowing hard. "The Starsent is gone, Kuzalem. Her nerash—"

"She isn't gone," Anna cooed into the spiraling darkness behind her lids. "Just out of sight."

Chapter 18

They worked to mend her flesh as though it were her, as though death meant the extinction of all she'd ever been. She watched it unfold with constant interest, marveling at the touch of a needle, the grace of a suturer's touch, the tears that twinkled upon eastern cheeks. The nerkoya gave it all a shapeless, gloomy pall, warping silhouettes into storms and candles into dim, guttering suns, distant stars through the nebulae, where whispers of the old worlds bled through the veil....

But a form's end could merely be stalled, never averted.

They moved her through lavender-smelling halls with pearl and violet tiles, past windows with rain that had beaded into the cosmos upon its glass, into quarters that were so distant and tranquil that they must've envisioned it as beyond death's reach.

Two women—Halshaf sisters, judging by their tongue—loomed at Anna's bedside, chanting, praying, weeping....

After a bout of dreamless sleep, she opened her eyes and sat up in ashen darkness. Pain tore across the sutures in her gut. She ignored the host of hands that flurried to calm her, to ease her back into the sleep that would become death.

"Let me up," Anna said firmly. "I must go to her."

But their voices were strained and timid, possessed by the fearful ignorance that had guided Anna for so long. Stay, sleep. They were bestial impulses now, equally fit to be taken or discarded by the mind that perceived them. After all, what was an instinct but an urge to avoid death? When one saw its inevitability, its looming shadow, there was nothing to avoid, nothing to chase.

Only what had to be done.

"Please," one of the Halshaf attendants said amid a chorus of whispers, "you're still sedated, Knowing One. This isn't the—"

Anna stared at the woman, through the woman. Slivers of hayat worked through the woman's flesh, like cracks in a vast dam...."I am Matrasa, seer of all things and none," she said. "The world is moving through its final breaths. You will seek out the commander of this garrison, and you will bring me to them. This is your path."

The gathering's chatter was severed in an instant, replaced by rapt, fanatical silence. Their wine-blot eyes grew engorged with—

With *what?* Anna marveled at their strangeness, the way they threaded the boundaries of terror and devotion. "Do you understand?"

Yet before she could finish her question, the attendant was a passing shadow in the corridor, a single star in the constellation of destiny.

* * * *

Deep within her own being, Anna sensed the omens of a gathering storm. It stood apart from the wind that howled over the walls and the rain that battered knuckle-thick windows. Her awareness was the dry, heavy air that pooled atop autumn fields, crackling with the peal of distant thunder. And she saw the thunder's sister—lightning, bright and forked—in the sigil of everyone she passed. She saw it in their eyes and their chattering teeth and their scrunched hands, the way the fighters carried their weapons and the hall-mothers recited their prayers.

But she was not afraid of the storm.

She *was* the storm.

"You really should rest," a gangly sister pleaded, even as she led Anna to the chamber's walnut door and rested her hand upon its knob. She exchanged glances with several attendants in the small, yet vocal crowd that had trailed Anna from the suturer's wing. "They're quite busy, and if—"

Anna stared at the doorknob. She excised everything from consciousness until there was only a shape, a bronze gleam, a set of faded prints that had been left by a nervous captain. She sensed the hands of a metalworker and the salt he'd been paid and the family he had fed with his meager earnings. She traced the device back to the man's foundry, then back to the quarry, to the earth, to the very cosmos that had delivered it.

The doorknob shifted.

Gasping, the sister jerked her hand away and clutched it near her chest. Her eyes were brimming with the ignorant terror of a beast.

"Take your sisters to the prayer hall," Anna said quietly. "Thank you for all you've done." She moved past the attendants, entered the chamber, and shut the door.

Fear hung heavy in the air—hot, sour, tinged with the dread of sending men to die. It was aptly complemented by a duel of spiteful flatspeak and charts unfurled upon a round, varnished table, calling Anna's old mind back to days in the Nest and beyond. Even more familiar was a red-faced Nahoran officer with his fingers jutting toward an Alakeph captain.

Not just any captain—Rashig.

Neither of them seemed to notice Anna's arrival, however, and the officer carried on in spite of—or perhaps in defiance of—Rashig's composure, occasionally pounding the table with the flat of his fists.

"We have nothing to spare," he snapped, gesturing to one of his many maps, as though the point proved itself. "Where are you conjuring these additional columns from?"

"My order is prepared to evacuate the region," Rashig replied steadily, "but we'll require your nerashi."

"Ga'mir Ashoral's command was to find the girl by any means," the captain said.

"Do you not see their ploy? Jenis's forces are already in position to sweep the valley, and our line with it."

"The state does not waver in its resolve."

"Is this the time for dogma?" Rashig prodded. "My forces were summoned here and we came as a courtesy. If you'll—"

"We need to strike at their heart." Anna's voice carried a sharp, dispassionate edge she had never sensed before.

Both men's heads swiveled toward her in unison, their mouths ajar with words formed and abandoned in the same instant. Rashig scrunched his brow as though making sense of a mirage. The Nahoran officer, by contrast, pulled on a mask of vague fury.

"You can't be here," the officer barked. "If the others see you bleeding—"

"She's not well," Rashig said gently.

"Not well? She's dying. Where are your girls with the pox-wreaths?"

Rashig blinked at Anna. "They were watching her."

"Yes, I am dying," Anna said with quiet resolve, tracking a stream of warm blood as it crested her hip bone and flowed down the curve of her lower belly. "We are all moving toward this fate, second by second. Lifetime by lifetime. The cycle will continue unless you heed my words."

"Get one of your sisters," the officer hissed at Rashig.

Anna's attention snapped to a clatter of footfalls, a jumble of hands extending on the other side of the threshold, a bit of tempered brass.

The latch on the inner face of the chamber's door slid shut.

"Will you listen now?" she asked. "There is no time for division."

Thunder crashed in the distance.

"What was that?" the officer whispered. But his eyes, monstrous and suffused with terrible awe, answered that feeble question in his stead.

"It's true, then." A lump bobbed in Rashig's throat. "It's all true."

"You will assemble every column you can muster," Anna told them. "You will arrange them on the platforms and you will prepare your nerashi to fly within the hour. We must converge on Malchym. There is no alternative and there can be no failure."

Stalking toward Anna, the officer's shock ceded to indignation. "The Ga'mir's instructions—"

"Were to neutralize the Starsent by any means," Anna finished. Her stare lingered on the officer's lips, which she'd managed to cinch shut with little more than a flicker of attention. His entire body followed in short order. Pain burrowed through the lining of Anna's gut, through the nested spirals of tissue at the base of her brain—control came at a cost. "She died to ensure this sacred task. Know that my words, and indeed my actions, are truth given form. The Starsent's impurity will devour this world."

Rashig eyed the officer with faint disinterest. "Are you certain she's there?"

"Beyond any doubt," Anna replied. "Her presence heralds extinction."

"And this is the will of the World-Womb?"

"It is the will of everything." Anna's gaze swept away from the Nahoran.

Released from that murderous grasp, the officer winced, sagged, and toppled forth onto his hands and knees. He remained there for a long while, gasping until threads of spittle hung from his mouth.

"Brother Rashig," the officer spat as he struggled to stand. "We can't bow to this—this...."

"It will be as you command," Rashig said to Anna. He strode past her, collected yet fervent, his sigils humming with the song of the universe.

As Anna moved to follow him, she sensed a warm trickle upon her cheek. It was not a tear, no, but simply another piece of the puzzle drifting into place. She pressed a hand to her left eye, already knowing, already observing that which she would find upon surrendered flesh.

Her fingertips came away crimson.

* * * *

Hall-Mother Yuliena had taken Lukas to a dim, jasmine-smelling chamber with low ceilings and engraved motifs of the World-Womb. Nobody had told Anna this truth; she had gleaned it from the slivers that paraded through her mind's eye, continuous and alluring, like keyholes into a world that balanced on the cusp of formation. And so she made her way to that chamber, a witness to all that would come and all that had come before.

What's the worth of mere presence? the mind whispered to itself. It was generated of its own accord, an echo of sorts, but she tracked its procession nonetheless. You have seen this moment, Matrasa. You have known its sorrow.

But her feet moved tenderly, assuredly, toward that which had caused the old mind so much pain. Perhaps its agony had rippled back through the eons, binding their forms into a knot she could neither fathom nor escape….

Until now.

Amid darkness and the bellowing of nerashi on the platforms far above, she came to the crooked door with an herb bundle nailed to its center. Gazing into the faint rings of the wood grain, the visions began to manifest once more, shimmering in fractal arrangements—the words exchanged, the gaping wound, the emptiness in the core of her being.

She glanced over her shoulder, though the gesture immediately registered as nonsensical—she had demanded solitude and they had obeyed. Moreover, she had glimpsed this moment long before now.

For a moment, she thought to turn away, but this urge, too, she had witnessed.

Anna entered the chamber.

Lukas was lying upon a straw mattress, his scarred face glistening with sweat in dim candlelight. A nearby table held a set of scalpels, suturing needles, and bottles of brown tinctures. The man's eyelids stirred at the sound of the door's creaking, but he did not speak, nor did he shift his thin covering.

"We're departing soon," Anna said.

He opened his eyes, blinked at her. "Anna."

"Don't strain," she whispered. "Be at peace. This world and all its pains are fleeting."

But the Breaking was still fresh and stinging, and he could not cease the churning of his lips, the tears that welled up in swollen eyes, the frail, mechanical cycles of clutching and releasing his blanket. "I'm sorry."

"I know."

"Did I ever tell you that, Anna?"

Her gaze lingered on the tiled floor.

"Didn't need to come to me," he managed, wiping his nose with the back of his hand. "I don't deserve it."

"Nothing deserves to die alone."

"But I do. The Grove won't take me. Shouldn't take me, anyway."

"The past is rigid, but this moment is still living. Compassion never arrives too late."

"It's far gone," he said shakily. "All those days, those years...burned away."

Anna had a sense of being invisible, perhaps nowhere at all. There was only Lukas, alone with his grief, his horrible burdens.

"And you never came for me," Lukas said abruptly. "You could've come looking, but you never did, did you? Could've strung me up, and it would've been just."

"It wouldn't have brought him back," Anna said.

"And what?"

"There could be no justice," she said, "only more pain."

"I deserved to be butchered," he cried. "Your cuts stole away sleep—that little death without thinking-talk. Do you know what that's like, Anna? To live with everything you've done, every wink and every useless breath? To know they'll circle 'till ever-ever?"

"I do know," she said. "This was your penance. But it's over now. It's all over."

"Will I hear it there?" he asked. "In the grave, I mean?"

"No," Anna said, her mind circling with the halos of utter oblivion. "There will be only bliss."

Lukas nodded to himself. "What did you see in there, Anna?"

"You could not fathom it."

"Did you see the Grove?"

"And more," she said. "I saw the end of all fear and all desire. So take comfort in my words, Lukas. Do not be afraid of what approaches. Only love can endure the revolutions of eternity." She tucked her head to her chest, aware of—yet wholly unaffected by—a sour knot in her belly. Then she moved toward the door.

Lukas whimpered into his covering. "Don't leave me, Anna."

"I never have."

"But now, here, I—"

She paused in the threshold, knowing that Lukas would not finish his sentence. Knowing that he would sob for sixteen breaths, mumbling things she would never know, thinking thoughts of a world that should have been. It reached her ears as a symphony, at once tragic and transcendent.

"Thank you, Anna," he said finally, practically whispering. "Thank you."

Once in the corridor, she heard it all in perfect, unbidden sequence: the cloth rustling, the scalpel clattering against its tray, the flesh splitting. Air and blood rasped out through the wound. She did not turn back to look, for the mind's portrait had pained her well enough.

Where are they now?

The thought saturated her awareness as she moved toward rain-shrouded platforms.

Chapter 19

She could sense their fear as keenly as the rust gnawing away at panels beneath the nerash. It was a maddening, fatal strain of fear, the sort her old mind had bred when confronted with the certainty of death. It carried neither an odor nor a sound; it was a sphere that engulfed them all, burgeoning and seeping, devouring whatever roots the thinking mind had managed to sprout in the minds of violent men.

It raged against her stillness.

She studied the blackness behind her lids, the waterfall of every breath, the warmth of sensations flowering into being moment by moment. Several of the others—mainly Alakeph, but a scattered few Nahorans—had come to sit by her in the staging area, passing prayers under the thrum of the engines. Their breaths were sharp and ragged, too defiant to understand the whims of reality. She could not blame them for their fear. Once she had been them, and once she had killed them.

But analysis had passed into the realm of futility—now there was only action and with it, a sense of brutal resolve.

Anna listened to the wind buffeting in the abyss around the flock. Each rain droplet and wisp of cloud was apparent to her in the space of non-seeing, a living data point that vibrated against its kin. There were no variables in the shade of ignorance: speed, position, density. It would only be a few moments now. She discerned the subtle bursts and vacuums in the air far, far below, their origin leagues ahead of them, yet inexorably linked....

"Secure yourselves," Anna said, her eyes still shut. Murmurs drifted around her. "Do not dissect my words, brothers. Secure yourselves now."

The shells whirled up through the mist-veils. Each spiraled within a cone of fractured air, superheated and luminous, punching closer, closer—

Anna opened her eyes and stared out the nearest window.

A nerash dipped slightly—though not slightly enough—into the murky screen, then became annihilated in a flash of diamond light, a fleeting black tuft. Smoldering plates and crystalline glass and shrapnel cascaded down into seas of fog.

The old mind gazed with horror, but there was cutting knowledge behind it, an assurance that there could be no other path. She envisioned each fragment plummeting across waterlogged fields, drawing the temporary attention of both Starsons and the hollow-eyed, bogat-born children that the fighters had marched there to fill damp graves.

Another shell burst beneath the nerash. Two fighters slammed against the floor panels, flailing and kicking to regain their bearings. Crimson lights flooded the cabin and a horrible wheezing emanated from the craft's nose.

Anna remained kneeling on the floor, her hands pressed to her thighs, gazing out at the volley that had begun detonating in a string of dark blossoms.

One nerash's glass vented in a prismatic spray, while another had its wing sheared off, throwing it into a wild, flaming spin that lanced through the cloud cover.

"Can you aid them?" It was Rashig's voice, uncharacteristically shaken. Faithful, but confined in ignorance.

She watched the shells ripping through wings, engines, landing skids. "No."

Not yet.

"There won't be enough of us," Rashig pressed. "We may need to turn back."

Anna closed her eyes. "To what end? Death will not avert its gaze, brother."

"*Tel glohaim!*" a navigator roared over the supersonic pops.

Two leagues. Two leagues separating eternity from the void. The moments shrank away in a blur of visions—this world, the next, the former. There was no center, no inside, no outside. Her mind did not chase the numinous light, nor did it shrink away from landscapes of black, charred bodies, of endless night, of thousand-armed beings eviscerating her form. That which was unborn was undying. That which knew pain was not subject to it.

"Drop!"

Anna's eyes snapped open. She sprang to her feet and clutched a tether as the nerash screamed downward, weight and sound and air winking out for an instant, bucking against the strangeness of that empty sky.

Beyond the windows, the clouds ceded to patchwork fields, dark and smoldering, blotted with tracts of evergreens. Then came the vague form of a labyrinth: ramshackle buildings, rooftop ladders, crooked chimneys, streets that the old mind had known and feared and somehow sought. But they were moving with impossible speed, impossible recklessness. They swept over the blots of dogs and soot-faced girls and Huuri craftsmen, all huddling in the refuge of gated compounds, far away from the flames and murderous iron. And yet even in the nerash's haste, a passage so swift that one could not discern grins from grimaces, nor even the reality of what had been witnessed, there was a sense of terror.

Save us, it seemed to whisper.

Then the nerash pulled up from its vicious dive, screaming up and over the mossy battlements and crenellations of the old city, dancing through the maze of lacquered tiles and sandstone.

Anna's hands shook upon the tether. *Do not be afraid*, the mind whispered, *for the dreamer knows not that they dream.*

Dozens of dark spires appeared just ahead of the craft, jutting up from the cityscape like rows of meshing fangs. The central lodge. Nothing had ever seemed so majestic, so terrifying. She recognized it not by its form— it had not even existed in her childhood—but by its sense of prescience, beckoning her into completion. Three other nerashi swooped down past Anna's window, intent on the courtyard at the center of the compound. As they thundered across the forest of slate stone, the engines' groans reverberating amid the tendrils and soaring arches, Anna heard the familiar jangling of hands combing over vests and fingers unseating trigger locks.

Rashig pressed himself to the wall panel beside Anna, sparing only cursory glances at the lodge's brutish features. "Will you need a ruj?"

She shook her head. "All I need is your trust."

"My brothers have nothing else to spare," he said. "This is our calling, sister."

"Then be brave in this hour."

Ruji fire peppered the far side of the nerash moments before the landing skids hissed in deployment. Fighters shrank away from the windows, their weapons shouldered and eyes vigilant, all glancing nervously at the cabin's sealed doors. The nerash's underbelly flared its landing fuel, kicking upward through the floor panels. There was an instant of stillness, a soft whisper of winds and molten iron, suspended in a nest of churning saffron dust. Then the landing skids clapped across cobblestones. The haze gave way to high, vaulted walls in all directions, and to encroaching fighters, and to pools of bright blood where the lodge's old guard had been sentenced and ended.

A jumble of prayers and wild shouts filled the cabin. *The Knowing One, the deliverer, the State, the World-Womb.* Each cry was hopeful, fearful.

Anna accepted their words into the fold of her heart.

She wanted to embrace them all, to tell them that the end would be sweet and fitting, but—

Air hissed into the cabin, followed by the grating screech of the doors slamming back along rusted rails. Sparks exploded from walls and ceiling panels. Fighters rushed into the rain, screaming, struggling, shoving over the bodies of dead brothers and sisters.

Anna followed in their wake, her hands dangling at her sides. She stepped over blood and sizzling shards and bits of tissue, every breath full and free, unafraid of death and its certainty. Exiting the nerash, she shut her eyes to the dance of rain across her hair and shoulders. Dozens of ruji hissed around her, raking stone, slicing the air, punching out the windows of crafts that descended around her. But there was no fear. What could they do beyond killing a body?

"Anna," Rashig cried. She found him kneeling beside a legless body, his gaze trained on a string of Nahoran fighters dashing toward the far walls. "Where are we striking, sister?"

Peering into the mind's eye, she saw an endless tunnel, a shower of warm light....

"The western hall," Anna said, pointing at a towering dome just ahead. Iron whistled past her head. She glanced at the packs of enemy fighters strung out along the battlements and lower levels, all of them scrambling to increase the pressure on descending nerashi. They were streaming from the northern concourse, at once surprised and rabid. The most dangerous breed. "Lead your forces inside, brother. We can't secure this ground."

Rashig cut down a pair of Starsons making their way across the square. "We'll have no way to withdraw."

"Do you trust me, Rashig?"

He lowered his ruj, looked at her sidelong. "Always."

"Then lead your forces inside."

Nodding firmly, Rashig rose and whistled to rally the nearest brothers. A descending nerash swiveled in a whirl of amber grit, shielding his forces as they pushed toward the gates. They were joined by at least three other detachments of troops, a borzaq unit among them, though their numbers were nothing in comparison to the Starson hordes flooding out of the hive. In that murky veil, there was no distinction of creed, no distinction of form. All of their silhouettes were dim and fleeting, like gnats on a summer's eve....

A group of Nahoran fighters sprinted past Anna, calling out to her as they went. But her name hardly registered as her own. Even in following, stepping lightly, regretfully, over the bodies that lined her path, she did not know where her form ended and the carnage began.

Screams escaped from the western arch in a shrill, braying mass. The gateway roiled with smog like a hellish mouth, each body a black tooth in the maw, its silhouettes frozen by every spark and flash and flicker.

Anna did not hurry toward the slaughter, nor did her mind resist it. She advanced with silent trust, undaunted by the cylinders that pounded across the stones and the volleys that shredded the air, her fingers loose and accepting of all that came, of all that might end her. And as she approached that burning threshold, she stopped to kneel and kiss the foreheads of those who had fallen, who gasped for air through blood and prayers to their gods, who held the names of their mothers on their lips, who did not want to kill or die but to sleep in loving arms.

Each step through the gateway was another world, another glimpse of that which she had seen in forms long dissolved: hands straining toward sunlight, glimmering with strands of varnished beads. Plains of glass and fractal salt. A white-haired lover dangling their legs over mossy stone.

Yet her mind now eased into the portraits, surrendering to the weight of their immutability, embracing lives condensed into a mere moment, a bead of water. Her mind rested in its own completeness—there was nothing to resist, for there were neither separations of place nor flesh.

"We need to withdraw," an Alakeph brother screamed in Anna's periphery, his white garb caked with the blood of brothers and foes alike. He was not afraid, only logical.

But logic would not spare them.

Anna stood in the gateway and studied the endless succession of bodies—crowding, shifting, slumping over by the dozens, both sides unmoved by the other's butchery. Billows of woodsmoke and acrid fumes hung in the air. She made no sense of the devastation, the faceless nature of cylinders and fléchettes hurtling from being to being. Like all mindless things, it had to be ceased. She lowered her head and moved over the trampled corpses and pits and gouges lining the way.

"Sister!" Rashig's voice bit through the deafening chaos. "We cannot advance."

She listened to the ruji pellets flitting through the air, leaving ripples and scars in the vacuums they birthed. They did not seem to flow around her, but rather *through* her, within her, as though she were them and they were her, and—

The silence descended before she grasped her own intentions.

Wisps of smoke snaked out to greet her, dispelled in the same haunting way as the din that had clouded her mind moments before. In their place were bodies—ruptured, leaking bodies—and the eerie stillness of efficiency. Pulp drained from blackened walls and portcullis prongs.

Rashig's breathing was fierce and broken in her ear. "Sister?"

"Secure the outer hall with your brothers," Anna whispered. "Leave the inner chamber to me."

"What's happening, Anna?"

"Everything."

Then she was gone from them, a breeze wafting through a maze of mahogany and bronze-sheltered lanterns, her mind aimed, dagger-like, toward the heavy doors that separated her from all that she had been created to meet. Fantasies of childhood fluttered here and there, gossamer webs in the heat of summer: her mother's laughter, a bushel of unripe juniper berries, sap drooling down a patch of desiccated bark. Past, present, future—she resided in all of them, yet in none.

As her hands reached toward the doors, opalescent and shimmering, she noticed their freckles of blood. Her own blood, wrung out of her in exchange for the bending of this world. She marveled at it, almost smiled at it; was it inside or outside? It would be returned in short order, the mind assured her.

She turned the handles and opened the doors. First came the waves of stale heat, thick with the coppery stench of bile and vomit, of bodies being dismantled through unholy force. Then there was the blighted reality she had encountered before, yet averted in her mind's eye, too wicked to be perceived, to be accepted before this very moment.

The central aisle, winding up toward an arrangement of shadowed figures and elk-horn chandeliers, had been reduced to a bloody sprawl: mutilated bodies, bone fragments, pink entrails strung out in lumpy coils. Corpses and captives filled the terraced seating on either side of the chamber; the dead were slumped over chairs and writs and quills, some faceless and others twitching madly, while the captives sat doe-eyed and quivering, their arms raised to form a pale forest. Grimy light spilled down from the rafters and bathed the walls in shadow.

Anna's gaze swept the crowd, penetrating the mass of twisting sigils—spires, nonagons, lattices, all interwoven like a cosmic loom.

"Not another step." Ramyi's voice pierced the drone of whimpers and gargling, its timbre just as striking as her radiant form. She shouldered past her fighters at the crest of the assembly and peered down at Anna. Amid the patchwork of darkness and creeping stains, her form was a light from the heavens, a living mirror of Anna's own form. "You should have died with grace."

Anna met the stares of the waiting Starborn. She granted her attention to each tarnished ruji barrel, unmoved by the alluring dreams of yesteryear, of worlds that had not transpired. "How do we proceed?"

"I end this scourge," Ramyi whispered, "and a new world—our world—arises in its wake."

"A new world?"

"Our liberation is close at hand."

"Perhaps," Anna said, "but Jenis is gone now. Is it your desire to do this, Ramyi? Does it sleep in your heart?"

Muscles twitched along the underside of Ramyi's jaw. "Once, you hesitated to kill me. But I won't hesitate. Not now."

"Yet you do."

"We all have our weaknesses," Ramyi said. She let her head hang for a moment, eyes pinched in seeming contemplation of the sobs by her side. It was a man—an old, milk-sighted man who groped feebly at the barrel pressed to his forehead. "Should I feel something for you, Anna? What about for these people? For any of them? The ones who stocked their coffers and sowed their fields when we were starving, and the ones who never learned how it feels to bury their comrades? What should I feel for these *things*?"

"I don't know," Anna whispered. "But neither do you."

Nodding absently, Ramyi began to pace in a tight circle. With a deep breath, a drop of her shoulders, she snapped her fingers.

The ruj drilled through the old man's head, and then there was nothing—no milk-sight, no skull, no trembling lips. Screams drowned out the body's *thud*.

"Do I appear uncertain, Anna?" And indeed, it was clear that there was no question in her mind, for she was not the same girl who had slept in pitted trenches and cried on Anna's shoulder and wished for a boy to take her hands and sway with her under starlight. A form remained, of course, but where was *she?* Discarded in a mass grave somewhere, buried between the mockery and apathy of cruel men. Once she had been insufferable, so young and foolish that Anna had cursed her for coming into being and losing her footing so often. Now she was everything Anna had forgotten to love. She was precisely what had created her.

"If you release them," Anna said, "I can grant you what you desire most."

"You showed me your treachery, Anna. The time for bargaining died long ago."

"Then kill me. Ascend to whatever throne you wish. Here, there—
it won't matter where these exiles go. You've spilled enough blood to
seed your world."

"You know the nature of embers," Ramyi sighed. "If just one
catches the wind...."

Ramyi lifted her remaining hand and stared into Anna's soul and
snapped with the weight of imminent violence.

A hundred fingers squeezed upon a hundred pieces of cast iron in the
same instant, depressing rain-worn springs that had kissed the sands of
the Glass Sea and beyond, churning cogs forged by the hands of young
boys who could not buy their own shackles, slamming cylinders forth with
bellies full of chipped oxide, birthing sparks—those fleeting catalysts, the
hearts of prophetic stars—and launching the fated granules down those
canals of birth and death, fusing them into white-hot masses of ejecta not
witnessed since flakes of the cosmos rained down across desolate bogs....

Anna ceased it all.

The iron flecks hung in the air, revolving a hair's width from the flesh
of foreheads and collarbones. They were featureless planets, thrumming
in their own stasis, their own prison of fossilized inertia.

"Let them," Anna sputtered, blood dribbling over her lips and chin, "go."

Ramyi's lips parted. "Stop it, Anna."

Crimson sills pooled along her lower lids. "Let them go."

The Starborn fighters exchanged furtive, questioning glances, their
ruji barrels wavering, their hands growing slick and pale-knuckled. The
way they stood and breathed and shifted whispered their formation into
Anna's awareness:

A quiet boy spending his days in sun-starved fields, begging his
brothers to swallow their words as the tall men passed on horseback,
always tucking his eyes away from those who might harm him or harm
his father again, always crying into his pillows, always wishing he could
be strong, if only for a day....

A foundling with memories of his mother's breast, his mother's smile,
the songs he had been sung long before his flesh was bruised and his
name was burned....

A girl who was not afraid, who had never been afraid, for she had seen
what had been done to her sisters and how they had not cried out and how
stillness had come over them in their final moments....

Anna did not understand them; she was them.

She felt every thread of hayat binding them, animating them, manifesting as bodies and minds and memories, a thousand waves comprising a single sea....

"Again," Ramyi called.

But this time, fingers did not tense and triggers did not creak and springs did not rattle. Not even the eyes of the Starborn swiveled in their sockets. Each of their bodies oscillated where they stood, wreathed in a ghostly aura, a cycling phase of positions neither here nor there. Hayat flared along their skin in wild crevasses and fissures. Entire fragments of their being flickered out of existence—arms, jaws, ears. Mote by mote, their flesh drifted apart and dispersed in luminous spores.

One of Ramyi's attendants, lugging the vague form of a yuzel, shoved to the forefront of their assembly. They raised the weapon and loosed a scream, but the sound vanished in tandem with their intentions, their mind.

The body fluttered apart in a sphere of velvet blood and gristle.

"What are you?" Ramyi whispered. She stumbled forward, fell to her knees. "What is this, Anna?"

"Stand." She could hardly speak around the blood.

"You've come here for death, so kill me."

"I have not gone anywhere." She stared at Ramyi and at the girl she had once been. Every strand of her form and mind lay bare before Anna, as simple to unbind as a knot with its ends exposed, begging to be undone with a final dance of omnipotence. *And what then?* the mind whispered. In the twilight of violence, when every foul tongue had been silenced and every wicked heart had been stilled, what would remain? The vibrations were ceaseless, fraught with pain from conception to extinction. There could be no end to the cycle, just as there had been no creation.

The only escape was cessation.

Ramyi turned her palms toward the bone chandeliers. "End it."

But as Anna moved onto the first of the satin-draped steps, her body growing cold and turning away from the flame of existence, her impulses dissolved. Sounds plunged into a vacuum. She watched droplets of blood wadding up and cascading from her fingertips, only to find the crimson beads hanging in midair, pristine, a gallery of her basest components. There was no fear, no place, no time. Indeed, the world transpired in tranquil silence around her—a symphony of bodies trampling one another, hands clutching faces in disbelief, dust spiraling through the air.

With each step, the flow of the cosmos thickened further into an immutable mosaic. Spittle and tears crystallized in the light. Fingers tensed and grew rigid, the digits splayed out, packed into useless fists.

Even Anna's mind receded into a space devoid of thinking, deprived of the motions and reactive chains it so desperately craved.

Ramyi swiped at her eyes and surveyed the room. "What've you done to them?"

Rivulets of blood rolled across Anna's cheeks, streaming out into the open air like sanguine clouds....

Ramyi's hand fidgeted within the folds of her cloak. With a flush face and gritted teeth, she drew a short, serrated blade and struggled to her feet. Her gaze was thick with the wrath of beasts, the mindless panic of those who did not comprehend death. She stalked down the steps with a single mission.

Her *mission.*

The notion erupted spontaneously, miraculously, a lancing thought that blanketed Anna's awareness like virgin snow. She did not exist without Ramyi, nor could Ramyi exist without her. Each of them was a seed of their true nature, another perspective with which to explore all that they were. How simple was it? How long had it evaded her, buried under delusions of selfishness and survival? Now she faced it directly, studying the link that bound them, the undying tether that stretched back to the womb of this world's spark.

After eons of domination, of ruinous empires, of beings sheltering their own hearts against the misery of their kin, there could only be one panacea:

Surrender.

Anna smiled at Ramyi, birthing a crinkle of uncertainty in the northerner's eyes.

Suddenly, the pain did not matter. The rusted point dug into the tender gulf beneath Anna's sternum, plunging through innards, grazing her spinal column and sapping the strength from her ankles. She crumpled onto Ramyi's bandaged shoulder and pressed her lips to the girl's cheek and kissed her as a mother ought to kiss their child. Her breaths wafted through Ramyi's hair.

"I love you," Anna whispered.

She touched her fingers to Ramyi's throat and channeled the vibrancy that had slumbered for so long in her heart, unknown, unwanted. Hayat crept up the girl's face in glassy strands. More than hayat, she realized—it was *her,* all of her, the sacred light that had been granted corporeal form, a mere shard of the macrocosm of all-that-was. She flowed into Ramyi as Hayat's being had flowed into her, shedding the dull machine of a body as she went. *Rejoice in this sacred gift,* the mind whispered, though there was no longer a thinker to claim the thought as their own. There was only awareness of death, of rebirth, of *becoming*.

Ramyi's eyes grew engorged with that cool blue light, and she stared into Anna's eyes as though there was nothing else in all of existence. Their lips flowed in unison.

"Is this it?" they spoke.

A wolf met the eyes of a flailing elk.

A young boy lifted another from bloodstained earth.

A woman raised her arms toward a dying sun.

"Is this—"

Piece by piece, the chamber dissolved around them, falling away into an endless recession, a geometric horizon without boundaries or centers, devoid of inner and outer, above and below, being and nonbeing. The mesh enveloped them in radiant fractals, throttling them in and out of the space their form occupied, bearing all of eternity on the wingtips of a raven and the spindles within bloodshot eyes. All things collapsed into a moment, a sensation.

"—becoming?"

Then there was nothing—no light, no darkness, nothing to be done or seen or heard or known or forgotten.

Bliss pervaded. Love resonated in every particle of every space. It was a moment, a dream in a sleepless dimension, a splinter of omniscience beholden to nothing beyond its own innate perfection. But an echo congealed in that ageless expanse.

What are we?

It fractured.

Then, again, there were two:

Formless, boundless energies perceiving one another across the void.

Sorrow and joy were equally absent, for there were not yet words to describe their sundering. *They.* The term was still vacuous, aimless. In time *they* would bloom into trees and starlight and mewling pups, wracked by every malady and sorrow their own ignorance might breed. Yet within each of them, a playful, knowing force awakened and burned with the light of remembrance. The instant was one of serene cognition.

Eventually, they would remember.

Eventually, they would become.

Meet the Author

James Wolanyk is the author of the Scribe Cycle and a teacher from Boston. He holds a B.A. in Creative Writing from the University of Massachusetts, where his writing has appeared in its quarterly publication and *The Electric Pulp*. After studying fiction, he pursued educational work in the Czech Republic, Taiwan, and Latvia. Outside of writing, he enjoys history, philosophy, and boxing. His post-apocalyptic novel, *Grid*, was released in 2015. He currently resides in Riga, Latvia, and works as an English teacher.

Visit him online at jameswolanykfiction.wordpress.com.

Scribes

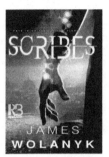

Pawns in an endless war, scribes are feared and worshipped, valued and exploited, prized and hunted. But there is only one whose powers can determine the fate of the world...

Born into the ruins of Rzolka's brutal civil unrest, Anna has never known peace. Here, in her remote village—a wasteland smoldering in the shadows of outlying foreign armies—being imbued with the magic of the scribes has made her future all the more uncertain.

Through intricate carvings of the flesh, scribes can grant temporary invulnerability against enemies to those seeking protection. In an embattled world where child scribes are sold and traded to corrupt leaders, Anna is invaluable. Her scars never fade. The immunity she grants lasts forever.

Taken to a desert metropolis, Anna is promised a life of reverence, wealth, and fame—in exchange for her gifts. She believes she is helping to restore her homeland, creating gods and kings for an immortal army—until she witnesses the hordes slaughtering without reproach, sacking cities, and threatening everything she holds dear. Now, with the help of an enigmatic assassin, Anna must reclaim the power of her scars—before she becomes the unwitting architect of an apocalyptic war.

Schisms

Three long years have passed since Anna, First of Tomas, survived the purge in Malijad after being forced to use her scribe sigils to create an army of immortals. Safely ensconced in the shelter of the Nest, a sanctuary woven by one of her young allies, Anna spends her days tutoring the gifted yet traumatized scribe, Ramyi—and coming to terms with her growing attachment to an expatriate soldier in her company.

Away from her refuge, war drums continue to beat. Thwarted in her efforts to locate the elusive tracker and bring him to justice, Anna turns to the state of Nahora and its network of spies for help. But Nahoran assistance comes with a price: Anna must agree to weaponize her magic for the all-out military confrontation to come.

Dispatched to the front lines with Ramyi in tow, Anna will find her new alliances put to the test, her old tormentors lying in wait, and the fate of a city placed in her hands. To protect the innocent, she must be willing to make the ultimate sacrifice. For even in this season of retribution, the gift of healing may be the most powerful weapon of all.

Printed in the United States
by Baker & Taylor Publisher Services